美国亚裔文学研究丛书

总主编　郭英剑

An Anthology of Asian American Literature

美国亚裔文学作品选

主编　郭英剑　张国庆　张龙艳

本研究受中国人民大学科学研究基金资助，
系2017年度重大规划项目“美国亚裔文学研究”（编号：17XNLG10）的阶段性成果。

中国人民大学出版社
·北京·

总序

美国亚裔文学的历史、现状与未来

郭英剑

一、何为“美国亚裔文学”？

“美国亚裔文学”（Asian American Literature），简言之，是指由美国社会中的亚裔群体作家所创作的文学作品的总称。也有人称之为“亚裔美国文学”。在我国台湾学术界，更多地称为“亚美文学”。

然而，“美国亚裔文学”这个由两个核心词汇——“美国亚裔”和“文学”——所组成的术语，远没有她看上去那么简单。说她极其复杂，一点也不为过。因此，要想对“美国亚裔文学”有基本的了解，就需要从其中的两个关键词入手。

首先，“美国亚裔”中的“亚裔”，是指具有亚裔血统的美国人，但其所指并非一个单一的族裔，其组成包括了美国来自亚洲各国（或者与亚洲各国有关联）的人员群体及其后裔，比如美国华裔（Chinese Americans）、日裔（Japanese Americans）、菲律宾裔（Filipino Americans）、韩裔（Korean Americans）、越南裔（Vietnamese Americans）、印度裔（Indian Americans）、泰国裔（Thai Americans）等等。

根据联合国的统计，亚洲总计有48个国家。除此之外，还有我国的台湾地区，以及香港、澳门特别行政区。因此，所谓“美国亚裔”自然包括在美国的所有这48个亚洲国家以及我国台湾、香港、澳门社会群体的后裔，或者有其血统的人员。由此所涉及的各国（以及地区）迥异的语言、不同的文化、独特的人生体验，以及群体交叉所产生的多样性，包括亚洲各国由于战争交恶所带给后裔及其有关人员的深刻影响，就构成了“美国亚裔”这一群体具有的极端的复杂性。在美国统计局的定义中，美国亚裔细分为“东亚”（East

Asia)、“东南亚”(Southeast Asia)和南亚(South Asia)。[1] 当然，也正由于其复杂性，到现在为止有些亚洲国家在美国的后裔或者移民，尚未形成一个相对固定的族裔群体。

其次，文学主要由作家创作，由于“美国亚裔”群体的复杂性，自然导致“美国亚裔”的“作家”群体同样处于极其复杂的状态，但也因此使这一群体的概念具有相当大的包容性。凡是身在美国的亚裔后裔、具有亚洲血统或者后来移民美国的亚裔作家，都可以称之为“美国亚裔作家”。

由于亚裔群体的语言众多，加上一些移民作家的母语并非英语，因此，“美国亚裔文学”一般指的是美国亚裔作家使用英语所创作的文学作品。但由于历史的原因，学术界也把最早进入美国时，亚裔用本国语言所创作的文学作品，无论是口头还是文字作品——比如 19 世纪中期，华人进入美国时遭到拘禁时所创作的诗句，也都纳入“美国亚裔文学”的范畴之内。同时，随着全球化时代的到来，各国之间的文学与文化交流日益加强，加之移民日渐增加，因此，也将部分发表时为亚洲各国语言，但后来被翻译成英语的文学作品，也同样纳入“美国亚裔文学”的范畴。

最后，“美国亚裔”的划分，除了语言、历史、文化之外，还有一个地理因素需要考虑。随着时间的推移与学术界研究【特别是离散研究(Diaspora Studies)】的进一步深化，“美国亚裔”中的“美国”(America)，也不单单指 the United States 了。我们知道，由于全球化时代所带来的人口流动性的极度增加，国与国之间的界限有时候变得模糊起来，人们的身份也变得日益具有多样性和流动性。比如，由于经济全球化的原因，美国已不单单是一个地理概念上的美国。经济与文化的构成，造就了可口可乐、麦当劳等商业品牌，它们都已经变成了流动的美国的概念。这样的美国不断在“侵入”其他国家，并对其不断产生巨大的影响。当然，一个作家的流动性，也无形中扩大了“美国”的概念。比如，一个亚洲作家可能移民到美国，一个美国亚裔作家也可能移民到其他国家。这样的流动性拓展了“美国亚裔”的定义与范畴。

为此，“美国亚裔文学”这一概念，有时候也包括一些身在美洲地区，但与美国有关联的作家用英语创作的作品，或者被翻译成英语的文学作品，也会被纳入这一范畴之内。

应该指出的是，由于“亚裔”群体进入美国的时间早晚不同，加上“亚裔”群体的复杂性，那么，每一个“亚裔”群体，都有其独有的美国族裔特征，比如华裔与日裔有所不同，印度裔与日裔也有所不同。如此一来，正如一些学者所认为的那样，各个族裔的特征最好应该分开来叙述和加以研究。[2]

---

1 参见：Karen R. Humes, Nicholas A. Jones, Roberto R. Ramirez (March 2011). “Overview of Race and Hispanic Origin: 2010” (PDF). United States Census Bureau. U.S. Department of Commerce.

2 参见：Chin, Frank, et al. “Preface” to *Aiiieeeee! An Anthology of Asian American Writers*. Edited by Frank Chin, Jeffery Paul Chan, Lawson Fusao Inada, and Shawn Wong. A Mentor Book. 1991. p.xi.

二、为何要研究“美国亚裔文学”？

虽然上文中提出，“美国亚裔”是个复杂而多元的群体，“美国亚裔文学”包含了极具多样化的亚裔群体作家，我们还是要把“美国亚裔文学”当做一个整体来进行研究。理由有三：

首先，“美国亚裔文学”与“美国亚裔作家”（Asian American Writers）最早出现时，即是作为一个统一的概念而提出。1974 年，赵健秀（Frank Chin）等学者出版了《哎咿！美国亚裔作家选集》。[3] 作为首部划时代“美国亚裔作家”的文学作品选集，该书通过发现和挖掘此前 50 年中被遗忘的华裔、日裔与菲律宾裔中的重要作家，选取其代表性作品，进而提出要建立作为独立的研究领域的“美国亚裔文学”（Asian American Literature）。[4]

其次，在亚裔崛起的过程中，无论是亚裔的无心之为，还是美国主流社会与其他族裔的有意为之，亚裔都是作为一个整体被安置在一起的。因此，亚裔文学也是作为一个整体而存在的。近年来，我国的“美国华裔文学”研究成为美国文学研究学界的一个热点。但在美国，虽然有“美国华裔文学”（Chinese American Literature）的说法，但真正作为学科存在的，则是“美国亚裔文学”（Asian American Literature），甚至更多的则是“美国亚裔研究”（Asian American Studies）。

再次，1970 年代之后，“美国亚裔文学”的发展在美国学术界逐渐成为研究的热点，引发了研究者的广泛关注。为此，旧金山州立大学、加州大学系统的伯克利分校、洛杉矶分校以及斯坦福大学率先设置了“美国亚裔研究系”（Department of Asian American Studies）或者“亚裔研究中心”，成为早期美国亚裔研究的重镇。随后包括宾夕法尼亚大学、哥伦比亚大学、布朗大学、哈佛大学、耶鲁大学等常青藤盟校在内的众多美国高校也都陆续增添了“美国亚裔研究”（Asian American Studies）专业，开设了丰富多彩的亚裔文学与亚裔研究方面的课程，教学与研究成果丰富多彩。在我国台湾地区，包括台湾“中央研究院”、台湾师范大学等在内的研究机构与高校，大都开设有亚裔文学与亚裔研究方面的课程，召开过众多的国际会议，研究成果丰富。

那么，我们需要提出的一个问题是：在中国语境下，研究“美国亚裔文学”的意义与价值究竟何在？我的看法如下：

第一，“美国亚裔文学”是“美国文学”的重要组成部分。不研究亚裔文学或者忽视甚至贬低亚裔文学，学术界对于美国文学的研究就是不完整的。如上文所说，亚裔文学的

3 Chin, Frank; Chan, Jeffery Paul; Inada, Lawson Fusao; Wong, Shawn. *Aiiieeeee! An Anthology of Asian-American Writers*. Howard University Press, 1974.

4 参见：Chin, Frank, et al. “Preface” to *Aiiieeeee! An Anthology of Asian American Writers*. Edited by Frank Chin, Jeffery Paul Chan, Lawson Fusao Inada, and Shawn Wong. A Mentor Book. 1991. pp.xi-xxii.

真正兴起是在 20 世纪六七十年代。美国六七十年代特殊的时代背景极大地促进了亚裔文学发展，自此，亚裔文学作品层出不穷，包括小说、戏剧、传记、短篇小说、诗歌等各种文学形式。在当下的美国，亚裔文学及其研究与亚裔的整体生存状态息息相关。种族、历史、人口以及政治诉求等因素促使被总称为“亚裔”的各个少数族裔联合发声，以期在美国政治领域和主流社会达到最大的影响力与辐射度。对此，学术界不能视而不见。

第二，我国现有的“美国华裔文学”研究，无法替代更不能取代“美国亚裔文学”研究。自从 1980 年代开始译介美国亚裔文学以来，我国国内的研究就主要集中在华裔文学领域，研究对象也仅为少数知名华裔作家及长篇小说创作领域。相较于当代国外亚裔文学研究的全面与广博，国内对于亚裔中其他族裔作家的作品关注太少。即使是那些亚裔文学的经典之作，如菲律宾裔作家卡洛斯·布洛桑（Carlos Bulosan）的《美国在我心中》（*America Is in the Heart*, 1946），日裔女作家山本久枝（Hisaye Yamamoto）的《第十七音节及其他故事》（*Seventeen Syllables and Other Stories*, 1949）、日裔约翰·冈田（John Okada）的《不—不仔》（*NO-NO Boy*, 1959），以及如今在美国文学界如日中天的青年印度裔作家裘帕·拉希莉（Jhumpa Lahiri）的作品，专题研究均十分少见。即便是像华裔作家任璧莲（Gish Jen）这样已经受到学者很大关注和研究的作家，其长篇小说之外体裁的作品同样没有得到足够的重视，更遑论国内学术界对亚裔文学在诗歌、戏剧方面的研究了。换句话说，我国学术界对于整个“美国亚裔文学”的研究来说还很匮乏，属于亟待开发的领域。实际上，在我看来，不研究“美国亚裔文学”，也无法真正理解“美国华裔文学”。

第三，在中国“一带一路”倡议与中国文化走出去的今天，作为美国文学研究的新型增长点，大力开展“美国亚裔文学”研究，特别是研究中国的亚洲周边国家如韩国、日本、印度等国在美国移民状况的文学表现，以及与华裔在美国的文学再现，使之与美国和世界其他国家以及我国台湾地区的“美国亚裔文学”保持同步发展，具有较大的理论意义与学术价值。

三、“美国亚裔文学”及其研究：历史与现状

从历史上看，来自亚洲国家的移民进入美国，可以追溯到 17 世纪。但真正开始较大规模的移民则是到了 19 世纪中后期。然而，亚裔一开始进入美国，就遭到了来自美国社会与官方的阻力与法律限制。从 1880 年代到 1940 年代这长达半个多世纪的岁月中，为了保护美国本土而出台的一系列移民法，都将亚洲各国人排除在外，禁止他们当中的大部分人进入美国大陆地区。直到 20 世纪 40 至 60 年代移民法有所改革时，这种状况才有所改观。其中的改革措施之一就是取消了国家配额。如此一来，亚洲移民人数才开始大规模上

升。根据 2010 年的美国国家统计局分析显示，亚裔是美国社会移民人数增长最快的少数族裔。[5]

"美国亚裔"实际是个新兴词汇。这个词汇的创立与诞生时间在 1960 年代后期。在此之前，亚洲人或者具有亚洲血统者通常被称为 Oriental（东方人）、Asiatic（亚洲人）和 Mongoloid（蒙古人、黄种人）。[6] 是美国历史学家市冈裕次（Yuji Ichioka）在 1960 年代末期，开创性地开始使用 Asian American 这个术语，[7] 从此，这一词汇开始被人们普遍接受和广泛使用。

与此同时，"美国亚裔文学"在随后的 1970 年代作为一个文学类别开始出现并逐步产生影响。1974 年，有两部著作几乎同时出版，都以美国亚裔命名。一部是《美国亚裔传统：散文与诗歌选集》，[8] 另外一部则是前面提到过的《哎咿！美国亚裔作家选集》。[9] 这两部著作，将过去长期被人遗忘的亚裔文学带到了聚光灯下，让人们仿佛看到了一种新的文学形式。其后，新的亚裔作家不断涌现，文学作品层出不穷。

最初亚裔文学的主要主题与主要内容为种族（race）、身份（identity）、亚洲文化传统、亚洲与美国或者西方国家之间的文化冲突，当然也少不了性别（sexuality）、社会性别（gender）、性别歧视、社会歧视等。后来，随着移民作家的大规模出现，离散文学的兴起，亚裔文学也开始关注移民、语言、家国、全球化、劳工、战争、帝国主义、殖民主义等问题。

如果说，上述 1974 年的两部著作代表着亚裔文学进入美国文学的世界版图之中，那么，1982 年著名美国亚裔研究专家金惠经（Elaine Kim）的《美国亚裔文学的创作及其社会语境》[10] 的出版，作为第一部学术著作，则代表着美国亚裔文学研究正式登上美国学术界的舞台。自此以后，不仅亚裔文学创作兴盛起来，亚裔文学研究也逐渐成为热点，成果不断推陈出新。

同时，人们对于如何界定"美国亚裔文学"等众多问题进行了深入的探讨，进一

---

5 参见：Wikipedia 依据"U.S. Census Show Asians Are Fastest Growing Racial Group" (NPR.org) 所得出的数据统计。https://en.wikipedia.org/wiki/Asian_Americans。

6 Mio, Jeffrey Scott, ed. (1999). *Key Words in Multicultural Interventions: A Dictionary*. ABC-Clio ebook. Greenwood Publishing Group. p.20.

7 K. Connie Kang, "Yuji Ichioka, 66; Led Way in Studying Lives of Asian Americans," *Los Angeles Times*, September 7, 2002. Reproduced at ucla.edu by the Asian American Studies Center.

8 Wand, David Hsin-fu, ed. *Asian American Heritage: An Anthology of Prose and Poetry*. New York: Pocket Books, 1974.

9 Chin, Frank; Chan, Jeffery Paul; Inada, Lawson Fusao; Wong, Shawn. *Aiiieeeee! An Anthology of Asian-American Writers*. Howard University Press, 1974.

10 Kim, Elaine. *Asian American Literature: An Introduction to the Writings and Their Social Context*. Philadelphia: Temple University Press, 1982.

步推动了这一学科向前发展。相关问题包括：究竟谁可以说自己是美国亚裔（an Asian America）？这里的 America 是不是就是单指“美国”（the United States）？是否可以包括“美洲”（Americas）？如果亚裔作家所写的内容与亚裔无关，能否算是“亚裔文学”？如果不是亚裔作家，但所写内容与亚裔有关，能否算在“亚裔文学”之内？

总体上看，早期的亚裔文学研究专注于美国身份的建构，即界定亚裔文学的范畴，以及争取其在美国文化与美国文学中应得的席位，是 20 世纪七八十年代亚裔民权运动的前沿阵地。早期学者如赵健秀、徐忠雄（Shawn Wong）等为领军人物。随后出现的金惠经、张敬珏（King-Kok Cheung）、骆里山（Lisa Lowe）等人均成为了亚裔文学研究领域的权威学者，他 / 她们的著作影响并造就了第二代美国亚裔文学研究者。90 年代之后的亚裔文学研究逐渐淡化了早期研究中对于意识形态的侧重，开始向传统的学科分支、研究方法以及研究理论靠拢，研究视角多集中在学术马克思主义（academic Marxism）、后结构主义、后殖民、女权主义以及心理分析等。

进入 21 世纪以来，“美国亚裔文学”研究开始向多元化、全球化与跨学科方向发展。随着亚裔文学作品爆炸式的增长，来自阿富汗、印度、巴基斯坦、越南等族裔作家的作品开始受到关注，极大丰富与拓展了亚裔文学研究的领域。当代“美国亚裔文学”研究的视角与方法也不断创新，战争研究、帝国研究、跨国研究、视觉文化理论、空间理论、身体研究、环境理论等层出不穷。新的理论与常规性研究交叉进行，不但开创了新的研究领域，而且对于经典问题（例如身份建构）的研究提供了新的解读方式与方法。

四、作为课题的“美国亚裔文学”研究及其丛书

“美国亚裔文学”研究，是由我担任课题负责人的 2017 年度中国人民大学科学研究基金重大规划项目。“美国亚裔文学”研究丛书，即是该项课题的结题成果。这是国内第一套较为完整的“美国亚裔文学”方面的系列丛书，由文学史、文学作品选、文学评论集、学术论著等所组成，由我担任该丛书的总主编。

“美国亚裔文学”研究在 2017 年 4 月立项。随后，该丛书的论证计划，得到了国内外专家的一致认可。2017 年 5 月 27 日，中国人民大学科学研究基金重大规划项目“美国亚裔文学研究”开题报告会暨“美国亚裔文学研究高端论坛”在中国人民大学隆重召开。参加此次会议的专家学者全部为美国亚裔文学研究领域中的顶尖学者，包括美国加州大学洛杉矶分校的张敬珏教授、南京大学海外教育学院前院长程爱民教授、南京大学海外教育学院院长赵文书教授、北京语言大学应用外语学院院长陆薇教授、北京外国语大学潘志明教授、解放军外国语学院石平萍教授等。在此次会议上，我向与会专家介绍了该项目的基本

情况、未来研究方向与预计出版成果。与会专家对该项目的设立给予高度评价，强调在当今时代加强“美国亚裔文学”研究的必要性，针对该项目的预计研究及其成果，也提出了一些很好的建议。

根据计划，这套丛书将包括文学史2部：《美国亚裔文学史》和《美国华裔文学史》；文学选集2部：《美国亚裔文学作品选》和《美国华裔文学作品选》；批评文选2部：《美国亚裔文学评论集》和《美国华裔文学评论集》；访谈录1部：《美国亚裔作家访谈录》；美国学术论著2部（中译本）：*Articulate Silences* 和 *Chinese American Literature Without Borders*。同时，还计划出版若干学术专著和国际会议的论文集等。

根据我的基本设想，《美国亚裔文学史》和《美国华裔文学史》的撰写，将力图体现研究者对美国亚裔文学的研究进入到了较为深入的阶段。由于文学史是建立在研究者对该研究领域发展变化的总体认识上，涉及文学流派、创作方式、文学与社会变化关系、作家间的关联等各方面的问题，我们试图通过对亚裔文学发展进行总结和评价，旨在为当前亚裔文学和华裔文学的研究和推广做出一定贡献。

《美国亚裔文学作品选》和《美国华裔文学作品选》，除了记录、介绍等基本功能，还将在一定程度发挥形成民族认同、促进意识形态整合等功能。作品选编是民族共同体想象性构建的重要途径，也是作为文学经典得以确立和修正的最基本方式之一。因此，这样的作品选编，也会对美国亚裔文学的研究起到重要的促进作用。

《美国亚裔文学评论集》和《美国华裔文学评论集》，将主要选编美国、中国以及世界上最有学术价值的学术论文，虽然有些可能因为版权问题而不得不舍弃，但我们努力使之成为中国学术界研究“美国亚裔文学”和“美国华裔文学”的重要参考书目。

《美国亚裔作家访谈录》、美国学者的著作汉译、中国学者的美国亚裔文学学术专著等，我们将力图促使中美两国学者之间的学术对话，特别是希望中国的“美国亚裔文学”研究，既在中国的美国文学研究界，也在美国和世界上的美国文学研究界发出中国学者的声音。“一带一路”倡议的实施，使得文学研究的关注发生了转变，从过分关注西方话语，到逐步转向关注中国（亚洲）话语，我们的美国亚裔（华裔）文学研究，正是从全球化视角切入，思考美国亚裔（华裔）文学的世界性。

那么，我们为什么要对“美国亚裔文学”进行深入研究，并要编辑、撰写和翻译这套丛书呢？

首先，虽然“美国亚裔文学”在国外已有较大的影响，学术界也对此具有相当规模的研究，但在国内学术界，出于对“美国华裔文学”的偏爱与关注，“美国亚裔文学”相对还是一个较为陌生的领域。因此本课题首次以“亚裔”集体的形式标示亚裔文学的存在，旨在介绍“美国亚裔文学”，推介具有族裔特色和代表性的作家作品。

其次，选择“美国亚裔文学”为研究对象，其中也有对“美国华裔文学”的研究，希望能够体现我们对全球化视野中华裔文学的关注，也体现试图融合亚裔、深入亚裔文学研究的学术自觉。同时，在多元化多种族的美国社会语境中，我们力主打破国内长久以来专注“美国华裔文学”研究的固有模式，转而关注包括华裔作家在内的亚裔作家所具有的世界性眼光。

最后，顺应美国亚裔文学发展的趋势，对美国亚裔文学的研究不仅是文学研究界的关注热点，也是我国外语与文学教育的关注焦点。我们希望为高校未来“美国亚裔文学”的课程教学，提供一套高水平的参考丛书。

五、“美国亚裔文学”及其研究的未来

如前所述，“美国亚裔文学”在 20 世纪 70 年代逐渐崛起后，使得亚裔文学从沉默走向了发声。到 21 世纪，亚裔文学呈现出多元化的发展特征，更重要的是，许多新生代作家开始崭露头角。单就这些新的亚裔作家群体，就有许多值得我们关注的话题。

2018 年 6 月 23 日，“2018 美国亚裔文学高端论坛 —— 跨界：21 世纪的美国亚裔文学”在中国人民大学隆重召开。参加会议的专家学者将近 150 人。演讲嘉宾除了国内的美国亚裔文学研究领域中的著名专家学者外，还包括了我国台湾“中央研究院”的特聘教授、欧美研究所前所长李有成先生；我国台湾“中央研究院”特聘教授、欧美研究所前所长、华人世界著名的美国亚裔研究学者单德兴先生；我国台湾“中央研究院”副研究员、现在中央美术学院的访问教授王智明先生等。

在此次会议上，我提出来：今天，为什么要研究美国亚裔文学？我们要研究什么？

正如我们在会议通知上所说，美国亚裔文学在一百多年的风雨沧桑中历经“沉默”、“觉醒”、走向“发声”，见证了美国亚裔族群的沉浮兴衰。21 世纪以来，美国亚裔文学在全球冷战思维升温和战火硝烟不断的时空背景下，不囿于狭隘的种族主义藩篱，以“众声合奏”与“兼容并蓄”之势构筑出一道跨洋、跨国、跨种族、跨语言、跨文化、跨媒介、跨学科的文学景观，呈现出鲜明的世界主义意识。为此，我们拟定了一些主要议题。包括：1. 美国亚裔文学中的跨洋书写；2. 美国亚裔文学中的跨国书写；3. 美国亚裔文学中的跨种族书写；4. 美国亚裔文学中的跨语言书写；5. 美国亚裔文学中的跨文化书写；6. 美国亚裔文学的翻译跨界研究；7. 美国亚裔文学的跨媒介研究；8. 美国亚裔文学的跨学科研究等。

事实上，21 世纪以来，亚裔群体、亚裔所面临的问题、亚裔研究都发生了巨大的变化。从过去较为单纯的亚裔走向了跨越太平洋（transpacific）；从过去的彰显美国身份（claiming

America）到今天的批评美国身份（critiquing America）；过去单一的 America，现在变成了复数的 Americas，这些变化都值得引起我们的高度重视。由此所引发的诸多问题，也需要我们认真对待。比如：如何在“21 世纪”这个特殊的时间区间内去理解“美国亚裔文学”这一概念？有关“美国亚裔文学”的概念构建，是否本身就存在着作家的身份焦虑与书写的界限？如何把握“美国亚裔文学”的整体性与区域性？“亚裔”身份是否是作家在表达过程中去主动拥抱的归属之地？等等。

展望未来，随着新生代作家的迭出，“美国亚裔文学”将会呈现出更加生机勃勃的生命力，“美国亚裔文学”研究也将迎来更加光明的前途。

2018 年 8 月 28 日定稿于哈佛大学

专家推荐语

“美国亚裔文学研究丛书”包括美国亚裔文学史、美国亚裔文学作品选读、美国亚裔文学评论集、美国亚裔文学研究专著等，具有基础性、综合性、前沿性的特点。从研究范围看，将美国华裔文学研究拓展到美国亚裔文学，呈现出一幅更为完整的美国少数族裔文学版图。从研究深度看，论著作者均为美国亚裔文学研究领域著名专家，学术积累丰厚，研究水平一流。作为中国人民大学科学研究基金重大规划项目的研究成果，“美国亚裔文学研究丛书”为我们开展美国亚裔文学教学、研究、翻译提供了亟需的学术资源，有助于促进我们国家对美国文学全面深入的研究。

——王守仁，中国外国文学学会副会长、南京大学人文社会科学资深教授

This series is a groundbreaking work not just for the Asian American literary field, but for literature on the whole. As the first series of books about Asian American literature in China, it will undoubtedly inspire an unprecedented scholarly movement and bring greater and deserved awareness to issues including—but by no means limited to—gender, sexuality, and race as depicted through the lens and narratives of Asians and Asian Americans, perspectives too little seen and heard until now.

—Henry Louis Gates, Jr., Alphonse Fletcher University Professor and Director of the Hutchins Center for African and African American Research at Harvard University

Chinese American literature, for the past hundred years or so, has always straddled at least two cultures: the American and the Chinese. This ambitious and impressive series edited by Prof. Yingjian Guo brings the complex world of Chinese American writers to a broader Chinese-language readership. Such scholarship will help broaden, for Chinese scholars and students, the horizons of literary discourse and the range of appreciation for the Chinese American experience. Asian American literature, when read in a comparative light, reveals aspects of an American and Chinese American cultural terrain which spans politics, law, culture, and more. This collection will be useful for those in China, the Chinese diaspora, as well as the Americas to understand the rich linguistic, generational, political, and gendered diversity within Chinese American literature.

—Russell C. Leong, Editor of UCLA's *Amerasia Journal* (1977-2010); Author of *Phoenix Eyes and Other Stories* (The American Book Award), and; Current Editor of CUNY FORUM, for the City University of New York

美国亚裔文学研究的第一本专书 1982 年于美国出版，中文世界有关美国华裔文学的学术研究也始于 1980 年代，在接近“不惑之年”之际，实有必要盘点以往的研究成果，了解当前的学科生态，并策划未来的研究发展。郭英剑教授担任总主编的“美国亚裔文学研究丛书”，经过审慎规划，是中文世界有关此领域的第一套具规模、有系统的出版品，内容涵盖文学作品、文学评论、学术专书、文学史与访谈录等，多方位、具深度地提供有关美国亚裔文学与研究的代表作品，值得高度肯定。

——单德兴，台湾“中央研究院”欧美研究所前所长、特聘研究员

“美国亚裔文学研究丛书”涵盖面甚广，有文学创作，有文学史，有学术论著，有文学评论等，属单一领域的多元呈现，为近年来大陆出版界所少见，颇能反映大陆学术教育界在美国亚裔文学研究方面的具体成就。

——李有成，台湾“中央研究院”欧美研究所前所长、特聘研究员

“美国亚裔文学研究丛书”内容涵括文学史著作、文学作品选读、文学批评选集、学术论著，为国内第一套全面性介绍亚裔美国文学的丛书，中文学术著作之外亦有英文著作译本，具有推广文学以及搜集研究资料的双重功能，对于华语世界的亚裔美国文学研究极其重要。

——冯品佳，台湾交通大学前教务长、特聘教授

前 言

“美国亚裔文学”研究，是由中国人民大学“杰出学者”特聘教授郭英剑先生担任课题负责人的2017年度中国人民大学科学研究基金重大规划项目。“美国亚裔文学研究丛书”是该项课题的结题成果，由郭英剑教授担任该套丛书的总主编。这是国内第一套较为完整的“美国亚裔文学”方面的系列丛书，由文学史、文学作品选、文学评论集、学术论著等组成。

“美国亚裔文学”的发展历史可以远溯至19世纪，但其真正的兴起是在20世纪六七十年代。当时特殊的时代背景极大地促进了“美国亚裔文学”的发展，自此，亚裔文学作品层出不穷，包括文集、小说、戏剧、传记、短篇小说、诗歌等等。同时，“美国亚裔文学”在美国学术界也逐渐升温，引发了研究者的大量关注，许多高校都专设了“美国亚裔文学”的课程。

虽然“美国亚裔文学”在国外具有相当大的学术与社会影响力，但在国内的研究中，由于人们对“美国华裔文学”的强烈关注，学者、研究者众多，成果也最为突出，但“美国亚裔文学”对于很多学者来说，还是一个较为陌生的领域。人们对亚裔作家了解甚少，读过其作品的人更是寥寥无几。

《美国亚裔文学作品选》旨在介绍“美国亚裔文学”，推介具有族裔特色和代表性的亚裔作家和作品。

《美国亚裔文学作品选》以历史为发展脉络，精选了40位美国亚裔作家的作品，并以作家的出生年代为顺序进行编目排列。主要收录了华裔、日裔、韩裔、菲律宾裔、印度裔、越南裔、伊朗裔、巴基斯坦裔等亚裔代表作家的经典作品和新兴作家的代表作品。作品选中的入选作品，时间跨度长达一个世纪。我们力图呈现“美国亚裔文学”的历史发展图景。

该作品选中，每个作家及其作品为一个章节，分为作者简介和作品选读两个主要部分。选读部分一般选取的是每位作家的两至三部代表作品的节选，包括了各种体裁，如自传、小说、诗歌和散文等。作者简介部分主要提供了所选作家的个人基本信息、创作经历与代表性作品，同时，对于入选的作品也做了简要的点评。我们希望这样的简介能够帮助读者尽快了解作家，也大致了解所选作品的中心思想与主要内容。

《美国亚裔文学作品选》除了记录、介绍等基本功能外，还将在一定程度上发挥形成民族认同、促进意识形态整合等功能。作品选编是民族共同体想象性构建的重要途径，也是作为文学经典得以确立和修正的最基本方式之一。因此，这样的作品选编，也会对“美国亚裔文学”的研究起到重要的促进作用。

我们希望,《美国亚裔文学作品选》能够成为中国学术界研究“美国亚裔文学”的重要参考书目。

编　者

2018 年 8 月 28 日

目 录

1

(Edith Maude Eaton, 1865—1914)

伊迪丝·莫德·伊顿

作者简介

伊迪丝·莫德·伊顿（Edith Maude Eaton, 1865—1914），笔名水仙花（Sui Sin Far），著名作家。伊顿出生在英国，经过在中国、欧洲、加拿大和牙买加等地的逗留或生活，她最终在美国定居，安度了晚年。她一生创作颇多，被认为是“最早的美国亚裔作家之一”。

她主要作品有自传体回忆录《一个欧亚混血儿的心理档案》（*Leaves from the Mental Portfolio of an Eurasian*, 1909）；短篇小说有《中国以实玛利》（*A Chinese Ishmael*, 1899）、《秋扇》（*An Autumn Fan*, 1910）、《爱之鸟》（*The Bird of Love*, 1910）与《中国稻田里的爱情故事》（*A Love Story from the Rice Fields of China*, 1911）等；短篇小说集有《春香夫人与其他故事》（*Mrs. Spring Fragrance and Other Writings*, 1912）。

伊顿所有作品中，短篇小说集《春香夫人与其他故事》是她最为经典、最具代表性的作品，被誉为“最早的一部在美国出版的，由华人和白人混血作家创作的小说集”。小说集主要展现了华裔家庭的喜怒哀乐以及中西文化之间的矛盾冲突，淋漓尽致地再现了华裔移民在两种文化夹缝中的困惑与挣扎。

《新之智慧》（“The Wisdom of the New”）与《蒲初的美国化》（“The Americanizing of Pau Tsu”）选自短篇小说集《春香夫人与其他故事》。《新之智慧》主要讲述了一对华裔夫妇就“儿子是否学习美国文化”而争执不下。然而，他们的儿子在一次事故中不幸遇难，丈夫最终也放弃了对“新”的追求，随妻子回到了中国。《蒲初的美国化》也同样讲述了在美国生活的丈夫把他在中国的童养媳接到了美国，试图让她过上“美国人”的生活。然而，从小在中国传统文化下长大的妻子无法融入美国文化与生活，使得她的丈夫不得不放弃对她的“美国化”。这两个故事共同表达了华裔移民对“美国梦”的追求以及中西文化之间的不相容性。

作品选读

The Wisdom of the New
(excerpt)

By Sui Sin Far

WOU SANKWEI stood behind his desk, busily entering figures in a long yellow book. Now and then he would thrust the hair pencil with which he worked behind his ears and manipulate with deft fingers a Chinese counting machine. Wou Sankwei was the junior partner and book keeper of the firm of Leung Tang Wou & Co. of San Francisco. He had been in America seven years and had made good use of his time. Self-improvement had been his object and ambition, even more than the acquirement of a fortune, and who, looking at his fine, intelligent face and listening to his careful English, could say that he had failed?

One of his partners called his name. Some ladies wished to speak to him. Wou Sankwei hastened to the front of the store. One of his callers, a motherly looking woman, was the friend who had taken him under her wing shortly after his arrival in America. She had come to invite him to spend the evening with her and her niece, the young girl who accompanied her.

After his callers had left, Sankwei returned to his desk and worked steadily until the hour for his evening meal, which he took in the Chinese restaurant across the street from the bazaar. He hurried through with this, as before going to his friend's house, he had a somewhat important letter to write and mail. His mother had died a year before, and the uncle, to whom he was writing, had taken his wife and son into his home until such time as his nephew could send for them. Now the time had come.

Wou Sankwei's memory of the woman who was his wife was very faint. How could it be otherwise? She had come to him but three weeks before the sailing of the vessel which had brought him to America, and until then he had not seen her face. But she was his wife and the mother of his son. Ever since he had worked in America he had sent money for her support, and she had proved a good daughter to his mother.

As he sat down to write he decided that he would welcome her with a big dinner to his countrymen.

"Yes," he replied to Mrs. Dean, later on in the evening, "I have sent for my wife."

"I am so glad," said the lady. "Mr. Wou"—turning to her niece—"has not seen his wife for seven years."

"Deary me!" exclaimed the young girl. "What a lot of letters you must have written!"

"I have not written her one," returned the young man somewhat stiffly.

Adah Charlton looked up in surprise. "Why—" she began.

"Mr. Wou used to be such a studious boy when I first knew him," interrupted Mrs. Dean, laying her hand affectionately upon the young man's shoulder. "Now, it is all business. But you won't forget the concert on Saturday evening."

"No, I will not forget," answered Wou Sankwei.

"He has never written to his wife," explained Mrs. Dean when she and her niece were alone, "because his wife can neither read nor write."

"Oh, isn't that sad!" murmured Adah Charlton, her own winsome face becoming pensive.

"They don't seem to think so. It is the Chinese custom to educate only the boys. At least it has been so in the past. Sankwei himself is unusually bright. Poor boy! He began life here as a laundryman, and you may be sure that it must have been hard on him, for, as the son of a petty Chinese Government official, he had not been accustomed to manual labor. But Chinese character is wonderful; and now after seven years in this country, he enjoys a reputation as a business man amongst his countrymen, and is as up to date as any young American."

"But, Auntie, isn't it dreadful to think that a man should live away from his wife for so many years without any communication between them whatsoever except through others."

"It is dreadful to our minds, but not to theirs. Everything with them is a matter of duty. Sankwei married his wife as a matter of duty. He sends for her as a matter of duty."

"I wonder if it is all duty on her side," mused the girl.

Mrs. Dean smiled. "You are too romantic, Adah," said she. "I hope, however, that when she does come, they will be happy together. I think almost as much of Sankwei as I do of my own boy."

III

PAU LIN, the wife of Wou Sankwei, sat in a corner of the deck of the big steamer, awaiting the coming of her husband. Beside her, leaning his little queued head against her shoulder, stood her six-year-old son. He had been ailing throughout the voyage, and his small face was pinched with pain. His mother, who had been nursing him every night since the ship had left port, appeared very worn and tired. This, despite the fact that with a feminine desire to make herself fair to see in the eyes of her husband, she had arrayed herself in a heavily embroidered purple costume, whitened her forehead and cheeks with powder, and tinted her lips with carmine.

He came at last, looking over and beyond her. There were two others of her countrywomen awaiting the men who had sent for them, and each had a child, so that for a moment he seemed somewhat bewildered. Only when the ship's officer pointed out and named her, did he know her as his. Then he came forward, spoke a few words of formal welcome, and, lifting the child in his arms, began questioning her as to its health.

She answered in low monosyllables. At his greeting she had raised her patient eyes to his face—the face of the husband whom she had not seen for seven long years—then the eager look of expectancy which had crossed her own faded away, her eyelids drooped, and her countenance assumed an almost sullen expression.

"Ah, poor Sankwei!" exclaimed Mrs. Dean, who with Adah Charlton stood some little distance apart from the family group.

"Poor wife!" murmured the young girl. She moved forward and would have taken in her own white hands the ringed ones of the Chinese woman, but the young man gently restrained her. "She cannot understand you," said he. As the young girl fell back, he explained to his wife the presence of the stranger women. They were there to bid her welcome; they were kind and good and wished to be her friends as well as his.

Pau Lin looked away. Adah Charlton's bright face, and the tone in her husband's voice when he spoke to the young girl, aroused a suspicion in her mind—a suspicion natural to one who had come from a land where friendship between a man and woman is almost unknown.

"Poor little thing! How shy she is!" exclaimed Mrs. Dean.

Sankwei was glad that neither she nor the young girl understood the meaning of the averted face.

Thus began Wou Sankwei's life in America as a family man. He soon became accustomed to the change, which was not such a great one after all. Pau Lin was more of an accessory than a part of his life. She interfered not at all with his studies, his business, or his friends, and when not engaged in housework or sewing, spent most of her time in the society of one or the other of the merchants' wives who lived in the flats and apartments around her own. She kept up the Chinese custom of taking her meals after her husband or at a separate table, and observed faithfully the rule laid down for her by her late mother-in-law: to keep a quiet tongue in the presence of her man. Sankwei, on his part, was always kind and indulgent. He bought her silk dresses, hair ornaments, fans, and sweetmeats. He ordered her favorite dishes from the Chinese restaurant. When she wished to go out with her women friends, he hired a carriage, and shortly after her advent erected behind her sleeping room a chapel for the ancestral tablet and gorgeous goddess which she had brought over seas with her.

Upon the child both parents lavished affection. He was a quaint, serious little fellow, small for his age and requiring much care. Although naturally much attached to his mother, he became also very fond of his father who, more like an elder brother than a parent, delighted in playing all kinds of games with him, and whom he followed about like a little dog. Adah Charlton took a great fancy to him and sketched him in many different poses for a book on Chinese children which she was illustrating.

"He will be strong enough to go to school next year," said Sankwei to her one day. "Later on I intend to put him through an American college."

"What does your wife think of a Western training for him?" inquired the young girl.

"I have not consulted her about the matter," he answered. "A woman does not understand such things."

"A woman, Mr. Wou," declared Adah, "understands such things as well as and sometimes better than a man."

"An American woman, maybe," amended Sankwei; "but not a Chinese."

From the first Pau Lin had shown no disposition to become Americanized, and Sankwei himself had not urged it.

"I do appreciate the advantages of becoming westernized," said he to Mrs. Dean whose influence and interest in his studies in America had helped him to become what he was, "but it is not as if she had come here as I came, in her learning days. The time for learning with her is over."

One evening, upon returning from his store, he found the little Yen sobbing pitifully.

"What!" he teased, "A man—and weeping."

The boy tried to hide his face, and as he did so, the father noticed that his little hand was red and swollen. He strode into the kitchen where Pau Lin was preparing the evening meal.

"The little child who is not strong—is there anything he could do to merit the infliction of pain?" he questioned.

Pau Lin faced her husband. "Yes, I think so," said she.

"What?"

"I forbade him to speak the language of the white women, and he disobeyed me. He had words in that tongue with the white boy from the next street."

Sankwei was astounded.

"We are living in the white man's country," said he. "The child will have to learn the white man's language."

"Not my child," answered Pau Lin.

Sankwei turned away from her. "Come, little one," said he to his son, "we will take supper tonight at the restaurant, and afterwards Yen shall see a show."

Pau Lin laid down the dish of vegetables which she was straining and took from a hook a small wrap which she adjusted around the boy.

"Now go with thy father," said she sternly.

But the boy clung to her—to the hand which had punished him. "I will sup with you," he cried, "I will sup with you."

"Go," repeated his mother, pushing him from her. And as the two passed over the threshold, she called to the father: "Keep the wrap around the child. The night air is chill."

Late that night, while father and son were peacefully sleeping, the wife and mother arose, and lifting gently the unconscious boy, bore him into the next room where she sat down with him in a rocker. Waking, he clasped his arms around her neck. Backwards and forwards she rocked him, passionately caressing the wounded hand and crooning and crying until he fell asleep again.

The first chastisement that the son of Wou Sankwei had received from his mother, was because he had striven to follow in the footsteps of his father and use the language of the stranger.

"You did perfectly right," said old Sien Tau the following morning, as she leaned over her balcony to speak to the wife of Wou Sankwei. "Had I again a son to rear, I should see to it that he followed not after the white people."

Sien Tau's son had married a white woman, and his children passed their grandam on the street without recognition.

"In this country, she is most happy who has no child," said Lae Choo, resting her elbow upon the shoulder of Sien Tau. "A Toy, the young daughter of Lew Wing, is as bold and free in her ways as are the white women, and her name is on all the men's tongues. What prudent man of our race would take her as wife?"

"One needs not to be born here to be made a fool of," joined in Pau Lin, appearing at another balcony door. "Think of Hum Wah. From sunrise till midnight he worked for fourteen years, then a white man came along and persuaded from him every dollar, promising to return doublefold within the moon. Many moons have risen and waned, and Hum Wah still waits on this side of the sea for the white man and his money. Meanwhile, his father and mother, who looked long for his coming, have passed beyond returning."

"The new religion—what trouble it brings!" exclaimed Lae Choo. "My man received word yesterday that the good old mother of Chee Ping—he who was baptized a Christian at the last baptizing in the Mission around the corner—had her head secretly severed from her body by the steadfast people of the village, as soon as the news reached there. 'Twas the first violent death in the records of the place. This happened to the mother of one of the boys attending the Mission corner of my street."

"No doubt, the poor old mother, having lost face, minded not so much the losing of her head," sighed Pau Lin. She gazed below her curiously. The American Chinatown held a strange fascination for the girl from the seacoast village. Streaming along the street was a motley throng made up of all nationalities. The sing-song voices of girls whom respectable merchants' wives shudder to name, were calling to one another from high balconies up shadowy alleys. A fat barber was laughing hilariously at a drunken white man who had fallen into a gutter; a withered old fellow, carrying a bird in a cage, stood at the corner entreating passersby to have a good fortune told; some children were burning punk on the curbstone. There went by a stalwart Chief of the Six Companies engaged in earnest confab with a yellow-robed priest from the joss house. A Chinese dressed in the latest American style and a very blonde woman, laughing immoderately, were entering a Chinese restaurant together. Above all the hubbub of voices was heard the clang of electric cars and the jarring of heavy wheels over cobblestones.

Pau Lin raised her head and looked her thoughts at the old woman, Sien Tau.

"Yes," nodded the dame, "'tis a mad place in which to bring up a child."

Pau Lin went back into the house, gave little Yen his noonday meal, and dressed him with care. His father was to take him out that afternoon. She questioned the boy, as she braided his queue, concerning the white women whom he visited with his father.

It was evening when they returned—Wou Sankwei and his boy. The little fellow ran up to her in high glee. "See, mother," said he, pulling off his cap, "I am like father now. I wear no queue."

The mother looked down upon him—at the little round head from which the queue, which had been her pride, no longer dangled.

"Ah!" she cried. "I am ashamed of you; I am ashamed!"

The boy stared at her, hurt and disappointed.

"Never mind, son," comforted his father. "It is all right."

Pau Lin placed the bowls of seaweed and chickens' liver before them and went back to the kitchen where her own meal was waiting. But she did not eat. She was saying within herself: "It is for the white woman he has done this; it is for the white woman!"

Later, as she laid the queue of her son within the trunk wherein lay that of his father, long since cast aside, she discovered a picture of Mrs. Dean, taken when the American woman had first become the teacher and benefactress of the youthful laundryman. She ran over with it to her husband. "Here," said she; "it is a picture of one of your white friends." Sankwei took it from her almost reverently, "That woman," he explained, "has been to me as a mother."

"And the young woman—the one with eyes the color of blue china—is she also as a mother?" inquired Pau Lin gently.

But for all her gentleness, Wou Sankwei flushed angrily.

"Never speak of her," he cried. "Never speak of her!"

"Ha, ha, ha! Ha, ha, ha!" laughed Pau Lin. It was a soft and not unmelodious laugh, but to Wou Sankwei it sounded almost sacrilegious.

Nevertheless, he soon calmed down. Pau Lin was his wife, and to be kind to her was not only his duty but his nature. So when his little boy climbed into his lap and besought his father to pipe him a tune, he reached for his flute and called to Pau Lin to put aside work for that night. He would play her some Chinese music. And Pau Lin, whose heart and mind, undiverted by change, had been concentrated upon Wou Sankwei ever since the day she had become his wife, smothered, for the time being, the bitterness in her heart, and succumbed to the magic of her husband's playing—a magic which transported her in thought to the old Chinese days, the old Chinese days whose impression and influence ever remain with the exiled sons and daughters of China.

The Americanizing of Pau Tsu (excerpt)

By Sui Sin Far

PAU TSU came with the spring, and Wan Lin Fo was one of the happiest and proudest bridegrooms. The tiny bride was really very pretty—even to American eyes. In her peach and plum colored robes, her little arms and hands sparkling with jewels, and her shiny black head decorated with wonderful combs and pins, she appeared a bit of Eastern coloring amidst the Western lights and shades.

Lin Fo had not been forgotten, and her eyes under their downcast lids discovered him at once, as he stood awaiting her amongst a group of young Chinese merchants on the deck of the vessel.

The apartments he had prepared for her were furnished in American style, and her birdlike little figure in Oriental dress seemed rather out of place at first. It was not long, however, before she brought forth from the great box, which she had brought overseas, screens and fans, vases, panels, Chinese matting, artificial flowers and birds, and a number of exquisite carvings and pieces of antique porcelain. With these she transformed the American flat into an Oriental bower, even setting up in her sleeping-room a little chapel, enshrined in which was an image of the Goddess of Mercy, two ancestral tablets, and other emblems of her faith in the Gods of her fathers.

The Misses Raymond called upon her soon after arrival, and she smiled and looked pleased. She shyly presented each girl with a Chinese cup and saucer, also a couple of antique vases, covered with whimsical pictures, which Lin Fo tried, his best to explain. The girls were delighted with the gifts, and having fallen, as they expressed themselves, in love with the little bride, invited her through her husband to attend a launch party, which they intended giving the following Wednesday on Lake Washington.

Lin Fo accepted the invitation in behalf of himself and wife. He was quite at home with the Americans and, being a young man, enjoyed their rather effusive appreciation of him as an educated Chinaman. Moreover, he was of the opinion that the society of the American young ladies would benefit Pau Tsu in helping her to acquire the ways and language of the land in which he hoped to make a fortune.

Wan Lin Fo was a true son of the Middle Kingdom and secretly pitied all those who were born far away from its influences; but there was much about the Americans that he admired. He also entertained sentiments of respect for a motto which hung in his room which bore the legend: "When in Rome, do as the Romans do."

"What is best for men is also best for women in this country," he told Pau Tsu when she wept over his suggestion that she should take some lessons in English from a white woman.

"It may be best for a man who goes out in the street," she sobbed, "to learn the new language, but of what importance is it to a woman who lives only within the house and her husband's heart?"

It was seldom, however, that she protested against the wishes of Lin Fo. As her mother-in-law had said, she was a docile, happy little creature. Moreover, she loved her husband.

But as the days and weeks went by the girl bride whose life hitherto had been spent in the quiet retirement of a Chinese home in the performance of filial duties, in embroidery work and lute playing, in sipping tea and chatting with gentle girl companions, felt very much bewildered by the novelty and stir of the new world into which she had been suddenly thrown. She could not understand, for all Lin Fo's explanations, why it was required of her to learn the strangers' language and adopt their ways. Her husband's tongue was the same as her own. So also her little maid's. It puzzled her to be always seeing this, and hearing that—sights and sounds which as yet had no meaning for her. Why also was it necessary to receive visitors nearly every evening?—visitors who could neither understand nor make themselves understood by her, for all their curious smiles and stares, which she bore like a second Vashti—or rather, Esther. And why, oh! Why should she be constrained to eat her food with clumsy, murderous looking American implements instead of with her own elegant and easily manipulated ivory chopsticks?

Adah Raymond, who at Lin Fo's request was a frequent visitor to the house, could not fail to observe that Pau Tsu's small face grew daily smaller and thinner, and that the smile with which she invariably greeted her, though sweet, was tinged with melancholy. Her woman's instinct told her that something was wrong, but what it was the light within her failed to discover. She would reach over to Pau Tsu and take within her own firm, white hand the small, trembling fingers, pressing them lovingly and sympathetically; and the little Chinese woman would look up into the beautiful face bent above hers and think to herself: "No wonder he wishes me to be like her!"

2

(Younghill Kang, 1898—1972)
姜镛讫

作者简介

姜镛讫（Younghill Kang, 1898—1972），美国朝鲜裔作家、评论家和翻译家，被誉为"美国朝鲜裔文学之父"。出生于一个书香门第，姜镛讫自幼起痴迷于中国传统文化，尤其是儒家经典，阅读了诸多相关的书籍。在日本侵略朝鲜期间，他辗转在日办学校和美国教会学校学习。这些学习经历为他日后的学习和创作奠定了良好的基础。由于朝鲜国内的政治动荡，1921 年姜镛讫在牧师的帮助下逃到了美国。他曾在波士顿大学学习，之后从哈佛大学获得了硕士学位。

在有生之年，他为美国亚裔文化和文学发展做出了杰出的贡献，担任过美国政府部门的亚洲顾问、参与大英百科全书的编辑、把大量朝鲜文学作品翻译成英文等。他荣获了哈柏林·卡明斯基奖（Halperine Kaminsky）、圣路易斯·魏斯纪念奖（Louis S. Weiss）和高丽大学荣誉博士称号等重要奖项与荣誉。

姜镛讫精通韩语、日语、英语和中文。起初，他用韩语和日语写作，自 1928 年开始，他转入全英文写作。他的著作有长篇小说《草堂》（*The Grass Roof*, 1931）、自传体小说《从东方到西方》（*East Goes West*, 1937）与一部未发表的戏剧《皇宫里的暗杀》（*Murder in the Royal Palace*）。

《草堂》是姜镛讫最为经典的一部作品。这部小说被认为是"第一部美国朝鲜裔小说"。小说从一名朝鲜少年的视角讲述了他不惧战争和死亡、一心求学的故事。这部小说是一部励志小说，激励人们克服万难，勇于探索学习的海洋。

第 12 章是本小说最精彩的部分之一，主要围绕主人公“向西方学习”话题而展开，表达主人公急切想要突破传统束缚、走向自由平等的西方世界的梦想和追求。

作品选读

The Grass Roof

Chapter XII

(excerpt)

By Younghill Kang

I was encouraged by an ardent and fiery young man of the new generation, Park Soo-San, or The Isolated Mountain. My uncle pak-sa had helped to bring him there from Seoul, and he had come to an out-lying province in order to escape spy detection. Already he had served jail sentence for printing a Korean history as a text-book. He was only twenty years old, but was a well-known mathematician in the country, and had written a text-book on algebra. Life at his school was very exciting. The Japanese government censored all studies, not only the native history which had always been taught before, but any historical account which dealt with independence movements, or emancipators. The books which told of Washington and Lincoln were contraband, of course. When inspection-day came around, Park Soo-San would be under the school-porch, burying history books in the clean white sand, until danger was over.

I was one of his favorites. He would make me entrancing lectures privately. Korea was just beginning to live again, he said. But we must never forget the task before us. We must master the entire learning of the West. He was like a prophet when he said this: his bright eyes behind scholarly spectacles full of terrible joy and courage, his slight body moved by waves of fierce emotion, his large head bold, well-shaped, poised with enthusiastic resolution. At whatever cost, he said. You knew that he would go through the hell-fire to go on with his work in education. In all that he spoke, he was like a hero. One night he mentioned to me the horrors which the intelligentsia of Korea might be called on to face at the hands of their Jap oppressors, before the

Western learning could be introduced throughout the land, uncurtailed and unrestricted. He told me of previous prison terms and hinted of the tortures, given him to extract testimony. He could not sleep at night for the throbbing agony of the after-effect. When he said this, I just cried for him.

"But Korea shall live again!" he repeated emphatically, catching me by the eyes.

"How can the people of Korea ever be happy again?" I echoed my father's words, "when this is how they are treated?"

"They are just waiting for leaders," he said solemnly, "they are waiting for leaders, leaders with Western education, Western ideals of progress."

These were words I had long been hungering for. I too was fascinated by the knowledge of the West.

"Japan has conquered Korea by Western science. We must regain our freedom by a superior knowledge of that science," Park Soo-San would say, and I would agree.

After this he spoke to me often about the future of Korea and about the Revolution for independence which was bound to come. Already there was a well-organized band of patriots throughout the land, and there were others in exile working for the country. He told me that always I must train my wits and use my social sense before these Jap spies which infested the nation. He gave me codes to memorize in communicating with other revolutionists, and I did not forget them.

At another time he spoke of America to me, America, the home of those queer missionaries of the market-place. Park Soo-San had become a liberal Christian, wishing to turn his back on the past, and his face toward the future; it was a very radical thing to do at that time. An education in America, for the greatest possible number, was the desideratum he always preached. Japan had government students there. China had too. Only Korea had not her quota there, because her national rights had been stolen before she could get the new ways. Yes, now Korea was being punished for her conservatism. Any who could must make their way to America. Others must go by the help of patriotic private citizens who yet had the means in hand. What glamour he cast over the great colleges in America, which held all that the West had ever thought or known, and the latest means for giving it in the diploma packet by the wholesale. An American education was for the few he preached; those few would reap the golden reward. He made me see that the road of a scholar's future prominence lay toward America like the shortest distance between two points... in a straight line.

As soon as I understood, my soul had the fixed goal, although I did not speak of it yet to anyone. It seemed too daring. But I studied with all the concentration and enthusiasm of the crazy-poet who would have died at any time for the great poets of the Tang and Sung dynasties; I studied with all the political and social fervor of my uncle pak-sa who made his name through pull and scholarship in Seoul; I studied with all the joie-de-vivre and recklessness of the prodigal-son who took his happiness at the expense of others; I studied with all the self-denial and earnestness of my father in slaving for three men's families; I studied with all the brains of my many ancestors who had been scholars and poets and officials beyond count or number.

The old Confucian school receded to the past, in my mind. It seemed to me more and more useless, as a bull-fight or a game of contract bridge, since I began to learn the law of gravitation, and Boyle's law and all the other laws. The study of the lives of Lincoln and Napoleon, and the geography of the World kindled my enthusiasm until sometimes I seemed just to be dazzled by stars in the head. The contrast of my inner world—an expanding cosmos that would admit no boundary—and my outer, that secluded village of the Han, with roots many centuries deep, growing down into the green earth, stimulated me to speculate and to speculate, and still I lived as in the starvation for more. As the wiseman of the East, I was led on by the star of Christian civilization, unaware then of the moral ambiguity in which its peoples live, or its industrial, mechanistic trend which makes cogs of their lives.

I cut my hair off short, like Park Soo-San's and a few others, without asking my father or my grandmother. I wanted to do something like a baptism. It was symbol to me of breaking away from the bondage of tradition, my oath that I had set myself toward Western learning and all the West had to give and to teach. Before I cut it, my hair was very long and thick, worn in two tight braids off the forehead, then tied with a ribbon and allowed to flow freely behind. This was girls' style and the style for the boy not yet reaching to manhood. As soon as men were married they put their hair up. Then it was worn in a top-knot high on the head. Park Soo-San was pleased when I cut my hair, and said it looked beautiful. He understood at once the symbol. He got me a Western hat too in the market-place. I loved that hat. To me it was almost like the cap of a great *pak-sa*, and meant that I was of those scholars sworn to obtain the degrees of the West. But I told no one of that.

Then I went home. Just outside the bamboo fence I had misgiving. It was not on my own behalf, but on behalf of my hat. I took it off and hid it under my overcoat. My grandmother was sitting on the floor of the kitchen, spinning, too sad even to sing a sad song. When she saw me she gave a sharp moan. My father heard her and came running out from the men's part of the house anxiously. My father, when he saw my short hair, made a kind of roaring noise. He went into savage rage in which he seemed to lose all mind.

"Monk's head! Monk's head!" he shouted, running toward me. It was as if I had joined the army of Japan. "How dare you take off the hair!" Then as I hid in my grandmother's skirt: "Let him out! Let him out! That Japanese widow!"

My grandmother threw her arms around me and tried to protect me. But my father took me and put me in a small cell where the husks of beans were kept. It smelled very good, but it was dark, and not pleasant waiting till my father came back with a long stick. Then my father beat me and beat me. He said it was his hair I had cut. How dared I cut his hair? At last he got tired, and rushed off, but still angry.

When I crept out, very sore, my grandmother wrung her hands. She was crying because I had been beaten. Some of her tears, too, were for my lost hair.

"Child, child!" my poor grandmother wailed. "What did you do with the hair?"

I said that I had thrown it all in the stove.

"Ai! Ai! But didn't you see the value of the hair? It was worth dozens and dozens of dollars. Such good hair, too!"

Hair was very expensive in Korea, because it was used so largely on brides. Dalpi, or tails of extra hair, were given to the girls about to be married and were in some way glued to the natural hair, and then elaborately arranged. Abundance of hair was the beauty of women, so if you hadn't much hair, or even if you had plenty, you added more. My childless aunt had the most luxurious Dalpi I ever saw; they had been given her by my uncle *pak-sa*, and cost a great deal of money. My grandmother was already saving hair for the dalpi of my future bride. Long threads of it, cut from the luxuriant heads of children in a place where it wouldn't show, were bound by men in the market-place to form home-made dalpi. Thus in three years, three dalpis had been taken from Ok-Dong-Ya'head. My grandmother kept all these and more in the drawer under the big chest. When a very respectable visitor came, she would show them.

"This one has a romantic history."

So for practical reasons she regretted the loss of my hair. It would have furnished several dalpi for my future wife. Already my father and my grandmother were talking about this person. I would hear them as I lay on the matting on my stomach, reading, in the room beyond the dining room. They had an informal agreement, they said to each other, with the family of a very nice and beautiful girl, living about ten miles away, and only a few years my senior. Some day I would be growing up, in three or four years now: at fifteen or sixteen they thought I ought to be married. My friend, Sur-Choon, I learned, was already formally betrothed, but this did not make me any better satisfied when I heard my elders speaking of my betrothal. Before I went to the Western school, I thought it would be nice to get married, but Park-Soo-San was not married, and all that now seemed to me old-fashioned. I began to disbelieve in marriage; it was waste of time, like the village school of Co-Mool where only dummies went. I wanted only to study.

My cutting of the hair was considered a family catastrophe, an insurmountable obstacle to early marriage. For the family honor I could not be married without my top-knot, even if the match-maker should keep my mutilation a secret from the family of the bride. My father flew into a rage at sight every time, and could not seem to get over it, so I had to run away to the village where my grandmother and my little aunt had lived before they were married. Here I hid seven weeks in exile, supported by a cousin and by Park Soo-San. At length my little aunt, the peace-maker of the family, came to get me. She had a way with her of smoothing everything over, making it soft and not so harsh. She said she was sure my father would forgive me if I would only let my hair grow; and she pretended that it wasn't much to do for your family, and would mean freedom in the long run. At last I agreed to compromise and let it grow half-way.

My little aunt carried back the news, and my family thankfully bought all kind of drugs and a turban to make the hair grow faster. Instead of feeding the water in which the rice was bathed to Dalksali, as formerly, my grandmother now saved it very carefully and washed my head in every week. Immediately after the washing of my hair, I would go to the top of Chak-Doo-Shay's garage, or place where the ox-carts were kept, to a kind of secret chamber and we would spread out the newspapers, and Chak-Doo-Shay would clip my hair all around a wee bit according to my direction. He was, very clever with the scissors.

Every ten days or so my elders would measure my hair. They were mystified at hair that stayed in the same place, never grew longer, never became shorter, day after day was just as before.

"This hair does not grow. I can't understand."

Nobody liked it short except Ok-Dong-Ya.

"Isn't it beautiful? I think it's cute! See that?" she passed her hand over my head. "If I were a boy, Chung-Pa, I would surely cut my hair off too."

Then she made up a song about how she hoped her husband would have short hair. My grandmother scolded her and even spoke bitterly about the younger generation.

"He! girls are losing modesty before their brothers, boys are cutting the hair. Where shall we be next? Even hair rebels against elders and will not grow."

Ok-Dong-Ya laughed into her sleeves, and ran off to see to the ribbons which were being sewed on her new dress. My little aunt laughed too very slyly. She knew the hair tonic didn't do any good though she rubbed it in faithfully according to my grandmother's directions, and never told her suspicions, even when my father said to my grandmother, "Do you know it has now been three months? His hair is bewitched. It won't grow."

I was eleven and a half years old. There was nothing more in Park Soo-San's school to learn. He said I was well prepared to go to any new high-school in Seoul, where there were five or six. I got all the advice from him about high-schools in Seoul. There were no high-schools near Song-Dune-Chi. I knew there was only one thing to be done; I must go South to Seoul, mysterious Seoul.

All my life I had heard of this city, but never until now was the centre in my country for the Western learning. My father, the crazy-poet and my uncle *pak-sa* had been there in official capacity, for formerly all young men of any standing went to Seoul to seek honor from the Emperor of the 10,000 isles, as he was called. Seoul, lying behind stone walls like every Eastern city, had held romance, adventure, sometimes glory for the wanderer, the spectacle of the glittering court and the fashionable poet-nobles, in the white stand gayest of silks, but before now, never the Western learning.

3

(Bienvenido Santos, 1911—1996)
比恩韦尼多·桑德斯

作者简介

比恩韦尼多·桑德斯（Bienvenido Santos, 1911—1996），美国菲律宾裔小说家、诗人和非小说作家，出生于菲律宾首都马尼拉。他曾在菲律宾大学（University of the Philippines）学习创意写作，并获得了文科学士学位。1941年他以政府学者（government pensionado）的身份被派送到美国，在伊利诺伊大学（University of Illinois）、哥伦比亚大学（Columbia University）和哈佛大学（Harvard University）就读和学习。他被誉为“美国亚裔先锋作家之一”。

他一生成果丰硕，创作了诸多小说、诗歌和非小说文类。他的小说有《火山》（*The Volcano*, 1965）与《祈祷的人》（*The Praying Man*, 1982）等；短篇小说集有《可爱的人》（*You Lovely People*, 1955）、《兄弟，我的兄弟》（*Brother, My Brother*, 1960）与《苹果的香味》（*Scent of Apples*, 1979）等；诗集有《受伤的雄鹿》（*The Wounded Stag*, 1956, 1992）等。非小说类作品有《记忆中的故事：个人历史》（*Memory's Fictions: A Personal History*, 1993）等。

作为多产的作家，比恩韦尼多·桑德斯斩获了颇多重要的荣誉和奖项，如古根海姆奖（Guggenheim Fellowship）、共和国文化遗产奖（Republic Cultural Heritage Award）、卡洛斯·帕兰卡纪念奖（Carlos Palanca Memorial Awards）与美国图书奖（American Book Award）等。

短篇小说集《苹果的香味》是比恩韦尼多·桑德斯最为经典的，也是唯一一部在美国出版的著作。这部小说集包含了他在20世纪40年代到70年代之间创作的短篇小说。这些作品主要表达了菲律宾人为了逃避国内的政治动荡，到美国寻求“美国梦”，然而经历了一场“美国噩梦”。这些作品以犀利的语言和精湛的文笔活灵活现地描绘出菲律宾人在美国的血泪历史。短篇小说《苹果的香味》（“Scent of Apples”）选自短篇小说集《苹果的香味》。这部小说主要讲述了在异国他乡的菲律宾人对自己母国的思念以及他们无法“回家”的心酸和遗憾之情。

作品选读

Scent of Apples

By Bienvenido Santos

When I arrived in Kalamazoo it was October and the war was still on. Gold and silver stars hung on pennants above silent windows of white and brick-red cottages. In a backyard an old man burned leaves and twigs while a grey-haired woman sat on the porch, her red hands quiet on her lap, watching the smoke rising above the elms, both of them thinking of the same thought perhaps, about a tall, grinning boy with blue eyes and flying hair, who went out to war: where could he be now this month when leaves were turning into gold and the fragrance of gathered apples was in the wind?

It was a cold night when I left my room at the hotel for a usual speaking engagement. I walked but a little way. A heavy wind coming up from Lake Michigan was icy on the face. It felt like winter straying early in the northern woodlands. Under the lampposts the leaves shone like bronze. And they rolled on the pavements like the ghost feet of a thousand autumns long dead, long before the boys left for faraway lands without great icy winds and promise of winter early in the air, lands without apple trees, *the singing and the gold!*

It was the same night I met Celestino Fabia, “just a Filipino farmer” as he called himself, who had a farm about thirty miles east of Kalamazoo.

“You came all that way on a night like this just to hear me talk?” I asked.

“I’ve seen no Filipino for so many years now,” he answered quickly. “So when I saw your name in the papers where it says you come from the Islands and that you're going to talk, I come right away."

Earlier that night I had addressed a college crowd, mostly women. It appeared that they wanted me to talk about my country; they wanted me to tell them things about it because my country had become a lost country. Everywhere in the land the enemy stalked. Over it a great silence hung; and their boys were there, unheard from, or they were on their way to some little known island on the Pacific, young boys all, hardly men, thinking of harvest moons and smell of forest fire.

It was not hard talking about our own people. I knew them well and I loved them. And they seemed so far away during those terrible years that I must have spoken of them with a little fervor, a little nostalgia.

In the open forum that followed, the audience wanted to know whether there was much difference between our women and the American women. I tried to answer the question as best as I could, saying, among other things, that I did not know much about American women, except that they looked friendly, but differences or similarities in inner qualities such as naturally belonged to the heart or to the mind, I could only speak about with vagueness.

While I was trying to explain away the fact that it was not easy to make comparisons, a man rose from the rear of the hall, wanting to say something. In the distance, he looked slight and old and very brown. Even before he spoke, I knew that he was, like me, a Filipino.

"I'm a Filipino," he began, loud and clear, in a voice that seemed used to wide open spaces, "I'm just a Filipino farmer out in the country." He waved his hand towards the door. "I left the Philippines more than twenty years ago and have never been back. Never will perhaps. I want to find out, sir, are our Filipino women the same like they were twenty years ago?"

As he sat down, the hall filled with voices, hushed and intrigued. I weighed my answer carefully. I did not want to tell a lie yet I did not want to say anything that would seem platitudinous, insincere. But more important than these considerations, it seemed to me that moment as I looked towards my countryman, I must give him an answer that would not make him so unhappy. Surely, all these years, he must have held on to certain ideals, certain beliefs, even illusions peculiar to the exile.

"First," I said as the voices gradually died down and every eye seemed upon me, "First, tell me what our women were like twenty years ago."

The man stood to answer. "Yes," he said, "you're too young... Twenty years ago our women were nice, they were modest, they wore their hair long, they dressed proper and went for no monkey business. They were natural, they went to church regular, and they were faithful." He had spoken slowly, and now in what seemed like an afterthought, added, "It's the men who ain't."

Now I knew what I was going to say.

"Well," I began, "it will interest you to know that our women have changed—but definitely! The change, however, has been on the outside only. Inside, here," pointing to the heart, "they are the same as they were twenty years ago. God-fearing, faithful, modest, and *nice*."

The man was visibly moved. "I'm very happy, sir," he said, in the manner of one who, having stakes on the land, had found no cause to regret one's sentimental investment.

After this, everything that was said and done in that hall that night seemed like an anti-climax; and later, as we walked outside, he gave me his name and told me of his farm thirty miles east of the city.

We had stopped at the main entrance to the hotel lobby. We had not talked very much on the way. As a matter of fact, we were never alone. Kindly American friends talked to us, asked us questions, said goodnight. So now I asked him whether he cared to step into the lobby with me and talk.

"No, thank you," he said, "you are tired. And I don't want to stay out too late."

"Yes, you live very far."

"I got a car," he said, "besides..."

Now he smiled, he truly smiled. All night I had been watching his face and I wondered when he was going to smile.

"Will you do me a favor, please," he continued smiling almost sweetly. "I want you to have dinner with my family out in the country. I'd call for you tomorrow afternoon, then drive you back. Will that be all right?"

"Of course," I said. "I'd love to meet your family." I was leaving Kalamazoo for Muncie, Indiana, in two days. There was plenty of time.

"You will make my wife very happy," he said.

"You flatter me."

"Honest. She'll be very happy. Ruth is a country girl and hasn't met many Filipinos. I mean Filipinos younger than I, cleaner looking. We're just poor farmer folk, you know, and we don't get to town very often. Roger, that's my boy, he goes to school in town. A bus takes him early in the morning and he's back in the afternoon. He's nice boy."

"I bet he is," I agreed. "I've seen the children of some of the boys by their American wives and the boys are tall, taller than the father, and very good looking."

"Roger, he'd be tall. You'll like him."

Then he said goodbye and I waved to him as he disappeared in the darkness.

The next day he came, at about three in the afternoon. There was a mild, ineffectual sun shining; and it was not too cold. He was wearing an old brown tweed jacket and worsted trousers to match. His shoes were polished, and although the green of his tie seemed faded, a colored shirt hardly accentuated it. He looked younger than he appeared the night before now that he was clean shaven and seemed ready to go to a party. He was grinning as we met.

"Oh, Ruth can't believe it. She can't believe it," he kept repeating as he led me to his car—a nondescript thing in faded black that had known better days and many hands. "I says to her, I'm bringing you a first class Filipino, and she says, aw, go away, quit kidding, there's no such thing as first class Filipino. But Roger, that's my boy, he believed me immediately. What's he like, daddy, he asks. Oh, you will see, I says, he's first class. Like you daddy? No, no, I laugh at him, your daddy ain't first class. Aw, but you are, daddy, he says. So you can see what a nice boy he is, so innocent. Then Ruth starts griping about the house, but the house is a mess, she says. True it's a mess, it's always a mess, but you don't mind, do you? We're poor folks, you know."

The trip seemed interminable. We passed through narrow lanes and disappeared into thickets, and came out on barren land overgrown with weeds in places. All around were dead leaves and dry earth. In the distance were apple trees.

"Aren't those apple trees?" I asked wanting to be sure.

"Yes, those are apple trees," he replied. "Do you like apples? I got lots of 'em. I got an apple orchard, I'll show you."

All the beauty of the afternoon seemed in the distance, on the hills, in the dull soft sky.

"Those trees are beautiful on the hills," I said.

"Autumn's a lovely season. The trees are getting ready to die, and they show their colors, proud-like."

"No such thing in our own country," I said.

That remark seemed unkind, I realized later. It touched him off on a long deserted tangent, but ever there perhaps. How many times did the lonely mind take unpleasant detours away from the familiar winding lanes towards home for fear of this, the remembered hurt, the long lost youth, the grim shadows of the years; how many times indeed, only the exile knows.

It was a rugged road we were travelling and the car made so much noise that I could not hear everything he said, but I understood him. He was telling his story for the first time in many years. He was remembering his own youth. He was thinking of home. In these odd moments there seemed no cause for fear no cause at all, no pain. That, would come later. In the night perhaps. Or lonely on the farm under the apple trees.

In this old Visayan town, the streets are narrow and dirty and strewn with corral shells. You have been there? You could not have missed our house, it was the biggest in town, one of the oldest, ours was a big family. The house stood right on the edge of the street. A door opened heavily and you enter a dark hall leading to the stairs. There is the smell of chickens roosting on the low-topped walls, there is the familiar sound they make and you grope your way up a massive staircase, the bannisters smooth upon the trembling hand. Such nights, they are no better than the days, windows are closed against the sun; they close heavily.

Mother sits in her corner looking very white and sick. This was her world, her domain. In all these years I cannot remember the sound of her voice. Father was different. He moved about. He shouted. He ranted. He lived in the past and talked of honor as though it were the only thing.

I was born in that house. I grew up there into a pampered brat. I was mean. One day I broke their hearts. I saw mother cry wordlessly as father heaped his curses upon me and drove me out of the house, the gate closing heavily after me. And my brothers and sisters took up my father's hate for me and multiplied it numberless times in their own broken hearts. I was no good.

But sometimes, you know, I miss that house, the roosting chickens on the low-topped walls. I miss my brothers and sisters. Mother sitting in her chair, looking like a pale ghost in a corner of the room. I would remember the great live posts, massive tree trunks from the forests. Leafy plants grew on the sides, buds pointing downwards, wilted and died before they could become flowers. As they fell on the floor, father bent to pick them and throw them out into the corral streets. His hands were strong. I have kissed those hands... many times, many times.

Finally we rounded a deep curve and suddenly came upon a shanty, all but ready to crumble in a heap on the ground, its plastered walls were rotting away, the floor was hardly a foot from the ground. I thought of the cottages of the poor colored folk in the south, the hovels of the poor everywhere in the land. This one stood all by itself as though by common consent all the folk that used to live here had decided to stay away, despising it, ashamed of it. Even the lovely season could not color it with beauty.

A dog barked loudly as we approached. A fat blonde woman stood at the door with a little boy by her side. Roger seemed newly scrubbed. He hardly took his eyes off me. Ruth had a clean apron around her shapeless waist. Now as she shook my hands in sincere delight I noticed shamefacedly (that I should notice) how rough her hands, how coarse and red with labor, how ugly! She was no longer young and her smile was pathetic.

As we stepped inside and the door closed behind us, immediately I was aware of the familiar scent of apples. The room was bare except for a few ancient pieces of second-hand furniture. In the middle of the room stood a stove to keep the family warm in winter. The walls were bare. Over the dining table hung a lamp yet unlighted.

Ruth got busy with the drinks. She kept coming in and out of a rear room that must have been the kitchen and soon the table was heavy with food, fried chicken legs and rice, and green peas and corn on the ear. Even as we ate, Ruth kept standing, and going to the kitchen for more food. Roger ate like a little gentleman.

"Isn't he nice looking?" his father asked.

"You are a handsome boy, Roger," I said.

The boy smiled at me. "You look like Daddy," he said.

Afterwards I noticed an old picture leaning on the top of a dresser and stood to pick it up. It was yellow and soiled with many fingerings. The faded figure of a woman in Philippine dress could yet be distinguished although the face had become a blur.

"Your..." I began.

"I don't know who she is," Fabia hastened to say. "I picked that picture many years ago in a room on La Salle Street in Chicago. I have often wondered who she is."

"The face wasn't a blur in the beginning?"

"Oh, no. It was a young face and good."

Ruth came with a plate full of apples.

"Ah," I cried, picking out a ripe one, "I've been thinking where all the scent of apples came from. The room is full of it."

"I'll show you," said Fabia.

He showed me a backroom, not very big. It was half-full of apples.

"Every day," he explained, "I take some of them to town to sell to the groceries. Prices have been low. I've been losing on the trips."

"These apples will spoil," I said.

"We'll feed them to the pigs."

Then he showed me around the farm. It was twilight now and the apple trees stood bare against a glowing western sky. In apple blossom time it must be lovely here, I thought. But what about wintertime?

One day, according to Fabia, a few years ago, before Roger was born, he had an attack of acute appendicitis. It was deep winter. The snow lay heavy everywhere. Ruth was pregnant and none too well herself. At first she did not know what to do. She bundled him in warm clothing and put him on a cot near the stove. She shoveled the snow from their front door and practically carried the suffering man on her shoulders, dragging him through the newly made path towards the road where they waited for the U.S. Mail car to pass. Meanwhile snowflakes poured all over them and she kept rubbing the man's arms and legs as she herself nearly froze to death.

"Go back to the house, Ruth!" her husband cried, "you'll freeze to death."

But she clung to him wordlessly. Even as she massaged his arms and legs, her tears rolled down her cheeks. "I won't leave you, I won't leave you," she repeated.

Finally the U.S. Mail car arrived. The mailman, who knew them well, helped them board the car, and, without stopping on his usual route, took the sick man and his wife direct to the nearest hospital.

Ruth stayed in the hospital with Fabia. She slept in a corridor outside the patients' ward and in the day time helped in scrubbing the floor and washing the dishes and cleaning the men's things. They didn't have enough money and Ruth was willing to work like a slave.

"Ruth's a nice girl," said Fabia, "like our own Filipino women."

Before nightfall, he took me back to the hotel. Ruth and Roger stood at the door holding hands and smiling at me. From inside the room of the shanty, a low light flickered. I had a last glimpse of the apple trees in the orchard under the darkened sky as Fabia backed up the car. And soon we were on our way back to town. The dog had started barking. We could hear it for some time, until finally, we could not hear it anymore, and all was darkness around us, except where the head lamps revealed a stretch of road leading somewhere.

Fabia did not talk this time. I didn't seem to have anything to say myself. But when finally we came to the hotel and I got down, Fabia said, "Well, I guess I won't be seeing you again."

It was dimly lighted in front of the hotel and I could hardly see Fabia's face. Without getting off the car, he moved to where I had sat, and I saw him extend his hand. I gripped it.

"Tell Ruth and Roger," I said, "I love them."

He dropped my hand quickly. "They'll be waiting for me now," he said.

"Look," I said, not knowing why I said it, "one of these days, very soon, I hope, I'll be going home. I could go to your town."

"No," he said softly, sounding very much defeated but brave, "Thanks a lot. But, you see, nobody would remember me now."

Then he started the car, and as it moved away, he waved his hand.

"Goodbye," I said, waving back into the darkness. And suddenly the night was cold like winter straying early in these northern woodlands.

I hurried inside. There was a train the next morning that left for Muncie, Indiana, at a quarter after eight.

4

(Carlos Bulosan, 1913—1956)
卡洛斯·布洛桑

作者简介

卡洛斯·布洛桑（Carlos Bulosan, 1913—1956），美国菲律宾裔小说家和诗人。他出生于菲律宾邦雅斯兰的一个农民家庭。由于家境贫寒，布洛桑孩童时期开始帮助父母务农或务工。在 1930 年，他离开菲律宾到了美国，在那里度过了噩梦般的余生。

布洛桑在有生之年创作出了很多重要的作品。长篇小说《我父亲的笑》（*The Laughter of My Father*, 1944）、《美国在心中》（*America Is in the Heart*, 1946）、《呐喊与奉献》（*The Cry and the Dedication*, 1995）、《所有的阴谋者》（*All the Conspirators*, 1998）、《我父亲的悲剧》（*My Father's Tragedy*, 2012）；短篇小说集《菲律宾在心中》（*The Philippines Is in the Heart*, 1978）与短篇小说《马格诺·卢比奥的浪漫》（*The Romance of Magno Rubio*, 1996）等；诗集《来自美国的一封信》（*Letter from America*, 1942）与《来自巴丹的声音》（*Voice of Bataan*, 1943）等；散文《如果你想了解我们》（*If You Want To Know What We Are*, 1983）等；文集《成为菲律宾人》（*On Becoming Filipino*, 1995）。

《美国在心中》（*America Is in the Heart*, 1946）是布洛桑半自传体小说。这部小说是"最早的一部从美国亚裔视角展现移民与劳工经历的作品之一"，被誉为"美国菲律宾裔经历的超文本"。小说讲述了布洛桑大半生的坎坷人生经历。在菲律宾，布洛桑一家过着穷困潦倒、朝不保夕的日子。为了更好的生计，布洛桑历尽千辛万苦到了美国。然而，他的"美国梦"演变成了"美国噩梦"。常年的饥寒交迫让他患上了肺结核。病痛与精神上的折磨最终让他在美国英年早逝，永远无法回到故乡。

小说第25章和26章中作者用犀利而又精妙的语言道出了所有菲律宾移民心中的“美国梦”，以及他们对故乡的思念，但又无法“回家”的心酸与苦楚。

作品选读

America Is in the Heart

Chapter XXV

By Carlos Bulosan

PASCUAL's condition was getting worse each day. His only desire now was to go back to the Philippines. His legs were paralyzed, but he could still move his hands. I knew that it was the end for him. But he had served his purpose. He belonged to yesterday. And although his socialistic ideas were vague and fumbling, I gained something vital from him. I was to add something new to it: a new significance and meaning.

As Pascual's days came to a close, I went to the Filipino camps and asked for contributions. Some of the agricultural workers came to town and sat around Pascual. He was dying, and he wanted to say something. He turned his face toward me and began to speak.

"It is for the workers that we must write," he said weakly. "We must interpret their hopes as a people desiring the fullest fulfillment of their potentialities. We must be strong of voice, objective of criticism, protest and challenge. There is no other way to combat any attempts to suppress individual liberty..."

It was Pascual's last message. When he died, his wife went to San Francisco with the newspaper and resumed its publication there with the co-operation of a farm worker who had become an editor. I never saw her again.

When the house was closed, I took a bus for Los Angeles. I found that my brother Macario and Nick, Jose's brother, were living together. They had started a literary magazine with a man named Felix Razon. To my amazement, he was the same peasant boy who had warned me to leave the rice fields in Tayug, before the Colorum revolted against the landlords.

I was becoming aware of the dynamic social struggle in America. We talked all night in my brother's room, planning how to spread progressive ideas among the Filipinos in California.

Macario had become more serious. When he talked, I noticed his old gentleness and the kind voice that had rung with sincerity at my sickbed in Binalonan. His words seized my imagination, so that years afterward I am able to write them almost word for word:

"It has fallen upon us to inspire a united front among our people," he said. "We must win the backward elements over to our camp; but we must also destroy that which is corrupt among ourselves. These are the fundamentals of our time; but there are also the realities that we must grasp in full."

"We must achieve articulation of social ideas, not only for some kind of economic security but also to help culture bloom as it should in our time. We are approaching what will be the greatest achievement of our generation: the discovery of a new vista of literature, that is, to speak to the people and to be understood by them."

"We must look for the main spring of democracy, but we must also destroy false ideals. We must discover the origin of our freedom and write of it in broad national terms. We must interpret history in terms of liberty. We must advocate democratic ideas, and fight all forces that would abort our culture."

"This is the greatest responsibility of literature: to find in our struggle that which has a future. Literature is a living and growing thing. We must destroy that which is dying, because it does not die by itself."

"We in America understand the many imperfections of the democracy and the malignant disease corroding its very heart. We must be united in the effort to make an America in which our people can find happiness. It is a great wrong that anyone in America, whether he be brown or white, should be illiterate or hungry or miserable."

"We must live in America where there is freedom for all regardless of color, station and beliefs. Great Americans worked with unselfish devotion toward one goal, that is, to use the power of the myriad peoples in the service of America's freedom. They made it their guiding principle. In this we are the same. We must also fight for an America where a man should be given unconditional opportunities to cultivate his potentialities and to restore him to his rightful dignity."

"It is but fair to say that America is not a land of one race or one class of men. We are all Americans that have toiled and suffered and known oppression and defeat, from the first Indian that offered peace in Manhattan to the last Filipino pea pickers. America is not bound by geographical latitudes, America is not merely a land or an institution, America is in the hearts of men that died for freedom; it is also in the eyes of men that are building a new world. America is a prophecy of a new society of men: of a system that knows no sorrow or strife or suffering. America is a warning to those who would try to falsify the ideals of freemen."

"America is also the nameless foreigner, the homeless refugee, the hungry boy begging for a job and the black body dangling on a tree. America is the illiterate immigrant who is ashamed that the world of books and intellectual opportunities is closed to him. We are all that nameless foreigner, that homeless refugee, that hungry boy, that illiterate immigrant and that lynched blackbody. All of us, from the first Adams to the last Filipino, native born or alien, educated or illiterate—*We are America!*"

"The old world is dying, but a new world is being born. It generates inspiration from the chaos that beats upon us all. The false grandeur and security, the unfulfilled promises and illusory power, the number of the dead and those about to die, will charge the forces of our courage and determination. The old world will die so that the new world will be born with less sacrifice and agony on the living..."

Chapter XXVI

The old world will die...

This was the new dictum of my life. I did not exactly know what it meant, but it was enough that my brother Macario had expressed it. It was a stirring law that governed my life and thoughts. And it did not matter who was going to die; it was enough that something horrible was to perish from the earth.

The simple beginning of my intellectual awakening—the tragic death of Pascual and the imprisonment of Jose, the sudden change of Macario into a personality passionately reaching out for understanding, and my second encounter with Felix Razon—all these influences were, enough to make my last few months of freedom useful and significant.

The first issue of *The New Tide* was with the printers; when it came out, Jose and I took a hundred copies and distributed them to some of the more literate farm workers. It did not create a sensation, but we did not expect anything spectacular. It was the first of its kind to be published by Filipinos in the United States, and it was fumbling and immature, but it promised to grow into something important in the history of Filipino social awakening.

The magazine was one of several publications that had arisen all over the nation, and had tried to grasp the social realities and to interpret them in terms of the needs of the decade. It sustained our lives, drowned our despair, and gave us hope. It broadened our scope and vision.

Then it went out of existence. Its founders tried to revive it. But like the other publications born overnight to rally behind anew social idea, it died a natural death. It was like a world that died. Felix Razon wanted to save it: he went to work in a hotel in Hollywood and lived in the basement in order to save it. Nick found an apartment house in Beverly Hills; he worked seven days a week for twenty-five dollars a month. Macario went to work in a restaurant but, upon my advice—since there was no hope for the magazine—he went to New Mexico hoping to attend the University there.

However, the magnificent spirit behind it did not die. It was born again, in a more dynamic form, when I acquired enough knowledge to revive the high idealism behind it. But what awed me, in those early days, were the sacrifices of the founders. I would ask myself why three starving men were willing to give up their hard-earned money to make an obscure magazine live, denying themselves the simple necessities of food and shelter. They had surrounded the publication as though it were a little life about to die, or dying, or dead—and breathed life into me after the other, looking desperate and lost when they realized that their efforts were futile. But it was an inspiring experience, watching these young men breathing life into a dead thing. Their efforts came to me again and again in the course of my struggle toward an intellectual clarification and a positive social attitude.

An old world literally died with the magazine. An old generation of writers died with it, too. A new generation was born with the same ideals, perhaps, but re-envigorated with new social attitudes. The labor movement was the paramount issue; it was winning the support of intellectual and the advanced sections of the proletariat. Listening and watching attentively, I knew that it was the dawn of a new morning. I did not have to wait for the birth of a new world, because what I had been told to fight for was here with its brilliant promises.

How was I to understand it? Could I help? I knew that the most forlorn man, in those rootless years, was he who knew that love was growing inside him but had no object on which to bestow it.

Upon my return to the Santa Maria Valley, I found that the Filipino Workers' Association, an independent union, was disintegrating. I rushed to join Jose in Lompoc, where he had gone with Gazamen to see if there was a possibility of establishing a workers' newspaper. The three of us decided to form a branch there and to make it the center of Filipino union activities in Central

California.

Salinas was still the general headquarters of the Association, but it was fast losing its authority and prestige. There was a mad scramble for power in the Association among the national officers, and their bitter rivalries wrecked our chance toward the establishment of a more cogent labor organization. Actually, however, it was the birth of progressive leadership in the Filipino labor movement.

The membership of the Filipino Workers' Association was tremendous, considering the myriad difficulties it met in the campaign to spread throughout the agricultural areas of California. The vigilant Filipino workers—their whole-hearted support of the trade union movement, their hatred of low wages and other labor discriminations—were the direct causes that instigated the persecutions against them, sporadic at first and then concerted, but destructive to the nation's welfare.

In Salinas, for instance, the general headquarters were burned after a successful strike of lettuce workers, and the president of the association was thrown in jail. Upon his release, he moved to Guadalupe, in the south, and campaigned for the purchase of a new building. Always alert, the Filipino agricultural workers throughout the valley rallied behind the proposal, and after a few months a new national office was established. Again, striking for better wages, the Filipino lettuce cutters and packers succeeded, but lost the building and their right to build another in Guadalupe.

Finally, Jose and I made the office in Lompoc the temporary general headquarters. It was unconstitutional, of course, out the moment called for drastic action. Our move was without precedent, but we hoped to accomplish something, and we did.

It was during our membership campaign that I came in contact with fascism in California. The sugar beet season was in full swing in Oxnard, but the Mexican and Filipino workers were split. The companies would not recognize their separate demands, and although there were cultural and economic ties between them, they had not recognized one important point: that the beet companies conspired against their unity.

I contacted a Filipino farm-labor contractor and a prominent Mexican, and Jose, who joined us later, planned a meeting in the town park. I felt a little elated; harmony was in the offing. But in the evening, when we were starting the program, deputy sheriffs came to the park and told us that our right to hold a meeting had been revoked. I did not know what to do. I was still a novice. An elderly Mexican told us that we could hold a meeting outside the city limit.

There was a large empty barn somewhere in the south end of Oxnard. A truck came and carried some of the men, but most of them walked with us on the highway. They were very serious. I glanced at Jose who was talking to three Filipinos ahead of me, and felt something powerful growing inside me. It was a new heroism: a feeling of growing with a huge life. I walked silently with the men, listening to their angry voices and to the magic of their marching feet.

I was frightened. But I felt brave, too. The Mexicans wanted a more inclusive union, but that would take time. We were debating the issue when I heard several cars drive into the yard. I signaled to the men to put out the lights and to take cover. They fanned out and broke through the four walls, escaping into the wide beet fields.

I rushed upon the improvised stage and grabbed Jose, whose wooden leg had become entangled in some ropes and wires.

"This is it!"

"Yeah!"

"Follow me!"

"Right!"

I jumped off the stage, Jose following me. Then there was the sudden patter of many feet outside, and shooting. I found a pile of dry horse manure in a comer of the barn. I told Jose to lie down; then I covered him with it, exposing only his nose. I lay beside him and covered myself with it, too. When I tried to talk, the manure went into my mouth and choked me. I lay still, waiting for the noise outside to subside.

A man with a flashlight came inside and stabbed the darkness with the steely light, cutting swiftly from corner to corner. He came near the pile of manure, spat on it, and searched the ceiling. A piece of manure tickled my throat, and I held my breath, bringing tears to my eyes. The man went outside, joined his companions, and drove off to town.

I pushed the dung away and jumped to my feet.

"Did you see his face?"

"No!"

"I saw it. He is a white man, all right."

"Let's run. There is still time."

I crept to the wall and crouched in the darkness. I wanted to be sure that every man had gone. The way was clear. Jose followed me outside. Then we were running across a beet field, our feet slapping against the broad leaves that got in our way. The moon came up and shone brightly in the night. As I ran, I looked up to see it sailing across the sky.

Then my fear was gone. I stopped running and sat down among the tall beats. Jose sat beside me. There were no words to describe the feeling in our minds and hearts. There was only our closeness and the dark years ahead. There was only the dark future.

We walked across the beet fields to Camarillo, five miles south. The town was quiet and dark. It was surrounded by orange groves. We went into the local school building and slept on the floor. A teacher found us there in the morning. She threatened to call the police, and we rushed outside. We walked in the morning sun, smelling the orange blossoms and the clean air. I looked at the tall mountains on our right and stopped, remembering the mountains in my village.

"You like the landscape?" Jose asked.

" It's like my village," I said.

"Tell me about it."

"Well, it is hard to describe it to you. But the farther I go from it, the more vivid it becomes to me. Perhaps I am sentimental. But my village is not like any other village. There are mountains on one side, and there is the wide river on the other. A tongue of land extends into the river and on this land are hills that are covered with guava trees. Now is the time for the guavas to bloom. I used to go there when I was a child and the smell of the blossoms followed me down into the valley. Between the mountains and the river, in the center of the valley, is a papaya grove. Papayas are in bloom now. Did you ever smell papaya blossoms? There is nothing like it. Someday I will go back and climb these guavas again. Someday I will make a crown of papaya blossoms. Do you think I am sentimental?"

"No," Jose said. "I know what you mean. We will go back someday. I will climb those guavas with you. We will swim in the river. The papayas are in bloom now, you say?"

The journey to Ventura was shortened. We were following the state highway when a police patrol stopped us and took us to the city jail and held us on charges of vagrancy. When we were released, three days afterward, we took a bus to Lompoc.

But another strike was in progress there. The lettuce workers had walked out three days before. I was informed that some of the men did not approve of the strike, but a white woman from Fresno had agitated them. Gazamen told me that she was staying at a local hotel, I asked Jose to go with me.

It was already one in the afternoon, but the hotel was very quiet. I knocked on the door. A short, stocky, ordinary-looking woman with dark hair stood before me.

"My name is Helen," she said, coming out with her overnight bag. "How is the strike this morning?"

"My name is Jose," Jose said. "We came to you to talk about it. I hope you don't mind our bothering you."

"Jose!" Helen was beaming. "You are the person I've been looking for in Lompoc. Mr. Magna in San Francisco recommended you—"

Jose's doubts vanished immediately. He knew Magna intimately. I walked eagerly with them to the office. But why did Helen talk as though this strike were a business? I was filled with doubts and premonitions.

5
(Hisaye Yamamoto, 1921—2011)
山本久枝

作者简介

山本久枝（Hisaye Yamamoto, 1921—2011），美国日裔作家，出生于南加利福尼亚州。家庭生活的窘困以及社会的动荡让山本久枝一家饱受煎熬。然而恰恰是这些磨难经历为山本久枝的写作提供了丰富的素材，铸就了一位著名的短篇小说家。她的小说主要围绕一世父母与二世子女之间的矛盾、一世女性的家庭地位以及美国日本集中营的生活展开。她曾荣获哥伦布前基金会美国图书奖终身成就奖（Before Columbus Foundation's American Book Award for Lifetime Achievement）、美国亚裔作家研究会颁发的终身成就奖（Asian American Writers Workshop's Lifetime Achievement Award）等重要奖项。

她的短篇小说有《十七音节》（*Seventeen Syllables*, 1949）、《笹川小姐传奇》（*The Legend of Miss Sasagawara*, 1950）、《米子的地震》（*Yoneko's Earthquake*, 1951）、《棕色的房子》（*The Brown House*, 1951）、《拉斯维加斯查理》（*Las Vegas Charley*, 1961）与《在小东京的一天》（*A Day in Little Tokyo*, 1986）等。

她最著名的短篇小说集《十七音节与其他小说》（*Seventeen Syllables and Other Stories*），在1988年出版面世，荣获美国亚裔研究协会颁发的文学奖（Association for Asian American Studies's Award for Literature）。这部小说集让山本久枝在美国名声大噪，作品也登上了各大主流媒体畅销书榜单。这部短篇小说集按小说创作的时间顺序收录了她的15部短篇小说，记录了山本久枝40年的写作生涯。小说主题涉及了一世父母与二世子女之间的文化冲突、一世女性的命运、第二次世界大战美国日本集中营的经历以及种族歧视等方面。

短篇小说《高跟鞋：回忆录》（“High-Heeled Shoes: A Memoir”）与《十七音节》（“Seventeen Syllables”）均选自短篇小说集《十七音节与其他小说》。《高跟鞋：回忆录》主要讲述了女性在社会上受到的不公待遇，如性骚扰等恶性事件，思考了女性的社会地位。《十七音节》讲述了母亲的“诗人梦”被父亲残忍扼杀的故事，关注了女性的家庭地位。

作品选读

High-Heeled Shoes: A Memoir

By Hisaye Yamamoto

In the middle of the morning, the telephone rings. I am the only one at home. I answer it. A man's voice says softly, "Hello, this is Tony."

I don't know anyone named Tony. Nobody else in the house has spoken of knowing any Tony. But the greeting is very warm. It implies, "There is a certain thing which you and I alone know." Evidently he has dialed a wrong number. I tell him so, "You must have the wrong number," and prepare to hang up as soon as I know that he understands.

But the man says this is just the number he wants. To prove it, he recites off the pseudonym by which this household, Garbo-like, goes in the directory, the address, and the phone number. It is a unique name and I know there is probably no such person in the world. I merely tell him a fragment of the truth, that there is no such person at the address, and I am ready to hang up again.

But the man stalls. If there is no such person available, it appears he is willing to talk to me, whoever I am. I am suddenly in a bad humor, suspecting a trap in which I shall be imprisoned uncomfortably by words, words, words, earnestly begging me to try some product or another, the like of which is unknown anywhere else in the world. It isn't that I don't appreciate the unrapturous life a salesman must often lead. And I like to buy things. If I had the money, I would buy a little from every salesman who comes along, after I had permitted him to run ably or ineptly (it doesn't really matter) through the words he has been coached to repeat. Then, not only in the pride of the new acquisition, but in the knowledge that he was temporarily encouraged, my own spirits would gently rise, lifted by the wings of the dove. At each week's end, surrounded knee-deep by my various purchases—the Fuller toothbrush, the receipt for the magazine subscription which will help a girl obtain a nine-week flying course which she eagerly, eagerly wants, the one dozen white eggs fresh from the farm and cheaper than you can get at the corner grocery, the first volume in the indispensable 12-volume Illustrated Encyclopaedia of Home Medicine, the drug sundries totalling at least two dollars which will help guarantee a youngish veteran a permanent job—I could sigh and beam. That would be nice. But I don't have the money, and this coming of ill temper is just as much directed at myself for not having it as it is at the man for probably intending to put me in a position where I shall have to make him a failure.

"And just what is it you want?" I ask impatiently.

The man tells me, as man to woman. In the stark phrasing of his urgent need, I see that the certain thing alluded to by the warmth of his voice is a secret not of the past, but, with my acquiescence, of the near future. I let the receiver take a plunge down onto the hook from approximately a one-foot height. Then, I go outside and pick some pansies for Margarita, as I had been intending to do just before the phone rang. Margarita is the seven-year-old girl next door. She has never known any mother or father, only *tias* and *tios* who share none of her blood. She has a face that looks as if it had been chiseled with utter care out of cream and pale pink marble. Her soft brown hair hangs in plaits as low as her waist. And these days, because the Catholic school is full and cannot take her, she wanders lonesomely about, with plenty of time for such amenities as dropping in to admire a neighbor's flowers. The pansies I pick for her, lemon yellow, deep purple, clear violet, mottled brown, were transplanted here last year by Wakako and Chester, a young couple we know who have a knack for getting things wholesale, and they are thriving like crazy this spring, sprawling untidily over their narrow bed and giving no end of blooms.

Later, there is a small, timid rat-tat-tat at the door. It's Margarita, bearing two calla lilies, a couple of clove pinks, and one tall amaryllis stalk with three brilliant brick-red flowers and a bud. She dashes off the porch, down the steps, and around the ivy-sprawled front fence before I can properly thank her. Oh, well. Taking the gift to the service porch, I throw out the wilting brown-edged callas she dashed over with last week, rinse out the blue potato glass, fill it with water, and stick in the new bouquet. But all the time the hands are occupied with these tokens of arrived spring and knowing Margarita, the mind recalls unlovely, furtive things.

When Mary lived with us, there was a time she left for work in the dark hours of the morning. On one of these mornings, about midway in her lonely walk past the cemetery to the P-car stop, a man came from behind and grabbed her, stopped her mouth with his hand, and, rather arbitrarily, gave her a choice between one kiss and rape. Terrified, she indicated what seemed to be the somewhat lesser requirement. He allowed her to go afterwards, warning her on no account to scream for help or look back, on penalty of death. When she arrived at her place of work, trembling and pale green, her office friends asked whether she was ill, and she told them of her encounter. They advised her to go to the police immediately.

She doubted whether that would help, since she had been unable to see the man. But, persuaded that a report, even incomplete, to the police was her duty to the rest of womankind, she reluctantly went to the nearest station with her story. She came back with the impression that the police had been much amused, that they had actually snickered as she left with their officially regretful shrug over her having given them nothing to go on. She told her boss and he called the police himself and evidently made his influence felt, for we had a caller that evening.

It was I who answered the knock. A policeman stepped in, and, without any preliminaries, asked, "Are you the girl that was raped?"

Making up with enough asperity for a sudden inexplicable lack of aplomb, I said, no, and no one had been raped, *yet*, and called Mary. She and the officer went out on the porch and talked in near whispers for a while. After he left, Mary identified him and his companion as the night patrol for our section of the city. He had promised that they would tell the dawn patrol to be hovering around about the time she left for work each morning. But Mary, nervously trying the dim walk a couple of more times, caught no sign of any kind of patrol. Thereafter, she and the rest of the women of the household took to traveling in style, by taxi, when they were called on to go forth at odd hours. This not only dented our budgets, but made us considerably limit our unescorted evening gadding.

There were similar episodes, fortunately more fleeting. What stayed with me longer than Mary's because it was mine, was the high-heeled shoes. Walking one bright Saturday morning to work along the same stretch that Mary had walked, I noticed a dusty blue, middle-aged sedan parked just ahead. A pair of bare, not especially remarkable legs was crossed in the open doorway, as though the body to them were lying on the front seat, relaxing. I presumed they were a woman's legs, belonging to the wife of some man who had business in the lumberyard just opposite, because they were wearing black high-heeled shoes. As I passed, I glanced at the waiting woman.

My presumption had been rash. It wasn't a woman, but a man, unclothed (except for *the high-heeled shoes, the high-heeled shoes*), and I saw that I was, with frantic gestures, being enjoined to linger awhile. Nothing in my life before had quite prepared for this: some Freud, a smattering of Ellis, lots of Stekel, and fat Krafft-Ebing, in red covers, were on my bookshelves, granted; conversation had explored curiously, and the imagination conjured bizarre scenes at the drop of a casual word. But reading is reading, talking is talking, thinking is thinking, and living is different. Improvising hastily on behavior for the occasion, I chose to pretend as though my heart were repeating Pippa's song, and continued walking, possibly a little faster and a little straighter than I had been, up to the P-car stop. When I got to the print shop, the boss said, "You look rather put upon this morning." I mustered up a feeble smile and nodded, but I couldn't bring myself to speak of the high-heeled shoes. This was nothing so uncomplicated as pure rape, I knew, and the need of the moment was to go away by myself, far from everybody, and think about things for awhile. But there were galleys and page proofs waiting to be read, and I set to with a sort of dedicated vengeance, for I had recently been reprimanded for getting sloppy again. When the hectic morning of poring over small print was over and my elbows black, letting my thoughts go cautiously but wholly back to the time between leaving the house and boarding the P-car, I found there was not much to think about. I had seen what I had seen. I had, admit it now, been thrown for a sickening loop. That was all. But the incongruity of a naked man in black high-heeled shoes was something the mind could not entirely dismiss, and there were times afterwards when he, never seen again, contributed to a larger perplexity that stirred the lees around and around, before more immediate matters, claiming attention, allowed them to settle again.

There was a man in the theatre with groping hands. There was a man on the streetcar with insistent thighs. There was a man who grinned triumphantly and walked quickly away after he trailed one down a drizzly street at dusk and finally succeeded in his aim of thrusting an unexpected hand under one's raincoat.

I remembered them as I plucked the pansies, took them over to Margarita's house, came back home, answered the door, received the amaryllis, the callas, the pinks, and arranged them in the blue potato glass on top of the buffet. I remembered another man, Mohandas Gandhi, probably a stranger to this company, not only because I had been reading on him of late, but because he seemed to be the only unimpeachable authority who had ever been called on to give public advice in this connection. When someone had delicately asked Gandhi, "What is a woman to do when she is attacked by miscreants?" naming the alternatives of violent self-defense and immediate flight, he had replied, "For me, there can be no preparation for violence. All preparation must be for non-violence if courage of the highest type is to be developed. Violence can only be tolerated as being preferable always to cowardice. Therefore I would have no boats ready for flight..." Then he had soared on to the nobler implications of non-violence, reproaching the world for its cowardice in arming itself with the atomic bomb.

I understood. When I first read these words, I had said, "Why, of course," smiling at the unnecessary alarms of some people. But I had read the words at a rarefied period, forgetting Mary, forgetting the high-heeled shoes. I decided now that the inspiration they gave to his probably feminine questioner was small potatoes. Of all the men suspected of sainthood, Gandhi, measured by his own testimony, should have been able to offer the most concrete comfort here. But he had evaded the issue. In place of the tangible example, vague words. Gandhi, in face of the ubiquitous womanly fear, was a failure. All he had really said was: don't even think about it. Then (I guessed), holding up his strong, bony brown hand, he had shaken his white-fuzzed, compactly-shaped head slowly back and forth and declined to hear the ifs and buts. The rest, as they say, was silence.

But could I have momentarily borrowed Gandhi's attitude to life and death, what would I have done as the man who called himself Tony rang my number? With enough straining, with maybe a resort to urgent, concentrated prayer, could I have found the gentle but effective words to make Tony see that there were more charming ways to spend a morning? I practiced this angle for awhile:

"I'm afraid you do have the wrong number." Soberly, hang up. Disconcerting enough, but rather negative.

"It's a nice day for the beach, sir. Why don't you go swimming? —might help you cool off a little." The voice with a compassionate smile. Too flippant.

"There are many lonely women in the world, and there are more acceptable ways to meet them than this. Have you tried joining a Lonely Hearts club? Don't you have any kind of hobby?" Condescending, as though I were forever above his need. Ambiguously worded, too, that last, fraught with the possibility of an abrupt answer.

"Listen, you know you aren't supposed to go around doing things like this. I think I know what made you do it, though, and I think a psychiatrist would help you quite a bit, if you'd cooperate." The enlightened woman's yap. Probably'd hang up on me.

Anyway, it was too late. And, after all, Gandhi was Gandhi, an old man, moreover dead, and I was I, a young woman, more or less alive. Since I was unable to hit on the proper pacifist approach, since, indeed, I doubted the efficacy of the pacifist approach in this crisis, should I, eschewing cowardice, have shouted bitter, indignant words to frighten Tony? Not that, either. Besides, I hadn't gauged his mood. He had spoken casually enough, but there had been an undertone of something. Restrained glee? Playfulness? Confidence? Desperation? I didn't know.

Then, to help protect my sisters, should I have turned toward the official avenues? Was it my responsibility to have responded with pretended warmth, invited him over, and had the police waiting with me when he arrived? Say I had sorrowfully pressed the matter, say Tony were consequently found guilty (of abusing his communication privileges, of course) —the omnipotent they (representing us) would have merely restricted his liberty for a while, in the name of punishment. What would he have done when he was let go, his debt to society as completely repaid as society, who had created his condition, could make him repay? Telephones in working order abound, with telephone books conveniently alongside them, containing any number of women's names, addresses, and numbers.

And what did Tony do when the sound of my receiver crashed painfully in his ear? Did he laugh and proceed to some other number? His vanity bruised, did he curse? Or perhaps he felt shame, thinking, "My God, what am I doing, what am I doing?" Whatever, whatever—I knew I had discovered yet another circle to put away with my collection of circles. I was back to what I had started with, the helpless, absolutely useless knowledge that the days and nights must surely be bleak for a man who knew the compulsion to thumb through the telephone directory for a woman's name, any woman's name; that this bleakness, multiplied infinite times (see almost any daily paper), was a great, dark sickness on the earth that no amount of pansies, pinks, or amaryllis, thriving joyously in what garden, however well-ordered and pointed to with pride, could ever begin to assuage.

The telephone rings. Startled, I go warily, wondering whether it might not be Tony again, calling perhaps to avenge the blow to pride by anonymous invective, to raise self-esteem by letting it be known that he is a practical joker. I hold my breath after I say, "Hello?"

It is the familiar voice, slightly querulous but altogether precious, of my aunt Miné. She says I am not to plan anything for supper. She has made something special, ricecakes with Indian bean frosting, as well as pickled fish on vinegared rice. She has also been able to get some yellowtail, to slice and eat raw. All these things she and Uncle are bringing over this evening. Is about five o'clock too early?

It is possible she wonders at my enthusiastic appreciation, which is all right, but all out of proportion.

(1948)

Seventeen Syllables (excerpt)

By Hisaye Yamamoto

She told him where her mother was and he came along with her, patting his face with an immaculate white handkerchief and saying something about the coolness of San Francisco. To her surprised mother and father, he bowed and introduced himself as, among other things, the haiku editor of the *Mainichi Shimbun*, saying that since he had been coming as far as Los Angeles anyway, he had decided to bring her the first prize she had won in the recent contest.

"First prize?" her mother echoed, believing and not believing, pleased and overwhelmed. Handed the package with a bow, she bobbed her head up and down numerous times to express her utter gratitude.

"It is nothing much," he added, "but I hope it will serve as a token of our great appreciation for your contributions and our great admiration of your considerable talent."

"I am not worthy," she said, falling easily into his style. "It is I who should make some sign of my humble thanks for being permitted to contribute."

"No, no, to the contrary," he said, bowing again.

But Rosie's mother insisted, and then saying that she knew she was being unorthodox, she asked if she might open the package because her curiosity was so great. Certainly she might. In fact, he would like her reaction to it, for personally, it was one of his favorite Hiroshiges.

Rosie thought it was a pleasant picture, which looked to have been sketched with delicate quickness. There were pink clouds, containing some graceful calligraphy, and a sea that was a pale blue except at the edges, containing four sampans with indications of people in them. Pines edged the water and on the far-off beach there was a cluster of thatched huts towered over by pine-dotted mountains of grey and blue. The frame was scalloped and gilt.

After Rosie's mother pronounced it without peer and somewhat prodded her father into nodding agreement, she said Mr. Kuroda must at least have a cup of tea after coming all this way, and although Mr. Kuroda did not want to impose, he soon agreed that a cup of tea would be refreshing and went along with her to the house, carrying the picture for her.

"Ha, your mother's crazy!" Rosie's father said, and Rosie laughed uneasily as she resumed judgment on the tomatoes. She had emptied six lugs when he broke into an imaginary conversation with Jesus to tell her to go and remind her mother of the tomatoes, and she went slowly.

Mr. Kuroda was in his shirtsleeves expounding some *haiku* theory he munched a rice cake, and her mother was rapt. Abashed in the great man's presence, Rosie stood next to her mother's chair until her mother looked up inquiringly, and then she started to whisper the message, but her mother pushed her gently away and reproached, "You are not being very polite to our guest."

"Father says the tomatoes..." Rosie said aloud, smiling foolishly.

"Tell him I shall only be a minute," her mother said, speaking the language of Mr. Kuroda.

When Rosie carried the reply to her father, he did not seem to hear and she said again, "Mother says she'll be back in a minute."

"All right, all right," he nodded, and they worked again in silence. But suddenly, her father uttered an incredible noise, exactly like the cork of a bottle popping, and the next Rosie knew, he was stalking angrily toward the house, almost running in fact, and she chased after him crying, "Father! Father! What are you going to do?"

He stopped long enough to order her back to the shed. "Never mind!" he shouted. "Get on with the sorting!"

And from the place in the fields where she stood, frightened and vacillating, Rosie saw her father enter the house. Soon Mr. Kuroda came out alone, putting on his coat. Mr. Kuroda got into his car and backed out down the driveway onto the highway. Next her father emerged, also alone, something in his arms (it was the picture, she realized), and, going over to the bathhouse woodpile, he threw the picture on the ground and picked up the axe. Smashing the picture, glass and all (she heard the explosion faintly), he reached over for the kerosene that was used to encourage the bath fire and poured it over the wreckage. I am dreaming, Rosie said to herself, I am dreaming, but her father, having made sure that his act of cremation was irrevocable, was even then returning to the fields.

Rosie ran past him and toward the house. What had become of her mother? She burst into the parlor and found her mother at the back window watching the dying fire. They watched together until there remained only a feeble smoke under the blazing sun. Her mother was very calm.

"Do you know why I married your father?" she said without turning.

"No," said Rosie. It was the most frightening question she had ever been called upon to answer. Don't tell me now, she wanted to say, tell me tomorrow, tell me next week, don't tell me today. But she knew she would be told now, that the telling would combine with the other violence of the hot afternoon to level her life, her world to the very ground.

It was like a story out of the magazines illustrated in sepia, which she had consumed so greedily for a period until the information had somehow reached her that those wretchedly unhappy autobiographies, offered to her as the testimonials of living men and women, were largely inventions: Her mother, at nineteen, had come to America and married her father as an alternative to suicide.

6

(Milton Murayama, 1923—2016)
弥尔顿·村山

作者简介

弥尔顿·村山（Milton Murayama, 1923—2016），美国日裔小说家和剧作家，出生于美国夏威夷。弥尔顿从夏威夷大学（University of Hawaii）获得了英语和哲学学士学位，从哥伦比亚大学（Columbia University）获得了中文与日文硕士学位。在求学期间，弥尔顿曾志愿服务于美国军队。作为第二代日本移民，弥尔顿在种植园的生活经历为他日后的写作提供了丰富的源泉。弥尔顿在 1980 年荣获美国图书奖（American Book Award），1991 年获得夏威夷文学奖（Hawaii Award for Literature）。

弥尔顿·村山一生创作的作品有长篇小说《我所求的是我的身体》（*All I Asking for Is My Body*, 1975）、《岩石上的五年》（*Five Years on a Rock*, 1994）、《种植园男孩》（*Plantation Boy*, 1998）与《客死异乡》（*Dying in a Strange Land*, 2008）；戏剧有《义经》（*Yoshitsune*, 1977）等。

弥尔顿的四部小说如同一幅连环画，生动地描绘了第二次世界大战前后不同时期日本移民在美国夏威夷种植园生活的血泪史。他用夏威夷地方特色的“皮钦语”（Pidgin English）写作，具有较高的文学和美学价值。

《岩石上的五年》是弥尔顿·村山的第二部小说，也是处女作《我所求的是我的身体》的续篇。与《我所求的是我的身体》不同的是，《岩石上的五年》更多地关照了日裔家庭中作为儿媳、妻子和母亲的女性的地位以及她们可悲的一生。

这部小说从主人公年轻时作为“照片新娘”被送到美国、嫁给日本丈夫开始，描写了主人公经历了人生大起大落，到晚年仍要奔波忙碌的心酸人生。本选篇为该小说第 24 章，是这部小说最精彩的部分之一。本章节主要表达了主人公在晚年之际思念家乡，但由于家庭经济的窘困不得不放弃这种“妄想”，继续为了生计而奔波劳碌。故事情节如同影视剧缓缓展开，让人不禁潸然泪下。

作品选读

Five Years on a Rock

Chapter 24

By Milton Murayama

I could no longer chew. My teeth wobbled.

“Your gums are infected. They all have to come out,” Dr. Hamaguchi said. “They’re loose, so pulling them won’t be difficult.” He advised pulling the lowers one week and the uppers the next. Was it cheaper pulling them all today? I asked. He said it would be $2 less.

“Please pull them all today,” I begged.

He injected Novocain into the backs of my lower gums, stuffed rolls of cotton beside them, and pulled out one tooth after another. The rolls of cotton dripped with blood.

“Would you like to stop?” he asked, after he’d pulled all the lowers.

“No,” I gurgled. I needed to *gaman* only a few more minutes to save $2.

Then he injected the corners of the upper gums, and the numbness spread to my cheekbones.

The uppers also came out easily, but now the blood gushed.

“There,” he said finally.

Just then my eyeballs rolled back and the lights went out.

***

I gag and cough, looking for somewhere to spit. A cup nearby is filled with blood.

Where am I? I hear my strange voice say.

You’re at my hospital. Dr. Kawamura peers at me behind his thick glasses.

I raise my head and the room spins and everything goes dark again.

It's pitch black when I wake up. Am I dead? I float up to the ceiling.

Kokua shite! Help me! Pull! I yell but I have no voice.

Then I'm playing tag with Toru, and Mother and Father are laughing.

When I awake, it's daylight and I'm back in bed. My mouth is swollen; my gums throb. There's nobody else in the three-bed hospital.

***

Then the bleeding stops and the pain returns. They take me home. I crawl out to the parlor and fight against the dizziness. I promised the kimono for the wedding.

"Why don't you sew something easy like pants or a dress?" Kiyoshi says.

"There's more money in a kimono."

"Why don't you sit on a chair or at the sewing machine where you can stretch your legs?"

"There's a proper way of doing everything."

But I get dizzy again and crawl back to the futon on the bedroom floor.

"Mother, Mother," a little girl's voice keeps calling. Oh, it's little Miwa, who's been assigned to baby-sit me.

"Mother, Mother? Oh, I think she's sleeping. Yeah, I can go," she says.

I hear steps leaving the veranda, the happy voices of her playmates. I remember scolding Takako, "You can't go out to play until you finish your sewing lesson!"

I feel guilty not having paid enough attention to Miwa. I never took her to the wharf or the playground at the kindergarten or played *karuta* with her. But she never acted up.

I get up and comb my disheveled hair and go back to my sewing.

Then it happens again.

***

When I awake, an oval face, a filigree of hair, hovers. Am I dead?

Oyama-san?

Hai—bowing upward to the angelic face.

The doctor says you're suffering from exhaustion and loss of blood. Otherwise, you're all right. You have no fever. So gambatte, ne? *You can't lose. You have to get well, ne?*

I'm sorry to be such a nuisance.

You're not a nuisance.

I'm so worthless.

You're not worthless. You're remarkable.

I wanted to borrow some of her flowing flapper dresses. They're simpler than kimonos, and I can charge more. But only she and the *haoles* wore them.

You have to want to get well, ne? It'd be mortifying to die in a strange land.

I'm sorry to be such trouble.

You're no trouble.

Was Madame Kanai really here? Or was it another dream? *Dying in a strange land*. It must've been her. Being childless, she has nobody to care for her if she dies here. It must worry her.

I hadn't fainted since I was a little child. I remember the terror of those little deaths. What if I don't wake up the next time? What if I wake up in a world of strangers?

***

They take me home again. I crawl out to the parlor.

"I'll tell them you can't do it! I'll ask them to give it to Nakai!" Isao yanks away the kimono.

"But I promised it for the wedding. Besides, they can't afford what a professional charges."

"You don't have the strength."

"But the rent is due."

"I've asked him for another extension!"

Please don't scold me; I need to be pampered. I can't sit up, anyway. The floor tilts and my head spins. Isao stays home and cooks and launders. He spoon-feeds me rice gruel and crushed fish. But the smell nauseates.

"*Gambatte, gambatte*," he says.

Why do we keep exhorting each other to persevere? We must lack stamina. My own father quit, then Mother Haru, and little brothers Toru and Kingo. No, the boys didn't quit. They pushed themselves till their bodies crumbled. They must've skimped on food and rest. *Yamato damashi* said the Japanese were special; we didn't need food or rest. Our spirit could overcome TB; even rotten teeth.

Isao says, "Don't worry; you worry too much. That's why you get sick."

"I wouldn't if you did!" I yell, and am startled awake. It irritated me the way he brushed off everything with a flick of the wrist.

It's so boring to be caged in a sick body. If only I could sleep; if I could soap off this sticky film of sweat and wake up cool and squeaky-clean. I miss the big *ohai* tree. Here the naked sun beats down on the roof and bakes the room. In Japan, no matter how sultry, October had always brought a respite. The skies turned brilliant, and chestnuts, grapes, and persimmons ripened, and the maple leaves turned crimson. I'd like so much to see it all once more.

Dr. Kawamura brings more pills and bottles.

I grimace. "They're not working."

"You need food more than medicines," he says.

"And rest. I wish I could go back to Kula." Talking contorts my face.

"You need to get fitted for dentures."

But I don't want to throw away money on a corpse! I think.

I don't feel dizzy the next time I get up. I go to the Singer and work on trousers. I get 50 cents a pair and I can knock one off in two hours. But I shake so much I have to lie down. My heart feels so tired. How can the body be so wasted and the mind so clear?

Oh, for a breath of winter chill! Deep winter, snow, and frozen toes. Unheated classrooms and hardship strengthened you. Numb fingers in calligraphy class, writing over and over: *Raku wa ku no tane, ku wa raku no tane*

樂は苦の種、苦は樂の種

"Luxury begets suffering, and suffering luxury."

Each proverb was illustrated with a story. When Confucius was a little boy, he lived next to fishmongers. All day long he imitated them, hawking fish. "We can't have this," his mother said, and moved the family next to a temple. He spent his days chanting like the bonzes. Finally his mother moved the family next to a college. Confucius imitated the scholars and grew up to become a great sage.

We have to move back to Kahana. They still celebrated the emperor's birthday there. Pepelau has too many *gaijins*, and the Japanese are scattered. Shame no longer works.

Mr. Omiya ran a monthly card game in his home behind the store. He hired Mrs. Morita from across town to pour *sake* for the gamblers. People had seen her, weaving her way home on Front Street early in the morning in her kimono and powdered face. "Doesn't Mr. Morita make enough on his salesman's commission?... A beautiful wife is a drawback," people said.

Mr. Yamashita on Front Street also had a beautiful wife. The bachelors went to his tailor shop just to gawk, and one of them, a rich fabric salesman, became a boarder. He was in love with Mrs. Yamashita, people whispered, and he supplied Mr. Yamashita with *sake* and much more. How else could Mr. Yamashita have sent all his children to high school and the boys on to college?

It was no wonder the boys were losing their manners. They've stopped saying, "*Gochiso sama!*", "*Tada-ima!*", and all the rituals of good manners. Rituals inculcated manners, and manners were morals. What would Confucius' mother have done?

It's another lie. Suffering does not beget luxury. When was our luxury? The three short years when Isao was *onaga* king? No, suffering begets more suffering, and death, death. Like Toru, like Kingo. Poor boys; they never had a chance. They were pushed by their mothers to succeed where their fathers had failed. Poor Mother Haru—marrying Father Takao only begat suffering. It happened in cycles of fours. *Shi* 死 "death" is *shi* 四 "four." I'm the fourth.

My comb falls out, and I pick it up without stepping on it first. Picking up a "comb," *kushi*, means also picking up the other *kushi*, or "painful death."

Isao yells, "I'm sick of all your puns. *Shi-shi* is also 'piss'!"

"I'm so worthless; I hope you think well of me after... " I *amaeru* to the children.

"Mama, don't worry about the debt. I'll be able to work full time in a few years. I'll help," Toshio says.

"Thank you so much." I bow upward, tears streaming down my temples. "Joji and Kiyoshi will help too, but I need to borrow your body most of all... " I cry so easily now. I'll be so happy if this makes him filial again, the way he was before I went to Kula.

"Why me? Why me?" I keep asking. "I must be chosen for somebody else's *bachi*."

"*Bakatare*. *Bachi* is superstition. Some bad luck is bound to happen to anybody if he waits long enough," Isao says quietly.

Kiyoshi is the only one who lets me *amaeru*. He understands we need to be pampered. He's been near death, too.

"We've never done anything that bad," he says.

"No, but a close relative might have. We can get punished as the substitute."

If only I could go back to Kula. I'll even force myself to eat the foul-smelling cheese. Their foods were so nutritious, I felt myself growing stronger day by day. Maybe that's why we keep exhorting, "Persevere, persevere." We lack the right foods. So we call on our spirit to make up for our poverty and poor diet. Dr. Hall, Dr. Sherwood, or Miss Wada could have saved Toru and Kingo. "Meddlesome bureaucrats" they were not. But then maybe only rich governments could afford to give free skin tests and X rays and dental inspections.

Mrs. Kato, now Mrs. Shimazu, returns from Japan and sits outside the barbershop, but her troubles no longer lessen my pain. It's so easy to just lie here and not get up. Mr. Noda, who worked at the pump station in Honokawai below Kahana, got a ride after work. He stood on the running board and an oncoming car hit him and killed him instantly. The eldest boy had to quit high school and go to work in the cane fields to support the family. Right in Omiya Camp, Mr.

Kosaka, a bonito fisherman, died of a heart attack. Tet-chan, who'd graduated with Toshio, took a job at the mill, 6:00 p.m. to 6:00 a.m. He looked ghostly pale from all the nightwork. Back in Kahana, Reverend Morimoto died of the Spanish flu, leaving Madame Morimoto with three girls. And there was Mr. Shinagawa, who picked at the sore in his nose and died at age thirty-six. His widow now worked with the women's gang, weeding and cutting cane seedlings. "Earthquake, thunder, fire, and father," they say in Japan, but the terror in Hawaii is to be left a widow with a houseful of children. But what if the wife died first? What will the children remember of me?

I tell Kiyoshi, "It's too bad you're not the number one son. You're wiser than Toshio and not a *kolohe* boy like Joji. See to it that Toshio and Father don't fight so much... "

I think about it afterward. *Why is Father so hard on Toshio? Why can't he treat him the way he treats Joji and Kiyoshi*? He takes Joji and Kiyoshi and their classmates out on his boat for a day of fishing. He takes them out again even if they got seasick the first time and begged him to take them back. *He's only wasting money on gas and baity,* I kept thinking, but he enjoyed entertaining the boys.Why can't he do the same for Toshio? Is that why Toshio hates fish so?

I tell Joji and Kiyoshi that we are Mr. Aoki's benefactor, so he'll keep extending us credit. "But we owe Tani Fish Market $1,000, the dentist... Dr. Kawamura... they're all in the ledger in the sewing machine drawer. Except for Mr. Aoki and Tani, you have to pay them at least $2 a month to show them you're sincere."

"Rest. Take care of the body," Joji said. "Toshio, Kiyoshi, and me, we'll be working in no time, and we'll pay off the debt."

"Thank you, thank you."

***

The heat is so oppressive. If I could only take off my flesh and lie down in my bones. What am I saying? I feel trapped, like Mrs. Kato (I keep calling her Mrs. Kato). "Why doesn't she leave?" people say. But how can she when *he* does not? It's Mr. Shimazu who doesn't know shame. It can't be helped. We're only women. We *gaman* too much, they pile too much on us; it's a Japanese disease.

***

"Oh, where's Father?" I woke one morning to find him gone.

"He went out to sea yesterday," Kiyoshi says.

"Why aren't you at school?"

"I thought I'd stay home."

"Is it all right?"

"I can catch up easily."

"You know, *Obaban* hasn't come to see me," I sigh. Sadao-san hasn't visited in months either. He's probably made new friends.

"Shall I go get her?"

"It costs too much to hire a taxi."

"I can phone the plantation store from Aoki Store and ask her to come. She doesn't know you're sick."

"I don't want to trouble her."

"I'll go get her," he says.

"*Sumimasen.* " I bow and drift off into half-sleep.

***

When I open my eyes, *Obaban's* fullness is at the doorway.

"Kitano-san?"

"Sawa-chan."

I sit up and we hold each other.

"I had to see you before I die!"

"You're not going to die."

"I can feel it."

"Your karma is decided the moment you're born. Your time is not now." Her voice is soft and deep.

"How do you know?"

"I know."

"What if I'm being chosen as a substitute for someone else's *bachi*?"

"Find another substitute," she laughs, "and you'll be spared."

"You know, I borrowed a handful of dirt from the San-O shrine when I came to Hawaii. I promised I'd return it without fail in five years. Could you return—" I catch myself. So stupid!

"You'll return it," she chuckles. "You'll go back for a visit some day. But life is better here. You're more free to be yourself. As hard as plantation life is, I think life in Japan is harder. We're often nostalgic for something that never existed."

"*Ah, so*?... "

"But first you must come back to Kahana. You have to tell your master. In a year he'll have been a fisherman for fifteen years. If he hasn't succeeded by then, he should give it up and return to the plantation... "

"Oh, thank you so much. I'm so worthless... "

"You're remarkable. People still talk about you in Kahana."

"But I'm so useless... "

"You get sick because you work too hard. Try to be lazy and really useless like the others," she laughs.

I feel light-headed afterward and drift off into a deep sleep. I dream Toru is just born and Father is so delighted he dances, cradling him. It stays with me. It was a happy time. But Mother and older sister Tomi were not in the dream! It was the dead beckoning me!

"I'm so relieved. I wanted to see Aunt Kitano one last time," I say to Isao when he comes home from sea.

"*Bakatare*," he says softly. "You'll outlive us all."

The next morning Mr. Tanji, the delivery man for Aoki Store, drives his pickup to the house in a cloud of dust. There was a phone call from the plantation store in Kahana. Aunt Kitano had suffered a stroke.

"But she was so healthy yesterday!"

"She wasn't feeling well this morning, so Mr. Kitano stayed home from work. She collapsed later," Mr. Tanji says.

Isao goes ahead.

Kahana has changed. There's a large Filipino camp now, and Filipino bachelors make up half of the work force. Tall eucalyptus ring the village, and every yard is an orchard of mango, avocado, banana, and papaya. The barracks have been replaced by detached wood frame houses with asphalt-shingle roofs. The air is bracing.

Aunt Kitano is already dead when we get there, and Sadao and his stepfather are standing face-to-face and shouting.

"That's why I came back, to look after her!" Sadao towers over him.

"I want her buried here so I can visit her!" Mr. Kitano shouts.

"I insist on cremating her!" Sadao shouts back down at him.

"I want her buried!"

"I want to take her with me!"

"I am her husband!"

"I am her son!"

Isao pulls Sadao aside. "Why don't you agree with him for now. After he dies, you can dig up her bones, cremate them, and take them with you."

I help wash and dress the body. I think of Madame Kanai's worrying about "dying in a strange land." You're fortunate, Kitano-san; you have people fighting over you.

"You should rest," Isao says.

"I have to do this last thing for her."

"She was your substitute," Kiyoshi says.

"I'm such a nobody, and twice I've been saved."

7

(John Okada, 1923—1971)
约翰·冈田

作者简介

约翰·冈田（John Okada, 1923—1971），美国日裔小说家，也被认为是第一个美国日裔小说家，代表作《不—不仔》（*No-No Boy*, 1957）。冈田出生于美国西雅图，曾就读于华盛顿大学（University of Washington）。珍珠港事件的爆发迫使冈田中断学业，随全家被迫迁往米尼多卡县的“重新安置中心”（Minidoka War Relocation Center）。冈田在放弃效忠日本天皇的问卷签字后，加入美国空军，并担任军队的日语翻译。第二次世界大战结束后，冈田重返校园，获得华盛顿大学英语学士学位和哥伦比亚大学硕士学位。

珍珠港事件后，在美的日本人都要接受“忠诚问卷”，其中两个问题是：你是否愿意服从美国当局命令随时加入美军作战？你愿意发誓永远无条件效忠美国，并保护她不受国内外势力的攻击，同时发誓抛弃对日本天皇或者其他任何国外政府、力量，和组织的服从和效忠吗？对这两个问题做出否定回答的日裔青年被称为“不—不仔”（No-No Boy）。他唯一的一部作品《不—不仔》就以第二次世界大战期间的美国西雅图为背景，记叙日裔青年“不—不仔”一郎（Ichiro）因拒绝服兵役在第二次世界大战期间和第二次世界大战后遭受的歧视、隔离和排斥，展现第二次世界大战对于日裔个人、家庭和社会造成的深刻影响。这部小说出版后一直受到冷落，直到20世纪70年代小说被亚裔作家重新发现，该小说才受到关注，并被视为美国亚裔文学的经典作品。

小说《不—不仔》第一章讲述日裔青年一郎（Ichiro）因第二次世界大战期间拒服兵役而入狱，两年后一郎返回家乡，在家乡的所见、所闻和所感。节选部分是一郎回家后路上偶遇曾经的朋友的情景。

作品选读

No-No Boy

1

(excerpt)

By John Okada

TWO WEEKS AFTER his twenty-fifth birthday, Ichiro got off a bus at Second and Main in Seattle. He had been gone four years, two in camp and two in prison.

Walking down the street that autumn morning with a small, black suitcase, he felt like an intruder in a world to which he had no claim. It was just enough he should feel this way, for, of his own free will, he had stood before the judge and said that he would not go in the army. At the time there was no other choice for him. That was when he was twenty-three, a man of twenty-three. Now, two years older, he was even more of a man.

Christ, he thought to himself, just a goddamn kid is all I was. Didn't I know enough to wipe my own nose. What the hell have I done? What am I doing back here? Best thing I can do would be to kill some son of a bitch and head back to prison.

He walked toward the railroad depot where the tower with the clocks on all four sides was. It was a dirty looking tower of ancient brick. It was a dirty city. Dirtier, certainly, than it had a right to be after only four years.

Waiting for the light to change to green, he looked around at the people standing at the bus stop. A couple of men in suits, half a dozen women who failed to arouse him even after prolonged good behavior, and a young Japanese with a lunch bucket. Ichiro studied him, searching in his mind for the name that went with the round, pimply face and the short-cropped hair. The pimples were gone and the face had hardened, but the hair was still cropped. The fellow wore green, army-fatigue trousers and an Eisenhower jacket—Eto Minato. The name came to him at the same time as did the horrible significance of the army clothes. In panic, he started to step off the curb. It was too late. He had been seen.

"Itchy!" That was his nickname

Trying to escape, Ichiro urged his legs frenziedly across the street.

"Hey, Itchy!" The caller's footsteps ran toward him.

An arm was placed across his back. Ichiro stopped and faced the other Japanese. He tried to smile, but could not. There was no way out now.

"I'm Eto. Remember?"Eto smiled and extended his palm. Reluctantly, Ichiro lifted his own hand and let the other shake it.

The round face with the round eyes peered at him through silver-rimmed spectacles."What the hell! It's been a long time, but not that long. How've you been? What's doing?"

"Well... that is, I'm... "

"Last time must have been before Pearl harbor. God, it's been quite a while, hasn't it? Three, no closer to four years, I guess. Lotsa Japs coming back to the Coast. Lotsa Japs in Seattle. You'll sake and see 'em around. Japs are funny that way. Gotta have their rice and other Japs. Stupid, I say. The smart ones went to Chicago and New York and lotsa places back east, but there's still plenty coming back out this way." Eto drew cigarettes from his breast pocket and held out the package. "No? Well, I'll have one. Got the habit in the army. Just got out a short while back. Rough time, but I made it. Didn't get out in time to make the quarter, but I'm planning to go to school. How long you been around?"

Ichiro touched his toe to the suitcase. "Just got in. Haven't been home yet."

"When'd you get discharged?"

A car grinding its gears started down the street. He wished he were in it. "I... that is... I never was in."

Eto slapped him good-naturedly on the arm. "No need to look so sour. So you weren't in. So what? Been in camp all this time?"

"No." He made an effort to be free of Eto with his questions. He felt as if he were in a small room whose walls were slowly closing in on him. "It's been a long time, I know, but I'm really anxious to see the folks."

"What the hell. Let's have a drink. On me. I don't give a damn if I'm late to work. As for your folks, you'll see them soon enough. You drink, don't you?"

"Yeah, but not now."

"Ahh." Eto was disappointed. He shifted his lunch box from under one arm to the other.

"I've really got to be going."

The round face wasn't smiling any more. It was thoughtful. The eyes confronted Ichiro with indecision which changed slowly to enlightment and then to suspicion. He remembered. He knew.

The friendliness was gone as he said: "No-no boy, huh?"

Ichiro wanted to say yes. He wanted to return the look of despising hatred and say simply yes, but it was too much to say. The walls had closed in and were crushing all the unspoken words back down into his stomach. He shook his head once, not wanting to evade the eyes but finding it impossible to meet them. Out of his big weakness the little ones were branching, and the eyes he didn't have the courage to face were ever present. If it would have helped to gouge out his own eyes, he would have done so long ago. The hate-churned eyes with the stamp of unrelenting condemnation were his cross and he had driven the nails with his own hands.

"Rotten bastard. Shit on you." Eto coughed up a mouthful of sputum and rolled his words around it: "Rotten, no-good bastard."

Surprisingly, Ichiro felt relieved. Eto's anger seemed to serve as a release to his own naked tensions. As he stooped to lift the suitcase a wet wad splattered over his hand and dripped onto the black leather. The legs of his accuser were in front of him. God in a pair of green fatigues, U.S. Army style. They were the legs of the jury that had passed sentence upon him. Beseech me, they seemed to say, throw your arms about me and bury your head between my knees and seek pardon for your great sin.

"I'll piss on you next time," said Eto vehemently.

He turned as he lifted the suitcase off the ground and hurried away from the legs and the eyes from which no escape was possible.

8

(Ronyoung Kim, 1926—1987)
金兰英

作者简介

金兰英（Ronyoung Kim, 1926—1987），美籍韩裔作家，出生于洛杉矶的一个韩国移民家庭。她的代表作《泥巴墙》（*Clay Walls*, 1987）获得普利策奖提名。

《泥巴墙》以金兰英父母的经历为原型：金兰英的父亲出生于韩国的农民阶层，而母亲来自贵族家庭，赴美后积极投身韩国独立运动。该小说被认为是“第一部讲述韩国移民和美籍韩裔居民的美国生活的小说”。小说讲述了一个韩国移民家庭从20世纪初到20世纪40年代的美国生活，展现了韩国人在第二次世界大战期间的生活经历，以及美国社会和韩国社会中不平等的种族、性别和阶级关系。1910年，韩国被日本占领后，父亲全（Chun）和母亲惠秀（Haesu）逃到美国，小说聚焦父母与子女因种族歧视和阶级差异而经历的艰难生活。小说分为三部分：第一部分讲述母亲惠秀的故事，母亲出生于韩国的贵族家庭，到美国后，积极参与韩国独立运动，不满意丈夫全对于革命的冷漠态度；第二部分聚焦出生于农民家庭的父亲全，父亲全来美国后努力赚钱养家，不理解妻子参与爱国活动，夫妻之间分歧日益增加。在妻子带儿女回韩国探亲的期间，他染上赌博的恶习，败光家产，抛弃妻子，最终客死他乡。探亲归来的母亲惠秀工作养家，被迫卖掉韩国的土地，切断与祖国的联系。小说第三部分讲述儿女们的故事。生在美国、长在美国的女儿费伊（Faye）和哥哥们对父母的祖国韩国没有过多感情，将自己视为美国人。珍珠港事件爆发后，她的哥哥们参军抵抗日本。

选读部分选自《泥巴墙》第三部分，叙述珍珠港事件爆发后，韩国人相互联系、诅咒日本人。他们决定帮助美国抗日，男子加入美国国民自卫队，有钱人买债券。听说韩国人也要被送往集中营后，一位韩国叔叔号召大家写信给国会议员，说明韩国人不同于日本人，最后韩国人幸免被送往集中营。

作品选读

Clay Walls
(excerpt)

By Ronyoung Kim

I walked over and turned down the volume of the radio. In the same loud voice she said, "The fools. They can't beat the United States. They'll get what they deserve. At last, Korea will have her independence."

The radio announcer spoke of sneak attacks, ships sinking, fires, deaths, war. He said nothing about Korean independence.

"Momma. War means we could all be killed."

"Oh no, don't you worry. They'll never touch us here. The Americans will smash them right away. The Japanese will be defeated. Now be quiet. I want to hear this," she said, turning up the volume.

It wasn't long before the phone began to ring. Koreans were getting in touch with their countrymen. They talked excitedly as they cursed the Japanese, cheered for the United States, and planned their country's independence. The telephone became inadequate and meetings were called. Momma pushed aside her work to attend. She told me about them later.

"We're going to get together. United Koreans to help the United States. Men are going to volunteer for the national guard. People with money will buy bonds. And we're going to wear badges saying we're Koreans."

"Badges?"

"You don't have to worry. You're an American citizen. But we might be mistaken for Japanese."

"That's nothing new," I said.

"The War is new. We don't want people to think we're our enemy."

Mama looked puzzled when I laughed. "There's an old saying about being one's own enemy," I explained.

"So?"

"Never mind. I don't know why it struck me as being funny. It has nothing to do with this," I said.

The Christmas dance was cancelled because of the war. No one would think of dancing when innocent people were dying. As news of bombings in Europe and invasions in the South Pacific flooded the radio and newsreels. I began to care about people I had never met, some living in places I never knew existed. Patriotism became the paramount virtue in the United States. It required hating the Japanese; I had had a lot of practice. Being at war with Japan meant mainstream Americans and I were on the same side.

Momma's group began to meet again. The smell of Momma's cooking and the sound of excitable voices filled the house once more. The war had given Koreans hope for regaining their country and reasons to organize.

"There's talk about sending the Japanese who live on the west coast to camps," Uncle Min said.

"What camps?" Momma asked.

"Somewhere away from the west coast. The government thinks the *wae nom* are spying for Japan," he said.

"Of course they are!" Uncle Lee declared. "A Japanese is always loyal to his emperor. It's in his blood."

"Does that make him patriotic?" I asked. I could not tell if Uncle Lee was praising them or damning them.

Uncle Yang laughed. "Before December seven, it made him a 'good' Japanese. After December seven, it made him a 'bad' American."

"Aeh!" Uncle Kim snapped. "*Sang noms* before and after any date," he said, calling them eternal bastards.

Uncle Yang took out a memo pad from his pocket and read from his notes. "A picket line at San Pedro to boycott Japanese goods, we need signs and lots of people. I'll be taking a carful. How about you, Faye?"

"What do I have to do?"

"Just walk around carrying a sign that says, 'Boycott Japan'."

"That sounds easy. Why not?" I said.

It was easy. A photographer from the *Los Angeles Times* was at the pier. He took a picture of me carrying a sign and printed it in the newspaper. Momma clipped it out and sent it to Harold, proud as if I were Joan of Arc.

Anything I did against the enemy made me a heroine. I was glad it wasn't Koreans who bombed Pearl Harbor.

I had gone to my room to read when the men arrived for the next meeting. The subject of "camps" came up immediately.

"There's talk of sending Koreans to camp with the Japanese," Uncle Min said.

"WHAT?" Uncle Lee barked.

I put down my book to listen.

"As far as the United States government is concerned, we are part of Japan," Uncle Min said.

"They can't do that. We can't let them do that," Uncle Yang said. I knew his eyes were blinking rapidly.

"Ignorance! Plain ignorance!" Uncle Lee spewed. "What do they think we've been screaming about all these years? Why do they think we've been demanding recognition as a separate nation?"

"It won't happen," Uncle Kim's voice was calm. "K. S. Ahn is in Washington talking to congressmen," he said.

"Yes, but will they listen?" Uncle Lee said.

"They'd better. No one's going to catch me going to camp with any Japanese," Uncle Kim said.

"Catch no Korean," Uncle Min said.

"I'm staying right here," Momma said. "No one can make me go anywhere."

"We'd better get everyone to send letters to congressmen and money to Ahn," Uncle Yang said. He paused. Probably writing notes, I thought. "We'll have to distribute the names and addresses of influential congressmen and senators to all Koreans in California," he continued.

"Senators. Good idea. Ahn needs all the support he can get," Uncle Kim said.

"Where's Rhee on this? He's known in Washington. What's he doing?" Uncle Min asked.

"Who cares?" Uncle Lee said, "Ahn's our man."

I was impressed. Letters to congressmen and senators in Washinton, D.C. Momma's group had a voice and the United States government was going to hear it.

Later, when the Koreans were informed they were excluded from the "relocation" program, K. S. Ahn became a hero.

Momma sighed deeply when she heard the news. "Justice, at last. No one will mistake us for Japanese. We will be moving about freely in California."

Bertha was the first to make me realize what it meant. I was surprised to see her at our door.

"I came to say goodbye and to let you know I think the whole thing stinks," she said.

"Where are you going?" I asked, holding the door open for her.

"I'm not going anywhere. You are the one. It's so dumb. Hauling everyone off to a camp because they can't tell who's spying."

Momma called me from the table. *"Nu gu wat ne?"*

"It's Bertha," I answered. Bertha beckoned me out and we sat on the porch steps. "Not us. The Japanese," I explained.

9

(Lawson Fusao Inada, 1938—)

劳森·稻田

作者简介

劳森·稻田（Lawson Fusao Inada, 1938— ），第三代美国日裔诗人，俄勒冈州第五位桂冠诗人。1938年5月26日，劳森·稻田出生于美国加利福尼亚州。第二次世界大战期间，他们全家被关在集中营里，辗转于加利福尼亚、阿肯色和科罗拉多的多个集中营。战后，他成为爵士乐手，演奏低音管，因此他的写作深受爵士乐和集中营经历的影响。他还曾在加州州立大学弗雷斯诺分校（California State University, Fresno）、俄勒冈大学（University of Oregon）以及爱荷华大学（University of Iowa）学习写作，并在新罕布什尔大学（University of New Hampshire）和南俄勒冈大学（Southern Oregon University）等高校任教。

劳森·稻田的诗集有《战前》（*Before the War: Poems As They Happen*, 1971）、《集中营传说》（*Legend from Camp*, 1993）和《划线》（*Drawing the Line*, 1997）。他的诗歌多以第二次世界大战为背景，特别是以集中营的经历为创作素材，因此被称为"集中营诗人"。他的第一部诗集《战前》是美国文学史上第一部亚裔作家出版的诗集，记录诗人被关在集中营前后的童年经历和情感，将个人、社会和家庭历史有机结合起来。《集中营传说》荣获1994年美国图书奖（American Book Award）。《划线》讲述了日裔后代在第二次世界大战时拒绝被关押集中营的故事。劳森·稻田的诗歌真实再现第二次世界大战期间美国日裔在集中营的悲惨经历，揭露美国社会根深蒂固的种族歧视。稻田的诗歌探讨日裔身份、历史和战争等主题，反思战争对于普通民众和国家造成的伤害和影响。稻田的诗歌句子简短，节奏活泼，通俗易懂。

除了集中营诗人的身份，劳森·稻田还是美国亚裔文学“哎咿—集团”的成员。他与赵健秀（Frank Chin）、陈耀光（Jeffery Paul Chan）和徐忠雄（Shawn Wong）合编亚裔美国作家文选《哎咿！美国亚裔作家选集》（*Aiiieeeee!: An Anthology of Asian-American Writers*, 1974）和《大哎咿！美国华裔与日裔文学选集》（*The Big Aiiieeeee!: An Anthology of Chinese-American and Japanese-American Literature*, 1990），这两部著作对美国亚裔文学具有重要的奠基意义，对美国亚裔文学批评的基本框架和理论命题的确立也有重要的先驱性。

诗歌《来自我们的相册》（“From Our Album”）选自诗集《战前》；诗歌《直到今天》（“To This Day”）和《记忆》（“Memory”）选自诗集《集中营传说》，诗歌记录日裔对于第二次世界大战期间所受不公正待遇的追问。

作品选读

From Our Album

By Lawson Fusao Inada

I. “Before the War”

“Before the war”
means Fresno, a hedged-in house,
two dogs in the family.

Blackie, the small one, mine,
lapped at his insides
on the floorboard, on the way to the doctor.

Jimmy, my father’s shepherd,
wouldn’t eat after the evacuation.
He wouldn’t live with another master

and pined away, skin and bone.

With feelings more than pride,
we call him our one-man dog.

II. Mud

Mud in the barracks—
a muddy room, a chamber pot.

Mud in the moats
around each barracks group.

Mud on the shoes
trudging to the mess hall.

Mud in the swamp
where the men chopped wood.

Mud on the guts
under a loaded wagon—

crushed in the mud by the wheel.

III. Desert Songs

1. ALL THAT WE GATHERED
Because there was little else to do,
they led us to the artillery range
for shells, all that we gathered,
and let us dig among dunes
for slugs, when they were through.

Because there was little else to do,
one of them chased a stray
with his tail between his legs
and shot him through the head.

2. SHELLS

A desert tortoise—
something mute and hard—

something to decorate
a desert Japanese garden:

gnarled wood, smooth
artillery shells for a border.

When a guard
smashes one, the shell

cracks open and the muscles ooze.

3. IT IS ONLY NATURAL

The pheasant is an Oriental creature,
so it is only natural
that one should fly into camp

and, famished by rations and cans,
break out in secret, native dance
over a fire, on a black coal stove.

4. SONG OF THE 442ND

Caged creatures
have curious moods.

Some of them choose
to be turned

loose in a group,
to take their chances

in the open.

5. STEERS
Because a dentist
logically drives a butcher truck,

I rode with my father
to the slaughterhouse on an afternoon.

Not hammers, not bullets,
could make him close his eyes.

6. HE TEACHES
He jerks the eyes
from birds, feet
from lizards,

and punishes
ants with the gaze
of a glass.

And with his sly
gaze, his child's face,
he teaches

what has its place,
and must be
passed on to others.

IV. Song of Chicago
When the threat lessened,
when we became tame,
my father and friends

took a train to Chicago

for factory work,
for packaging bolts.
One grew a mustache
and called himself Carlos.

And they all made a home
with those of their own—

rats, bedbugs, blacks.

To This Day

By Lawson Fusao Inada

Have you ever wondered
whatever happened to all the
barbed wire that defined
and confined the so-called
camp at Tule Lake?
That's a good question
we have a right to ask
as ordinary tax-paying citizens:
"Whatever happened
to all that barbed wire?"
When you think about it,
the very idea of fencing such an expense of land
was a daunting challenge

for all those concerned
because it wasn't easy
to coordinate "back East" planning
with "out West" implementation,
along with the manufacture
and transportation of materials
from all points in between.
And it was also
an innovative undertaking,
a historical precedent,
because this fence was to confine,
not cattle or criminals,
but residents of the American West,
who, in the western tradition,
were to be "rounded up",
and "herded" into fenced areas—
Tule Lake being but one such place.
Now, thinking about barbed wire,
it could be easy to consider
related matters that would
take us off into a tangent
about, oh, fence posts
and other such aspects
of construction, sidetracking us
into thinking about cutting
forests for fence posts,
and all the effort, energy, expense
involved in the overall venture—
including catered lunches
for planning meetings sequestered
in the "red tape" of D.C.—
so let's just focus on the wire
that arrived by train

on huge spools, I suppose,
ready to be unloaded
by many men with machines
who would then, over days,
depending on weather,
erect the barbed wire fence.
And let's keep going forward,
like the war effort,
not backward to the origins
of the wire that would include
iron ore, iron mines, steel mills,
all the sweat, smoke, steam,
shoveling, smelting, stamping
of the extensive process
of manufacturing wire
and then barbing it;
Yes, let's keep going forward,
like the war effort
not backward to the origins
of the war, or to the barb wire
trenches of the First World War,
but to the brand-new
barbed wire fence of Tule Lake.
The wire was gleaming in the sun!
And with all those barbs—
thousands upon thousands—
all those strands were sparkling!
As we can imagine—
the fence was really something!
And just imagine—
from the air, the shining structure
may have resembled—
a gigantic musical instrument,

that storms and raging winds would strum and pluck...
At any rate, whatever happened
to all that barbed wire? It's all gone somewhere, somehow,
obviously, which is a good thing;
otherwise, it would pose a hazard
for wildlife, and rusted barbs
could cause tetanus in humans...
especially children.
So perhaps it's immaterial
to dwell on such material matters
like rusted wire of the past;
rather, as we can imagine,
in this advanced day and age,
there just might be a mentality
among us, between us,
that, to this day,
serves to keep us separated
serves to keep us confined
between "them" and "us",
and this mentality, this condition,
invisible as it is,
intangible as it is,
can actually function
like actual barbed wire—
and it is up to everyone,
in the spirit of humanity,
in the name of mutuality,
to reach through the strands
with extended hands.

Memory

By Lawson Fusao Inada

Memory is an old Mexican woman
sweeping her yard with a broom.
She has grown even smaller now,
residing at that vanishing point
decades after one dies,
but at some times, given
the right conditions—
an ordinary dream, or practically
anything in particular—
she absolutely looms,
assuming the stature
she had in the neighborhood.

This was the Great Valley,
and we had swept in
to do the grooming.
We were on the move, tending
what was essentially
someone else's garden.
Memory's yard was all that
in miniature, in microcosm:
rivers for irrigation,
certain plants, certain trees
ascertained by season.
Without formal acknowledgment,
she was most certainly
the head of a community, American.

Memory had been there forever.
We settled in around her;
we brought the electricity
of blues and baptized gospel,
ancient adaptations of icons,
spices, teas, fireworks, trestles,
newly acquired techniques
of conflict and healing, common
concepts of collective survival...

Memory was there all the while.
Her house, her shed, her skin,
were all the same—weathered—
and she didn't do anything, especially,
except hum as she moved;
Memory, in essence, was unmemorable.

Yet, ask any of us who have long since left,
who have all but forgotten that adulterated place
paved over and parceled out by the powers that be,
and what we remember, without even choosing to,
is an old woman humming, sweeping, smoothing her yard: Memory.

10

(Bharati Mukherjee, 1940—2017)
巴拉蒂·慕克吉

作者简介

巴拉蒂·慕克吉（Bharati Mukherjee, 1940—2017），美国著名小说家和社会评论家。慕克吉 1940 年生于印度加尔各答（Calcutta, India），自幼接受英国传统式教育。慕克吉 1959 年从加尔各答大学（University of Calcutta）毕业，1961 年获英语和印度古代文化硕士学位，同年入读爱荷华大学作家工坊（Iowa Writers' Workshop），1969 年获得爱荷华大学比较文学博士学位。慕克吉本打算返回印度，但她在爱荷华与加拿大/美国作家克拉克·布莱兹（Clark Blaise）相识，随后两人决定成婚。慕克吉获得博士学位后，在加拿大麦克吉尔大学等高校执教十余年，后返回美国定居。她曾在纽约城市大学（City University of New York）和加州大学伯克利分校（University of California, Berkeley）任教。

慕克吉著有小说和散文。她的主要作品有长篇小说《老虎的女儿》(*The Tiger's Daughter*, 1971)、《妻子》(*Wife*, 1975)、《茉莉花》(*Jasmine*, 1989)、《坐拥世界》(*The Holder of the World*, 1993)、《称心的女儿》(*Desirable Daughters*, 2002）和短篇小说集《黑暗》(*Darkness*, 1983)、《中介》(*The Middleman and Other Stories*, 1988)。慕克吉另与克拉克·布莱兹合著回忆录《加尔各答的日日夜夜》(*Days and Nights in Calcutta*, 1986）和《悲情与恐怖：印度航空公司惨案遗事》(*The Sorrow and the Terror: The Haunting Legacy of the Air India Tragedy*, 1987)。慕克吉曾凭借短篇小说集《中介》获 1988 年美国国家图书评论界奖（National Book Critics Circle Award)。慕克吉坚持小说创作，笔耕不辍。慕克吉认为自己是一名美国作家，而非印度移民作家。她的作品描写印度移民在美国的生活，不仅表

现了作者对保持印度传统的自豪感，也反映了她融入美国的喜悦之情。

《房客》(“The Tenant”）选自短篇小说集《中介》，获评1987年美国最佳短篇小说（The Best American Short Stories 1987），小说女主人公玛雅（Maya Sanyal）在美国大学教授世界文学，自认为是美国人，可是却受到印度传统文化的束缚，小说塑造一个“解放的”印度女性形象，反映印度移民在两种文化中的孤独感和漂泊感。节选部分讲述经历婚姻失败、倍感孤独的玛雅在异国他乡联系征婚人的故事。小说《称心的女儿》具有自传色彩，讲述出生印度上层社会的三姐妹从古老印度到现代美国的不同的人生旅程，小说融合家族历史、三姐妹的童年回忆与成年的自我发现之旅。小说情节扣人心弦，可读性强。选读部分选自《称心的女儿》第一章，介绍三姐妹中最小的妹妹塔拉（Tara）的包办婚姻。

作品选读

The Tenant
(excerpt)

By Bharati Mukherjee

The next day, Monday, instead of getting a ride home with Fran—Fran says she likes to give rides, she needs the chance to talk, and she won't share gas expenses, absolutely not—Maya goes to the periodicals room of the library. There are newspapers from everywhere, even from Madagascar and New Caledonia. She thinks of the periodicals room as an asylum for homesick aliens. There are two aliens already in the room, both Orientals, both absorbed of homes, in the politics and gossip of their far off homes.

She goes straight to the newspaper from India. She bunches her raincoat like a bolster to make herself more comfortable. There is so much to catch up on. A village headman, a known-congress party worker, has been shot at by scooter-riding snipers. An Indian pugilist has won an international medal in Nepal. A child drawing well water—the reporter calls the child "a neo-Buddhist, a convert from the now-outlawed untouchable caste"—has been stoned. An editorial explains that the story stoning is not a story about caste but about failed idealism; a story about promises of green fields and clean, portable water broken, a story about bribes paid and wells not dug. But no, thinks Maya, it's about caste.

Out here, in the heartland of the new world, the India of serious newspapers unsettles. Maya longs again to feel what she had felt in the Chatterjis' living room: virtues made physical. It is a familiar feeling, a longing. Had a suitable man presented himself in the reading room at that instant, she would have seduced him. She goes on to the stack of *India Abroads*, reads through matrimonial columns, and steals an issue to take home.

Indian men want Indian brides. Married Indian men want Indian mistresses. All over America, "handsome, tall, fair"engineers, doctors, data processors—the new pioneers—cry their eerie love calls.

Maya runs a finger down the first column; her finger tip, dark with newsprint, stops at random.

Hello! Hi! Yes, you *are* the one I'm looking for. You are the new emancipated Indo-American woman. You have a zest for life. You are at ease in USA and yet your ethics are rooted in Indian tradition. The man of our dreams has come. Yours truly is handsome, ear-nose-throat specialist, well-settled in Connecticut. Age is 41 but never married, physically fit, sportsmanly, and strong. I adore idealism, poetry, beauty. I abhor smugness, passivity, caste system. Write with recent photo. Better still, Call!!!

Maya calls. Hullo, hullo, hullo! She hears immigrant lovers cry in crowded shopping malls. Yes, you who are at ease in both worlds, you are the one. She feels she has a fair chance.

A man answers. "Ashoke Mehta speaking."

She speaks quickly into the bright-red mouthpiece of her telephone. He will be in Chicago, in transit, passing through O'Hare. United counter, Saturday, two p.m. As easy as that.

"Good," Ashoke Mehta says. "For these encounters I, too, prefer a neutral zone."

On Saturday at exactly two o'clock the man of Maya's dream floats toward her as lovers used to in shampoo commercials. The United counter is a loud, harassed place but passengers and piled-up luggage fall away from him. Full-cheeked and fleshy-lipped, he is handsome. He hasn't lied. He is serene, assured, a Hindu god touching down in Illinois.

She can't move. She feels ugly and unworthy. Her adult life no longer seems miraculously rebellious; it is grim, it is perverse. She has accomplished nothing. She has changed her citizenship but she hasn't broken through into the light, the vigor, the *bustle* of the New World. She is stuck in dead space.

"Hullo, hullo!" Their fingers touch.

Oh, the excitement! Ashoke Mehta's palm feels so right in the small of her back. Hullo, hullo, hub. He pushes her out of the reach of anti-Khomeini Iranians, Hare Krishnas, American Fascists, men with fierce wants, and guides her to an empty gate. They have less than an hour.

"What would you like, Maya?"

She knows he can read her mind, she knows her thoughts are open to him. *You*, she's almost giddy with the thought, with simple desire. "From the snack bar," he says, as though to clarify. "I'm afraid I'm starved."

Below them, where the light is strong and hurtful, a Boeing is being serviced. "Nothing," she says.

He leans forward. She can feel the nap of his scarf—she recognizes the Cambridge colors—she can smell the wool of his Icelandic sweater. She runs her hand along the scarf, then against the flesh of his neck. "Only the impulsive ones call," he says.

The immigrant courtship proceeds. It's easy, he's good with facts. He knows how to come across to a stranger who may end up a lover, a spouse. He makes over a hundred thousand. He owns a house in Hartford and two income properties in Newark. He plays the market but he's cautious. He's good at badminton but plays handball to keep in shape. He watches all the sports on television. Last August he visited Copenhagen, Helsinki and Leningrad. Once upon a time he collected stamps but now he doesn't have hobbies, except for reading. He counts himself an intellectual, he spends too much on books. Ludlum, Forsyth, MacInns; other names she doesn't catch. She suppresses a smile, she's told him only she's a graduate student. He's not without his vices. He's a spender, not a saver. He's a sensualist: good food—all foods, but easy on the Indian—good wine. Some temptations he doesn't try to resist.

And I, she wants to ask, do I tempt?

"Now tell me about yourself, Maya." He makes it easy for her. "Have you ever been in love?"

"No."

"But many have loved you, I can see that." He says it no unkindly. It is the fate of women like her, and men like him. Their karmic duty, to be loved. It is expected, not judged. She feels she can see them all, the sad parade of need and demand. This isn't the time to reveal all.

And so the courtship enters a second phase.

When she gets back to Cedar Falls, Ted Sumikiski is standing on the front porch. It's late at night, chilly. He is wearing a down vest. She's never seen him on the porch. In fact there's no chair to sit on. He looks chilled through. He's waited around a while.

"Hi." She has her keys ready. This isn't the night to offer the six-pack in the fridge. He looks expectant, ready to pounce.

"Hi." He looks like a man who might have aimed the dart at her. What has he done to his wife, his kids? Why isn't there at least a dog? "Say, I left a note upstairs."

The note is written in Magic Marker and thumb-tacked to her apartment door. DUE TO PERSONAL REASONS, NAMELY REMARRIAGE, I REQUEST THAT YOU VACATE MY PLACE AT THE END OF THE SEMESTER.

Maya takes the note down and retacks it to the kitchen wall. The whole wall is like a bulletin board, made of some new, crumbly building-material. Her kitchen, Ted Sumikiski had told her, was once a child's bedroom. Sumnski in love: the idea stuns her. She has misread her landlord. The dart at her window speaks of no twisted fantasy. The landlord wants the tenant out.

She gets a glass out of the kitchen cabinet, gets out of a tray of ice, pours herself a shot of Fran's bourbon. She is happy for Ted Sumikiski. She is. She wants to tell someone how moved she'd been by Mrs. Chatterji's singing. How she'd felt in O'Hare, even about Dr. Rab Chatterji's in the car. But Fran is not the person. No one she's ever met is the person. She can't talk about the dead space she lives in. She wishes Ashoke Mehta would call. Right now.

Weeks pass. Then two months. She finds a new room, signs another lease. Her new landlord calls himself Fred. He has no arms, but he helps her move her things. He drives between Ted Sumikiski's place and his twice in his station wagon. He uses his toes the way Maya uses her fingers. He likes to do things. He pushes garbage sacks full of Maya's clothes up the stairs.

"It's all right to share," Fred says. "Hell, I would."

That first afternoon in Fred's rooming house, they share a Chianti. Fred wants to cook her pork chops but he's a little shy about Indians and meat. Is it beef, or pork? Or any meat? She says it's okay, any meat, but not tonight. He has an ex-wife in Des Moines, two kids in Portland, Oregon. The kids are both normal; he's the only freak in the family. But he's self-reliant. He shops in the supermarket like anyone else, he carries out the garbage, shovels the snow off the sidewalk. He needs Maya's help with one thing. Just one thing. The box of Tide is a bit too heavy to manage. Could she get him the giant size every so often and leave it in the basement?

The dead space need not suffocate. Over the months, Fred and she will settle into companionship. She has never slept with a man without arms. Two wounded people, he will joke during their nightly contortions. It will shock her, this assumed equivalence with a man so strikingly deficient. She knows she is strange, and lonely, but being Indian is not the same, she would have thought, as being a freak.

One night in spring, Fred's phone rings. "Ashoke Medhta speaking." None of this "do you remember me?" nonsense. The god has tracked her down. He hasn't forgotten. "Hullo," he says, in their special way. And because she doesn't answer back, "Hullo, hullo, hullo." She is aware of Fred in the back of the room. He is lighting a cigarette with his toes.

"Yes," she says, "I remember."

"I had to take care of a problem," Ashoke Mehta says, "You know that I have my vices. That time at O'Hare I was honest with you."

She is breathless.

"Who is it, May?" asks Fred.

"You also have a problem," says the voice. His laugh echoes. "You will come to Hartford, I know."

When she moves out, she tells herself, it will not be the end of Fred's world.

Desirable Daughters

Chapter One (excerpt)

By Bharati Mukherjee

In the mind's eye, a one-way procession of flickering oil lamps sways along the muddy shanko between rice paddies and flooded ponds, and finally disappears into a distant wall of impenetrable jungle. Banks of fog rise from warmer waters, mingle with smoke from the cooking fires, and press in a dense sooty collar, a permeable gray wall that parts, then seals, igniting a winter chorus of retching coughs and loud spitting. Tuberculosis is everywhere. The air, the water, the soil are septic. Thirty-five years is a long life. Smog obscures the moon and dims the man-made light to faintness deeper than the stars'. In such darkness perspective disappears. It is a two-dimensional world impossible to penetrate. But for the intimacy of shared discomfort, it is difficult even to estimate the space separating each traveler.

The narrow, raised trail stretches ten miles from Mishtigunj town to the jungle's edge. In a palanquin borne by four servants sit a rich man's three daughters, the youngest dressed in her bridal sari, her little hands painted with red lac dye, her hair oiled and set. Her arms are heavy with dowry gold; bangles ring tiny arms from wrist to shoulder. Childish voices chant a song, hands clap, gold bracelets tinkle. I cannot imagine the loneliness of this child. A Bengali girl's happiest night is about to become her lifetime imprisonment. It seems all the sorrow of history, all that is unjust in society and cruel in religion has settled on her. Even constructing it from the merest scraps of family memory fills me with rage and bitterness.

The bride-to-be whispers the "Tush Tusli Brata," a hymn to the sacredness of marriage, a petition for a kind and generous husband:

What do I hope for in worshipping you? That my father's wisdom be endless, My mother's kindness bottomless. May my husband be as powerful as a king of gods. May my future son-in-law light up the royal court. Bestow on me a brother who is learned and intellectual, A son as handsome as the best-looking courtier, And a daughter who is beauteous. Let my hair-part glow red with vermilion powder, as a wife's should. On my wrists and arms, let bangles glitter and jangle. Load down my clothes-rack with the finest saris. Fill my kitchen with scoured-shiny utensils. Reward my wifely virtue with a rice-filled granary. These are the boons that this young virgin begs of thee.

In a second, larger palki borne by four men sit the family priest and the father of the bride. Younger uncles and cousins follow in a vigilant file. Two more guards, sharp-bladed daos drawn, bring up the rear. Two servants walk ahead of the eight litter-bearers, holding naphtha lamps. No one has seen such brilliant European light, too strong to stare into, purer white than the moon. It is a town light, a rich man's light, a light that knows English invention. If bandits are crouching in the gullies they will know to strike this reckless Hindu who announces his wealth with light and by arming his servants. What treasures lie inside, how much gold and jewels, what target ripe for kidnapping? The nearest town, where such a wealthy man must have come from, lies behind him. Only the jungle lies ahead. Even the woodcutters desert it at night, relinquishing it to goondahs and marauders, snakes and tigers.

The bride is named Tara Lata, a name we almost share. The name of the father is Jai Krishna Gangooly. Tara Lata is five years old and headed deep into the forest to marry a tree.

I have had the time, the motivation, and even the passion to undertake this history. When my friends, my child, or my sisters ask me why, I say I am exploring the making of a consciousness. Your consciousness? They tease, and I tell them, No. Yours.

On this night, flesh-and-blood emerges from the unretrievable past. I have Jai Krishna's photo, I know the name of Jai Krishna's father, but they have always been ghosts. But Tara Lata is not, nor will her father be, after the events of this special day. And so my history begins with a family wedding on the coldest, darkest night in the Bengali month of Paush—December/January—in a district of the Bengal Presidency that lies east of Calcutta—now Kolkata—and south of Dacca—now Dhaka—as the English year of 1879 is about to shed its final two digits, although the Hindu year of 1285 still has four months to run and the Muslim year of 1297 has barely begun.

(......)

And so, the story of the three great-granddaughters of Jai Krishna Gangooly starts on the day of a wedding, a few hours before the palki ride where fates have already been decided, in the decorated ancestral house of the Gangoolys on the river in Mishtigunj town. The decorations signify a biye-bari, a wedding house. Beggars have already camped in the alleys adjacent to the canopy under which giant copper vats of milk, stirred by professional cooks, have been boiling and thickening for sweetmeats, and where other vats, woks, and cauldrons receive the chunks of giant hilsa fish netted fresh from the river and hold the rice pilao, lamb curry, spiced lentils, and deep-fried and sauce-steeped vegetables, a feast for a thousand invited guests and the small city of self-invited men, women, and children camped outside the gates.

The astrologers have spoken; the horoscopes have been compared. The match between Jai Krishna's youngest daughter and a thirteen-year-old youth, another Kulin Brahmin from an upright and pious family from a nearby village, has been blessed. The prewedding religious rites have been meticulously performed, and the prewedding stree-achar, married women's rituals, boisterously observed. To protect the husband-to-be from poisonous snakebite, married women relatives and Brahmin women neighbors have propitiated Goddess Manasha with prescribed offerings. All of this has been undertaken at a moment in the evolution of Jai Krishna from student of Darwin and Bentham and Comte and practitioner of icy logic, to reader of the Upanishads and believer in Vedic wisdom. He had become a seeker of truth, not a synthesizer of cultures. He found himself starting arguments with pleaders and barristers, those who actually favored morning toast with marmalade, English suits, and leather shoes. Now nearing forty, he was in full flight from his younger self, joining a debate that was to split bhadra lok society between progressives and traditionalists for over a century.

A Dacca barrister, Keshub Mitter, teased him for behaving more like a once-rich Muslim nawab wedded to a fanciful past and visions of lost glory than an educated, middle-class Hindu lawyer. Everyone knew that the Indian past was a rubbish heap of shameful superstition. Keshub Mitter's insult would have been unforgivable if it hadn't been delivered deftly, with a smile and a Bengali lawyer's wit and charm. My dear Gangooly, English is but a stepping-stone to the deeper refinement of German and French. Where does our Bangla language lead you? A big frog in a small, stagnant pond. Let us leave the sweet euphony of Bangla to our poets, and the salvation-enhancement of Sanskrit to our priests. Packet boats delivered Berlin and Paris papers to the Dacca High Court, along with the venerated *Times*.

The cases Jai Krishna pleaded in court often cast him as the apostle of enlightenment and upholder of law against outmoded custom, or the adjudicator of outrages undefined and unimaginable under British law. The majesty of law was in conflict with Jai Krishna's search for an uncorrupted, un-British, un-Muslim, fully Hindu consciousness. He removed his wife and children from cosmopolitan Dacca and installed them in Mishtigunj. He sought a purer life for himself, English pleader by day, Sanskrit scholar by night. He regretted the lack of a rigorous Brahminical upbringing, the years spent in Calcutta learning the superior ways of arrogant Englishmen and English laws, ingesting English contempt for his background and ridicule for babus like him. He had grown up in a secularized home with frequent Muslim visitors and the occasional wayward Englishman. In consideration of non-Hindu guests, his father had made certain that his mother's brass deities and stone lingams stayed confined in the closed-off worship-room.

On the morning of Tara Lata's wedding, female relatives waited along the riverbank for the arrival of the groom and his all-male wedding party. The groom was Satindranath Lahiri, fifth son of Surendranath Lahiri, of the landowning Lahiri family; in his own right, a healthy youth, whose astrological signs pointed to continued wealth and many sons. Back in Dacca, Jai Krishna had defended the ancient Hindu practices, the caste consciousness, the star charts, the observance of auspicious days, the giving of a dowry, the intact integrity of his community's rituals. His colleague, Keshub Mitter, to be known two decades later as Sir Keshub, and his physician, Dr. Ashim Lal Roy, both prominent members of the most progressive, most Westernized segment of Bengali society, the Brahmo Samaj, had attempted to dissuade him. The two men had cited example after example of astrologically arranged marriages, full of astral promise, turning disastrous. The only worthwhile dowry, they'd proclaimed, is an educated bride. Child-marriage is barbarous. How could horoscopes influence lives, especially obscure lives, in dusty villages like Mishtigunj? Jai Krishna knew these men to be eaters of beef and drinkers of gin.

"I consider myself a student of modern science," Jai Krishna had explained, "and because I am a student of modern science, I cannot reject any theory until I test it." And so far, the tests had all turned out positive. His two older daughters, seven and nine, were successfully married and would soon be moving to their husbands' houses and living as wives, then as mothers. They were placid and obedient daughters who would make loving and obedient wives. Tara Lata, his favorite, would be no exception.

In the wintry bright hour just before twilight blackens Mishtigunj, the decorated bajra from the Lahiri family finally sailed into view. The bride's female relatives stood at the stone bathing-steps leading from the steep bank down to the river as servants prepared to help the groom's party of two hundred disembark. Women began the oo-loo ululation, the almost instrumental, pitched-voice welcome. Two of Jai Krishna's younger brothers supervised the unrolling of mats on the swampy path that connected the private dock and Jai Krishna's two-storied brick house.

The bajra anchored, but none on board rushed to the deck railings to be ceremoniously greeted by the welcoming party of the bride's relatives. The bridegroom's father and uncles had a servant deliver a cruel message in an insulting tone to the bride's father. They would not disembark on Jai Krishna's property for Jai Krishna and his entire clan were carriers of a curse, and that curse, thanks to Jai Krishna's home-destroying, misfortune-showering daughter, had been visited on their sinless son instead of on Jai Krishna's flesh-and-blood. They demanded that Jai Krishna meet them in the sheltered cabin of the bajra.

Jai Krishna ordered the wedding musicians to stop their shenai playing and dhol beating. His women relatives, shocked at the tone in which the servant repeated his master's message to Jai Krishna babu, the renowned Dacca lawyer, had given up their conch shell blowing and their ululating on their own. For several minutes, Jai Krishna stood still on the bathing-steps, trying to conceal at first his bewilderment, then his fury, that the man who was to have full patriarchal authority over his beloved daughter had called her names. Then he heard a bullying voice from inside the cabin yell instructions to the boatmen to pull up anchor.

"They're bargaining for more dowry," muttered one of Jai Krishna's brothers.

"No beggar is as greedy as that Lahiri bastard!" spat another brother.

Two boatmen played at reeling in ropes and readying the bajra to sail back.

11

(Maxine Hong Kingston, 1940—　)
汤亭亭

作者简介

汤亭亭（Maxine Hong Kingston, 1940—　）出生于美国加利福尼亚斯托克顿。1958年进入加利福尼亚大学伯克利分校（University of California, Berkeley）读工程学，后转读英语文学；1962年毕业后与演员厄尔·金斯顿结婚。曾在夏威夷大学（University of Hawaii）教授英语、加利福尼亚大学伯克利分校教授创意写作。现为加利福尼亚大学荣休教授。

作为当代美国重要作家，汤亭亭获得过多种奖项，作品被选入多种文学选集或教材。处女作《女勇士》（*The Woman Warrior*, 1976）使她一举成名，获得1976年美国国家书评人协会奖（纪实文学类）（National Book Critics Circle Award for Nonfiction）。《中国佬》（*China Men*, 1980）获得1981年美国国家图书奖（纪实文学类）（National Book Award for Nonfiction）。其他作品还有《孙行者：他的即兴曲》（*Tripmaster Monkey: His Fake Book*, 1989）、《第五部和平之书》（*The Fifth Book of Peace*, 2003）、《我喜欢自己的生活有充分的余地》（*I Love a Broad Margin to My Life*, 2011），编辑出版《战争老兵，和平老兵》（*Veterans of War, Veterans of Peace*, 2006）。荣获美国艺术文学院奖（American Academy and Institute of Arts and Letters Literature Award）、国家人文勋章（National Humanities Medal）、美国国家图书基金会授予的美国文学杰出贡献奖（Medal for Distinguished Contribution to American Letters from the National Book Foundation）、国家艺术勋章（National Medal of Arts）等。

《女勇士》（*The Woman Warrior: Memoirs of a Girlhood Among Ghosts*, 1976）是一部自传体小说，是汤亭亭的成名作。小说以极富想象力的虚构与简洁白描，展示了一个生活在异乡的华人女孩的所思所想，讲述几代在美华人的酸甜苦辣和融入异域文化的心路历程。

《白老虎》(“White Tigers”) 选自《女勇士》。在故事中作者改写了中国传统民间故事“花木兰替父从军”和“岳母刺字”，让读者耳目一新，感受别具一格的阅读体验。

作品选读

The Woman Warrior: Memoirs of a Girlhood Among Ghosts

White Tigers
(excerpt)

By Maxine Hong Kingston

When I reached my village, my father and mother had grown as old as the two whose shapes I could at last no longer see. I helped my parents carry their tools, and they walked ahead so straight, each carrying a basket or a hoe not to overburden me, their tears falling privately. My family surrounded me with so much love that I almost forgot the ones not there. I praised the new infants.

“Some of the people are saying the Eight Sages took you away to teach you magic,” said a little girl cousin. “They say they changed you into a bird, and you flew to them.”

“Some say you went to the city and became a prostitute,” another cousin giggled.

“ You might tell them that I met some teachers who were willing to teach me science,” I said.

“I have been drafted,” my father said.

“No, Father,” I said. “I will take your place.”

My parents killed a chicken and steamed it whole, as if they were welcoming home a son, but I had gotten out of the habit of meat. After eating rice and vegetables, I slept for a long time, preparation for the work ahead.

In the morning, my parents woke me and asked that I came with them to the family hall. "Stay in your night clothes," my mother said. "Don't change yet." She was holding a basin, a towel and and a kettle of hot water. My father had a bottle of wine, an ink block and pens, and knives of various sizes. "Come with us," he said. They had stopped the tears with which they had greeted me. Forebodingly I caught a smell—metallic, the iron smell of blood, as when a woman gives birth, as at the sacrifice of a large animal, as when I menstruated and dreamed red dreams.

My mother put a pillow on the floor before the ancestors. "Kneel here," she said. "Now take off your shirt." I kneeled with my back to my parents so none of us felt embarrassed. My mother washed my back as if I had left for only a day and were her baby yet. "We are going to carve revenge on your back," my father said. "we'll write our oaths and names."

"Wherever you go, whatever happens to you, people will know our sacrifice." my mother said. "And you'll never forget either." She meant that even if I got killed, the people could use my dead body for a weapon, but we do not like to talk out loud about dying.

My father first brushed the words in ink, and they fluttered down my back row after row. Then he began cutting to make fine lines and points he used thin blades, for the stems, large blades.

My mother caught the blood and wiped the cuts with a cold towel soaked in wine. It hurts terribly—the cuts sharp; the air burning; the alcohol cold, then hot—pain so various. I gripped my knees. I released them. Neither tension nor relaxation helped. I wanted to cry. If not for the fifteen years of training, I would have writhed on the floor; I would have had to he held down. The list of grievances went on and on. If an enemy should flay me, the light would shine through my skin like lace.

At the end of the last word, I fell forward. Together my parents sang what they had written, then let me rest. My mother fanned my back. "We'll have you with us until your back heals," she said.

When I could sit up again, my mother brought two mirrors, and I saw my back covered entirely with words in red and black files, like an army, like my army. My parents nursed me just as if I had fallen in battle after many victories. Soon I was strong again.

A white horse stepped into the courtyard where I was polishing my armor. Though the gates were locked tight, through the moon door it came—a kingly white horse, I wore a saddle and bridle with red, gold, and black tasses dancing. The saddle was just my size with tigers and dragons tooled in swirls. The white horse pawed the ground for me to go. On the hooves of its near forefoot and hindfoot was the ideograph "to fly".

My parents and I had waited for such a sign. We took the fine saddlebags off the horse and filled them with salves and herbs blue grass for washing my hair, extra sweaters, dried peaches. They gave me a choice of ivory or silver chopsticks. I took the silver ones because they were lighter. It was like getting wedding presents. The cousins and villagers came bearing bright orange jams, silk dresses, silver embroidery scissors. They brought blue and white porcelain bowls filled with water and carp—the bowls painted with carp, fins like orange fire. I accepted all the gifts—the tables, the earthenware jugs—though I could not possibly carry them with me, and culled for travel only a small copper cooking bow. I could cook in it and eat out of it and would not have to search for bowl-shaped rocks or tortoise shells.

I put on my men's clothes and armor and tied my hair in a man's fashion. "How beautiful you look," the people said. "How beautiful she looks."

A young man stepped out of the crowd. He looked familiar to me, as if he were the old man's son or the old man himself when you looked at him from the corners of your eyes.

"I want to go with you." he said.

"You will be the first soldier in my army," I told him.

I leapt onto my horse's back and marveled at the power and height it gave to me. Just then, galloping out of nowhere straight at me came a rider on a black horse. The villagers scattered except for my one soldier, who stood calmly in the road. I drew my sword. "Wait!" shouted the rider, raising weaponless hands. "Wait. I have travelled here to join you."

Then the villagers relinquished their real gifts to me—their sons. Families who had hidden their boys during the last conscription volunteered them now. I took the ones their families could spare and the ones with hero-fire in their eyes, not the young fathers and not those who would break hearts with their leaving.

We were better equipped than many founders of dynasties had been when they walked north to dethrone an emperor; they had been peasants like us. Millions of us had laid our hoes down on the dry ground and faced north. We sat in the fields, from which the dragon had withdrawn its moisture, and sharpened those hoes. Then, though it be ten thousand miles away, we walked to the palace. We would report to the emperor. The emperor, who sat facing south, must have been very frightened—peasants everywhere walking day and night toward the capital, toward Peiping. But the last emperors of dynasties must not have been facing in the right direction, for they would have seen us and not let us get this hungry. We would not have had to shout our grievances. The peasants would crown as emperor a farmer who knew the earth or a beggar who understood hunger.

"Thank you, Mother. Thank you, Father," I said before leaving. They had carved their names and address on me and I would come back.

Often I walked beside my horse to travel abreast of my army. When we had to impress other armies—marauders, columns of refugees filing past one another, boy gangs following their martial arts teachers—I mounted and rode in front. The soldiers who owned horses and weapons would pose fiercely on my left and right. The small bands joined us, but sometimes armies of equal or larger strength would fight us. Then screaming a mighty scream and swinging two swords over my head, I charged the leaders; I released my bloodthirsty army and my straining war-horse. I guided the horse with my knees, freeing both hands for sword work, spinning green and silver circles all around me.

I inspired my army, and I fed them. At night I sang to them glorious songs that came out of the sky and into my head. When I opened my mouth, the songs poured out and were loud enough for the whole encampment to hear, my army stretched out for a mile. We sewed red flags and tied the red scraps around arms, legs, horses' tails. We wore our red clothes so that when we visited a village, we would look as happy as for New Year's Day. Then people would want to join the ranks. My army did not rape, only taking food where there was an abundance. We brought order wherever we went.

When I won over a goodly number of fighters, I built up my army enough to attack fiefdoms and to pursue the enemies I had seen in the water gourd.

My first opponent turned out to be a giant, so much bigger than the toy general I used to peep at. During the charge, I singled out the leader, who grew as he ran toward me. Our eyes locked until his height made me strain my neck looking up, my throat so vulnerable to the stroke of a knife that my eyes dropped to the secret death points on the huge body. First I cut off his leg with one sword swipe, as Chen Luan-feng had chopped the leg of the thunder god. When the giant stumped toward me, I cut off his head. Instantly he reverted to his true self, a snake and slithered away hissing. The fighting around me stopped as the combatants' eyes and mouths opened wide in amazement. The giant's spells now broken, his soldiers, seeing that they had been led by a snake, pledged their loyalty to me.

In the stillness after battle I looked up at the mountaintops: perhaps the old man and woman were watching me and would enjoy my knowing it. They'd laugh to see a creature winking at them from the bottom of the water gourd. But on a green ledge above the battlefield I saw the giant's wives crying. They had climbed out of their palanquins to watch their husband fight me, and now they were holding each other weeping. They were two sisters, two tiny fairies against the sky, widows from now on. Their long undersleeves, which they had pulled out to wipe their tears, flew white mourning in the mountain wind. After a time, they got back into their sedan chairs, and their servants carried them away.

I led my army northward, rarely having to sidetrack; the emperor himself sent the enemies I was hunting chasing after me. Sometimes they attacked us on two or three sides; sometimes they ambushed me when I rode ahead. We would always win, Kuan Kung, the god of war and literature riding before me. I would be told of in fairy tales myself. I overheard some soldiers—and now there were many who had not met me—say that whenever we had been in danger of losing, I made a throwing gesture and the opposing army would fall, hurled across the battlefield. Hailstones as big as heads would shoot out of the sky and the lightning would stab like swords, but never at those on my side. "On *his* side," they said. I never told them the truth. Chinese executed women who disguised themselves as soldiers or students, no matter how bravely they fought or how high they scored on the examinations.

One spring morning I was at work in my tent repairing equipment, patching my clothes, and studying maps when a voice said, "General, may I visit you in your tent, please?"As if it were my own home, I did not allow strangers in my tent. And since I had no family with me, no one ever visited inside. Riverbanks, hillsides, the cools sloped rooms under the pine trees—China provides her soldiers with meeting places enough. I opened the tent flap. And there in the sunlight stood my own husband with arms full of wildflowers for me. "You are beautiful," he said, and meant it truly. "I have looked for you everywhere. I've been looking for you since the day that bird flew away with you." We were so pleased with each other, the childhood friend found at last, the childhood friend mysteriously grown up. "I followed you, but you skimmed over the rocks until I lost you."

"I've looked for you too," I said, the tent now snug around us like a secret house when we were kids. "Whenever I heard about a good fighter. I went to see if it were you," I said. "I saw you marry me. I'm so glad you married me."

He wept when he took off my shirt and saw the scar words on my back. He loosened my hair and covered the words with it. I turned around and touched his face, loving the familiar first.

So for a time I had a partner—my husband and I, soldiers together just as when we were little soldiers playing in the village. We rode side by side into battle. When I became pregnant, during the last four months, I wore my armor altered so that I looked like a powerful big man. As a fat man, I walked with the foot soldiers so as not to jounce the gestation. Now when I was naked, I was a strange human being indeed—words carved on my back and the baby large in front.

I hid from battle only once, when I gave birth to our baby. In dark and silver dreams I had seen him falling from the sky, each night closer to the earth, his soul a star. Just before labor began, the last star rays sank into my belly. My husband would talk to me and not go, though I said for him to return to the battlefield. He caught the baby, a boy, and put it on my breast "What are we going to do with this?" he asked, holding up the piece of umbilical cord that had been closest to the baby.

"Let's tie it to a flagpole until it dries," I said. We had both seen the boxes in which our parents kept the dried cords of all their children. "This one was yours, and this yours," my mother would say to us brothers and sisters, and fill us with awe that she could remember.

We made a sling for the baby inside my big armor and rode back into the thickest part of the fighting. The umbilical cord flew with the red flag and made us laugh. At night inside our own tent, I let the baby ride on my back. The sling was made of red satin and purple silk, the four paisley straps that tied across my breasts and around my waist ended in housewife's pockets lined with a coin, a seed, a nut, and a juniper leaf. At the back of the sling I had sewn a tiny quilted triangle, red at its center against two shades of green, it marked the baby's nape for luck. I walked bowed, and the baby warmed himself against me, his breathing in rhythm with mine, his heart beating like my heart.

When the baby was a month old, we gave him a name and shaved his head. For the full-month ceremony my husband had found two eggs, which we dyed red by boiling them with a flag. I peeled one and rolled it all over the baby's head, his eyes, his lips, off his bump of a nose, his cheeks, his dear bald head and fontanel. I had brought dried grapefruit peel in my saddlebag, and we also boiled that. We washed our heads and hands in the grapefruit water, dabbing it on the baby's forehead and hands. Then I gave my husband the baby and told him to take it to his family, and I gave him all the money we had taken on raids to take to my family. "Go now," I said, "before he is old enough to recognize me." While the blur is still in his eyes and the little fists shut tight like buds, I'll send my baby away from me. I altered my clothes and became again the slim young man. Only now I would get so lonely with the tent so empty that I slept outside.

My white horse overturned buckets and danced on them; it lifted full wine cups with its teeth. The strong soldiers lifted the horse in a wooden tub, while it danced to the stone drums and flute music. I played with the soldiers, throwing arrows into a bronze jar. But I found none of these antics as amusing as when I first set out on the road.

It was during this lonely time, when any high cry made the milk spill from my breasts, that I got careless. Wildflowers distracted me so that I followed them, picking one, then another, until I was alone in the woods. Out from behind trees, springing off branches came the enemy, their leader looming like a genie out of the water gourd. I threw fists and feet at them, but they were so many, they pinned me to the earth while their leader drew his sword. My fear shot forth— a quick, jabbing sword that slashed fiercely, silver flashes, quick cuts wherever my attention drove it. The leader stared at the palpable sword swishing unclutched at his men, then laughed aloud. As if signaled by his laughter, two more swords appeared in midair. They clanged against mine, and I felt metal vibrate inside my brain. I willed my sword to hit back and to go after the head that controlled the other swords. But the man fought well, hurting my brain. The swords opened and closed, scissoring madly, metal zinging along metal. Unable to leave my sky sword to work itself, I would be watching the swords move like puppets when the genie yanked my hair back and held a dagger against my throat. "Aha!" he said. "What have we here?" He lifted the bead pouch out of my shirt and cut the string. I grabbed his arm, but one of his swords dived toward me, and I rolled out of the way. A horse galloped up, and he leapt on it, escaping into the forest, the beads in his fist. His swords fought behind him until I heard him shout, "I am here!" and they flew to his side. So I had done battle with the prince who had mixed the blood of his two sons with the metal he had used for casting his swords.

I ran back to my soldiers and gathered the fastest horsemen for pursuit. Our horses ran like the little whitewater horses in the surf. Across a plain we could see the enemy, a dust devil rushing toward the horizon. Wanting to see, I focused my eyes as the eagles had taught me, and there the genie would be—shaking one bead out of the pouch and casting it at us. Nothing happened. No thunder, no earthquake that split open the ground, no hailstones big as heads.

"Stop!" I ordered my riders. "Our horses are exhausted, and I don't want to chase any farther south." The rest of the victories would be won on my own, slow and without shortcuts.

I stood on top of the last hill before Peiping and saw the roads below me flow like living rivers. Between roads the woods and plains moved too; the land was peopled—the Han people, the People of One Hundred Surnames, marching with one heart, our tatters flying. The depth and width of joy were exactly known to me: the Chinese population. After much hardship a few of our millions had arrived together at the capital. We faced our emperor personally. We beheaded him, cleaned out the palace, and inaugurated the peasant who would begin the new order. In his rags he sat on the throne facing south, and we, a great red crowd, bowed to him three times. He commended some of us who were his first generals.

I told the people who had come with me that they were free to go home now, but since the Long Wall was so close, I would go see it. They could come along if they liked. So, loath to disband after such high adventures, we reached the northern boundary of the world, chasing

Mongols en route.

I touched the Long Wall with my own fingers, running the edge of my hand between the stones, tracing the grooves the builders' hands had made. We lay our foreheads and our cheeks against the Long Wall and cried like the women who had come here looking for their men so long building the wall. In my travels north, I had not found my brother.

Carrying the news about the new emperor, I went home, where one more battle awaited me. The baron who had drafted my brother would still be bearing sway over our village. Having dropped my soldiers off at crossroads and bridges, I attacked the baron's stronghold alone. I jumped over the double walls and landed with swords drawn and knees bent, ready to spring. When no one accosted me. I sheathed the swords and walked about like a guest until I found the baron. He was counting his money, his fat ringed fingers playing over the abacus.

"Who are you? What do you want?" he said, encircling his profits with his arms. He sat square and fat like a god.

"I want your life in payment for your crimes against the villagers."

"I haven't done anything to you. All this is mine. I earned it. I didn't steal it from you. I've never seen you before in my life. Who are you?"

"I am a female avenger."

Then—heaven help him—he tried to be charming, to appeal to me man to man. "Oh, come now. Everyone takes the girls when he can. The families are glad to bend of them. 'Girls are maggots in the rice.' 'It is more profitable to raise geese than daughters.'" He quoted to me the savings I hated.

"Regret what you've done before I kill you," I said.

"I haven't done anything other men—even you—wouldn't have done in my place."

"You took away my brother."

"I free my apprentices."

"He was not an apprentice."

"China needs soldiers in wartime."

"You took away my childhood."

"I don't know what you're talking about. We've never met before. I've done nothing to you."

"You've done this," I said, and ripped off my shirt to show him my back. "You are responsible for this." When I saw his startled eyes at my breasts, I slashed him across the face and on the second stroke cut off his head.

I pulled my shirt back on and opened the house to the villagers. The baron's family and servants hid in closets and under beds. The villagers dragged them out into the courtyard, where they tried them next to the beheading machine. "Did you take my harvest so that my children had to eat grass?" a weeping farmer asked.

"I saw him steal seed grain," another testified.

"My family was hiding under the thatch on the roof when the bandits robbed our house, and we saw this one take off his mask." They spared those who proved they could be reformed. They beheaded the others. Their necks were collared in the beheading machine which slowly clamped shut. There was one last-minute reprieve of a bodyguard when a witness shouted testimony just as the vise was pinching blood. The guard had but recently joined the household in exchange for a child hostage. A slow killing gives a criminal time to regret his crimes and think of the right words to prove he can change.

I searched the house, hunting out people for trial. I came upon a locked room.When I broke down the door, I found women, cowering, whimpering women. I heard shrill insect noises and scurrying. They blinked weakly at me like pheasants that have been raised in the dark for soft meat. The servants who walked the ladies had abandoned them, and they could not escape on their little bound feet. Some crawled away from me, using their elbows to pull themselves along. These women would not be good for anything. I called the villagers to come identify any daughters they wanted to take home, but no one claimed any. I gave each woman a bagful of rice, which they sat on. They rolled the bags to the road. They wandered away like ghosts. Later, it would be said they turned into the band of swordswomen who were a mercenary army. They did not wear men's clothes like me, but rode as women in black and red dresses. They bought up girl babies so that many poor families welcomed their visitations. When slave girls and daughters-in-law ran away, people would say they joined these witch amazons. They killed men and boys. I myself never encountered such women and could not vouch for their reality.

After the trials we tore down the ancestral tablets. "We'll use this great hall for village meetings," I announced. "Here we'll put on operas, we'll sing together and talk-story." We washed the courtyard; we exorcised the house with smoke and red paper. "This is a new year," I told the people, "the year one."

I went home to my parents-in-law and husband and son. My son stared, very impressed by the general he had seen in the parade, but his father said, "It's your mother. Go to your mother." My son was delighted that the shiny general was his mother too. She gave him her helmet to wear and her swords to hold.

Wearing my black embroidered wedding coat, I knelt at my parents-in-law's feet, as I would have done as a bride. "Now my public duties are finished," I said. "I will stay with you, doing farmwork and housework, and giving you more sons."

"Go visit your mother and father first," my mother-in-law said, a generous woman. "They want to welcome you."

My mother and father and the entire clan would be living happily on the money I had sent them. My parents had bought their coffins. They would sacrifice a pig to the gods that I had returned. From the words on my back, and how they were fulfilled, the villagers would make legend about my perfect filiality.

12

(Jessica Hagedorn, 1949—)
杰西卡·哈格多恩

作者简介

杰西卡·哈格多恩（Jessica Hagedorn, 1949— ），美国菲律宾裔剧作家、作家、诗人和多媒体表演艺术家，出生于菲律宾首都马尼拉。在 1963 年，哈格多恩一家举家搬迁到旧金山，之后她在美国戏剧学院（American Conservatory Theater）就读，开启了她的艺术和创作生涯。她善于运用混杂的风格来创作她的诗歌、作品形象和口语对话。

她创作了很多音乐剧、话剧、诗歌、散文、小说等不同题材和风格的文学作品。舞台作品有《芒果探戈》（*Mango Tango*, 1977）、《公寓里的爱人》（*Tenement Lover*, 1985）等；诗歌与散文集《险与美》（*Danger and Beauty*, 1993）；长篇小说有《食狗肉的人》（*Dogeaters*, 1990）、《爱的强盗》（*The Gangster Of Love*, 1996）与《毒理学》（*Toxicology*, 2011）等。她的作品荣获了包括戈尔博特与休利特基金会剧作奖（Gerbode, Hewlett Foundations' Playwriting Award）在内的诸多奖项和荣誉。

长篇小说《食狗肉的人》是哈格多恩最为著名的作品之一。这部小说在 1990 年荣获了美国图书奖（American Book Award），1991 年提名美国国家图书奖（American National Book Award）。小说是以 20 世纪 50 年代菲律宾为背景，讲述了当时菲律宾各个社会阶层人们的生活以及他们的精神状态，展现了在美国文化影响下当时菲律宾社会、政治和文化等方面的问题以及当时菲律宾人的迷茫和空虚。

章节《情书》（"Love Letters"）与《天堂》（"Paradise"）选自长篇小说《食狗肉的人》。《情书》主要围绕一部广播连续剧"情书"展开，通过描述菲律宾人对这部剧的痴迷，折射出美国对菲律宾的殖民影响。《天堂》讲述了菲律宾社会高层不顾底层人民的安危，贪图享乐和虚荣，迷失了自己，迷失了身份的故事。

作品选读

Love Letters

By Jessica Hagedorn

Love Letters has been on the air for years, the most popular radio serial in Manila. Even the President boasts of being an avid fan. Many of the episodes have been adapted into successful movies by Mabuhay Studios. Top movie stars still perform as guests on the show, including the biggest and most beloved—Nestor Noralez and Barbara Villanueva. Nestor and Barbara are engaged to marry in real life but keep postponing the wedding. Nestor sadly admits in numerous interviews that for him, "Hard work and Lady Success come first." Barbara is just as understanding and loyal to Nestor as the characters she portrays.

My grandmother's crazy for *Love Letters* because the plots are so sad and complicated. Every week, there's a new story, which always involves a love letter. An episode comes on every night of the week, each story beginning on a Sunday and ending on a Saturday. Everyone weeps at the inevitable, tragic conclusion on the seventh night.

According to my father, *Love Letters* appeals to the lowest common denominator. My Uncle Agustin's version of the lowest common denominator is the "bakya crowd." It's the same reason the Gonzagas refuse to listen to Tagalog songs, or go to Tagalog movies. I don't care about any of that. As far as *Love Letters* goes, I'm hooked—and though I'd definitely die if cousin Pucha ever found out, I cry unabashedly in the company of *Lola* Narcisa and all the servants.

Without fail, someone dies on *Love Letters*. There always a lesson to be learned, and it's always a painful one. Just like our Tagalog movies, the serial is heavy with pure love, blood debts, luscious revenge, the wisdom of mothers, and the enduring sorrow of Our Blessed Virgin Barbara Villanueva. It's a delicious tradition, the way we weep without shame. If Pucha could see me, I'd never hear the end of it. She has no use for Barbara Villanueva, Patsy Pimentel, or Nestor Noralez, whom she calls "The King of Corny." She has no use for anyone who isn't Kim Novak, or Rock Hudson.

LOVE LETTERS #99

Dalisay (Barbara Villanueva) is a beautiful young servant who's been deflowered by the handsome Mario (Cesar Carmelo), the son of wealthy landowner Don Pedro de Leon (Nestor Noralez) and his wife, the haughty mestiza Doña Hilda (Patsy Pimentel).

Dalisay writes Mario a love letter as soon as she discovers she is pregnant. Mario is away at a military school in Baguio. To make matters worse, Dalisay must function in her role as servant in Don Pedro's hacienda as if nothing has happened, especially under the suspicious scrutiny of the arrogant and possessive Doña Hilda, who calls her only son "a gift from God." Dalisay, of course, has no one to turn to or confide in.

The letter is intercepted by the snoopy headmaster Pating (Nestor Noralez) at Mario's military school. Pating doesn't tell Mario about the letter, but instead sends it back to Mario's horrified parents. Don Pedro and Doña Hilda have their hearts set on their son marrying Elvira (Patsy Pimentel), the daughter of the town mayor. Elvira is actually in love with a soldier of humble origins, but she is willing to marry Mario to please her parents.

The beautiful young servant is cruelly thrown out of the house on a stormy night, and there is no place she can run to but her widower father's hut on the outskirts of town. Dalisay's father, Mang Berto (Nestor Noralez), is a poor tenant farmer who works Don Pedro's land. Mang Berto vows to take care of his innocent daughter, and accepts responsibility for the care of her unborn child. Everyone in the small town is scandalized, and treats the miserable Dalisay with scorn.

Mario wants to come home for Christmas and profess his love for the poor servant girl at the risk of being disowned by his powerful father. He still has no idea about Dalisay's condition. Doña Hilda is worried about the possible outcome of her beloved son's impending visit, and decides the only practical solution is to get rid of Dalisay by staging an accident. The unsuspecting young girl awaits the birth of her child, meekly resigned to the fact that Mario refuses to see her.

Meanwhile...

Barbara Villanueva's melodious voice sings an ominous invocation against witches: "*Asin, suca / get-teng, luya / bawang, lasona*"... "Salt, vinegar / scissors, ginger / garlic, onion"... An invocation against death, to protect her unborn child.

It is raining outside, a torrential rain, a sign that the typhoon season is about to begin. I can smell the rain, a thickness in the air. The furious downpour clatters against the tiles on our roof, beating a mist up from the ground. I pray the streets will flood and there will be no school tomorrow. It is a godsend, this sudden storm, this lightning and thunder and static on the radio. My *yaya* Lorenza is terrified and cowers in the kitchen every time the thunder crackles and explodes. She is tearfully cleaning grains of rice, picking out the tiny pebbles and white worms before the rice can be cooked by Pacita. "*Dios ko, dios ko, dios ko*" she mutters, biting her lip and making signs of the cross. She will be the last to join us in my grandmother's room, where we are all concentrating hard on the story inside the radio. My parents and brother seem distant and harmless, although they are only a few rooms away. My mother has forgotten all about me and assumes Lorenza has put me to bed. I am curled up under the crocheted bed spread on my *lola's* bed. *Lola* Narcisa rocks in her chair. Aida, Pacita, Fely, and the chauffeur Macario sit or stand in various corners of the room, straining to listen.

I try to blot from my mind the image of my grandfather Whitman sick in the hospital, the shabby American Hospital with its drab green walls, drab green smells, and the hovering presence of the hospital's supervising staff of melancholy American doctors. Like my grandfather, they are leftovers from recent wars, voluntary exiles whose fair skin is tinged a blotchy red from the tropical sun or too much alcohol; like his, their clothes and skin reek of rum and Lucky Strikes. It is not an unpleasant scent, something soothing I associate with old American men and my grandfather Whitman, whom I love.

My *Lola* Narcisa claims that her husband is the first white man stricken with *bangungot*. She seems almost proud of his nightmare sickness, a delirious fever in which he sweats, sleeps, and screams. Most *bangungot* victims die overnight in their sleep. It is a mysterious illness which usually claims men. My grandfather's case is even stranger than most—he's been sick like this for weeks. At first, the American doctors diagnosed malaria. After a week, they patroled the corridor outside my grandfather's private room, consulting each other worriedly and coming up with more far-fetched theories. *Bangungot* is ruled out of the picture by the chief of staff, Dr. Leary, who dismisses the tropical malady as native superstition, a figment of the overwrought Filipino imagination.

I have been to the hospital only once, with my *lola* and the cook Pacita. My parents have forbidden me to go back; when I ask why, my father replies, "You are much too young to be around sick people. It's best to remember your grandfather as a healthy man." What they don't seem to understand is that unlike Raul, I'm not afraid.

When *Love Letters* is over, the servants file out of the room, murmuring good-night and thanks to my grandmother. Lorenza even comes back with another bowl of snacks for *Lola* Narcisa:

minced red salted duck eggs dabbed with vinegar, more rice with crunchy *dilis*. Happy and lost in her radio reverie, my grandmother nods and smiles at no one in particular. Lorenza turns to give me one last warning before leaving the room. "Rio, if you don't go to bed in your own room, your mother will chop my head off." I grin at her and put my finger to my lips. "I won't tell, Lorenza. Promise."

My grandmother dabs her eyes with one of my grandfather's oversized handkerchiefs. The *Love Letters* theme song is playing, a saccharine instrumental melody replete with organ and violins. The somber voice of the male announcer in tones, "Tune in for the next episode of *Love Letters* at the same time tomorrow night. And so, until then... "

Hunching her bony shoulders, *Lola* Narcisa leans in closer to the radio, as if by doing so she can prolong her precious drama one more second. An eerie, high-pitched sound is followed by the voice of the same radio announcer, this time more cheery and impersonal. "This is DZRK, Radiomanila, signing off for the evening. At the sound of the tone, it's exactly twelve midnight, in the Blessed Year of the Family Rosary. Remember: The family that prays together, stays together."

Forgotten not just by my mother but by everyone, I sit drowsily on the lumpy bed watching my grandmother eat and cry. Tomorrow they'll find me asleep, next to her. I know I should go down the hallway to my own room, but the house is too big and dark, all the lights turned off by the reliable Fely and Lorenza. As I watch my rapt grandmother, I too begin to cry.

It's another movie. *A Place in the Sun*—condemned by the Archdiocese of Manila as vile and obscene. I don't understand the commotion, why Pucha and I have to sneak off and pretend we're going to see Debbie Reynolds in *Bundle of Joy*. Fortunately for us, Pucha's older brother Mikey is our chaperone for the day. He wants to see Elizabeth Taylor naked.

We are all bewildered by the movie, which is probably too American for us. Mikey falls asleep halfway through it, after Shelley Winters drowns. I decide that even if I don't understand it, I *like* this movie. In my eyes, it is unjust that Montgomery Clift is executed for Shelley Winters' murder. While Mikey snores away, Pucha and I sit tensely in the dark, waiting for the obscene images that never appear. Pucha is enthralled, although I don't think she gets it either. She has found a new idol in Montgomery Clift. All she can say afterward at the Cafe España is, "Shelley Winters is so ordinary. She deserves to die. *Que pobrecito*, Montgomery!" All Mikey can say is, "You owe me one, girls... "

The bark of Montgomery Clift's shoulder in giant close-up on the movie screen. Elizabeth Taylor's breath-taking face is turned up toward him, imploring a forbidden kiss. They are drunk with their own beauty and love, that much I understand. Only half of Elizabeth Taylor's face is visible—one violet eye, one arched black eyebrow framed by her snort, glossy black hair. She is glowing, on fire in soft focus.

Jane Wyman bends over a comatose Rock Hudson. She tells him she loves him, she will be with him forever in the rustic cottage by the frozen lake. He finally opens his eyes. A deer wanders up to the picture window. Sentimental music interrupts the pastoral silence, swelling to a poignant crescendo as the closing credits roll along. As no doctor ever could, the power of Jane Wyman's love has cured Rock Hudson and pulled him from death, like Sleeping Beauty.

I try to imagine *Lola* Narcisa bending over my grandfather's bed like Jane, an angel of mercy whispering so softly in his ear that none of us can make out what she is saying. My grandfather the white man tosses his head from side to side, still locked in his eternal nightmare after all these years. He barks like a dog, grunts and sputters like an old car. My grandmother wipes the drool from the corners of his mouth while my Rita Hayworth mother, Dolores Logan Gonzaga, stands as far away from her father's bed as possible. She seems terrified and bewildered by this image of her dying father.

He groans *Chicago*, *Chicago*, *Chicago*, with such longing I shut my eyes and the movie projector goes off in my head. Concrete, glass, and in the background, cardboard cut-out skyscrapers. June Allyson descends from a winding staircase, wearing a ballgown made of gold-flecked, plastic shower curtains. My grandfather mutters repeatedly in his frenzied sleep: *Chicago*, *Chica-go*...

He shrieks, as if someone or something has finally caught up with him. The anguish in his voice, in the way his body twists and jerks epileptically on the hospital bed, is unbearable. The anxious American doctors have been waiting for a sign. They rush into the room, trailed by eager nurses ready with gleaming, stainless steel bedpans, ominous catheters, and intravenous attachments bursting with glucose and pints of fresh black blood. My mother Dolores covers her eyes. She is shaking and sobbing with grief. "DON'T TOUCH HIM!" my *Lola* Narcisa screams in English at Doctor Leary. Everyone stops dead in their tracks, stunned that the shriveled brown woman has so loudly and finally spoken.

I am confused by the thought of Elizabeth Taylor's one violet eye luminous in black and white, the pristine illusion of elegant deer peacefully grazing outside Rock Hudson's picture window. In this hospital room, there is only our sense of foreboding, heightened by the grayness of bedsheets and medical uniforms, the dim fluorescent lights, the lizards watching from the corners of the ceiling. My grandfather is dying. My mother has been tranquilized and waits for my father, who has telephoned the nurse's station to let her know he is on his way. Our family priest, Father Manuel, has been summoned. No one seems to remember or care that my grandfather Whitman is an avowed atheist, that his hatred for the Catholic clergy runs deep. "Don't wake him," *Lola* Narcisa keeps pleading in English. "If you wake him, he dies. Uh-hmmm." She nods her head. "Better to leave him dreaming."

Typhoon rages outside. She waits in the chair next to the bed, eyes glazed and gone. Buzzing static emanates from the radio. She rocks, ever so slightly. It is a rhythm only she can feel and hear. The air is crackling, electric. I feel a chill, and cover myself with one of my grandmother's shawls. Above my *lola's* head, a speckled lizard disappears behind the safety of the velvet painting. On a tin plate resting on the windowsill, the *katol* incense has burned down into an ashy, smoldering heap, the smoke still dense and fragrant. The ancient Philco radio is alive, hissing and humming to my *Lola* Narcisa, its dreadful music somehow soothing her.

Paradise (excerpt)

By Jessica Tarahata Hagedorn

The Manila International Film Festival is the First Lady's latest whim. She orders the city and slums rejuvenated with fresh coats of paint, windows and doorways lined with pots of plastic flowers, the streets swept and reswept by women in red and yellow sweatshirts with "MetroManila Aide" printed in big black letters on the back and front. Even uncle's shack gets the treatment. Funny thing is, it all looks fake. Painted scenery in a slum no one's going to bother visiting—but what the hell, we all get a big bang out of it. Uncle laughs the hardest, shaking his head in disbelief. Fucking crazy bitch, he calls the First Lady. *Talagang sirang ulo*.

A bunch of new buildings have been built right next to the Magsaysay Pavilion on Roxas Boulevard. She's calling the whole thing a *cultural center*, whatever that means. Movies, ballerinas, and opera *daw*. The workers are busy day and night, trying to finish the complex for the film festivals opening night, which is scheduled in a few weeks. Toward the end, one of the structures collapses and lots of workers are buried in the rubble. Big news. Cora Camacho even goes out there with a camera crew, "Manila's Worst Disaster!" A special mass is held right there in Rizal Park, with everyone weeping and wailing over the rubble. The Archbishop gives his blessing, the First Lady blows her nose. She orders the survivors to continue building; more cement is poured over dead bodies; they finish exactly three hours before the first foreign film is scheduled to be shown. Hoy—I'm impressed. Someday, maybe I'll stroll over there and see it for myself.

Along with other honored guests of the government, the German director is flown in, first class, on Philippine Air Lines. He is housed in some big shot's three-story mansion in Forbes Park, right nextdoor to the Alacran estate. Arriving in Manila early in the morning, the German cruises CocoRico later that same night, looking for action. The hair dresser Chiquiting takes him around, introducing him to Andres. Chiquiting is in his glory. He swoops through the door of CocoRico, making sure everyone sees him dragging the German by his elbow. "Darlings! Look who I've brought for you this evening!" he announces. You'd think he was the German's fiancé or pimp.

The German spots me right away, spinning my records. He is intrigued, watching me dance with myself in front of mirrored walls. I'm the best dancer I know; I don't like dancing with other people. What's the point, anyway? Even with partners, we dance alone. That's why I hate playing slow songs; sentimental love songs make me sick, I hate watching the desperate way people grab on to each other in the dark. If Andres insists, or someone gives me a tip, I'll play one or two ballads a night. That's all I can stand. I know I have to do it—Andres gets so pissed off when I don't. He won't admit it, but he loathes real rock'n'roll. He only tolerates it because of all the money he's making. If he could have it his way, you'd be dancing to "The Way We Were" or "I Will Survive" all night long.

I'm on display. The German is watching me from the bar, pretending to listen to Chiquiting blither in his ear. I'm high, lost in the music and moving cool and sexy. During my break, Chiquiting comes up to me. Trying hard to conceal his resentment, he says some important foreigner wants to meet me, buy me a drink. "Joey," Andres informs me, as soon as he gets a chance, "you'd better take advantage of the situation—that guy's famous!" We call Andres the Minister of Information around here, for good reason. He's sure if I play my cards right, the German director will cast me in his next movie. All my problems will be over, ha-ha. Andres is visibly excited, fussing over the famous director. Every time Andres pours him a drink, he wipes up the counter with one of his rags.

I slide onto a stool next to Prince Charming. Andres gives me one of his looks. "Your usual?" he asks me casually, pulling out the Remy Martin. I nod. Andres pours me a double, trying to maintain his composure. I'm following his script tonight. Andres has urged me to order cognac around foreigners, so he'll make more money and they'll be impressed by my expensive taste. "Instead of that cheap rum you're always drinking," he nags. What the fuck, tonight's the night. I'll try anything once. I turn to face the German, real cool, taking my time. He shakes my hand, introduces himself as *Rainer*. "Like Grace Kelly's husband," Andres gushes, "how unusual..." He gazes at the German with reverence. Not exactly, the German says, with an embarrassed smile. "Rain or shine, *di ba*?" I tease him, flash him one of my killer grins.

He's around forty, who knows. Pale and flabby, baggy clothes, a drooping moustache and the smell of cigarettes, straggly reddish blond hair. I'm not sure I can bear to see him naked. It's one thing if he was just an old man. I'd expect to see his flesh hang loose like an elephant; I'd be prepared. That's when I imagine I'm in my movie. I'm the strong young animal—I'm the panther. Or else I'm the statue of a magnificent young god in a beautiful garden. The old man with elephant skin drools. Maybe he's God the Father, lost in paradise. He can't get over how perfect I am; he can't get over the perfection of his own creation. He falls in love with me. They always do. I'll admit, I can get off with some old man that way. I need my own movies, with their flexible endings. Otherwise, it's just shit. Most sex is charity, on my part. I'd rather dance alone.

13

(Karen Tei Yamashita, 1951—)
山下凯伦

作者简介

山下凯伦（Karen Tei Yamashita, 1951— ）是当代美国日裔作家中的代表作家。她生于加州奥克兰市，是第三代日裔移民后代，目前在加州大学圣克鲁兹分校（University of California, Santa Cruz）执教，主讲创意写作和美国亚裔文学课程。

山下凯伦主要创作小说与戏剧，以小说为主。山下凯伦迄今已出版五部反映文化交融背景下日裔移民在美洲生活的小说，即《穿越雨林之弧》（*Through the Arc of Rain Forest*, 1990）、《巴西－马鲁》（*Brazil-Maru*, 1992）、《橘子回归线》（*Tropic of Orange*, 1997）、《K圈循环》（*Circle K Cycles*, 2001）与《国际旅社》（*I Hotel*, 2010）。其中，处女作《穿越雨林之弧》获得美国图书奖等奖项，《国际旅社》获得美国图书奖并进入 2010 年美国国家图书奖的决选名单。她的多部戏剧收录在戏剧集《公共动漫：表演的虚构》（*Anime Wong: Fictions of Performance*, 2014）。山下凯伦的作品具有跨国视野，她笔下的人物从来不局限于某个族裔群体。山下凯伦在亚裔作家中的独特之处在于她超越了历史维度上的东－西方文化差异的关注，将目光投向 20 世纪以来更趋向多元化、全球化、更复杂更有趣的“南－北”美洲地理维度上的日裔移民的生活全景差异，以及巴西日裔返归日本经历中产生的新的文化失落。山下凯伦的作品体现强烈的后现代主义色彩，例如语言的杂糅、超现实主义的叙事声音、多媒体的文本展示方式等。山下凯伦在作品中娴熟地使用日语、葡萄牙语和英语，以语言的混杂来表现移民杂糅的文化身份。

山下凯伦的处女作《穿越雨林之弧》讲述了巴西热带雨林地区在经济开发中覆灭的故事，浓郁的拉美魔幻现实主义风格和冷峻的政治讽刺奇妙的结合在一起。《巴西—马鲁》讲述日本移民在巴西建立殖民社会的故事，展现了理想主义乌托邦的建立和瓦解。《橘子回归线》以洛杉矶为背景，被认为是一部魔幻现实主义作品。《橘子回归线》以美国洛杉矶和墨西哥为背景，由七个人物讲述一周发生的事情，《拼车——城区立体交叉道》（“Rideshare—Downtown Interchange”）选自第八章，讲述美籍日裔第三代曼扎那（Manzanar）在洛杉矶一条高速公路上指挥交通的场景。山下凯伦十年磨一剑写成的小说《国际旅社》展现了 1968—1977 年旧金山地区波澜壮阔的亚裔权利运动。该书夹杂了戏剧、漫画、新闻、宣传材料，使这部作品呈现复杂的立体感，将历史和想象巧妙地融入文本中。选读部分描绘了亚裔在国际旅社（I Hotel）附近游行示威的场面。

作品选读

Tropic of Orange

Rideshare—Downtown Interchange

By Karen Tei Yamashita

Manzanar lifted and dipped his baton, feeling his way carefully through the early morning traffic. It was a red convertible Porsche. The two young men wended their way north toward Hollywood, peeling oranges, bouncing flippant ideas for a storyboard back and forth. It was overcast but so what; the forecast was always sun. Not that Manzanar knew; he was just a conductor. The terrible pain of this moment flashed: the screech of tires, the groaning wail of the monstrous semi pulling 40,000 pounds of liquid propane under pressure in its shiny stainless steel interior—its great twisting second-half tumbling and thundering over itself, and the horror in the face of the driver who knew the consequences of this payload. All this played against the metallic crash and crunch of the unfortunate who shared the same lanes, the snap of delicate necks, the squish of flesh and blood. In both directions of the freeway, spread across ten lanes, hundreds of cars piled one onto the other in an almost endless jam of shrieking notes. Perhaps, perhaps someone had caught it all on video. There was always someone out there catching unsightly things on video. Perhaps not. In any case, Manzanar had fearlessly recorded everything—every horrible, terrifying thing in music. The sad refrain, not meant to be insipid, was the gentle notes of ridesharing. He had seen the friendship of the two young, and indeed beautiful men, their brief encounter with happiness, and the possibility of success.

Ridesharing, when it was practiced in greater proportions, alleviated flow, increased rhythm while enhancing and deepening tone. Manzanar, for one, was grateful. The complexity of human adventure over lines of transit fascinated him. The mass of people flowing to work and play, the activity of minds muddling over current affairs, love affairs, the absence of affairs, in automatic, toward destinations beyond streets, parking lots, or driveways: Manzanar followed it all conscientiously.

Long ago, Manzanar had been a skilled surgeon. His work had entailed careful incisions through layers of living tissue, excising tumors, inserting implants, facilitating transplants. At what point the baton replaced the knife, he could no longer remember. Perhaps the skill had never left his fingers, but the will had. He could as easily have translated his talents to that of a sculptor in clay, wood, or even marble any sort of inanimate substance, but strangely, it was the abstraction of music that engulfed his being. One day, he left a resident to sew up a patient, removed his mask, gloves, and gown, strode through the maze of corridors, down the elevator, through patient waiting, to become a statistic under *missing persons*.

Manzanar imagined himself a kind of recycler. After all he, like other homeless in the city, was a recycler of the last rung. The homeless were the insects and scavengers of society, feeding on leftovers, living in residue, collecting refuse, carting it this way and that for pennies. In the same manner, who would use the residue of sounds in the city if Manzanar did not? This was perhaps a simplistic interpretation of his work, as simplistic as, for example, the description of his utilizing the sounds of cars whooshing down freeways to imitate the sound of the ocean. Poetic, but false. Everything had its own sound. Genius disguised, as always, with innocent simplicity.

There are maps and there are maps and there are maps. The uncanny thing was that he could see all of them at once, filter some, pick them out like transparent windows and place them even delicately and consecutively in a complex grid of pattern, spatial discernment, body politic. Although one might have thought this capacity to see was different from a musical one, it was really one and the same. For each of the maps was a layer of music, a clef, an instrument, a musical instruction, a change of measure, a coda.

But what were these mapping layers? For Manzanar they began within the very geology of the land, the artesian rivers running beneath the surface, connected and divergent, shifting and swelling. There was the complex and normally silent web of faults—cracking like mud flats baking under a desert sun, like the crevices in aging hands and faces. Yet, below the surface, there was the man-made grid of civil utilities: Southern California pipelines of natural gas; the unnatural waterways of the Los Angeles Department of Water and Power, and the great dank tunnels of sewage; the cascades of poisonous effluents surging from rain-washed streets into the Santa Monica Bay; electric currents racing voltage into the open watts of millions of hungry energy-efficient appliances; telephone cables, cable TV, fiber optics, computer networks.

On the surface, the complexity of layers should drown an ordinary person, but ordinary persons never bother to notice, never bother to notice the prehistoric grid of plant and fauna and human behavior, nor the historic grid of land usage and property, the great overlays of transport sidewalks, bicycle paths, roads, freeways, systems of transit both ground and air, a thousand natural and man-made divisions, variations both dynamic and stagnant, patterns and connections by every conceivable definition from the distribution of wealth to race, from patterns of climate to the curious blueprint of the skies.

As far as Manzanar was concerned, it was all there. A great theory of maps, musical maps, spread in visible and audible layers—each selected sometimes purposefully, sometimes at whim, to create the great mind of music. To the outside observer, it was a lonely business; it would seem that he was at once orchestra and audience. Or was he indeed? Unknown to anyone, a man walking across the overpass at that very hour innocently hummed the recurrent melody of the adagio.

I Hotel
(excerpt)

By Karen Tei Yamashita

By the time we got the red alert to place our bodies in a human barricade around an old hotel that held seventy years of our city's hotel history, we were already the displaced people in the city's plan to impose a particular meaning of *home* and a particular meaning of *nation.* Since our hotel life was considered suspect morally and socially, our hotels should naturally be replaced by proper single-family houses built in locations distant from the city, and our hotels and all our businesses that serviced us should be replaced with what the city was properly useful for: trading posts, jails, courthouses, and saloons. And no one should be allowed to live over a saloon unless he was just passing through. A commercial room was simply not a dwelling. These edicts were substantiated by zoning and blight laws allowing the city to use eminent domain to liberate our homes for the public good, even if the public good meant giving up our property for the wealthy few. Almost as quickly as an earthquake, our neighborhoods located in the Fillmore and South of Market were already razed and being replaced by forty-eight-story multinational corporate trading posts. Even if we were expected to build, maintain, clean, and service these posts, we weren't expected to live anywhere nearby. Be at work promptly at eight a.m., but please, please disappear by five p.m. But this was an impossible request because we could not leave, and we had nowhere to go. So that night in August, far past our five p.m. curfew and into the next morning, we gathered around the I-Hotel to face four hundred officers of the police, sheriffs, and fire departments all dressed up in riot gear, to demonstrate that we had not disappeared and that we were finally fed up. What was the total cost to us as taxpayers, not just in overtime and equipment, but everything—everything it took over how many months in anticipation to deploy the full force of the city's and county's final retribution? No doubt more than a million dollars, the insipid worth of the structure we defended.

Had we not ourselves elected these men of good intentions: the mayor who ran out of promises, the judge who ruled for eviction despite a hung jury, and the sheriff who carried out a law he thought to be unjust? Did these elected officials also think that our city was only useful for trading posts, a courthouse, and a jail?

Armed with only our bodies, we faced our officers of the law—heavily protected by face helmets, gloves, sticks, given height by their tall animals, speed by their motorcycles, reach by their aerial ladders, and ultimately power by their deadly weapons. We saw the barricades part for the Sheriff himself, driving up to the I-Hotel. He emerged from his vehicle as if it were his powerful steed and stood in the blinding spotlights of that evening, young and handsome, dressed informally in a gold turtleneck sweater and casual jacket, bidding his dinner partner a sweet good-night. Perhaps it was a brash double-oh-seven gesture lost to our angry chanting. We knew he had been convicted for contempt of court, spending five days in his own jail for refusing in January to carry out the court order of eviction of the tenants of the I-Hotel. Was he not one of our own people, our own gallant knight, and would he not once again take a stand in our favor? Had he not himself complained that the laws of our society were written to protect those with property and money? Would he later justify his part in the eviction based on having, as an officer of the law, to carry out the law, just or unjust as it may be?

As two thousand of us were eventually bullied away from the hotel entrance, we saw our sheriff enter at the head of his deputies, leading them into the hotel and the final phase of the eviction, breaking into the doors of each of the hotel tenants and ordering them to leave their homes. And yes, we knew that each room was a tiny home, a place of final refuge for a lifetime of work, and that the room, though housed in a hotel, was still a home.

So when we saw our sheriff place his sledgehammer to the first door, banging and splintering the old dark wood into jagged pieces, we were ourselves diminished by every stroke of his hammer. We heard the wretched sobbing cry of horror, an anguished plea but also a warning, *No! Don't do it! Don't do it!* But our sheriff had made his decision, perhaps, he justified, to take responsibility by being an actor in this painful event, to mitigate what he imagined could have been a more violent end. But we would never forget his violent presence on that night and the sad betrayal of his actions.

Shame! Shame! Shame! we cried.

Where will you live when you get old?

Where will we live when we get old?

14

(Amy Tan, 1952—)
谭恩美

作者简介

谭恩美（Amy Tan, 1952— ），生于美国加利福尼亚州奥克兰，曾就读于林菲尔德学院（Linfield College）、圣何塞城市学院（San Jose City College）、圣何塞州立大学（San Jose State University）等多所大学，取得语言学硕士学位，现主要居住于加利福尼亚州和纽约，专门从事文学创作。

谭恩美的主要作品有《喜福会》（*The Joy Luck Club*, 1989）、《灶神之妻》（*The Kitchen God's Wife*, 1991）、《通灵女孩》（*The Hundred Secret Senses*, 1995）、《接骨师之女》（*The Bonesetter's Daughter*, 2001）、《我的缪斯》（*The Opposite of Fate: A Book of Musings*, 2003）、《拯救沉没之鱼》（*Saving Fish from Drowning*, 2005）、《惊奇山谷》（*The Valley of Amazement*, 2013）、《往昔之始：作家回忆录》（*Where the Past Begins: A Writer's Memoir*, 2017）等。她的作品不仅长期占据《纽约时报》等多个媒体畅销书排行榜，而且荣获"英联邦金奖（Commonwealth Gold Award）"等大奖。

《喜福会》是谭恩美的处女作，也是她最著名的作品之一。这部小说在1989年《纽约时报》畅销书排行榜连续9个月上榜，共销出275 000多本精装本，使谭恩美在美国文坛及读者之中名声大噪。小说以"喜福会"麻将聚会为主线展开四位华裔母亲与她们美国出生的女儿之间的关系，表达母女关系、身份诉求、中西文化冲突、移民困境等主题。

在《喜福会——吴晶梅》（"The Joy Luck Club——Jing Mei Woo"）这一章节中作者围绕我替代母亲加入"喜福会"为中心，突出中国母亲与美国出生的女儿之间的隔阂与矛盾。

本段巧妙地将“母女”关系搬到麻将桌上，让本为严肃的话题顿时变得诙谐幽默，同时不乏深刻内涵。

作品选读

The Joy Luck Club

The Joy Luck Club——Jing Mei Woo
(excerpt)

By Amy Tan

Joy Luck was an idea my mother remembered from the days of her first marriage in Kweilin, before the Japanese came. That's why I think of Joy Luck as her Kweilin story. It was the story she would always tell me when she was bored, when there was nothing to do, when every bowl had been washed and the Formica table had been wiped down twice, when my father sat reading the newspaper and smoking one Pall Mall cigarette after another, a warning not to disturb him. This is when my mother would take out a box of old ski sweaters sent to us by unseen relatives from Vancouver. She would snip the bottom of a sweater and pull out a kinky thread of yarn, anchoring it to a piece of cardboard. And as she began to roll with one sweeping rhythm, she would start her story. Over the years, she told me the same story, except for the ending, which grew darker, casting long shadows into her life, and eventually into mine.

"I dreamed about Kweilin before I ever saw it," my mother began, speaking Chinese. "I dreamed of jagged peaks lining a curving river, with magic moss greening the banks. At the tops of these peaks were white mists. And if you could float down this river and eat the moss for food, you would be strong enough to climb the peak. If you slipped, you would only fall into a bed of soft moss and laugh. And once you reached the top, you would be able to see everything and feel such happiness it would be enough to never have worries in your life ever again.

"In China, everybody dreamed about Kweilin. And when I arrived, I realized how shabby my dreams were, how poor my thoughts. When I saw the hills, I laughed and shuddered at the same time. The peaks looked like giant fried fish heads trying to jump out of a vat of oil. Behind each hill, I could see shadows of another fish, and then another and another. And then the clouds would move just a little and the hills would suddenly become monstrous elephants marching slowly toward me! Can you see this? And at the root of the hill were secret caves. Inside grew hanging rock gardens in the shapes and colors of cabbage, winter melons, turnips, and onions. These were things so strange and beautiful you can't ever imagine them.

"But I didn't come to Kweilin to see how beautiful it was. The man who was my husband brought me and our two babies to Kweilin because he thought we would be safe. He was an officer with the Kuomintang, and after he put us down in a small room in a two-story house, he went off to the northwest, to Chungking.

"We knew the Japanese were winning, even when the newspapers said they were not. Every day, every hour, thousands of people poured into the city, crowding the sidewalks, looking for places to live. They came from the East, West, North, and South. They were rich and poor, Shanghainese, Cantonese, northerners, and not just Chinese, but foreigners and missionaries of every religion. And there was, of course, the Kuomintang and their army officers who thought they were top level to everyone else.

"We were a city of leftovers mixed together. If it hadn't been for the Japanese, there would have been plenty of reason for fighting to break out among these different people. Can you see it? Shanghai people with north-water peasants, bankers with barbers, rickshaw pullers with Burma refugees. Everybody looked down on someone else. It didn't matter that everybody shared the same sidewalk to spit on and suffered the same fast-moving diarrhea. We all had the same stink, but everybody complained someone else smelled the worst. Me? Oh, I hated the American air force officers who said habba-habba sounds to make my face turn red. But the worst were the northern peasants who emptied their noses into their hands and pushed people around and gave everybody their dirty diseases.

"So you can see how quickly Kweilin lost its beauty for me. I no longer climbed the peaks to say, How lovely are these hills! I only wondered which hills the Japanese had reached. I sat in the dark corners of my house with a baby under each arm, waiting with nervous feet. When the sirens cried out to warn us of bombers, my neighbors and I jumped to our feet and scurried to the deep caves to hide like wild animals. But you can't stay in the dark for so long. Something inside of you starts to fade and you become like a starving person, crazy-hungry for light. Outside I could hear the bombing. Boom! Boom! And then the sound of raining rocks. And inside I was no longer hungry for the cabbage or the turnips of the hanging rock garden. I could only see the dripping bowels of an ancient hill that might collapse on top of me. Can you imagine how it is, to want to be neither inside nor outside, to want to be nowhere and disappear?

"So when the bombing sounds grew farther away, we would come back out like newborn kittens scratching our way back to the city. And always, I would be amazed to find the hills against the burning sky had not been torn apart.

"I thought up Joy Luck on a summer night that was so hot even the moths fainted to the ground, their wings were so heavy with the damp heat. Every place was so crowded there was no room for fresh air. Unbearable smells from the sewers rose up to my second-story window and the stink had nowhere else to go but into my nose. At all hours of the night and day, I heard screaming sounds. I didn't know if it was a peasant slitting the throat of a runaway pig or an officer beating a half-dead peasant for lying in his way on the sidewalk. I didn't go to the window to find out. What use would it have been? And that's when I thought I needed something to do to help me move.

"My idea was to have a gathering of four women, one for each corner of my mah jong table. I knew which women I wanted to ask. They were all young like me, with wishful faces. One was an army officer's wife, like myself. Another was a girl with very fine manners from a rich family in Shanghai. She had escaped with only a little money. And there was a girl from Nanking who had the blackest hair I have ever seen. She came from a low-class family, but she was pretty and pleasant and had married well, to an old man who died and left her with a better life.

"Each week one of us would host a party to raise money and to raise our spirits. The hostess had to serve special *dyansyin* foods to bring good fortune of all kinds—dumplings shaped like silver money ingots, long rice noodles for long life, boiled peanuts for conceiving sons, and of course, many good-luck oranges for a plentiful, sweet life.

"What fine food we treated ourselves to with our meager allowances! We didn't notice that the dumplings were stuffed mostly with stringy squash and that the oranges were spotted with wormy holes. We ate sparingly, not as if we didn't have enough, but to protest how we could not eat another bite, we had already bloated ourselves from earlier in the day. We knew we had luxuries few people could afford. We were the lucky ones.

"After filling our stomachs, we would then fill a bowl with money and put it where everyone could see. Then we would sit down at the mah jong table. My table was from my family and was of a very fragrant red wood, not what you call rosewood, but *hong mu*, which is so fine there's no English word for it. The table had a very thick pad, so that when the mah jong *pai* were spilled onto the table the only sound was of ivory tiles washing against one another.

"Once we started to play, nobody could speak, except to say '*Pung*!' or '*Chr*!' when taking a tile. We had to play with seriousness and think of nothing else but adding to our happiness through winning. But after sixteen rounds, we would again feast, this time to celebrate our good fortune. And then we would talk into the night until the morning, saying stories about good times in the past and good times yet to come.

"Oh, what good stories! Stories spilling out all over the place! We almost laughed to death. A rooster that ran into the house screeching on top of dinner bowls, the same bowls that held him quietly in pieces the next day! And one about a girl who wrote love letters for two friends who loved the same man. And a silly foreign lady who fainted on a toilet when firecrackers went off next to her.

"People thought we were wrong to serve banquets every week while many people in the city were starving, eating rats and, later, the garbage that the poorest rats used to feed on. Others thought we were possessed by demons—to celebrate when even within our own families we had lost generations, had lost homes and fortunes, and were separated, husband from wife, brother from sister, daughter from mother. Hnnnh! How could we laugh, people asked.

"It's not that we had no heart or eyes for pain. We were all afraid. We all had our miseries. But to despair was to wish back for something already lost. Or to prolong what was already unbearable. How much can you wish for a favorite warm coat that hangs in the closet of a house that burned down with your mother and father inside of it? How long can you see in your mind arms and legs hanging from telephone wires and starving dogs running down the streets with half-chewed hands dangling from their jaws? What was worse, we asked among ourselves, to sit and wait for our own deaths with proper somber faces? Or to choose our own happiness?

"So we decided to hold parties and pretend each week had become the new year. Each week we could forget past wrongs done to us. We weren't allowed to think a bad thought. We feasted, we laughed, we played games, lost and won, we told the best stories. And each week, we could hope to be lucky. That hope was our only joy. And that's how we came to call our little parties Joy Luck."

My mother used to end the story on a happy note, bragging about her skill at the game. "I won many times and was so lucky the others teased that I had learned the trick of a clever thief," she said. "I won tens of thousands of *yuan*. But I wasn't rich. No. By then paper money had become worthless. Even toilet paper was worth more. And that made us laugh harder, to think a thousand-*yuan* note wasn't even good enough to rub on our bottoms."

I never thought my mother's Kweilin story was anything but a Chinese fairy tale. The endings always changed. Sometimes she said she used that worthless thousand-*yuan* note to buy a half-cup of rice. She turned that rice into a pot of porridge. She traded that gruel for two feet from a pig. Those two feet became six eggs, those eggs six chickens. The story always grew and grew.

And then one evening, after I had begged her to buy me a transistor radio, after she refused and I had sulked in silence for an hour, she said, "Why do you think you are missing something you never had?" And then she told me a completely different ending to the story.

"An army officer came to my house early one morning," she said, "and told me to go quickly to my husband in Chungking. And I knew he was telling me to run away from Kweilin. I knew what happened to officers and their families when the Japanese arrived. How could I go? There were no trains leaving Kweilin. My friend from Nanking, she was so good to me. She bribed a man to steal a wheelbarrow used to haul coal. She promised to warn our other friends.

"I packed my things and my two babies into this wheelbarrow and began pushing to Chungking four days before the Japanese marched into Kweilin. On the road I heard news of the slaughter from people running past me. It was terrible. Up to the last day, the Kuomintang insisted that Kweilin was safe, protected by the Chinese army. But later that day, the streets of Kweilin were strewn with newspapers reporting great Kuomintang victories, and on top of these papers, like fresh fish from a butcher, lay rows of people—men, women, and children who had never lost hope, but had lost their lives instead. When I heard this news, I walked faster and faster, asking myself at each step, Were they foolish? Were they brave?

"I pushed toward Chungking, until my wheel broke. I abandoned my beautiful mah jong table of *hong mu*. By then I didn't have enough feeling left in my body to cry. I tied scarves into slings and put a baby on each side of my shoulder. I carried a bag in each hand, one with clothes, the other with food. I carried these things until deep grooves grew in my hands. And I finally dropped one bag after the other when my hands began to bleed and became too slippery to hold onto anything.

"Along the way, I saw others had done the same, gradually given up hope. It was like a pathway inlaid with treasures that grew in value along the way. Bolts of fine fabric and books. Paintings of ancestors and carpenter tools. Until one could see cages of ducklings now quiet with thirst and, later still, silver urns lying in the road, where people had been too tired to carry them for any kind of future hope. By the time I arrived in Chungking I had lost everything except for three fancy silk dresses which I wore one on top of the other."

"What do you mean by 'everything'?" I gasped at the end. I was stunned to realize the story had been true all along. "What happened to the babies?"

She didn't even pause to think. She simply said in a way that made it clear there was no more to the story: "Your father is not my first husband. You are not those babies."

When I arrive at the Hsus' house, where the Joy Luck Club is meeting tonight, the first person I see is my father. "There she is! Never on time!" he announces. And it's true. Everybody's already here, seven family friends in their sixties and seventies. They look up and laugh at me, always tardy, a child still at thirty-six.

I'm shaking, trying to hold something inside. The last time I saw them, at the funeral, I had broken down and cried big gulping sobs. They must wonder now how someone like me can take my mother's place. A friend once told me that my mother and I were alike, that we had the same wispy hand gestures, the same girlish laugh and sideways look. When I shyly told my mother this, she seemed insulted and said, "You don't even know little percent of me! How can you be me?" And she's right. How can I be my mother at Joy Luck?

"Auntie, Uncle," I say repeatedly, nodding to each person there. I have always called these old family friends Auntie and Uncle. And then I walk over and stand next to my father.

He's looking at the Jongs' pictures from their recent China trip. "Look at that," he says politely, pointing to a photo of the Jongs' tour group standing on wide slab steps. There is nothing in this picture that shows it was taken in China rather than San Francisco, or any other city for that matter. But my father doesn't seem to be looking at the picture anyway. It's as though everything were the same to him, nothing stands out. He has always been politely indifferent. But what's the Chinese word that means indifferent because you can't *see* any differences? That's how troubled I think he is by my mother's death.

"Will you look at that," he says, pointing to another nondescript picture.

The Hsus' house feels heavy with greasy odors. Too many Chinese meals cooked in a too small kitchen, too many once fragrant smells compressed onto a thin layer of invisible grease. I remember how my mother used to go into other people's houses and restaurants and wrinkle her nose, then whisper very loudly: "I can see and feel the stickiness with my nose."

I have not been to the Hsus' house in many years, but the living room is exactly the same as I remember it. When Auntie An-mei and Uncle George moved to the Sunset district from Chinatown twenty-five years ago, they bought new furniture. It's all there, still looking mostly new under yellowed plastic. The same turquoise couch shaped in a semicircle of nubby tweed. The colonial end tables made out of heavy maple. A lamp of fake cracked porcelain. Only the scroll-length calendar, free from the Bank of Canton, changes every year.

I remember this stuff, because when we were children, Auntie An-mei didn't let us touch any of her new furniture except through the clear plastic coverings. On Joy Luck nights, my parents brought me to the Hsus'. Since I was the guest, I had to take care of all the younger children, so many children it seemed as if there were always one baby who was crying from having bumped its head on a table leg.

"You are responsible," said my mother, which meant I was in trouble if anything was spilled, burned, lost, broken, or dirty. I was responsible, no matter who did it. She and Auntie An-mei were dressed up in funny Chinese dresses with stiff stand-up collars and blooming branches of embroidered silk sewn over their breasts. These clothes were too fancy for real Chinese people, I thought, and too strange for American parties. In those days, before my mother told me her Kweilin story, I imagined Joy Luck was a shameful Chinese custom, like the secret gathering of the Ku Klux Klan or the tom-tom dances of TV Indians preparing for war.

But tonight, there's no mystery. The Joy Luck aunties are all wearing slacks, bright print blouses, and different versions of sturdy walking shoes. We are all seated around the dining room table under a lamp that looks like a Spanish candelabra. Uncle George puts on his bifocals and starts the meeting by reading the minutes:

"Our capital account is $24,825, or about $6,206 a couple, $3,103 per person. We sold Subaru for a loss at six and three-quarters. We bought a hundred shares of Smith International at seven. Our thanks to Lindo and Tin Jong for the goodies. The red bean soup was especially delicious. The March meeting had to be canceled until further notice. We were sorry to have to bid a fond farewell to our dear friend Suyuan and extended our sympathy to the Canning Woo family. Respectfully submitted, George Hsu, president and secretary."

That's it. I keep thinking the others will start talking about my mother, the wonderful friendship they shared, and why I am here in her spirit, to be the fourth corner and carry on the idea my mother came up with on a hot day in Kweilin.

But everybody just nods to approve the minutes. Even my father's head bobs up and down routinely. And it seems to me my mother's life has been shelved for new business.

Auntie An-mei heaves herself up from the table and moves slowly to the kitchen to prepare the food. And Auntie Lin, my mother's best friend, moves to the turquoise sofa, crosses her arms, and watches the men still seated at the table. Auntie Ying, who seems to shrink even more every time I see her, reaches into her knitting bag and pulls out the start of a tiny blue sweater.

The Joy Luck uncles begin to talk about stocks they are interested in buying. Uncle Jack, who is Auntie Ying's younger brother, is very keen on a company that mines gold in Canada.

"It's a great hedge on inflation," he says with authority. He speaks the best English, almost accentless. I think my mother's English was the worst, but she always thought her Chinese was the best. She spoke Mandarin slightly blurred with a Shanghai dialect.

"Weren't we going to play mah jong tonight?" I whisper loudly to Auntie Ying, who's slightly deaf.

"Later," she says, "after midnight."

"Ladies, are you at this meeting or not?" says Uncle George. After everybody votes unanimously for the Canada gold stock, I go into the kitchen to ask Auntie An-mei why the Joy Luck Club started investing in stocks.

"We used to play mah jong, winner take all. But the same people were always winning, the same people always losing," she says. She is stuffing wonton, one chopstick jab of gingery meat dabbed onto a thin skin and then a single fluid turn with her hand that seals the skin into the shape of a tiny nurse's cap. "You can't have luck when someone else has skill. So long time ago, we decided to invest in the stock market. There's no skill in that. Even your mother agreed."

Auntie An-mei takes count of the tray in front of her. She's already made five rows of eight wonton each. "Forty wonton, eight people, ten each, five row more," she says aloud to herself, and then continues stuffing. "We got smart. Now we can all win and lose equally. We can have stock market luck. And we can play mah jong for fun, just for a few dollars, winner take all. Losers take home leftovers! So everyone can have some joy. Smart-hanh?"

I watch Auntie An-mei make more wonton. She has quick, expert fingers. She doesn't have to think about what she is doing. That's what my mother used to complain about, that Auntie An-mei never thought about what she was doing.

"She's not stupid," said my mother on one occasion, "but she has no spine. Last week, I had a good idea for her. I said to her, Let's go to the consulate and ask for papers for your brother. And she almost wanted to drop her things and go right then. But later she talked to someone. Who knows who? And that person told her she can get her brother in bad trouble in China. That person said FBI will put her on a list and give her trouble in the U.S. the rest of her life. That person said, You ask for a house loan and they say no loan, because your brother is a communist. I said, You already have a house! But still she was scared.

"Auntie An-mei runs this way and that," said my mother, "and she doesn't know why."

As I watch Auntie An-mei, I see a short bent woman in her seventies, with a heavy bosom and thin, shapeless legs. She has the flattened soft fingertips of an old woman. I wonder what Auntie An-mei did to inspire a lifelong stream of criticism from my mother. Then again, it seemed my mother was always displeased with all her friends, with me, and even with my father. Something was always missing. Something always needed improving. Something was not in balance. This one or that had too much of one element, not enough of another.

The elements were from my mother's own version of organic chemistry. Each person is made of five elements, she told me.

Too much fire and you had a bad temper. That was like my father, whom my mother always criticized for his cigarette habit and who always shouted back that she should keep her thoughts to herself. I think he now feels guilty that he didn't let my mother speak her mind.

Too little wood and you bent too quickly to listen to other people's ideas, unable to stand on your own. This was like my Auntie An-mei.

Too much water and you flowed in too many directions, like myself, for having started half a degree in biology, then half a degree in art, and then finishing neither when I went off to work for a small ad agency as a secretary, later becoming a copywriter.

I used to dismiss her criticisms as just more of her Chinese superstitions, beliefs that conveniently fit the circumstances. In my twenties, while taking *Introduction to Psychology*, I tried to tell her why she shouldn't criticize so much, why it didn't lead to a healthy learning environment.

"There's a school of thought," I said, "that parents shouldn't criticize children. They should encourage instead. You know, people rise to other people's expectations. And when you criticize, it just means you're expecting failure."

"That's the trouble," my mother said. "You never rise. Lazy to get up. Lazy to rise to expectations."

"Time to eat," Auntie An-mei happily announces, bringing out a steaming pot of the wonton she was just wrapping. There are piles of food on the table, served buffet style, just like at the Kweilin feasts. My father is digging into the chow mein, which still sits in an oversize aluminum pan surrounded by little plastic packets of soy sauce. Auntie An-mei must have bought this on Clement Street. The wonton soup smells wonderful with delicate sprigs of cilantro floating on top. I'm drawn first to a large platter of *chaswei*, sweet barbecued pork cut into coin-sized slices, and then to a whole assortment of what I've always called finger goodies—thin-skinned pastries filled with chopped pork, beef, shrimp, and unknown stuffings that my mother used to describe as "nutritious things".

Eating is not a gracious event here. It's as though everybody had been starving. They push large forkfuls into their mouths, jab at more pieces of pork, one right after the other. They are not like the ladies of Kweilin, who I always imagined savored their food with a certain detached delicacy.

And then, almost as quickly as they started, the men get up and leave the table. As if on cue, the women peck at last morsels and then carry plates and bowls to the kitchen and dump them in the sink. The women take turns washing their hands, scrubbing them vigorously. Who started this ritual? I too put my plate in the sink and wash my hands. The women are talking about the Jongs' China trip, then they move toward a room in the back of the apartment. We pass another room, what used to be the bedroom shared by the four Hsu sons. The bunk beds with their scuffed, splintery ladders are still there. The Joy Luck uncles are already seated at the card table. Uncle George is dealing out cards, fast, as though he learned this technique in a casino. My father is passing out Pall Mall cigarettes, with one already dangling from his lips.

And then we get to the room in the back, which was once shared by the three Hsu girls. We were all childhood friends. And now they've all grown and married and I'm here to play in their room again. Except for the smell of camphor, it feels the same—as if Rose, Ruth, and Janice might soon walk in with their hair rolled up in big orange-juice cans and plop down on their identical narrow beds. The white chenille bedspreads are so worn they are almost translucent. Rose and I used to pluck the nubs out while talking about our boy problems. Everything is the same, except now a mahogany-colored mah jong table sits in the center. And next to it is a floor lamp, a long black pole with three oval spotlights attached like the broad leaves of a rubber plant.

Nobody says to me, "Sit here, this is where your mother used to sit." But I can tell even before everyone sits down. The chair closest to the door has an emptiness to it. But the feeling doesn't really have to do with the chair. It's her place on the table. Without having anyone tell me, I know her corner on the table was the East.

The East is where things begin, my mother once told me, the direction from which the sun rises, where the wind comes from.

Auntie An-mei, who is sitting on my left, spills the tiles onto the green felt tabletop and then says to me, "Now we wash tiles." We swirl them with our hands in a circular motion. They make a cool swishing sound as they bump into one another.

"Do you win like your mother?" asks Auntie Lin across from me. She is not smiling.

"I only played a little in college with some Jewish friends."

"Annh! Jewish mah jong," she says in disgusted tones. "Not the same thing." This is what my mother used to say, although she could never explain exactly why.

"Maybe I shouldn't play tonight. I'll just watch," I offer.

Auntie Lin looks exasperated, as though I were a simple child: "How can we play with just three people? Like a table with three legs, no balance. When Auntie Ying's husband died, she asked her brother to join. Your father asked you. So it s decided."

"What's the difference between Jewish and Chinese mah jong?" I once asked my mother. I couldn't tell by her answer if the games were different or just her attitude toward Chinese and Jewish people.

"Entirely different kind of playing," she said in her English explanation voice. "Jewish mah jong, they watch only for their own tile, play only with their eyes."

Then she switched to Chinese: "Chinese mah jong, you must play using your head, very tricky. You must watch what everybody else throws away and keep that in your head as well. And if nobody plays well, then the game becomes like Jewish mah jong. Why play? There's no strategy. You're just watching people make mistakes."

These kinds of explanations made me feel my mother and I spoke two different languages, which we did. I talked to her in English, she answered back in Chinese.

"So what's the difference between Chinese and Jewish mah jong?" I ask Auntie Lin.

"Aii-ya," she exclaims in a mock scolding voice, "Your mother did not teach you anything?"

Auntie Ying pats my hand. "You're a smart girl. You watch us, do the same. Help us stack the tiles and make four walls."

I follow Auntie Ying, but mostly I watch Auntie Lin. She is the fastest, which means I can almost keep up with the others by watching what she does first. Auntie Ying throws the dice and I'm told that Auntie Lin has become the East wind. I've become the North wind, the last hand to play. Auntie Ying is the South and Auntie An-mei is the West. And then we start taking tiles, throwing the dice, counting back on the wall to the right number of spots where our chosen tiles lie. I rearrange my tiles, sequences of bamboo and balls, doubles of colored number tiles, odd tiles that do not fit anywhere

"Your mother was the best, like a pro," says Auntie An-mei while slowly sorting her tiles, considering each piece carefully.

Now we begin to play, looking at our hands, casting tiles, picking up others at an easy, comfortable pace. The Joy Luck aunties begin to make small talk, not really listening to each other. They speak in their special language, half in broken English, half in their own Chinese dialect.

15

(David Mura, 1952—)
戴维·穆拉

作者简介

戴维·穆拉（David Mura, 1952— ），美国日裔作家、诗人、小说家、剧作家、评论家和表演艺术家，出生于美国芝加哥。他从格林内尔学院（Grinnell College）获得文学学士学位，从佛蒙特美术学院（Vermont College of Fine Arts）获得创意写作硕士学位。他曾在明尼苏达大学（University of Minnesota）、圣奥拉夫学院（St. Olaf College）和俄勒冈大学（The University of Oregon）任教。他以优秀的作品和杰出的贡献荣获了国家艺术基金会文艺奖（National Endowment for the Arts–Literature Fellowships）与美日创意艺术家奖（U.S.–Japan Creative Artist Fellowship）等重要奖项。

他的作品有诗集《最后的咒语》（*The Last Incantations*, 2014）、《燃烧天使》（*Angels for the Burning*, 2004）与《欲望的颜色》（*The Colors of Desire*, 1995）等；小说《日本帝国闻名于世的自杀》（*Famous Suicides of the Japanese Empire*, 2008）；回忆录《身体与记忆相触的地方：一个关于种族、性别和身份的奥德赛》（*Where the Body Meets Memory: An Odyssey of Race, Sexuality and Identity*, 1995）等。

在诗集《燃烧天使》中穆拉一方面表达了日裔美国家庭中一世、二世和三世之间的家庭矛盾，另一方面把所有美国亚裔人作为一个整体，展现了他们在美国的辛酸经历。

诗歌《年轻的亚洲女人》（“The Young Asian Women”）和《集中营书信》（“Internment Epistles”）选自诗集《燃烧天使》。《年轻的亚洲女人》通过对亚洲女性外表和身体的描写，折射出美国人眼中“低俗”和“劣等”的亚洲人形象。《集中营书信》通过书信的形式描写日本移民在集中营生活的血泪历史。

作品选读

The Young Asian Women

By David Mura

The young Asian women are shaving their heads,
piercing eyelids and ears. They stare holes
in curators, shop clerks and geisha chasers,
bubble gum snapping like caps in their jaws.
Their names? Juliana, Vong, Lee, and Lily.
Could be Mina from the outskirts of Tokyo
but more likely she's Nkauj'lis of the famous
or infamous Lyfongs (depending on your clan
and your anti-Communist persuasions).
Check out that siren named Sonia, too in love
with her looks, a nasty curl of Seoul
in her smile. Or if her name is Hoa,
she's tough as her mother, bad girl, bitch,
it doesn't matter, she'll survive like nettles,
flower in what ditch she finds herself, with
or without a man, or her lesbian lover who left
for Alaska, the smell of bear shit on the trail.
With her Taiwanese aunt, digs tales of Toisan
ladies, dragons and the water marsh where bandit
ghosts steal years with a kiss, talking tongues
down your throat to your belly, slipping
a demon seed inside you to grow. Oh, they're
like that, these young women, their art alive
like Thai hot sauce on your tongue, hurtling hurt
with a half pint gleaming on the night stand.
They know how mysteriously the body is written,

how thundering colors of Benetton befit
statistics on garment workers in the Third
and First Worlds. They know *Woman Warrior*,
bell hooks, how the moon waxes red like
the sheets where they write out scripts, stories,
and poems, unwrapping their dreams before
you, a palm of paint, pearls, I-Ching stones.
With boots black and buckled, their jeans frayed,
lips bruised purple or incandescent red,
their bodies at the dance club cut into hip-hop.
Their voices are hoarse after nights on the floor,
their faces smeared with sweat. Their cheeks aglow.
They scare the pants off the young men they know.

Internment Epistles

By David Mura

Dear Hanaye,

A cold snap blew in today, stinging
our faces as we trudged to mess,
rifling my coat like a guard.

The slop they serve sickens me.
Why eat? (And yet I know, I know:
At this same moment millions starve.)

Frost whitens the windowpane

with intricate leafy designs,
and I conjure there rows of tomatoes

or strawberries, blossoms of color
as I travel in my mind backwards
to the fields we harvested

together, you so young and shy
still, a beautiful beautiful bride
who braved an ocean for this harsh

and lush land and the raw callused
hands of a farmer who dreamed
of *Bon O-dori* celebrations, his sons

pounding *taiko*, daughters
dancing *buyo*, chrysanthemums
bursting from rippling kimonos:

Why did you come? Why did I stay?
Such thoughts slip like icy winds
through the cracks, and I cannot

hold them back. And yet,
in a Mason jar on my desk,
swims a baby whitefish

by a sprig of snapdragon,
saved from the fall, as if I
still owned a glorious garden.

Take these coal-black characters,
Hanaye, take them as footsteps

across a frozen white tundra

and know that as the salmon
spears against the cold current,
I am forever flailing toward you...

My dear husband,

Received two letters and one postcard.
I cannot apologize enough for my silence.

Fever and coughing keep me up at night,
yet my dreams are worse than illness,
unsettling images of fire, temples

and houses crushed like a boy's kite
and ants scurrying out from hissing flames:
Last night one possessed my mother's face.

She held out her hands, each palm a pyre,
and asked me to drink and be saved.
Father Fukuda says pay these no mind;

he begs me to pray to his Jesus,
nailed to a post, a beast on a gibbet,
as if torture required tortuous belief.

I try to think of the bodhisattva shade
where Buddha sat, a hissing cobra
at his back, contemplating No-Mind:

His cobra slithered away. Mine does not.
(Like these barracks my thoughts overflow,

couples arguing, babies bawling, love sounds at night...)

Christmas was lonely. I cried and cried.
George at training camp, Kimiko at college.
You in that prison they won't call a prison.

Me, a bird in a cage, who's stopped her singing...
They have given me a single room now.
For my nerves. For my nerves I knit,

but sometimes as I pearl and stitch,
the yarn tangles and I forget
for whom I web this scarf.

I tell myself it is you.
But when I try to bring back your face,
that is when my No-Mind appears.

Forgive me, dear husband.
I shouldn't be telling you all this.
I will try to write more next time.

I will try to heal...

Dear Hanaye,

Waiting anxiously to receive your reply
to the important matters in my letter
of December 7. (*How that date*

now chimes inside me: pounding at
the door, the men in their dark raincoats
striding like bandits into our living room,

yanking open my desk, the dressers,
rummaging our closets, letters
I sent you after our omiyai;

the plaque from the Japanese
literary society proclaiming
my triumph in haiku

and the map Kimiko scrawled
for a high-school assignment
of the Panama canal—

all that incriminated us
in their eyes: Not one of them
thought to take off his hat.)

I received the chocolates you sent,
so I assume you must be okay.
Perhaps my letter has gone astray.

My appeal and other documents
to file with the Attorney General
are ready, but without a word

from you, I'm at a loss.
Perhaps you are ill,
I think, and my mind goes wild

with images I sever
to prevent following
where they may lead.

I tell myself it must be Christmas

and preparations for *Bon O-dori*
that keeps you busy, as this

last day of the year it rains:
I am carving a model boat,
a tiny anchor of sandstone.

Hanaye, let us sail away
from all this, and anchor
our craft in Haname bay...

My dear husband,

I received your letter yesterday.
A thousand apologies. Please
do not read into my silence.
Yes, I've been ill. But now

I am gaining weight. I force
myself to the *magusa* they serve
and though sometimes I feel
like a pig at a trough, I chew

and swallow and think of slices
of *maguro* and *hamachi*,
unagi unrolled across a bed
of rice, golden sliced orbs

of *tsukemono*, like tiny suns:
And my belly grows warmer
as if another child grew
there, as we so often wished.

Dr. Mitsumori, Ishibashi,
even the Pastor have helped me so.
And your lovely model ship.
Surely you are my anchor.

I do suffer some insomnia.
Perhaps it's simply old age.
I don't need my dreams anymore.
I know what they amount to.

Uncle Koike still acts strangely.
I try to talk to him though.
He keeps losing his money.
He tells me its the gambling

and sake, so drunk on the way
home, someone beat
and robbed him of everything
he owned. I laugh and tell him:

Ojii-chan, it was just a dream.
It was just a dream...
He looks at me as if I'm
the crazy one. *Bakkatare*,

he mutters. But I know
he doesn't mean it.
Yesterday, though, he tried
to kiss me, calling me Sachiko,

and I kept telling him Sachiko's
dead, Sachiko's dead. He
let go of me and stared

at his hands, and with his left

traced the lifeline of his right
as if searching for where
she went. He began weeping
then, into his cupped palms...

Iwao, my hands are shaking.
I can’t write any longer.
I thank Buddha for my blessings,
what strength I still possess.

Dear Hanaye,

Tadao-san wove this cigarette case
from the strands of a potato sack.
I roiled the cigarettes myself.

I will think of you sitting
on the barracks steps, smoking:
Blow, for me, a few smoke rings.

We’ll communicate like the Indians
from a great distance,
and I’ll know you’re all right.

My rehearing’s next week.
I try not to think about it.
I’m almost as restless

as when Yukio—I mean George—
was born (isn’t it strange
how so many sons assume this name

as if they too could give birth
to this country. Better
to borrow the name Geronimo,

who refused his prison
and vanished in mountains
where none could find him.)

In the shallows of the river
near camp, Tadao and I
dug up clams and kelp.

We roasted the clams
on a tin drum and pickled
the kelp into *tsukudani*

and ate them with mushrooms
we found by the willows:
their texture, earthy and dark,

reminded me of my hands
and how they must have smelled
to you, and I found both shame

and delight in that.
Tadao-san laughed we were a pair
of *ronin*, growing fat

off the land. Not fat,
I said, but skinny, skinny
as two scavenging crows,

and for a moment

as the juice of the clams
dribbled down our chins

I forget where we are.
It will get colder soon.
Another season passes

and we are still apart.
Please be more careful now.
I can't but feel it's almost done.

My dear husband,

Thank you for the dried salmon.
And the candy and the "Jimminy Cricket."
The salmon was salty and pungent and tough.

I devoured it like a woman, alone and starving.
You know, one of those witches in Noh,
with her hut deep in the forest, who foresees

all that has passed, all that will come,
and traps journeyers with her beauty
and elegant dance and delicate kimono.

But when the night falls
and she unchignons her hair
and the silk cloth drops at her feet,

no flesh steps forth, just glittering scales
and a serpent's hiss, the tongue seeking
a companion for punishment and eternity—

I'm afraid sometimes that trapped traveler
is you. Such a gentle and simple pilgrim,
a woodsman who's labored years

for a pittance, and yet, will not give up
his cutting and hauling, though all he gathers
the flames devour, transmogrifying

to black black ash. So I pray for green
sagebrush to cover the white mountains
which stand before me like sentinels

that bar the way and trap me
with these days that pass shamelessly
as my eyes flutter and blink

and cannot believe what they see
and so believe what surfaces at night
when they are closed and witches dream.

Perhaps this is merely age. Or nerves.
Or simply an old lady's unsettling moods.
I pray for your health. I'll write when I'm better...

Dear Hanaye,

I have just received the telegram.
I ripped the star from the window.
Wept from a place inside I did not know.

But when I stopped—but it has not stopped—
I picked up the crumpled cloth strip,
smoothed it out and hung it up again.

Once I believed in the weaver girl
and the herd boy who, torn
apart in their constellations

up in the black black sky, once yearly,
across the spaces of the universe
and the River of Heaven,

came together and held each
other's hand, so briefly
it must have mattered.

Now, Hanaye, you must not let go.
There is a new star there.
It will not fall again...

Dear Hanaye,

It's bitter cold. Minus sixteen.
In these rickety barracks
my breath forms frozen clouds

as if my lungs only gave out ghosts.
There's the smell of leftover
Kikkoman in my tiny room

as if a feast had just been devoured
and the partyers vanished
and the silence is fuller

for the echoes it holds.
How have you been feeling
lately? I tell myself you're better.

And for once I don't know
whether it is or is not a lie.
As I told you before

it won't be long before the sun
shines upon us both
as it did that day I took your hand

at Tokyo Bay and pointed east
and across the silver scales
of sea glittering in the sun,

mirroring our glorious future,
our home, and our children lay.
So far away that time,

our flesh so close I could sense
your breathing and matched it
with mine and my imaginings.

Beneath the far peaks
snowy fields wait like a blank page
for me to write one last message:

No wonder you slipped.
It's a sea of ice, you know.
Sparkling in sunlight.

You should have warned me.
Old woman of white,
you have to be alive to tell the tale...

16

(Cynthia Kadohata, 1956—   )

辛西娅·角畑

作者简介

辛西娅·角畑（Cynthia Kadohata, 1956—   ），美国日裔儿童文学家，出生于美国伊利诺伊州。她从南加利福尼亚大学（University of Southern California）获得新闻学学士学位，并在匹兹堡大学（University of Pittsburgh）和哥伦比亚大学（Columbia University）学习研究生写作课程。由于她突出的写作天赋，荣获过怀丁作家奖（Whiting Writers' Award）、纽伯瑞奖（Newbery Medal）与美国国家图书奖（American National Book Award）等诸多重要奖项。

辛西娅·角畑是一名多产的作家，著作有小说《漂浮的世界》（*The Floating World*, 1989）、《在爱之谷的中心》（*In the Heart of the Valley of Love*, 1992）、《玻璃山》（*The Glass Mountains*, 1995）、《亮晶晶》（*Kira-Kira*, 2004）、《野草花》（*Weedflower*, 2006）、《侦探犬克拉克》（*Cracker! The Best Dog in Vietnam*, 2007）、《外在美》（*Outside Beauty*, 2008）、《一百万道阴影》（*A Million Shades of Gray*, 2010）、《明天会有好运气》（*The Thing About Luck*, 2013）、《半个世界之外》（*Half a World Away*, 2014）与《阻截》（*Checked*, 2018）。她在《纽约客》（*New Yorker*）和《密西西比评论》（*The Mississippi Review*）等重要期刊上发表过一些短篇故事。

《亮晶晶》是辛西娅·角畑的处女作，也是她的成名作。这部小说荣获2005年的纽伯瑞奖（Newbery Medal）和美国亚太文学奖（Asian/Pacific American Award for Literature）。小说讲述了一位日裔美国少女面对贫困、种族歧视、亲人的离去等接踵而至的逆境时，选择用乐观和勇敢的态度去面对天灾与人祸的故事。

小说第 13 章讲述了主人公一家在美国过着穷困潦倒和祸不单行的日子。主人公姐姐的生病使本来就很拮据的生活“雪上加霜”。父母整日超负荷工作，但仍然无济于事，家庭经济每况愈下。作者巧妙地用儿童语言展现出生动活泼的画面，然而故事背后残酷的现实却催人泪下。

作品选读

Kira-Kira
Chapter 13

By Cynthia Kadohata

BECAUSE OF LYNN'S medical bills, soon my parents were getting behind on the mortgage. All they did was work. My mother came home only to sleep, and my father did not come home at all. Auntie or Mrs. Kanagawa stayed with Lynn and Sammy during the day when I was at school. My parents were so exhausted, I wasn't sure they even realized what arrangements we were making each day. Some days *nobody* stayed with us.

Most of the time Lynn slept, but anytime she was awake, she wanted attention. She wanted a bedpan, or food, or water, or sometimes just a little company. But sometimes she didn't know what she wanted. In fact, it seemed that at least once a day she didn't know what she wanted. That was the most exhausting thing. She would want me to read to her, and then she wouldn't like the book and would want me to read something else. And then she still wouldn't like the book and would want me to sing for her. But she wouldn't like that, either. My teacher had commented on the black circles under my eyes. A couple of mornings I even made myself coffee.

Sammy and I slept in the room with her now, because somebody needed to be with her all the time. Once, Lynn woke up in the middle of the night, the way she often did.

"Katie?" she said.

I almost never slept deeply anymore—as soon as she said my name, I always sat up immediately, no matter how tired I was. But that night I was completely exhausted. I could barely pull myself up.

"Katie?" she said, more impatiently.

"Uh-huh." I sat up. "Yeah, okay."

"I want some milk."

"Now? Are you sure?"

"What do you mean, am I sure? I want some milk."

I got up and went to the kitchen and brought back a glass of milk. I pulled her up and picked up the bolster from the floor and used it to support her back. She took one sip of milk and made a face. "Can I have water instead?"

"I thought you said you were sure!"

She looked as if she might cry. "I said I'm thirsty!" She dropped the cup to the floor. I just stood there a moment, watching her small rug soak up the milk.

I suddenly felt angry at her. "Dad had to buy you that rug, you know."

"I want water!"

I went to the kitchen and came back with water, a soapy dishrag, and a towel. I handed her the water without comment. Sammy's eyes were open wide, watching me. I cleaned up the rug.

Lynn cried out, "There's soap on this water glass!" She flung it to the floor.

I stared at the cup for a moment. Then I whipped around. "You're ruining everything!" I said. "We got a new house, and you're ruining everything! Mom and Dad worked so hard to get this house. *You're* ruining it!"

She looked really hurt for a moment, but then she got angry. She said, "*I want milk*."

I said, "No."

"I *hate* you."

"I hate *you*!"

Sammy said, "Katie?"

"Shut up!" I snapped at him, and he was still.

I finished cleaning up and got in bed. Sammy was still awake, staring at me. I told him to go to sleep. Lynn started to cry, but only for about fifteen minutes.

Then she started to make a soft, mournful, squeaky noise, kind of like "heeah... heeah... heeah," every time she exhaled. She didn't sound like Lynn, she sounded like an animal. Since she never seemed to inhale deeply anymore, her breathing was quick and shallow. She made the noise on and on, weakly. She didn't cry again, she just kept making the noise. It sounded really sad. Sammy's face looked scared in the glow from the Rabbit on the Moon night-light Auntie

Fumi had given Lynn.

I ignored my sister and brother, just lay there and listened to Lynnie in the dim light. Usually while I lay in bed, I liked to think of new things I could do for Lynnie. Maybe I could let her try my pillow to see if she liked it better. Or I could bring her a new cracker she'd never tried. Or maybe I could even find a new book that she'd never heard of and read it to her, even though she had heard of every book in the world. That night I knew that nothing I could do would make her feel better. So I lay in bed and listened to her mournful noise and didn't feel love or hate or anger or anything at all except despair.

For Thanksgiving weekend my parents needed a break from me and Sammy, and we needed a break from them. No one felt like eating turkey. My parents arranged for Uncle to take us on a camping trip. He took his kids camping almost every weekend, even when it rained. He called every Friday night and asked whether we wanted to come. We always said no. I wanted to stay with Lynn. But this time my parents made me go.

We left early on a Saturday morning. My parents seemed relieved to see us go. It made me surprised and guilty to find how glad I felt to get out of the house where everything reminded me of my sister. I felt guilty whenever I left my sister's side, but at the same time I could not be with her every moment. If I had been, I would have lost my mind. Maybe I *was* losing my mind. Sometimes, even just for three minutes, even when it was my turn to be with Lynnie, I had to step outside. I had to look at the sky. I had to be anywhere else but in that sad room with her.

In addition to Sammy and me, Uncle was bringing his family, my friend Silly, and his friend Jedda-Boy, a local land surveyor. Silly and I rode in the truck with Uncle. Amazingly, it was the same truck he had driven us to Georgia in years earlier. It didn't go more than twenty-five miles an hour, so Jedda-Boy's truck lost us in the first ten minutes. Unfortunately, Uncle had never been to our destination before. We were going to one of Jedda-Boy's favorite campsites. Uncle got lost and refused to stop for directions because, he kept saying, he knew the way, which he obviously didn't.

At one point we went down a small road that ended at a cliff. The truck got stuck and wouldn't back up. I could literally see down into a canyon before us. If we went forward, we would fall to our deaths. Then Lynn would miss me and might get sicker. Uncle wanted Silly and me to sit in the truck bed to get better traction. So she and I got in back and prayed that my uncle wouldn't go forward by accident.

The truck revved and revved and shook and shook, but it was still stuck. Then Uncle tried to explain to me how to use a clutch, so that I could back up the truck while he and Silly sat in the bed, since he was heavier than I was and would give us better traction. I couldn't figure out the clutch. In fact, at one point while I was learning, the truck jolted forward several inches. Uncle screamed a scream as high-pitched as a girl's and rammed his foot on top of mine on the brake. He taught Silly instead. She was like Lynn in that she could do anything, including crazy stuff like learning how to use a clutch.

Uncle and I climbed in back. Silly turned once to look at us. She crossed her fingers and then turned forward. The truck shook and rattled, and then we backed up.

Uncle was sweating. He seemed to think we would all be dead if he hadn't slammed his foot on mine. My toes still hurt. He looked at me with new respect, I guess over just how much trouble I was capable of causing. He got in and started driving again. We pulled around a corner, and I felt myself totter uncertainly and then lean into the door. He'd told me the door came loose sometimes. I tried to stop myself, but the door fell open. The next thing I knew, my back was scraping along rocks on the roadside.

Unbelievably, no one noticed, not even Silly. They rolled merrily along while I lay on the road and watched the truck recede. I screamed, "Wait for me!" In a moment the truck came slowly down the road from the opposite direction. I saw Silly point at me excitedly, and the truck pulled over. I got in the truck and refused to talk to Uncle Katsuhisa. My shirt was torn in back. Basically, there were already about a thousand things I could snitch on Uncle for if I wanted.

He seemed to realize that, because he handed me a piece of rice candy and said, "I'd like to give you this." I continued to shun him. "All right, then, here," he said. He handed me the whole pack of rice candy plus a Hershey's bar. I took the rice candy, handing the Hershey's bar to Silly.

"Now, don't you tell your parents you fell out of the truck."

"I won't."

He shook his head. "I still remember when I could bribe you for half a stick of gum."

At the campgrounds Jedda-Boy had already set up camp. When I started to tell the story of the cliff, Uncle frowned at me, so I didn't say anything. He smiled innocently at Auntie Fumi.

David, Daniel, Silly, and I ran off to play a game we called Hunter and Hunted with water guns. At first I hadn't felt like playing, but they begged me. Silly and I chose to be the deer first; David and Daniel would hunt us with their water guns. I found I loved pretending to be a deer, loping through the forest as the boys counted to one hundred. Silly and I moved as quickly and quietly as we could. We had to balance our movements between speed and noise. Silly was like an animal, with perfect animal instincts about where to go and how to move gracefully. We heard David and Daniel call out, "Here we come, deer!"

I thought I could feel the blood rushing through my body. For a moment I forgot I was human. We moved very quietly. Then we stopped moving and just listened. We couldn't hear a thing. Suddenly, there was a huge crashing nearby, and we crashed away in the opposite direction. I found myself laughing crazily as I ran. I felt so free!

Silly and I split up in different directions. I heard Daniel yelling, "I'll get Silly!" I ran desperately through the woods. There was a sudden open area, and I ran and ran across. I felt like a real deer, graceful and fast. I saw an arc of water by my side. It missed me! Then water splattered on my head. I collapsed to the ground and groaned the way I thought an animal might. David ran up and put his foot on my stomach and pounded his chest and said, "For I am the greatest hunter *alive*!"

We turned to watch Silly running into the woods chased by Daniel. In a minute he came out of the woods looking confused. He stood still to listen. David and I helped him look for Silly. About ten minutes later we still hadn't found her. Daniel yelled, "Ollie, Ollie, ocean free!" Silly appeared right where we'd just come from. I was so proud of her.

Then it was the boys' turn to be the deer. They went to hide. We didn't chase them. Instead, we returned to camp to play cards in our tent. We were so funny! When the boys finally figured out where we were, they refused to speak to us. So we refused to speak to them.

David said, "How can you not speak to us when you're the ones who played the trick?" But we didn't answer because we weren't speaking to them!

When night approached, Uncle made us a fire, and I lay near it and felt the heat on my body. I stared at the sky, as I had done so many times with my sister. I was surprised to realize that I hadn't thought of my sister for nearly an hour—the whole time we were playing and about half an hour after. That was the longest I hadn't thought about her for a while. I felt refreshed, as if I could now sit with her for ten years straight if necessary to help her get well.

Auntie and Sam sat next to me. David, Daniel, and Silly were playing some game. Uncle and Jedda-Boy took a couple of surveying instruments and discussed mud and sand and other important surveying matters. Jedda-Boy was talking about how once when he lived in Nevada, he got helicoptered to a secret location to measure some land. The land was in the desert near where nuclear bomb tests had been held. He finished the job even though the area was probably radioactive, because a self-respecting surveyor always finishes a job no matter what it involves, including, he said, wild dogs, gunshots from angry neighbors mixed up in a property dispute, snakes and alligators, and radioactivity.

I said quietly, "Auntie, when is Uncle Katsuhisa going to quit his job at the hatchery and become a land surveyor?"

She pushed back my hair and said sadly, "Sweetheart, nobody in Georgia is going to hire a Japanese man to be a land surveyor."

"How do you know?"

"He's been turned down for five jobs."

"But he can be whatever he wants. Lynn is going to be either a rocket scientist or a famous writer."

"It's different for you children. You're younger, the world is changing."

Jedda-Boy was talking loudly. "The first time I got chased by an alligator, I was scared, I admit that. But I finished the job later."

Sammy smiled serenely and looked at the beautiful sky. Lynn liked to say the stars were the ultimate thing you could describe as *kirakira*. The second most ultimate thing was the way the sun glittered off the ocean. Of course, she had never seen this, but she could imagine exactly how it would look.

Uncle came and sat down with us. I said, "Uncle, can't you become a land surveyor?"

He drank from his canteen and wiped his mouth. He didn't answer for a long time. Everyone was quiet. After a time he said, "I remember that when I was a boy, I thought I was going to grow up and map the world."

Auntie stroked his face.

Uncle saw Sammy gazing at the sky, and he looked at the sky too. "Would you look at those stars! I can really see how the ancient Egyptians or whoever the hell it was said, 'Goddamnit, let's name those goddamn stars and go down in history!'"

I didn't know what the ancient Egyptians had said, but I doubted they had said exactly that.

Uncle's face got wistful as he stared into the sky. Auntie kissed his face. He put his arm around her, and they leaned against each other. I saw in their faces how happy they were, and sad, too, because Uncle Katsuhisa would never be a land surveyor.

New Year's is the biggest holiday of the year for the Japanese. Every year since we'd lived in Georgia, Mrs. Muramoto held a big party. She served *sake* and *mochi* and a couple dozen different snacks. We would usually stay until about ten and then go home. Just before dawn I would get up and write down my *hatsu-yume*, first dream of the new year. Then we would meet the other families and go to the empty lot nearby with our lawn chairs to watch the sunrise. Watching the first sunrise is the traditional way to celebrate New Year's in Japan. The last few years, though, nobody had bothered getting up for the sunrise. The fathers were all too tired for such a celebration.

Mrs. Kanagawa stayed with Lynn and Sammy while I went to Mrs. Muramoto's for just half an hour before returning to sit with Lynn. Mrs. Kanagawa told me Lynn had been very peaceful. We made quiet small talk about the party, and then Mrs. Kanagawa left. Lynn continued to sleep, her breath catching heart-breakingly, as if breathing had become a hardship for her body. Her hair had grown stringy. I moved a strand of hair from her forehead, then pulled a chair to the window and spied on Mr. and Mrs. Miller's party next door. It was quite a bit noisier than the party at Mrs. Muramoto's. Everybody seemed drunk. All at once the men started to put bows on their foreheads and run out the front door. I had no idea what they were doing. I hurried into the alcove and peeked out our front window. The men ran down the street shouting "Happy New Year!" with the bows on their foreheads. Even though I was in a sad mood, I couldn't help smiling at these crazy white people.

I went into the kitchen and called my parents at the party and told them Lynn was sleeping peacefully. Someday when Lynn got better, we were going to get her a phone for the bedroom. Gregg and Amber both used to call all the time, so when she got better and made more friends, she would need a phone.

I put on my pajamas around 11:30 and lay on the floor next to Lynn's bed. The Rabbit on the Moon looked so pretty shining in the outlet.

"Katie?" Lynn said softly. She hadn't talked all day.

I sat up. "Yes?"

"You have to try to get better grades. Promise?"

"Okay."

"You should go to college. Promise?"

"I'll think about it."

"Promise?"

"Yes."

"Take care of Mom and Dad and Sammy."

"Okay, I promise." I hesitated. "When you get better, you can help me take care of them."

"Okay, I promise." She laughed very softly, almost soundlessly.

The phone rang, and she seemed to perk up a bit. But it stopped after just one ring, and she seemed to deflate. It was amazing that as sick as she was, she could still be interested in something as small as the ring of a phone.

She groaned suddenly. "Can we open the window?"

I jumped up to open the window. She closed her eyes, and I sat next to the bed and stared at her. Her skin looked almost purely white, like the white of the ghost of Brenda I'd seen at the swamp. She opened her eyes again.

"It's too dark in here," she said.

I turned on the light. A little brown moth flitted in. It wasn't big, not even an inch long. It landed on the ceiling. Lynn stared at it. Then it flitted toward the lamp and away again. Lynn kept watching. For a moment the party next door quieted down. Our room was so quiet, I could just make out the sound of the moth's wings. Lynn didn't move, except for her eyes. Her eyes moved this way and that as she watched the moth. It was strange because although her eyes showed no emotion or interest, she must have been interested in order to be watching the moth so closely. She couldn't take her eyes off that little bug as it sailed across the room and back again, across and back. And then I thought I saw something in her eyes, some emotion or interest, but I wasn't sure what it was.

The moth settled down, and she went to sleep. I closed my eyes and tried to sleep on the floor with the lights on. I didn't like to sleep in my bed because it was too far from Lynnie, several feet away.

For some reason my mother didn't make me go back to my cot that night. I couldn't sleep deeply so I didn't have a *hatsu-yume.* When it was almost sunrise, I sat up and watched Lynn sleep for a few minutes. Then I took a lawn chair and a blanket down to the empty lot on the corner. I was alone. I thought about getting dressed, but I wasn't expecting to see anybody. I stared east, at the giant tire over the tire store across from the lot. The giant tire looked just like the giant doughnut over the doughnut store on Main Street, except that the tire was black and the doughnut was brown.

It was cold out. Here are the sounds I heard:

1. An old piece of newspaper fluttering in the breeze.
2. A mechanical whirring—I didn't know what was making that sound.
3. A bird chirping.
4. A quick *click-clicking* from a bug light at the tire store.

We lived below what Georgians called the gnat line, meaning all the gnats in the world lived in town with us. My uncle claimed that more bugs lived per square mile in southern Georgia than anywhere in the state. Even in winter, there were bugs.

Those were the only noises.

Here are the things I saw:

1. The tire store—through a window, I saw tires piled inside.
2. A lonely tree outside the store.
3. The gray sky.
4. A crow sitting on the giant tire.

I cried and cried. For a while as I cried I hated my parents, as if it were their fault that Lynn was sick. Then I cried because I loved my parents so much.

Then I didn't feel like crying anymore. I just felt barren, my eyes felt dry. The sky was still gray. Everything was gray, the sky and the store and even my hand when I held it out in front of myself. I wondered if anyone else in history had ever been as sad as I was at that moment. As soon as I wondered that, I knew the answer was yes. The answer was that millions of people had been that sad. For instance, what about the people of the great Incan city of Cuzco, which was ransacked by foreigners in the sixteenth century? I wrote a paper about that for school. And then there were all the millions of people in all the many wars throughout history and throughout the world, and all the millions of people with loved ones killed by millions of other people.

A lot of people had been as sad as I was. Maybe a billion of them had been this sad. As soon as I realized this, I felt like I was no longer a little girl but had become a big girl. What being a big girl meant exactly, I wasn't sure.

I watched a swatch of the sky turn red. The red spread like blood in the sea: red, red, red, and then less and less red, until there was only blue left. I squinted as the sun rose. I must have fallen asleep, because when I woke up, my father was carrying me into the house. Sam walked beside us carrying the lawn chair, which seemed almost as big as he was.

Inside the living room my father laid me on my cot. "She's gone," he said.

17

(Chitra Banerjee Divakaruni, 1956—　)
奇塔·蒂娃卡鲁尼

作者简介

奇塔·蒂娃卡鲁尼（Chitra Banerjee Divakaruni, 1956—　），著名美籍印度裔诗人、小说家。蒂娃卡鲁尼出生于印度，获得印度加尔各答大学（University of Calcutta）学士学位。美国莱特州立大学（Wright State University）硕士学位、加州大学伯克利分校（University of California, Berkeley）博士学位。蒂娃卡鲁尼现居德州，在休士顿大学（University of Houston）教授创意写作课程。

蒂娃卡鲁尼凭借诗歌踏入文坛，早期诗集有《旱金莲的原因》（*The Reason for Nasturtiums*, 1990）、《黑色蜡烛》（*Black Candle*, 1991）、《离开尤巴城》（*Leaving Yuba City*, 1997）等，荣获芭芭拉·戴明纪念奖（Barbara Deming Memorial Award）以及艾伦·金斯伯格奖（Allen Ginsberg Award）等多个奖项。2005 年她凭借短篇小说集《媒妁婚姻》（*Arranged Marriage*, 1995）获得美国图书奖（American Book Award）和湾区书评奖（Bay Area Book Reviewers Award）。她的其他重要作品还有《香料情妇》（*The Mistress of Spices*, 1997）、《我心姐妹》（*Sister of My Heart*, 1999）、《欲望的藤蔓》（*Vine of Desire*, 2002）、《美梦女王》（*Queen of Dreams*, 2004）、《一件美事》（*One Amazing Thing*, 2010）、《幻影宫殿》（*The Palace of Illusions: A Novel*, 2008）、《夹竹桃女孩》（*Oleander Girl*, 2013）和《在我们拜访女神之前》（*Before We Visit the Goddess*, 2016）。其中，《香料情妇》和《我心姐妹》分别被改编为电影和电视剧。《幻影宫殿》和《在我们拜访女神之前》也是畅销书。她也创作青少年小说。《海螺护卫》（*The Conch Bearer*, 2003）、《火与梦之镜》（*The Mirror of*

Fire and Dreaming, 2005）和《影子土地》（*Shadowland,* 2009）组成畅销的海螺兄弟系列（The Brotherhood of the Conch）。印度和美国的双重文化身份使得她的作品总是聚焦于印度经历和当代美国社会。蒂娃·卡鲁尼擅长描绘移民的心理与处境。她的作品情节精巧，感情细腻动人，她的文字揉合东西方传统，兼具印度的乡愁、英诗的优美等特点，富含诗韵。

诗歌《切割太阳》（“Cutting the Sun”）选自诗集《离开尤巴城》。小说《我心姐妹》讲述一对来自印度上层社会的表姐妹在经历世事变故后仍然互相关爱、互相支持的故事。《苏哈》（“Sudha”）选自《我心姐妹》第一章，介绍两个命运相连的表姐妹安珠（Anju）和苏哈（Sudha）的基本信息。《海螺护卫》讲述12岁的印度少年阿南德（Anand）在聪明勇敢的小伙伴尼莎（Nisha）和神秘人Abadhyatta的陪伴下将一颗具有魔力的海螺送回其家乡的冒险故事。《深夜访客》（“The Night Visitor”）选自《海螺护卫》，讲述一个夜晚来到阿南德家的不速之客。

作品选读

Cutting the Sun

By Chitra Banerjee Divakaruni

After Francesco Clemente’s *Indian Miniature #16*

The sun-face looms over me, gigantic-hot, smelling
of iron. Its rays striated,
rasp-red and muscled as the tongues
of iguanas. They are trying to lick away
my name. But I
am not afraid. I hold in my hands
(where did I get them)
enormous blue scissors that are
just the color of sky. I bring
the blades together, like
a song. The rays fall around me

curling a bit, like dried carrot peel. A far sound
in the air—fire
or rain? And when I've cut
all the way to the center of the sun
I see
flowers, flowers, flowers.

Sister of My Heart

Chapter One Sudha
(excerpt)

By Chitra Banerjee Divakaruni

They say in the old tales that the first night after a child is born, the Bidhata Purush comes down to earth himself to decide what its fortune is to be. That is why they bathe babies in sandalwood water and wrap them in soft red malmal, color of luck. That is why they leave sweetmeats by the cradle. Silver-leafed sandesh, dark pantuas floating in golden syrup, jilipis orange as the heart of a fire, glazed with honey-sugar. If the child is especially lucky, in the morning it will all be gone.

"That's because the servants sneak in during the night and eat them," says Anju, giving her head an impatient shake as Abha Pishi oils her hair. This is how she is, my cousin, always scoffing, refusing to believe. But she knows, as I do, that no servant in all of Calcutta would dare eat sweets meant for a god.

The old tales say this also: In the wake of the Bidhata Purush come the demons, for that is the world's nature, good and evil mingled. That is why they leave an oil lamp burning. That is why they place the sacred tulsi leaf under the baby's pillow for protection. In richer households, like the one my mother grew up in, she has told us, they hire a brahmin to sit in the corridor and recite auspicious prayers all night.

"What nonsense," Anju says. "There are no demons."

I am not so sure. Perhaps they do not have the huge teeth, the curved blood-dripping claws and bulging red eyes of our Children's Ramayan Picture Book, but I have a feeling they exist. Haven't I sensed their breath, like slime-black fingers brushing my spine? Later, when we are alone, I will tell Anju this.

But in front of others I am always loyal to her. So I say, bravely, "That's right. Those are just old stories."

It is early evening on our terrace, its bricks overgrown with moss. A time when the sun hangs low on the horizon, half hidden by the pipal trees which line our compound walls all the way down the long driveway to the bolted wrought-iron gates. Our great-grandfather had them planted one hundred years ago to keep the women of his house safe from the gaze of strangers. Abha Pishi, one of our three mothers, has told us this.

Yes, we have three mothers—perhaps to make up for the fact that we have no fathers.

There's Pishi, our widow aunt who threw herself heart-first into her younger brother's household when she lost her husband at the age of eighteen. Dressed in austere white, her graying hair cut close to her scalp in the orthodox style so that the bristly ends tickle my palms when I run my hands over them, she's the one who makes sure we are suitably dressed for school in the one-inch-below-the-knee uniforms the nuns insist on. She finds for us, miraculously, stray pens and inkpots and missing pages of homework. She makes us our favorite dishes: luchis rolled out and fried a puffy golden-brown, potato and cauliflower curry cooked without chilies, thick sweet payesh made from the milk of Budhi-cow, whose owner brings her to our house each morning to be milked under Pishi's stern, miss-nothing stare. On holidays she plaits jasmine into our hair. But most of all Pishi is our fount of information, the one who tells us the stories our mothers will not, the secret, delicious, forbidden tales of our past.

There's Anju's mother, whom I call Gouri Ma, her fine cheekbones and regal forehead hinting at generations of breeding, for she comes from a family as old and respected as that of the Chatterjees, which she married into. Her face is not beautiful in the traditional sense—even I, young as I am, know this. Lines of hardship are etched around her mouth and on her forehead, for she was the one who shouldered the burden of keeping the family safe on that thunderclap day eight years ago when she received news of our fathers' deaths. But her eyes, dark and endless-deep—they make me think of Kalodighi, the enormous lake behind the country mansion our family used to own before Anju and I were born. When Gouri Ma smiles at me with her eyes, I stand up straighter. I want to be noble and brave, just like her.

Lastly (I use this word with some guilt), there's my own mother, Nalini. Her skin is still golden, for though she's a widow my mother is careful to apply turmeric paste to her face each day. Her perfect-shaped lips glisten red from pain, which she loves to chew—mostly for the color it leaves on her mouth, I think. She laughs often, my mother, especially when her friends come for tea and talk. It is a glittery, tinkling sound, like jeweled ankle bells, people say, though I myself feel it is more like a thin glass struck with a spoon. Her cheek feels as soft as the lotus flower she's named after on those rare occasions when she presses her face to mine. But more often when she looks at me a frown ridges her forehead between eyebrows beautiful as wings. Is it from worry or displeasure? I can never tell. Then she remembers that frowns cause age lines and smoothes it away with a finger.

Now Pishi stops oiling Anju's hair to give us a wicked smile. Her voice grows low and shivery, the way it does when she's telling ghost stories. "They're listening, you know. The demons. And they don't like little eight-year-old girls talking like this. Just wait till tonight... "

Because I am scared I interrupt her with the first thought that comes into my head. "Pishi Ma, tell no, did the sweets disappear for us?"

Sorrow moves like smoke-shadow over Pishi's face. I can see that she would like to make up another of those outrageous tales that we so love her to tell, full of magic glimmer and hoping. But finally she says, her voice flat, "No, Sudha. You weren't so lucky."

I know this already. Anju and I have heard the whispers. Still, I must ask one more time.

"Did you see anything that night?" I ask. Because she was the one who stayed with us the night of our birth while our mothers lay in bed, still in shock from the terrible telegram which had sent them both into early labor that morning. Our mothers, lying in beds they would never again share with their husbands. My mother weeping, her beautiful hair tangling about her swollen face, punching at a pillow until it burst, spilling cotton stuffing white as grief. Gouri Ma, still and silent, staring up into a darkness which pressed upon her like the responsibilities she knew no one else in the family could take on.

To push them from my mind I ask urgently, "Did you at least hear something?"

Pishi shakes her head in regret. "Maybe the Bidhata Purush doesn't come for girl-babies." In her kindness she leaves the rest unspoken, but I've heard the whispers often enough to complete it in my head. For girl-babies who are so much bad luck that they cause their fathers to die even before they are born.

Anju scowls, and I know that as always she can see into my thoughts with the X-ray vision of her fiercely loving eyes. "Maybe there's no Bidhata Purush either," she states and yanks her hair from Pishi's hands though it is only half-braided. She ignores Pishi's scolding shouts and stalks to her room, where she will slam the door.

But I sit very still while Pishi's fingers rub the hibiscus oil into my scalp, while she combs away knots with the long, soothing rhythm I have known since the beginning of memory. The sun is a deep, sad red, and I can smell, faint on the evening air, wood smoke. The pavement dwellers are lighting their cooking fires. I've seen them many times when Singhji, our chauffeur, drives us to school: the mother in a worn green sari bent over a spice-grinding stone, the daughter watching the baby, keeping him from falling into the gutter. The father is never there. Maybe he is running up a platform in Howrah station in his red turban, his shoulders knotted from carrying years of trunks and bedding rolls, crying out, "Coolie chahiye, want a coolie, memsaab?" Or maybe, like my father, he too is dead.

Whenever I thought this my eyes would sting with sympathy, and if by chance Ramur Ma, the vinegary old servant woman who chaperones us everywhere, was not in the car, I'd beg Singhji to stop so I could hand the girl a sweet out of my lunch box. And he always did.

The Conch Bearer

The Night Visitor

By Chitra Banerjee Divakaruni

It was dark by the time Anand got off work, and he was very angry. Haru was supposed to let him go by 4 p.m., but he often found an excuse to keep Anand longer. Today he had claimed that Anand had not wiped the tables properly and made him do them all over again.

Anand had scrubbed the pocked wood of the tables furiously, biting his lip to make himself stay silent. Arguing, he knew, would only earn him a slap. Now he was going to be late for the market! Today was payday, and he had promised his mother that he would stop at the vegetable bazaar. For days now they'd had nothing to eat except potatoes and white radish boiled with rice, and he was tired of it. He had hoped to get a bunch of fresh, crisp spinach, or some sheem beans to fry up with chilies. But by now most of the pavement vendors would be gone. If only I had the power to run my hands over the tables and make them new and shiny! he thought. But no, if I knew how to work that kind of changing magic, I'd start with Haru's black heart.

Bone tired though he was, Anand ran all the way to the vegetable market. Just as he had feared, the bazaar was deserted, the ground littered with wilted cabbage leaves and banana peels. Only the big stall with the neon lights, the one that charged extra for everything and had a big red sign that said NO BARGAINING, was still open. Anand walked up to it warily, knowing that most of the items there were beyond his budget. But maybe there would be something not so fresh. Then his eyes were caught by the pile of mangoes. Mangoes in winter! Where had the storekeeper found them? They were plump and soft and just the right ripeness, their skins a glowing orange streaked with red. How long had it been since Anand had eaten a mango? He swallowed, imagining the sweet juice that would fill his mouth when he took a big bite, and asked how much they were.

"Two rupees each," said the storekeeper in a bored voice. Obviously, he didn't think the ragged boy standing in front of him could afford the price.

Anand opened his mouth to protest. Why, the storekeeper was charging twice as much as what the pavement vendors would have charged! But he said nothing. The man would only shrug insolently and tell him to go elsewhere. He hesitated, then took out the meager bundle of rupee notes he had tucked into his waistband and peeled off two of them. He carefully picked the biggest, fattest mango, hefting it in his palm. Wouldn't Meera be amazed when he showed up with this beauty!

By now it was late and windier than ever, and Anand had to keep his head lowered to avoid the dust and debris flying through the air. Thankfully, he didn't feel cold. Why, he thought in surprise, he hadn't felt cold all day, not since he gave the old man his tea! He hoped the old man had found a place to shelter himself for the night. It looked like it was going to be a rough one.

The streets were strangely empty as Anand made his way home. Was it because it was dinnertime, or was it this unpleasant wind? The small businesses that lined the street—the printing presses and machine shops—had turned off their lights, padlocked their gates, and sent their employees home. With a brief pang of envy, Anand imagined them safe in their warm, lighted houses, listening to songs on the radio or sitting around a table, eating a hot meal, maybe a chicken curry with rice. After dinner the children would crowd around their father, begging for a story. The mother would bring bowls of sweet milk pudding from the kitchen. That was how it had been with his family, too, before...

Anand shook his head to clear the memories. What use was it to long for what was no longer there? He'd better concentrate on getting home quickly. He'd have to start the cooking because Mother wouldn't be home until much later, and Meera couldn't be trusted to light the kerosene stove on her own. She couldn't do much of anything since the bad-luck accident, that's how he thought of it, had happened to her. He hoped she had remembered to wash the plates and fill the big earthen pitcher with water from the tenement's tube well. Sometimes when he came home, she would still be sitting on her bedding with a vacant look on her face, and he knew she hadn't moved from there since morning. But he never had the heart to scold her.

He passed the cigarette shop, surprised to see that it, too, was closed. Before today, no matter how late he had been in coming back from work, it had always been open, its shiny radio blaring hits from the latest Hindi movies. There was always a crowd of young men around it, joking and jostling around, smoking beedis or chewing on betel leaves and spitting out the red juice wherever they pleased. But today, with its shutters pulled down and locked, the shop looked abandoned and eerie, and Anand walked past it as quickly as he could.

Right around then he became aware that someone was following him. He wasn't sure how he knew it. There were no sounds—not that he would have heard footsteps in all this wind. Nor was there anyone behind him when he forced himself to whirl around and look. The street was empty and dark—a streetlight had burned out—and Anand realized that he was at the same crossing where Meera had been when the accident that had turned her strange and silent had occurred. He pushed the thought away from him with a shiver and quickened his steps. There's no one behind me, no one, he said to himself over and over, and, under that, Mustn't fall, mustn't fall. Because then, whatever was behind him would catch up.

There's no one behind me. Mustn't fall.

He was running now. There was a fog all around him, obscuring the shapes of the shacks and turning the alleys into unfamiliar, yawning tunnels. His foot caught on something, and he went sprawling. The mango fell from his hand and rolled into the darkness. Oh no! Not the mango he'd spent two whole hard-earned rupees on! He scrabbled desperately for it, but felt nothing but asphalt and dirt. He wanted to search more, but something told him it wasn't safe to delay any longer. Where had the fog come from, anyway? How could it be windy and foggy at the same time? Was this his street? Where was his house, then? He looked around wildly, not recognizing anything. Help me! He called inside his head, not knowing to whom he called. Help! He was ashamed to be acting this way, like a child. The fog in front of him thinned for a moment. Ah! There was his shack with its warped tin door! He had never been so happy to see it. He knocked frantically on the door, calling to Meera to open up, hurry, hurry. He heard her unsteady steps, then the bolt sliding across. He threw himself inside, slammed the door behind him, and bolted it again. He leaned his back against the door, his heart pounding. Meera stared at him, a startled look on her face.

He forced himself to smile because he didn't want to scare her. "Don't worry, Meera," he said, though his throat was so dry he could barely speak. "Everything's all right."

Then he heard the knocking. Tap, tap, tong. Someone was hitting the door with... a stick? A piece of metal? He could feel the vibration against his shoulder blades. He jumped away from the door and looked around for a weapon, something with which to defend himself and his sister. In the flickering light of the small oil lamp, he could see nothing except an old bonti, its blade dulled from years of cutting vegetables. Somehow he didn't think it would stop whoever was outside.

Then he heard the voice, deep and rusty, as if it had been at the bottom of a river for a long time.

"Anand," it said. "Let me in."

Anand didn't know how long he stood in the middle of the room, eyes squinched shut, heart pounding madly. But the knocking didn't stop, as he had hoped. There it was again. Tap, tap, tong.

"Go away," he whispered through dry lips.

"Let me in, Anand," the voice said. "I won't hurt you."

Right! Anand thought. That's what all the evil beings in his storybooks said, the monsters and witches, the dakinis who drank blood.

"I don't believe you! I don't even know who you are!" he shouted. "Go away now, before I yell for the neighbors."

"Your neighbors won't come. They won't even hear you over the wind. And even if they did, they'd be too scared, because of the killing—"

"How did you know about the... killing?" Anand asked, astonished, stumbling over the word. No one in the neighborhood spoke of it, not out loud like this, anyway. Like Anand, they all called it "the accident", as though renaming it could make it into something less dangerous.

The voice didn't answer his question. "In any case, you do know who I am," it said instead with a little laugh. "I'm the old man to whom you gave your tea."

Perhaps it was the laugh, or the memory of the old man's hand, light as a bird's foot in his hand, but Anand felt less scared. He wasn't completely convinced, though.

"Why did you follow me home?" he asked.

"Don't you know? You called for me—for us—and we came."

"I never called anyone," Anand said. Then he added, suspiciously, "What do you want from me?"

"Did you not call for help a little while ago?" the old man said.

"But that was in my head—"

"Exactly," said the man, a smile in his voice. "But you're right. I do want something. And in return I have something to offer you. But I can't discuss these things with a closed door between us. Please?"

Wondering if he was making a terrible mistake, Anand motioned to Meera to get behind him. What if it's a trick?

A voice inside him whispered. Ignoring it, he raised a trembling hand and unbolted the door. It was only when the door had creaked open on its hinges that he remembered that the man had said "we came."

But thank heavens, the old man was alone. Perhaps I misheard him, Anand thought. Something about him was different, though. Was it Anand's imagination, or did he seem straighter and taller? His white hair and beard glowed eerily in the dim light from the lamp as he stepped into the room, and there was a brightness in his eyes. The cloth bag was slung over his shoulder.

"Thank you," he said with a slight bow. "The wind was becoming rather unpleasant." As Anand watched, he walked to each corner of the room and made the same strange motion with his hand that Anand had seen him make earlier. Then he sat down on the mat the boy had spread out for him.

"It's very unusual for it to be so windy here," Anand said, mostly because he didn't know what else to say. He wondered if it had been the old man whom he had felt following him earlier. Somehow he didn't think so. The old man was strange, but Anand didn't feel scared when he looked at him. If anything, he felt happy. That was odd. Why should he feel happy looking at this ragged stranger whom he'd never met before today?

"I'm afraid I'm partly responsible for that the old man was saying with a rueful grin.

What do you mean? Did you... make... the wind happen?" As soon as he said it, Anand felt stupid. People didn't make winds happen.

But the old man didn't seem to think it was a stupid question. "I didn't," he replied. "Someone who wanted to stop me did. But before I explain things, is it possible to get a bite to eat? I'm starving. Only had a glass of tea all day, you know, and a few pooris!"

Anand jumped to his feet, embarrassed. "Of course! I'll start the rice and lentil stew right away.

That's all we have, I'm afraid." He hunted around in the corner for the pot. Thankfully Meera had remembered to wash it today. He glanced at Meera, who was unusually quiet. She had crept close to the old man as he talked and was watching him intently. This surprised him. Ever since the killing, she'd been terrified of strangers, and on the few occasions when they had neighbors visiting them, she had curled up on her pallet in the far corner of the room, with the bedclothes drawn over her head.

Anand lit the stove, threw a few handfuls of rice and lentils into the pot, and added water, salt, turmeric, and chili powder. In twenty minutes, it would form a bubbly stew. Once again, he wished he'd been able to pick up a few vegetables. And that mango! If he hadn't dropped it, he could have cut each of them a slice to eat after dinner. He wanted to kick himself for being so clumsy.

The lamp in the corner flickered and the flame grew small. Anand could tell it was running out of oil. He reached for the bottle to refill it, then remembered that it was empty. He'd been supposed to buy some oil, too, on his way home, but the wind and the fog and the fear had driven it out of his mind.

The lamp wavered and went out. Now there were only the blue flames from the kerosene stove.

"Maybe I can help," the old man said. He rummaged in his bag and came up with the stub of a candle. It wasn't much, Anand thought as he lighted it, but at least it would last through dinner.

"I've a couple of other things here that you may be able to use," the man said. He held up a small yellow squash and a handful of green beans, and Anand thankfully chopped them up and threw them into the pot. The room began to fill with a delicious smell. As though, Anand thought, he'd put lots of expensive spices into the pot. They sat in the small golden circle of light thrown out by the candle stub, waiting for the lentils to cook. As they waited, the old man told them his story.

18
(Don Lee, 1959—　)
多恩·李

作者简介

多恩·李（Don Lee, 1959—　），美籍韩裔小说家。李是第三代美籍韩裔，在日本东京和韩国首尔度过童年时代，本科毕业于加州大学洛杉矶分校（University of California, Los Angeles），后获得爱默生学院（Emerson College）写作硕士学位（MFA）。多恩·李目前任教于坦普尔大学（Temple University），并且创办网上文学期刊 *TINGE*，同时也是《佐治亚评论》（*Georgia Review*）、《新英格兰评论》（*New England Review*）和文学杂志与出版社协会（CLMP）等文学期刊的顾问。

李的作品有短篇小说集《黄色》（*Yellow*, 2001），长篇小说《起源之国》（*Country of Origin,* 2005）、《破坏和毁灭》（*Wrack and Ruin*, 2008)、《集体》（*The Collective,* 2012）和《我们面前的孤独》（*Lonesome Lies Before Us: A Novel*, 2017）。李荣获欧·亨利短篇小说奖和手推车奖（Pushcart Prize）。短篇小说集《黄色》讲述一个虚构小镇上几个美国亚裔青年的故事，荣获苏·考夫曼奖（Sue Kaufman Prize for First Fiction）；小说《起源之国》获得埃德加奖（Edgar Award for Best First Novel）和美国图书奖（American Book Award）；《集体》荣获亚裔 / 太平洋美国文学奖（Asian/Pacific American Award for Literature ）。

小说《集体》是一部关于友谊、艺术、背叛与种族的成长小说，讲述亚裔作家埃里克·赵（Eric Cho）、画家杰西卡·蔡（Jessica Tsai）和小说家约书亚·尹（Joshua Yoon）从本科到研究生期间的友情与成长，探讨艺术梦想的追求、理想与现实的差距、亚裔身份的困惑等严肃主题。第一章选自《集体》，记叙才华横溢的小说家约书亚（Joshua）的自杀。

作品选读

The Collective

Chapter 1

By Don Lee

There's a road in Sudbury, on the outskirts of Boston, called Waterborne. Famous for the great blue herons that nest there, the road cuts through the immediate floodplain of the Sudbury River. It's lined with red maple, white oak, and dead ash yellows, long ago decimated by a virus. It curves and dips, wending through hills and an alluvial marsh, rising once again past meadows and farmland, then descending in a series of hairpin turns. It's a beautiful road—smooth, continuous, unsullied by houses or businesses—and therefore popular with bikers, runners, and drivers in a hurry. To no one's surprise, hardly a month goes by without some sort of accident on Waterborne.

It was around three o'clock on a Saturday afternoon in late September 2008, partly cloudy and unseasonably warm at seventy-six degrees, the tincture of fall edging the flora. Joshua Yoon, thirty-eight, was on his afternoon run on Waterborne, hugging the road's left edge so he could watch for approaching cars. He had intended nothing for that day. The week before, in fact, he had arrived upon the method he'd use, suggested by a group on the Internet: he was going to put a clear plastic bag over his head, fasten the bottom of it around his neck with Velcro, open two canisters that would pump helium through tubes into the bag, and within minutes he would be unconscious and dead. Painless, quick, and efficient.

Once you decide to kill yourself, studies have said, there is clarity. You become focused. Your mood brightens. You're blessed with a profound state of well-being. These sorts of decisions, momentous as they are, come willy-nilly. They begin as passing whims, an indulgence of reverie, and then, unbidden, they sharpen and coalesce within you, and you begin to fixate, and plan. You pay your bills, you write letters of instruction, you update your will, make funeral arrangements, buy an urn, label all your keys. There are only two things left to be determined—how and when.

You have choices. You feel relief and joy.

This is not to say that Joshua was entirely lucid then. He was taking pills, so many pills. He was on antidepressants, anti-anxiety meds, mood stabilizers, sleeping pills, and painkillers, their effects aggravated by a recent experiment with robo tripping, something he'd learned teenagers were doing, spinning a bottle of Robitussin centrifugally on a string to distill pure DXM to the top. He was high, perhaps even hallucinating—not that it mitigates anything.

He was running on a stretch of Waterborne where drivers are slingshot out of a curve and accelerate. He heard a car coming, and, rather than keeping to the edge of the road, he drifted a few feet onto it.

Did he really mean to do it, to be hit by someone and killed? Could he have been so callous, willing to burden an anonymous driver, through no fault of his own, with a lifetime of trauma?

To this day, I am not sure. I go over and over it, and still I don't know. Maybe Joshua, my old friend, had only wanted to feel the whoosh and rev of the car as it went by, the inches between death and continuance, how arbitrary the sway can be between the two. Maybe he had yawed drunkenly into the car's path without volition or meditation. Yet the impulse had probably come across Joshua before, more than once, running on that road, to step in front of a speeding car, ending everything right then and there. Whatever the case, there was a witness, a driver approaching from the other direction, who claimed she saw Joshua veer abruptly and unmistakably into the path of the car.

The timing of it, the multiple, trivial interruptions that could have prevented any of it from happening: a stoplight, a phone call, a detour for ice cream, a playmate needing a ride home. A few seconds would have made all the difference.

A few seconds before the car came out of the turn, the little girl in the backseat, three months shy of her fourth birthday, had unbuckled herself and climbed out of her safety chair to pick up a book she had dropped. Her father was driving too fast, a bit impaired himself, having had a few drinks earlier at lunch. He disliked seat belts and would have eschewed them altogether if not for the insistent warning beeps. That day, he had compromised by clicking in the lap belt and flipping the shoulder strap behind his back. He turned around to yell at the girl to get back in her chair right this minute. Then he glanced around and saw Joshua, ten feet in front of him on the road, too late to do anything, but swerving on instinct to avoid hitting him head-on. The car swiped out Joshua's legs at an angle, crushing one of them and snagging the other on something, maybe the bumper, so his foot disarticulated at the ankle, much like twisting a chicken bone off at the joint. The impact vaulted his body into the air in deranged cartwheels, and the car itself flipped and rolled in the other direction, tumbling repeatedly and brutally, until it squashed to a rest against a stand of white oak. By then, the man and the little girl were slowly dying inside the car. Joshua was luckier, if one could call it that.

He landed on his head on the asphalt, and the blunt-force trauma to his brain killed him instantly.

19

(Thrity Umrigar, 1961—)
斯瑞迪 · 里加

作者简介

斯瑞迪 · 里加（Thrity Umrigar, 1961— ），美籍印度裔记者、小说家、评论家。里加出生于印度孟买，21 岁时移民美国。里加获得孟买大学（Bombay University）学士学位、俄亥俄州立大学（Ohio State University）硕士学位和肯特州立大学（Kent State University）英语博士学位。她做过记者，目前在凯斯西储大学（Case Western Reserve University）任教，同时也为《华盛顿邮报》、《赫芬顿邮报》和《波士顿环球报》（*The Boston Globe*）等报纸撰写文章。

里加著有小说《孟买时间》（*Bombay Time*, 2001）、《我们之间的空间》（*The Space Between Us*, 2006）、《如果今天是甜蜜的》（*If Today Be Sweet*, 2007）、《天堂的重量》（*The Weight of Heaven*, 2009）、《我们发现的世界》（*The World We Found*, 2012）、《故事时刻》（*The Story Hour*, 2014）和《每个人的儿子》（*Everybody's Son*, 2017）与回忆录《清晨的宠儿：印度童年回忆录》（*First Darling of the Morning: Selected Memories of an Indian Childhood*, 2004）。她的小说出版后颇受好评，被翻译成多种语言，在超过 15 个国家出版。《我们之间的空间》入围笔会 / 超越边界奖（PEN/Beyond Margins Award），回忆录《清晨的宠儿：印度童年回忆录》进入米兰达作家协会奖决选名单。斯瑞迪 · 里加获得多项荣誉，包括克利夫兰艺术奖（Cleveland Arts Prize）、朗姆达文学奖（Lambda Literary award）和赛斯 · 罗森伯格奖（Seth Rosenberg Prize）。斯瑞迪 · 里加受到约翰斯坦 · 贝克、海明威、弗吉尼亚 · 伍尔夫和威廉 · 福克纳等文学巨匠的影响。她的作品以印度和美国为背景，既探讨家庭、爱、死亡等主题，也探讨种族、性别、阶级、宗教等话题。她的作品文字流畅生动，可读性强，人物刻画栩栩如生。

小说《我们之间的空间》以印度孟买为背景，中上层社会的富孀赛拉（Sera）和下层的贫苦女佣皮马（Bhima）的故事交叉进行，阶级和性别的影响、传统与现代的碰撞在小说中上演，故事情节跌宕起伏，引人入胜。此处选自小说《我们之间的空间》第一章，本章讲述年逾花甲的印度女佣皮马面对未婚先孕的外孙女玛雅（Maya）的复杂心理活动。散文《天使在美国》（"Angels in America"）最初发表于 1994 年 12 月 25 日的《阿克伦灯塔杂志》（*Akron Beacon Journal*），文章讲述作者在美国过圣诞节的经历，指出美国民众就是善良、仁慈、友善的天使。

作品选读

The Space Between Us

Chapter One

(excerpt)

By Thrity Umrigar

Although it is dawn, inside Bhima's heart it is dusk.

Rolling onto her left side on the thin cotton mattress on the floor, she sits up abruptly, as she does every morning. She lifts one bony hand over her head in a yawn and a stretch, and a strong, mildewy smell wafts from her armpit and assails her nostrils. For an idle moment she sits at the edge of the mattress with her callused feet flat on the mud floor, her knees bent, and her head resting on her folded arms. In that time she is almost at rest, her mind thankfully blank and empty of the trials that await her today and the next day and the next... To prolong this state of mindless grace, she reaches absently for the tin of chewing tobacco that she keeps by her bedside. She pushes a wad into her mouth, so that it protrudes out of her fleshless face like a cricket ball.

Bhima's idyll is short-lived. In the faint, delicate light of a new day, she makes out Maya's silhouette as she stirs on the mattress on the far left side of their hut. The girl is mumbling in her sleep, making soft, whimpering sounds, and despite herself, Bhima feels her heart soften and dissolve, the way it used to when she breast-fed Maya's mother, Pooja, all those years ago. Propelled by Maya's puppylike sounds, Bhima gets up with a grunt from the mattress and makes her way to where her granddaughter lies asleep. But in the second that it takes to cross the small hut, something shifts in Bhima's heart, so that the milky, maternal feeling from a moment ago is replaced by that hard, merciless feeling of rage that has lived within her since several weeks ago. She stands towering over the sleeping girl, who is now snoring softly, blissfully unaware of the pinpoint anger in her grandmother's eyes as she stares at the slight swell of Maya's belly.

One swift kick, Bhima says to herself, one swift kick to the belly, followed by another and another, and it will all be over. Look at her sleeping there, like a shameless whore, as if she has not a care in the world. As if she has not turned my life upside down. Bhima's right foot twitches with anticipation; the muscles in her calf tense as she lifts her foot a few inches off the ground. It would be so easy. And compared to what some other grandmother might do to Maya—a quick shove down an open well, a kerosene can and a match, a sale to a brothel—this would be so humane. This way, Maya would live, would continue going to college and choose a life different from what Bhima had always known. That was how it was supposed to be, how it had been, until this dumb cow of a girl, this girl with the big heart and, now, a big belly, went and got herself pregnant.

Maya lets out a sudden loud snort, and Bhima's poised foot drops to the floor. She crouches down next to the sleeping girl to shake her by the shoulders and wake her up. When Maya was still going to college, Bhima allowed her to sleep in as late as possible, made gaajar halwa for her every Sunday, gave her the biggest portions of dinner every night. If Serabai ever gave Bhima a treat—a Cadbury's chocolate, say, or that white candy with pistachios that came from Iran—she'd save it to bring it home for Maya, though, truth to tell, Serabai usually gave her a portion for Maya anyway. But ever since Bhima has learned of her granddaughter's shame, she has been waking the girl up early. For the last several Sundays there has been no gaajar halwa, and Maya has not asked for her favorite dessert. Earlier this week, Bhima even ordered the girl to stand in line to fill their two pots at the communal tap. Maya had protested at that, her hand unconsciously rubbing her belly, but Bhima had looked away and said the people in the Basti would soon enough find out about her dishonor anyway, so why hide it?

Maya rolls over in her sleep, so that her face is inches away from where Bhima is squatting. Her young, fat hand finds Bhima's thin, crumpled one, and she nestles against it, holding it between her chin and her chest. A single strand of drool falls on Bhima's captive hand. The older woman feels herself soften. Maya has been like this from the time she was a baby—needy, affectionate, trusting. Despite all the sorrow she has experienced in her young life, Maya has not lost her softness and innocence. With her other free hand, Bhima strokes the girl's lush, silky hair, so different from her own scanty hair.

The sound of a transistor radio playing faintly invades the room, and Bhima swears under her breath. Usually, by the time Jaiprakash turns his radio on, she is already in line at the water tap. That means she is late this morning. Serabai will be livid. This stupid, lazy girl has delayed her. Bhima pulls her hand brusquely away from Maya, not caring whether the movement wakes her up. But the girl sleeps on. Bhima jumps to her feet, and as she does, her left hip lets out a loud pop. She stands still for a moment, waiting for the wave of pain that follows the pop, but today is a good day. No pain.

Bhima picks up the two copper pots and opens the front door. She bends so that she can exit from the low door and then shuts it behind her. She does not want the lewd young men who live in the slum to leer at her sleeping granddaughter as they pass by. One of them is probably the father of the baby... She shakes her head to clear the dark, snakelike thoughts that invade it.

Angels in America

By Thrity Umrigar

When I first came to this country as a young student, I had numbers on my mind. Test scores. GPAs. How many beers I could drink at one time.

But as I look back on those years, I realize that those are no longer the numbers I am proud of.

The number of which I am now the most proud is the number of Christmases I have spent in America. Because I have never spent one alone.

See, when you move to a country you have never even visited before, weird fears cross your mind. Like: What if everybody at Ohio State goes home for the holidays and I'm the only person left on the whole campus?

Like I said, weird. But real.

However, there was one thing I hadn't counted on. And that was America.

Land of friendly strangers and large-hearted people. Where a stranger can become a friend in a heartbeat. Where a baby-boom generation of gypsies make and create new families wherever they go. Where a new generation, living away from hometowns and biological families, has introduced a new concept—that of choosing your own families.

I am happy to say that over the years, I have belonged to several families. Being in America has changed my concept of what family is—from the feudal concept of family-is-what-you-were born-into, to the post-modern definition of family-is-who-you-chose-to-spend-your-time-with.

This is not to say that I am not close to my family of origin. If anything, getting older only makes me appreciate them more than I ever did in my angst-filled teen-age years.

But America has allowed me to keep adding new members to my family.

And over the years, I have spent my Christmases with my different families.

My first few Christmases, while I was a student at Ohio State, I spent in a small farmhouse in rural Georgia. I had been in America for only four months and here I was, a child of the city from India, romping around in the woods and eating grits for breakfast.

How did that happen, you ask?

The answer is—America. For what is America but the endless opportunity to re-create yourself?

Georgia was the beginning of a long journey that finally ended with my becoming an American citizen. It was in Georgia that I first realized that life's supply of friends was not limited but as abundant as the leaves on a maple tree. It was there that I realized that it is possible to have more than one home in this world. It was there that I learned that it was my decision whether to live in my new home, America, as a guest or as a family member.

I went to Georgia at the invitation of my friend Peggy, whom I had met on my second day at Ohio State when I stopped her to ask for street directions. We had talked, walked, exchanged phone numbers, had a few beers together several days later, and stayed friends. Then four months later, I went to Peggy's family home with her.

Good thing, too. Peggy's family is black and after spending 10 days with these good, hard-working, honest, country folks, I'll never believe another racist stereotype in my life. Not that I was likely to anyway, but racism is a virus. Best to keep getting your immunity shots against it.

One stereotype was true. Peggy's family did live on the wrong side of the tracks. Despite working hard all their lives, her parents were poor. Still, you'd never know that if you saw the gifts they bought me for Christmas. Not just her parents, but her whole extended family. I was so choked up, I could hardly manage a thank-you.

The funny thing is, I can't remember any of those gifts now. Because I'm still awe-struck by the biggest one they gave me—the gift of affection, of inclusion.

The gift of family.

One night stands out in my mind from those days in Georgia. We were driving down a long country road on a moonlit winter's night. There was a lull in the conversation and John Lennon's Happy Xmas (War is Over) came on the radio. I remember listening to that song in silence, as the beautiful, still, night scenery flew past. A sweet, sad, peace came over me. It was one of those moments you know you will always remember, even while you are in it.

Fast forward a few years. Peggy now lived in California and I was working at a small paper near Cleveland. A colleague from work asked me to spend Christmas Day with her family. Not knowing what I was agreeing to, I said yes.

I felt as if I had stumbled into the movie *The Sound of Music*, as I walked into that living room. Jokes, quips and laughter flew across that room, which was filled with exuberant, laughing, screaming adults and children. My friend and her many siblings were hugging and yelling, "Merry Christmas," to each other. Little children were squealing with joy as they were tossed in the air. My friend's mother, trying to control her brood, was as helpless as a conductor trying to tame an orchestra gone mad.

I watched in amazement, with an only-child's envy and wonder, while these high-spirited people renewed their family ties and caught up with each other's lives. But I barely had time to think of this. Because the roaring, cheerful beast spread its tentacles and drew me into its fold. Suddenly, I, too, was talking at the top of my voice, laughing loudly, swapping quips. The distance between me and them collapsed, as they spun the easy webs of friendship around me.

Soon, the clamor of the children to open their gifts reached its crescendo. And the colorful boxes, with their smiling bows, begged to be opened.

At first, the gift-opening was slow, polite and dignified. But soon a happy chaos took over. Siblings tossed their gift boxes to each other like footballs. There was loud laughter over the gag gifts. There were "Oohs" and "Aahs" over the good ones.

The pile of gift wrap under my own feet grew. All of my friend's siblings had bought me something. And her mother had knitted me a beautiful blue and pink winter scarf. Each time I wear that scarf today, the memories of that Christmas come rushing past.

Finally, it was time to unwrap my friend's gift. I gasped as I saw Bruce Springsteen's five-record box set. With tears in my eyes, I looked up. I saw my friend grinning broadly at my obvious surprise and pleasure.

For Christmas dinner we sat at a beautiful table that was big enough to have served King Arthur and his knights. And as I eyed the twinkling glasses, the sparkling wine, the plates groaning with food, I thought for a brief and shining moment about Camelot.

Other Christmases also stand out in my mind. I remember one because of its simplicity, in contrast to the boisterous Christmases I had been used to.

It was after I started working at the *Beacon Journal*. I accepted the invitation of a friend who was away from home herself and had invited me to a meal with herself and her teen-aged son. When I got to her house, she was in a frazzled mood. Dinner wasn't ready, her son was in a grumpy mood, and she was feeling the pressure of making Christmas perfect.

"Hey, it's only me, remember?" I reminded my friend. "You don't have to stand on ceremony with me."

She visibly relaxed.

Well, dinner turned to be fine, her son stunned us both with his charming table manners and Christmas was perfect after all. We sat at a beautiful table chatting about everything from James Agee to The Three Stooges to what our individual families were doing on that day.

After dinner, my friend suggested we go to a movie. I agreed, certain that the three of us would be the only people at the theater on Christmas Day. But when we got there, the large crowd of moviegoers, surprised me.

And, suddenly, standing in that crowd of strangers, I felt an incredible sense of community. All those people—a counter-culture band of nomads, misfits and mavericks—were redefining the traditional rituals of Christmas in their own, silent way.

This wasn't the Christmas found on Hallmark cards—the Christmas of snowy woods and fat, jolly old men in red suits. This popcorn-buying Christmas crowd resembled not the old-fashioned, quaint citizens of Norman Rockwell's America, but the cosmopolitan, eclectic, mad-cap citizens of David Letterman's America. This scene said as much about the diversity and easy casualness of contemporary America as did anything else.

Two years ago, I celebrated Christmas with the family of another friend. There was a twinge of melancholy woven into the day. My friend's mother, a brave, feisty, gruff woman, was dying of cancer. All her children had chipped in to buy her a gold ring.

I watched the woman's weathered face as she opened the box and saw her gift. Her face shone as brightly as the ring, with pride and satisfaction.

All around her stood her children, their faces shiny with love, their eyes saying all the things their lips could not. They were saying good-bye and they were saying thank-you—two of the hardest things to say.

Despite the hair that she lost to chemotherapy, despite the weight she had lost and the pain she was in, I know my friend's mother had a good Christmas—her last. The ring on her finger, a symbol of her children's love, was all the wealth she needed.

Later on, I gave my friend's mother my Christmas gift. It was a stone angel.

I like to give angels to people. But I have a preference. I like my angels to be cracked. Or chipped. Just damaged slightly, in some way.

I know this sounds strange. Let me explain. See, perfection bewilders me. Being human, I only understand humanity, not divinity. Angels as ethereal creatures with wings and harps mean little to me. I want my angels to be human, to tread on the same mortal Earth that I do. I want my angels to earn their wings, not be born with them. I want them to try to fly as high as they can, to fall flat on their face, and then, to try again. I prefer my angels cracked.

I had not been able to find a cracked angel for her. But after my friend's mom died in 1993, her family gave me back the angel in remembrance of her. Within days of getting it back, the angel fell off my mantelpiece. It is now cracked.

Last Christmas, my friend's family was subdued. The old woman's absence was a strong presence during dinner. Conversations revolved around her favorite recipes, childhood family stories, funny things she had said during her life. The children seemed a little lost, as if a compass had been misplaced.

All that day, I wished I had a cracked angel for all of them. To remind them that their mother had led a good, brave life and had now earned her wings. To console them that they had all done their part in lighting her way to heaven.

And to tell them, that in their silent sorrow and loss, they were actually marking the true spirit of Christmas.

Because, after all, isn't it for a cracked angel who lived, suffered and died 2,000 years ago that we mark this Christmas Day?

20

(Daniyal Mueeenuddin, 1963—　)

戴尼亚尔·穆伊努丁

作者简介

戴尼亚尔·穆伊努丁（Daniyal Mueenuddin, 1963—　），美籍巴基斯坦裔作家。父亲是巴基斯坦裔的印度公务员，母亲是第二代美籍挪威裔，任《华盛顿邮报》记者。穆伊努丁出生于洛杉矶，在巴基斯坦度过童年，13 岁时父母离异，他随母亲移民美国。达特茅斯学院（Dartmouth College）毕业后，他返回巴基斯坦帮父亲料理家族农场。1993 年，他返回美国就读于耶鲁法学院（Yale Law School），就读其间担任《耶鲁国际法期刊》主编。穆伊努丁毕业后在国际人权组织短暂工作，后从事律师和企业法律顾问工作。后来，他厌倦律师工作，立志成为作家，于是攻读亚利桑那大学（University of Arizona）创意写作硕士课程，于 2004 年获得学位。

他的第一部短篇小说集《别人的房间，别样的风景》（*In Other Rooms, Other Wonders*, 2009）斩获多个奖项，包括 2010 年英联邦作家奖（Commonwealth Writers' Prize），并进入 2009 年的国家图书奖和普利策奖决选名单。这部小说集被翻译成 16 种语言。他的作品受短篇小说巨匠契科夫的影响，善于运用细节来刻画人物。这些短篇小说呈现一个从传统向现代过渡的巴基斯坦，生动展现巴基斯坦的风土人情和社会百态、逐渐瓦解的封建制度与西化的生活方式的碰撞、日渐式微的封建贵族与崛起的商业群体，巴基斯坦底层社会与权势阶层的生活状况。穆伊努丁的短篇故事描绘了巴基斯坦底层人的生存境况，以及他们对生活低微的欲求，生动逼真的细节刻画使小说画面感十足，人物形象跃然纸上，使读者感慨命运、贫穷对于人生影响的同时，去深入地思考人性。

《电工纳瓦布丁》(“Nawabdin Electrician—The Life of a Wily Pakistani Electrician”)选自短篇小说集《别人的房间，别样的风景》，入选2008年美国最佳短篇小说选集(The Best American Short Stories of 2008)，讲述电工努力赚钱养家。节选部分讲述电工在一个夜晚骑摩托车回家遭劫匪抢劫未遂后，受伤的两人被赶来的村民送往诊所。《我们的巴黎女士》(“Our Lady of Paris”)选自短篇小说集《别人的房间，别样的风景》，讲述一对巴基斯坦父母拆散儿子与美国女友的恋情，节选部分讲述美国女孩海伦(Helen)初次见男友苏海尔(Sohail)父母哈鲁尼(Hayatullah)和拉菲亚(Rafia)的场景。

作品选读

Nawabdin Electrician
——The Life of a Wily Pakistani Electrician
(excerpt)

By Daniyal Mueenuddin

It seemed very peaceful. In the distance, the dogs kept barking, and all around the cicadas called, so many of them that they blended into a single gentle sound. In a mango orchard across the canal, some crows began cawing, and he wondered why they were calling at night. Maybe a snake up in the tree, in the nest. Fresh fish from the spring floods of the Indus had just come onto the market, and he kept remembering that he had wanted to buy some for dinner, perhaps the next night. As the pain grew worse, he thought of that, the smell of frying fish.

Two men from the village came running up, one much younger than the other, both of them bare-chested. The elder, potbellied, carried an ancient single-barrelled shotgun, the butt mended crudely with wire.

“Oh God, they’ve killed him. Who is it?”

The younger man kneeled down next to the body. “It’s Nawab, the electrician, from Nurpur Harouni.”

“I’m not dead,” Nawab said insistently, without raising his head. He knew these men, a father and son—he had arranged the lighting at the son's wedding. "The bastard's right there in those reeds."

Stepping forward, aiming into the center of the clump, the older man fired, reloaded, and fired again. Nothing moved among the green leafy stalks, which were head high and surmounted by feathers of seed.

"He's gone," the young man said, sitting next to Nawab, holding his arm.

The father walked carefully forward, holding the gun to his shoulder. Something moved, and he fired. The robber fell forward into the open ground. He called, "Mother, help me," and got up on his knees, holding his hands to his waist. Walking up to him, the father hit him once in the middle of the back with the butt of the gun, and then threw down the gun and dragged him roughly by his collar onto the road. Raising the bloody shirt, he saw that the robber had taken half a dozen buckshot pellets in the stomach—black angry holes seeping blood in the light of the torch. The robber kept spitting, without any force.

The son got up and started the motorcycle by pushing it down the road with the gears engaged, until the engine came to life. Shouting that he would get some transport, he raced off, and Nawab winced, hearing the man, in his hurry, shifting without using the clutch.

"Do you want a cigarette, Uncle?" the old villager said to Nawab, offering the pack.

Nawab rolled his head back and forth. "Fuck, look at me."

In the silence, a forgotten thought kept bothering Nawab, something important. Then he remembered.

"Find the guy's revolver, Bholay. You're going to need it for the cops."

"I can't leave you," he said. But after a minute he threw away his cigarette and got up.

The old man was still searching in the reeds when the lights of a pickup materialized at the canal headworks and bounced wildly down the road. The driver, doubtful of the whole affair, stood by while the father and son lifted Nawab and the motorcycle thief into the back. They drove to Firoza, to a private clinic there, run by a mere pharmacist, who nevertheless kept a huge clientele because of his abrupt and sure manner and his success at healing all the prevalent diseases with the same few medicines.

The clinic smelled of disinfectant and of bodily fluids, a heavy sweetish odor. Four beds stood in a room, dimly lit by a fluorescent tube. As the father and son carried him in, Nawab, alert to the point of strain, observed blood on some rumpled sheets, a rusty blot. The pharmacist, who lived above the clinic, had come down wearing a loincloth and undershirt. He seemed perfectly unflustered, if anything slightly cross at having been disturbed.

"Put them on those two beds."

"*As salaam aleikum*, Dr. Sahib," said Nawab, who felt as if he were speaking to someone very far away. The pharmacist seemed an immensely grave and important man, and Nawab spoke to him formally.

"What happened, Nawab?"

"He tried to snatch my motorbike, but I didn't let him."

The pharmacist pulled off Nawab's shalwar, got a rag, and washed away the blood, then poked around quite roughly, while Nawab held the sides of the bed and willed himself not to scream. "You'll live," he said. "You're a lucky man. The bullets all went low."

"Did it hit..."

The pharmacist dabbed with the rag. "Not even that, thank God."

The robber must have been hit in the lung, for he kept breathing up blood.

"You won't need to bother taking this one to the police," the pharmacist said. "He's a dead man."

"Please," the robber begged, trying to raise himself up. "Have mercy, save me. I'm a human being also."

The pharmacist went into the office next door and wrote the names of drugs on a pad, sending the villager's son to a dispenser in the next street.

"Wake him and tell him it's Nawabdin the electrician. Tell him I'll make sure he gets the money."

Nawab looked over at the robber for the first time. There was blood on his pillow, and he kept snuffling, as if he needed to blow his nose. His thin and very long neck hung crookedly on his shoulder, as if out of joint. He was older than Nawab had thought, not a boy, dark-skinned, with sunken eyes and protruding yellow smoker's teeth, which showed whenever he twitched for breath.

"I did you wrong," the robber said weakly. "I know that. You don't know my life, just as I don't know yours. Even I don't know what brought me here. Maybe you're a poor man, but I'm much poorer than you. My mother is old and blind, in the slums outside Multan. Make them fix me, ask them to and they'll do it." He began to cry, not wiping away the tears, which drew lines on his dark face.

"Go to hell," Nawab said, turning away. "Men like you are good at confessions. My children would have begged in the streets."

The robber lay heaving, moving his fingers by his sides. The pharmacist seemed to have gone away somewhere.

"They just said that I'm dying. Forgive me for what I did. I was brought up with kicks and slaps and never enough to eat. I've never had anything of my own, no land, no house, no wife, no money, never, nothing. I slept for years on the railway-station platform in Multan. My mother's blessing on you. Give me your blessing, don't let me die unforgiven." He began snuffling and coughing even more, and then started hiccupping.

Now the disinfectant smelled strong and good to Nawab. The floor seemed to shine. The world around him expanded.

"Never. I won't forgive you. You had your life, I had mine. At every step of the road I went the right way and you the wrong. Look at you now, with bubbles of blood stuck in the corner of your lips. Do you think this isn't a judgment? My wife and children would have wept all their lives, and you would have sold my motorbike to pay for six unlucky hands of cards and a few bottles of poison home brew. If you weren't lying here now, you would already be in one of the gambling camps along the river."

The man said, "Please, please, please," more softly each time, and then he stared up at the ceiling. "It's not true," he whispered. After a few minutes, he convulsed and died. The pharmacist, who had come back in by then and was cleaning Nawab's wounds, did nothing to help him.

Yet Nawab's mind caught at this, at the man's words and his death, like a bird hopping around some bright object, meaning to peck at it. And then he didn't. He thought of the motorcycle, saved, and the glory of saving it. Six shots, six coins thrown down, six chances, and not one of them had killed him, not Nawabdin Electrician.

Our Lady of Paris
(excerpt)

By Daniyal Mueenuddin

At dusk the following day, Sohail sat watching Helen dress for their first dinner with his parents. He wore a sports jacket, a black cashmere turtleneck, and pleated trousers; she rolled black stockings over her legs, which were pink and damp from the shower. She walked to the closet, naked but for the stockings, removed a black dress that she had hung up the night before, stepped into it, and pulled it over the flare of her hips. She turned her back to him, and he zipped it.

They walked past the half-hearted Christmas tree in front of Notre Dame and then along the left bank of the Seine, among the headlights of scooters and cars, the crowds rushing home into the twilight, the tourists everywhere taking pictures, the Parisians with buttoned-down faces. The wet streets glittered. Helen walked beside Sohail, keeping up with him, her heels clicking. She drank in the city around them, moving so quickly, so differently.

A barge passed, going upstream, long and fast, smoking into the night, the lit cabin cozy and cheerful above the cold black water.

"You know," she said thoughtfully, "the Seine doesn't divide Paris, it keeps the city together. It's just the right width, not a little stream but a public place in the heart of the city."

Sohail leaned down and kissed her. "That's a great image, the river *not* dividing Paris."

"It's yours," said Helen. "For your next poem."

His parents were staying in an apartment on the Quai des Grands Augustins, overlooking the Seine. Sohail and Helen went up to the second floor, found the door, and he had just touched the bell when a voice called, "Coming."

"Hello, darling," said his mother, presenting her cheek to kiss, looking past him to Helen. She had a husky, attractive voice and was dressed quite plainly, a long white cotton tunic embroidered in white over slim-fitting pants.

Helen extended her hand, palm flat, and looked Sohail's mother in the eye, directly and ingenuously. "Hello, Mrs. Gurmani. I'm Helen."

"And I'm Rafia. Welcome." She had fixed a stiff smile on her face.

Sohail's father stood to one side, a smallish man with a little moustache, precisely dressed in a thick brown tweed suit with a vest and muted tie and brilliantly shined shoes of a distinctive tan color. As he took Helen's coat, he said, "Welcome, welcome. Thank you for coming." But his statement appeared to be reflexive, without connection to his mental processes. Putting the coat on a hanger, he looked at her closely, with shrewd eyes. Sohail had thrown his coat on a chair near the door.

"Very nice," said Sohail, looking around at the apartment, which had high ceilings and diminutive fittings. A woman on the stereo sang in French, and his mother had lit candles.

"It belongs to Brigadier Hayatullah," said his father, sitting down again in front of the fire.

Rafia and Helen had moved into the living room. The mother leaned down and looked at Helen's necklace, an Afghan tribal piece, silver with lapis.

"Isn't that pretty."

"Sohail gave it to me. It's one of my favorite things."

Rafia said to Sohail, turning and smiling at him, "Will you get Helen and yourself whatever you want—it's in the kitchen." Then to Helen, "Come sit here by me."

Sohail brought a drink for Helen and one for himself. His father sat back in the sofa, his drink on his knee, and looked sedately about the room. Rafia began.

"I promised Sohail not to embarrass him, not to say how much I've heard about you." She had little dimples when she smiled. "But it's true, he keeps telling me about you, it's sweet."

"Ma, please. That makes me sound like I'm fifteen," said Sohail.

"It's the simple truth. And why shouldn't I say it, it's nice to see you happy. But please come help me with dinner. Bring your drink."

As mother and son went into the kitchen, Helen heard Rafia whisper to Sohail, "But she's *so* pretty."

Helen was left with Mr. Gurmani, who did not seem disposed to conversation. He looked complacently at the fire, his glass sweating. After hesitating to have a drink, Helen had accepted a white wine, reminding herself that she was an adult. Now she took a sip of the wine, trying to relax. She had been sitting up erect, halfway forward in the seat.

Still looking into the fire, Mr. Gurmani said speculatively, "Sohail was very happy at Yale." She waited for more, but the father seemed to be content placing this statement on the table between them, a sufficient offering.

"He really was, Mr. Gurmani. He's been happy as long as I've known him." She wanted to be as straight with his parents as possible.

"Please, call me Amjad." The thick tweed of his suit and the smallness of his hands and feet made him appear to Helen like an expensive toy. He spoke very quietly.

She decided to press on, to maintain even this slight momentum of conversation. "His life in Pakistan is so different, at least from what I know. But he has an American side, what I think of as American. He's very gentle—I don't mean Americans are gentle, they're not. But it's easier to be gentle in a place where there's order."

She paused, took a sip of her wine, waited for a moment.

"Go on," said Mr. Gurmani.

"He and my mother got along well, even though—she's a secretary in a little Connecticut town, and she has a house with cats and a garden. He liked that. At first I thought he was pretending, but he wasn't."

"It's a wonderful country. There's nothing you people can't do when you put your minds to it. I admire the Americans tremendously." He sipped from his glass, the ice cubes clattering. "So many of our young people want to live in America—I suppose Sohail as well."

"He talks about it," she said cautiously. "But he talks about Pakistan a lot too. When he and I first met he told me stories about Pakistan for hours."

"And what about you? What would you like to do?"

"I want to be a doctor. I just sent out my applications to medical school." She blushed as she said this, the color unevenly creeping up her fine-grained cheekbones.

"On the East Coast?"

"In New York, maybe. When I was little my mother would drive me to the city, to the Museum of Natural History or the Met, or sometimes we would just walk around looking at the stores and the people. I've always wanted to live there." She paused again, conscious that she might sound pathetic. "It feels like the center of everything. And it's not the way it used to be, it's safe and clean, you can walk through the Park at midnight."

The father looked at her with an expressionless face. "Perhaps Sohail can set up a branch of our company there."

Sohail had come in and heard this last part of the conversation. He sat down on the arm of Helen's chair, put his hand on her shoulder, and said, "Now you've seen it, Helen. That's as close as my father comes to humor." He leaned forward, took his father's empty glass, and stood up.

"I warn you, this man has more factories than your mother has cats. Watch out for him. Stick to name, rank, and serial number."

Mr. Gurmani smiled appreciatively.

"We both want the same thing—what's best for you," said Helen in a flirtatious tone quite new to her. "Why would I need to be careful?"

They had dinner at a small table under a spiky modern chandelier painted with gold leaf, Mr. Gurmani sitting at the head and filling their bowls with bouillabaisse, saffroned and aromatic. Rafia tasted hers from the tip of her spoon and said, "It's good. It's from Quintessence—that's the new chic place, supposedly." Sohail poured the wine and then turned down the lights, so that the table was illuminated by candles.

A bateau mouche glided by on the Seine, its row of spotlights trained on the historic buildings along the quay, throwing patterned light through the blinds onto the living room wall. For a moment they carefully sipped the hot stew.

Helen felt she should break the silence. Just as she was to begin, Rafia turned to her.

"Do you know, Sohail was almost born in Paris?" She sipped from her spoon, looking at Helen sideways. "I was in London to have the baby, and I was enormous and felt like an elephant—so I begged Amjad to come over with me and let me pick out some outrageous outfits. I thought I'd have my girlish figure back the day after I delivered."

Sohail beamed across at Helen, his face framed by two wavering candles. "You can tell this is one of my mother's tall tales—by the simple fact that she's never begged my father for anything. If she had said she ordered my father to Paris it might have been true."

"In any case, you were almost born here, in the Hotel d'Angleterre."

"I wish it had happened," said Sohail. "For a Pakistani being born in London is about as exciting as being born in Lahore. Paris would be glamorous."

Rafia tilted her head toward Helen. "Where would you have liked to be born?"

"I've never thought of that. The first time I met Sohail we talked about where we'd like to be buried."

"In seven years of dating that line has never once failed." Sohail appeared to be saying the first thing that came into his head, filling up the gaps in the conversation.

"Don't be flip, Sohail. Amjad, where would you like to have been born?"

The father, who had been drinking his stew with the equanimity of a solitary patron in a busy café, looked up from under his brows.

"I suppose in the happiest possible home. And not in India, I think. And not in Europe. Perhaps in America."

This interested Helen, relieving her of an irritation at the conversation between mother and son, which seemed too practiced, as if they were performing together, and in their display excluding her.

"Why America?" she asked. Her oval face reflected the light of the candles.

Placing his forearms on the table, still holding his spoon, Mr. Gurmani looked for a moment over his wife's head at the opposite wall. "You know or you correctly assume that I was born into a comfortably well-off family. All my life I've been lucky, my business succeeded, I've had no tragedies, my wife and I are happy, we have a wonderful son. The one thing I've missed, I sometimes feel, is the sensation of being absolutely free, to do exactly what I like, to go where I like, to act as I like. I suspect that only an American ever feels that. You aren't weighed down by your families, and you aren't weighed down by history. If I ran away to the South Pole some Pakistani businessman would one day crawl into my igloo and ask if I were the son of K. K. Gurmani."

Rafia touched his arm. "Darling, you're too old to be menopausal. Americans aren't more free than anyone else. Just because an American runs away, to Kansas or Wyoming, doesn't mean that he succeeds in escaping whatever it is he left behind. Like all of us he carries it with him." She turned to Helen. "Let me ask you. Do you think you're free?"

"I'm not old enough yet to know. I think that at twenty-one many girls think they are."

"Brilliant!" said Sohail. He poured more wine for himself and for his parents; Helen put her hand over the mouth of her glass.

After a moment Mr. Gurmani stood up and began gathering their dishes. He prevented Sohail from rising to help him, saying, "No, no, you sit, let me do this."

"You have to admit, my dad's pretty evolved," said Sohail. "He even likes to cook."

Her mind cooling, prickly from the wine, Helen listened to Sohail and his mother talking about their plans for the next few days, museums and the ballet on Christmas Eve. Rafia had a slight British accent, but softer than that, more rounded—as if the accent had been bred by the personality, as one of her individual characteristics. *So this is how Sohail grew up*, Helen thought. She wondered what lay beneath the angularities of Rafia's character—a woman so imposing not only in her speech but in her manner, the way in which she moved her hands, the angle at which she held her head. In any case, Helen would manage with Rafia, they would make their peace.

21

(Chang-rae Lee, 1965—)
李昌来

作者简介

李昌来（Chang-rae Lee, 1965— ），美国韩裔小说家，生于韩国汉城（现改名为首尔），三岁时移民美国。李昌来于1987年从耶鲁大学毕业，获得英语学士学位，后获俄勒冈大学（University of Oregon）硕士学位。李昌来先后在纽约城市大学、普林斯顿大学教授创意写作课程，现在斯坦福大学任教。

李昌来是重要的当代韩裔作家，他的作品有长篇小说《说母语者》（*Native Speaker*, 1995）、《手势人生》（*A Gesture Life*, 1999）、《在高处》（*Aloft*, 2004）、《投降者》（*The Surrendered*, 2010）和《在浩瀚大海上》（*On Such a Full Sea*, 2014）。李昌来的处女作《说母语者》出版后好评如潮，并获得海明威笔会奖（Hemingway Foundation/PEN Award）、美国图书奖（American Book Award）等多个文学大奖。他的第二部小说《手势人生》获得美国亚裔文学奖（Asian American Literary Award）。李昌来凭借这两部小说被《纽约客》杂志评为20位40岁以下的最佳作家。小说《投降者》荣获2011年代顿文学和平奖（Dayton Literary Peace Prize），并进入2011年普利策小说奖的决选名单；《在浩瀚大海上》被提名2014年美国国家图书评论奖。李昌来的小说以移民身份、离散、同化、历史等为主题。李昌来也从事短篇小说和散文创作，他的短篇小说和散文发表在《纽约客》等杂志上，并被收入一些短篇小说选集。

散文《不动的盛宴》（"Immovable Feast"）最初发表于2014年11月3日的《纽约客》，文章回忆作者在私立中学的时光，语言幽默。小说《投降者》讲述朝鲜孤女琼

（June）、美国士兵赫克托（Hector）和美国妇女赛尔维（Sylvie）之间的故事，反思战争、创伤与爱。选读部分选自小说《投降者》第一章，讲述朝鲜战争期间，少女琼携带两个年幼的弟弟逃难的场景，结尾是琼被迫抛下身负重伤的弟弟，自己搭乘逃命的列车。

作品选读

Immovable Feast

By Chang-rae Lee

I never minded eating in the dining halls. This was at Phillips Exeter Academy, in the early eighties. Let's be clear: I didn't love it—nobody could, unless you were clinically insane or had just been airlifted there from the Soviet bloc. The food was not good. But, then, it wasn't meant to be good, at least not by the standards of the outside world, and surely not compared with my mother's cooking, which would cause my nose to sweat, or compel me to haste so that I scalded my tongue. Her braised pig trotters with sweetened *gochujang* could make me giggle and cry.

The dining-hall fare was mostly New England-inflected, heavy and creamy, unpredictably salty or sweet. Still, my dorm mates and I would find ourselves wandering across the quad and arriving at the dining hall just after the doors opened, at 5:30 *P.M.* We were fifteen-year-old boys, and we were hungry. If weekly menus were posted, we never looked at them. Why bother? There were two dining halls, one at each end of the campus, but somehow they cloned the food perfectly, and there was no choice but the one meal on offer. You could fix yourself a basic salad or a bowl of cornflakes, but I always wanted hot food for dinner, and still do. A cold supper, for me, is like being dipped in a melancholy sauce.

We pulled our trays from the stack and shook off the excess dishwater; the tiled floor there got slimy by the end of the meal service, and if you rushed in late you could end up on your ass. It was calmer early. We moved down the line, wondering what the wombats would dole out to us. That's what the dining staff—all older ladies—were called, after the rotund, earth-burrowing marsupial. Apparently, there used to be tunnels connecting the dorms, where the meals were once served, and the staff carted everything back and forth underground; thus the name. The cooks were all men, salty, grater-voiced dudes whose jeans hung loosely below their aprons as they smoked butts outside.

Their repertoire, I came to learn, was classic. Baked-haddock squares with a bright-orange crumb topping. Chipped beef on toast, a.k.a. shit on a shingle. Fried-clam strips that could double as a kind of seafood jerky. The mains were always accompanied by a form of potato or other starch and a spent, long-suffering vegetable. The Irish stew was pretty tasty, perhaps because I imagined that it was laced with stout. I always ate two cheeseburgers, no matter that the meat was studded with hard nits of gristle. I picked off the bacon, as it smelled exactly like the fetal pigs we dissected in biology class.

You washed it all down with milk. Always plenty of milk; it was dispensed, as it is in most dining halls, from a refrigerated unit that held five-gallon bags, the milk coming out of a white rubber hose that was un-pinched when you lifted the metal paddle. There was always some joker who tried to sneak a suck straight from the teat-like end, to see how long he could go before having to spew. Desserts were probably the best offerings, sugar clearly being the kitchen's favored spice. But I was never a sweets eater, preferring, if anything, a piece of fruit, and sometimes I found myself idly paring an apple the way my mother had when I was little, and making bunny ears with the skin.

In the dorm after curfew, you might have pizza delivered. But, being from New York, I didn't like the local style; it was too doughy, too cheesy, the sauce not right. It got expensive, besides, and I felt guilty spending extra money when I could have had more helpings in the dining hall. My parents didn't qualify for financial aid, but I knew the tuition was a reach for them. Still, they sent me money for "treats." So I supplemented the meals, not with the chips and cookies most of the others would buy but with chub salamis and port-wine cheese balls, which I'd have on Saltines. I'd keep the perishables in the window well, which in New Hampshire was a natural refrigerator from October to April, though sometimes freak weather would hit and I'd have to trash most of a salami. I discovered that you could pare the mold from cheese to salvage it. When I felt like a splurge, I'd buy smoked oysters canned in oil, popping the slick nubs down with twenty-five-cent ginger ale from the dorm's soda machine.

But, mostly, I got my fill in the dining halls. I felt that it was my duty to eat there, plain good form. There's a certain fellowship when everybody gets the same thing. I've visited my old school over the years, and see now that it's serving dishes like Panang curry and grilled-chicken pesto; plus, there's a wok station and daily vegan choices and a self-serve sandwich bar, all of which is great. Still, I don't know. Sometimes being catered to is not the most satisfying thing.

Yes, your particular tastes were never recognized. You had few choices, hardly any liberties. But you dreamed.

The Surrendered

Chapter One

(excerpt)

By Chang-rae Lee

Korea, 1950

THE TRAIN HAD SETTLED into a steady pace, moving through the flat of the darkened valley at the speed of a fast horse trot, the locomotive's rhythm and the radiant warmth of her siblings' bodies finally ushering June into a state of virtual sleep. It was not wholly sleep because she did not yet dream—she never quite dreamed anymore. Instead, her mind rode alongside itself in a state of animal vigilance, such that she could see the three of them nested in the dull gray wrap of the blanket, their heads and feet tucked inside so that it looked like some huge spider's or moth's downy egg sac affixed on the boxcar, placed so that it might travel freely and survive. These last of their kind. If there were any purposeful thoughts bracing her now they simply marked the distances they were covering, the meter of the wheels upon the rails, the shriek of the turns, and the idea that if they could keep moving like this it would be their best chance of remaining together, staying sound. Her one resolve, just before falling sleep, was that they should stay on this train for as long as it would go, for as far as it might take them. There was almost no prospect of getting food on the train, as there would be at some camp; it was difficult to steal or beg anything inside the cars and all but impossible on top. But they were ground down by the road, and she calculated it might be worth eating nothing at all if they could stay cocooned like this and reach Pusan in the next couple of days. If she could administer a potion to make them sleep right through and so blunt the pangs in their bellies she would do so even if it meant them sliding dangerously close to death. For in every village there was a purveyor of herbal medicines who made teas for sleep—even the deepest sleep, if one wished, for the pained and dying.

But what would June in fact do if she had some of that tea now? She would not be afraid that they might drink too much. Maybe she would even steal some sugar or honey to make the drink delicious and sweet, have them gulp it and then lay them down just like this, clinging to her belly like they were her own children, and tell them a colorful story about the grand meal they'd soon enjoy with their cousins. She would give her life for them, but she had begun to understand that the other face of that will was that she could allow them to suffer only so much. They were in a grave condition. Their cheekbones, like her own, were sharply drawn now and jutting, but their bellies were unnaturally distended, the skin drum-tight and shiny. Ji-Young's hair was beginning to fall out and Hee-Soo had a weeping rash on her back that was festering as it spread. Both of them were listless, dull-eyed, growing quieter by the hour, and they'd even ceased to wonder about their mother and sister; after the attack by the planes they'd asked constantly about where they might have gone, as June had told them their truck had sped off before the planes swooped in and that they would make their way to Pusan soon, if they weren't there already. But in the last few days neither mentioned Hee-Sung or their mother, as if the privation had clarified their minds as much as their bodies, rendered away all infantile hope and wish and belief to leave only the unmysterious, the unmistakable, the real.

And yet June would not yet speak aloud what they already knew was the truth. It was not for them she delayed, but for herself. She cast a stony front to the world but in her sleep's throes it was for the moment vanquished and she was once again the child she had been on the eve of the war, a too-tall, soft-spoken girl of eleven who was content to play with much younger children, who was still too shy to look the village boys in the eyes, who wanted nothing more than to sit in her father's lap and hum along with his records while he drew on his corncob pipe, the smoke hanging fatly and sweetly about them. And the deep warmth she felt was not of her sleeping siblings but the heat of the ondol floor nearest the kitchen hearth, where in winter she often lay with a book, the housekeeper stoking the fire so hot that June was sure she'd be seared to the tiles if she read another page. In her sleep she could still believe that all of them would eventually reunite, for she hadn't actually witnessed her mother's and sister's deaths, or, for that matter, her father's. And then, for all she knew, her older brother, despite the surety of her instinct, might very well be hiking north through the hills with the Communists, beleaguered but alive. This was the waking picture in her mind. And even if she knew that all of this was illusory, perhaps the most perilous kind of self-lie, the kind that made one giddy and angry and desperate all at once, she might still choose to crawl inside of it anyway for as long as she could, let it have her breath if it wanted, let it extinguish her outright.

Her chest heaved at the close, used-up air beneath the tight dome of the blanket, and she involuntarily turned from her siblings and craned against the corner of the fabric so that the wind rushed over her eyes and nose. The air was frigid and tainted by the coally exhaust of the locomotive but she took it in and let it flood her lungs. She shivered terribly. The night sky was dying, brightening quickly with the light. She was awake but did not yet want to open her eyes. She wanted to sleep, to sleep a little bit again. But the train suddenly and violently bucked, sending her hurtling against the metal rib on the front side of the well. She struck it head first and was dazed for a second and when she opened her eyes she was half hanging off the edge between the cars. The train lurched forward once more and then finally stopped. Her nose felt as if it was smashed. It was only when she checked her own skin for blood that she realized they were gone. Her brother and her sister. She peered down and saw the blanket draped over the coupling, their satchel broken open beside the shiny rail, their few worthless possessions scattered in the dirt.

She screamed: "Ji-Young-a! Hee-Soo-na!"

She climbed down the ladder and jumped to the ground. But they weren't there, not on either side of the boxcars. They were in a wide, dusky valley, no buildings or houses or even a road within sight.

"Ji-Young-a! Where are you? Hee-Soo-na! Answer me! Answer me!"

She got on her knees and looked under the wheels but they weren't there. Other people had climbed down as well and were running toward the rear; the train had rolled a short distance before halting, perhaps the length of three or four cars. Some terrible shouting came now, and June followed it even though it was a grown man's voice, running in her bare feet—her shoes had come off—and when she came upon him he was grasping his arm in a funny way. He had been thrown off the train as well and had broken it, the lower part of his arm bent grotesquely backwards, as if he had an extra elbow. He asked her for help but she didn't answer because she heard the report of Ji-Young's voice weakly calling, Noo-nah, noo-nah.

He was two cars down, lying close to the train. A woman was kneeling before him. She didn't see Hee-Soo. At first it looked as if the woman were fitting her brother for a shoe, but when June got closer she saw what had happened and stopped a few paces short, unable to move on.

"Noo-nah... " Ji-Young said again.

"This is your little brother?" the woman said to June. June nodded.

"Then come here and help me! Well? Come on, girl, right now!"

June stepped forward and knelt down. "When I say so, pinch his leg with your hands, here, just below the knee. As hard as you can."

June readied her hands.

"Now!"

Ji-Young moaned sharply with the pressure, crying miserably. The woman seemed to know what she had to do. She kept telling him not to look down, to keep his eyes closed, saying there was nothing to see. June would always think later that that was perversely right: for his foot was gone. The amputation was very clean. The stump was bleeding fitfully, the flow alternately stanched and then surging as the woman tried to bind his thin calf with a belt. The light was coming up now and the blood showed its pure color, while all else—the woman's clothes, the arid ground—was washed out, depleted. It was then that June looked away from the tracks and noticed a figure lying belly down near the weedy field. It was Hee-Soo; she could tell by her thick mop of hair. For a moment June was sure that she was all right because her face was turned to her and her eyes were open, her mouth in a faint, if somewhat confused, smile. But she was dead. Both her legs were cut off. She had crawled all that way, and all her blood had run out.

The wheels of the train squealed and it began to inch forward, as though the locomotive was now pushing off the rails whatever obstacle it had struck. Then the train stopped for a moment before moving again. The woman's own children, who sat on top of the boxcar, yelled for her to get back on. But the woman couldn't cinch the belt tightly enough, and Ji-Young was bleeding freely again. The train kept moving, a little faster now, and the woman's children began to shriek for their mother, high panic in their wails. She looked June in the eye and said to her, "You should get back on, child."

"Please help us."

"I'm sorry... I'm sorry... " She got up, pausing ever so slightly, and then hustled to the car where her children were, climbing quickly aboard.

Ji-Young was quiet now, breathing shallowly, as though he wasn't very pained at all. June wound the belt around his leg and looped it through itself before pulling on it as hard as she could. Ji-Young screamed and momentarily fainted. But the bleeding stopped, and with all her strength she lifted her brother and cradled him. He was no heavier than kindling. And she began to run. One of the boxcar's doors was partly open and she could catch it and hand him up to the people packed inside. Some of them were waving her on, beckoning her. The train was speeding up, beginning to leave her behind. It was their only chance now. But it was then that the belt came loose from Ji-Young's leg and slipped off. The blood poured out as if from a spigot and she squeezed the stump as she ran, but one hand wasn't strong enough. She could not do it. So she halted and laid him on the ground, gripping the stump again with two hands. The cars were slowly rolling past them, only a third of the train remaining.

"How come you stopped?" he murmured.

"I can't run anymore."

"Oh." He was losing consciousness, the color draining from his face. "Will you come back for me?"

June nodded.

"You promise?"

She nodded again.

"It's okay. You don't have to."

She let go his still-warm hand, kissed his still-warm face. She stayed with him as long as she could. But when the last car of the train passed her she rose to her feet and steadied herself. And then she ran for her life.

22
(Khaled Hosseini, 1965—　)
卡勒德 · 胡赛尼

作者简介

卡勒德 · 胡赛尼（Khaled Hosseini, 1965—　），美籍阿富汗裔小说家、医生。胡赛尼于 1965 年生于阿富汗喀布尔市，父亲是阿富汗外交官，母亲是喀布尔女子学校的教师。1980 年，全家移民美国。胡赛尼毕业于美国加州大学圣地亚哥分校医学院（University of California San Diego School of Medicine），后成为一名内科医生。胡赛尼现居住在加州，全职从事创作。

胡赛尼主要作品有小说《追风筝的人》（*The Kite Runner*, 2003）、《灿烂千阳》（*A Thousand Splendid Suns*, 2007）、《群山回唱》（*And The Mountains Echoed*, 2013）。他的三部小说都成为美国畅销书，并被翻译成多种语言，畅销世界各地。胡赛尼受西方文学、波斯诗歌和阿富汗口述文学影响颇深，将西方叙述技巧与诗意的语言融为一体。胡赛尼获得约翰 · 斯坦贝克文学奖、加利福尼亚图书奖银奖等多个文学奖项。2006 年，因其作品巨大的国际影响力，胡赛尼获得联合国人道主义奖，并受邀担任联合国难民署亲善大使。

《追风筝的人》因栩栩如生的人物刻画、震撼人心的情节安排、感人肺腑的真挚情感，出版后好评如潮，并跃居美国各大畅销书排行榜，2007 年被改编成同名电影。小说以友谊与爱、背叛与赎罪为主题，围绕喀布尔富家少爷阿米尔（Amir）和仆人哈桑（Hassan）长达数十年的友谊展开，将阿富汗君主制的终结、塔利班当权、“9 · 11”等政治事件融合在小说生活背景中，揭开了阿富汗的神秘面纱，展现了阿富汗的风土人情和文化传统。选读部分选自《追风筝的人》第二十五章，讲述阿米尔重返饱受战火蹂躏的阿富汗，历尽千辛将哈桑的儿子索拉博（Sohrab）带回美国，饱受创伤的孤儿索拉博在来到美国后将自己封闭起来，直到某个下午再次做在故乡最爱的活动——放风筝，象征着索拉博和阿米尔开始新的生活。选读部分是索拉博放风筝的场景。

《灿烂千阳》将关注点放到阿富汗妇女身上，小说讲述两个阿富汗妇女的不幸经历，反映阿富汗女性在家庭、婚姻和社会生活中遭受的压迫、欺凌和虐待。选读部分选自《灿烂千阳》第一章，介绍女主人公玛丽雅姆（Mariam）的私生女身份。

作品选读

The Kite Runner

Chapter 25

(excerpt)

By Khaled Hosseini

By three o'clock, the rain had stopped and the sky was a curdled gray burdened with lumps of clouds. A cool breeze blew through the park. More families turned up. Afghans greeted each other, hugged, kissed, exchanged food. Someone lighted coal in a barbecue and soon the smell of garlic and morgh kabob flooded my senses. There was music, some new singer I didn't know, and the giggling of children. I saw Sohrab, still in his yellow raincoat, leaning against a garbage pail, staring across the park at the empty batting cage.

A little while later, as I was chatting with the former surgeon, who told me he and Baba had been classmates in eighth grade, Soraya pulled on my sleeve. "Amir, look!?"

She was pointing to the sky. A half-dozen kites were flying high, speckles of bright yellow, red, and green against the gray sky.

"Check it out," Soraya said, and this time she was pointing to a guy selling kites from a stand nearby.

"Hold this," I said. I gave my cup of tea to Soraya. I excused myself and walked over to the kite stand, my shoes squishing on the wet grass. I pointed to a yellow seh-parcha. "Sawl-e-nau mubabrak," the kite seller said, taking the twenty and handing me the kite and a wooden spool of glass tar. I thanked him and wished him a Happy New Year too. I tested the string the way Hassan and I used to, by holding it between my thumb and forefinger and pulling it. It reddened with blood and the kite seller smiled. I smiled back.

I took the kite to where Sohrab was standing, still leaning against the garbage pail, arms crossed on his chest. He was looking up at the sky.

"Do you like the seh-parcha?" I said, holding up the kite by the ends of the cross bars. His eyes shifted from the sky to me, to the kite, then back. A few rivulets of rain trickled from his hair, down his face.

"I read once that, in Malaysia, they use kites to catch fish," I said. "I'll bet you didn't know that. They tie a fishing line to it and fly it beyond the shallow waters, so it doesn't cast a shadow and scare the fish. And in ancient China, generals used to fly kites over battlefields to send messages to their men. It's true. I'm not slipping you a trick." I showed him my bloody thumb. "Nothing wrong with the tar either."

Out of the corner of my eye, I saw Soraya watching us from the tent. Hands tensely dug in her armpits. Unlike me, she'd gradually abandoned her attempts at engaging him. The unanswered questions, the blank stares, the silence, it was all too painful. She had shifted to "Holding Pattern," waiting for a green light from Sohrab. Waiting.

I wet my index finger and held it up. "I remember the way your father checked the wind was to kick up dust with his sandal, see which way the wind blew it. He knew a lot of little tricks like that," I said. Lowered my finger. "West, I think."

Sohrab wiped a raindrop from his earlobe and shifted on his feet. Said nothing. I thought of Soraya asking me a few months ago what his voice sounded like. I'd told her I didn't remember anymore.

"Did I ever tell you your father was the best kite runner in Wazir Akbar Khan? Maybe all of Kabul." I said, knotting the loose end of the spool tar to the string loop tied to the center spar. "How jealous he made the neighborhood kids. He'd run kites and never look up at the sky, and people used to say he was chasing the kite's shadow. But they didn't know him like I did. Your father wasn't chasing any shadows. He just... knew."

Another half-dozen kites had taken flight. People had started to gather in clumps, teacups in hand, eyes glued to the sky.

"Do you want to help me fly this?" I said.

Sohrab's gaze bounced from the kite to me. Back to the sky.

"Okay." I shrugged. "Looks like I'll have to fly it tanhaii." Solo.

I balanced the spool in my left hand and fed about three feet of tar. The yellow kite dangled at the end of it, just above the wet grass. "Last chance," I said. But Sohrab was looking at a pair of kites tangling high above the trees.

"All right. Here I go." I took off running, my sneakers splashing rainwater from puddles, the hand clutching the kite end of the string held high above my head. It had been so long, so many years since I'd done this, and I wondered if I'd make a spectacle of myself. I let the spool roll in my left hand as I ran, felt the string cut my right hand again as it fed through. The kite was lifting behind my shoulder now, lifting, wheeling, and I ran harder. The spool spun faster and the glass string tore another gash in my right palm. I stopped and turned. Looked up. Smiled. High above, my kite was tilting side to side like a pendulum, making that old paper-bird-flapping-its-wings sound I always associated with winter mornings in Kabul. I hadn't flown a kite in a quarter of a century, but suddenly I was twelve again and all the old instincts came rushing back. I felt a presence next to me and looked down. It was Sohrab. Hands dug deep in the pockets of his raincoat. He had followed me.

"Do you want to try?" I asked. He said nothing. But when I held the string out for him, his hand lifted from his pocket. Hesitated. Took the string. My heart quickened as I spun the spool to gather the loose string. We stood quietly side by side. Necks bent up.

Around us, kids chased each other, slid on the grass. Someone was playing an old Hindi movie soundtrack now. A line of elderly men were praying afternoon *namaz* on a plastic sheet spread on the ground. The air smelled of wet grass, smoke, and grilled meat. I wished time would stand still.

Then I saw we had company. A green kite was closing in. I traced the string to a kid standing about thirty yards from us. He had a crew cut and a T-shirt that read THE ROCK RULES in bold block letters. He saw me looking at him and smiled. Waved. I waved back.

Sohrab was handing the string back to me.

"Are you sure?" I said, taking it.

He took the spool from me.

"Okay," I said. "Let's give him a *sabagh*, teach him a lesson, nay?" I glanced over at him. The glassy, vacant look in his eyes was gone. His gaze flitted between our kite and the green one. His face was a little flushed, his eyes suddenly alert. Awake. Alive. I wondered when I had forgotten that, despite everything, he was still just a child.

The green kite was making its move. "Let's wait," I said. "We'll let him get a little closer." It dipped twice and crept toward us. "Come on. Come to me," I said.

The green kite drew closer yet, now rising a little above us, unaware of the trap I'd set for it. "Watch, Sohrab. I'm going to show you one of your father's favorite tricks, the old lift-and-dive."

Next to me, Sohrab was breathing rapidly through his nose. The spool rolled in his palms, the tendons in his scarred wrists like rubab strings. Then I blinked and, for just a moment, the hands holding the spool were the chipped-nailed, calloused hands of a harelipped boy. I heard a crow cawing somewhere and I looked up. The park shimmered with snow so fresh, so dazzling white, it burned my eyes. It sprinkled soundlessly from the branches of white-clad trees. I smelled turnip qurina now. Dried mulberries. Sour oranges. Sawdust and walnuts. The muffled quiet, snow-quiet, was deafening. Then far away, across the stillness, a voice calling us Home, the voice of a man who dragged his right leg.

The green kite hovered directly above us now. "He's going for it. Anytime now," I said, my eyes flicking from Sohrab to our kite.

The green kite hesitated. Held position. Then shot down. "Here he comes!" I said.

I did it perfectly. After all these years. The old lift-and-dive trap. I loosened my grip and tugged on the string, dipping and dodging the green kite. A series of quick sidearm jerks and our kite shot up counterclockwise, in a half circle. Suddenly I was on top. The green kite was scrambling now, panic-stricken. But it was too late. I'd already slipped him Hassan's trick. I pulled hard and our kite plummeted. I could almost feel our string sawing his. Almost heard the snap.

Then, just like that, the green kite was spinning and wheeling out of control.

Behind us, people cheered. Whistles and applause broke out. I was panting. The last time I had felt a rush like this was that day in the winter of 1975, just after I had cut the last kite, when I spotted Baba on our rooftop, clapping, beaming.

I looked down at Sohrab. One corner of his mouth had curled up just so.

A smile.

Lopsided.

Hardly there.

But there.

Behind us, kids were scampering, and a melee of screaming kite runners was chasing the loose kite drifting high above the trees. I blinked and the smile was gone. But it had been there. I had seen it.

"Do you want me to run that kite for you?"

His Adam's apple rose and fell as he swallowed. The wind lifted his hair. I thought I saw him nod.

"For you, a thousand times over," I heard myself say.

Then I turned and ran.

It was only a smile, nothing more. It didn't make everything all right. It didn't make anything all right. Only a smile. A tiny thing. A leaf in the woods, shaking in the wake of a startled bird's flight.

But I'll take it. With open arms. Because when spring comes, it melts the snow one flake at a time, and maybe I just witnessed the first flake melting.

I ran. A grown man running with a swarm of screaming children. But I didn't care. I ran with the wind blowing in my face, and a smile as wide as the Valley of Panjsher on my lips.

I ran.

The End

A Thousand Splendid Suns

Chapter 1

By Khaled Hosseini

Mariam was five years old the first time she heard the word *harami*.

It happened on a Thursday. It must have, because Mariam remembered that she had been restless and preoccupied that day, the way she was only on Thursdays, the day when Jalil visited her at the *kolba*. To pass the time until the moment that she would see him at last, crossing the knee-high grass in the clearing and waving, Mariam had climbed a chair and taken down her mother's Chinese tea set. The tea set was the sole relic that Mariam's mother, Nana, had of her own mother, who had died when Nana was two. Nana cherished each blue-and-white porcelain piece, the graceful curve of the pot's spout, the hand-painted finches and chrysanthemums, the dragon on the sugar bowl, meant to ward off evil.

It was this last piece that slipped from Mariam's fingers, that fell to the wooden floorboards of the *kolba* and shattered.

When Nana saw the bowl, her face flushed red and her upper lip shivered, and her eyes, both the lazy one and the good, settled on Mariam in a flat, unblinking way. Nana looked so mad that Mariam feared the *jinn* would enter her mother's body again. But the *jinn* didn't come, not that time. Instead, Nana grabbed Mariam by the wrists, pulled her close, and, through gritted teeth, said, "You are a clumsy little *harami*. This is my reward for everything I've endured. An heirloom-breaking, clumsy little *harami*."

At the time, Mariam did not understand. She did not know what this word harami (bastard) meant. Nor was she old enough to appreciate the injustice, to see that it is the creators of the *harami* who are culpable, not the *harami*, whose only sin is being born. Mariam did surmise, by the way Nana said the word, that it was an ugly, loathsome thing to be a *harami*, like an insect, like the scurrying cockroaches Nana was always cursing and sweeping out of the *kolba*.

Later, when she was older, Mariam did understand. It was the way Nana uttered the word not so much saying it as spitting it at her that made Mariam feel the full sting of it. She understood then what Nana meant, that a *harami* was an unwanted thing; that she, Mariam, was an illegitimate person who would never have legitimate claim to the things other people had, things such as love, family, home, acceptance.

Jalil never called Mariam this name. Jalil said she was his little flower. He was fond of sitting her on his lap and telling her stories, like the time he told her that Herat, the city where Mariam was born, in 1959, had once been the cradle of Persian culture, the home of writers, painters, and Sufis.

"You couldn't stretch a leg here without poking a poet in the ass," he laughed. Jalil told her the story of Queen Gauhar Shad, who had raised the famous minarets as her loving ode to Herat back in the fifteenth century. He described to her the green wheat fields of Herat, the orchards, the vines pregnant with plump grapes, the city's crowded, vaulted bazaars.

"There is a pistachio tree," Jalil said one day, "and beneath it, Mariam jo, is buried none other than the great poet Jami." He leaned in and whispered, "Jami lived over five hundred years ago. He did. I took you there once, to the tree. You were little. You wouldn't remember."

It was true. Mariam didn't remember. And though she would live the first fifteen years of her life within walking distance of Herat, Mariam would never see this storied tree. She would never see the famous minarets up close, and she would never pick fruit from Herat's orchards or stroll in its fields of wheat. But whenever Jalil talked like this, Mariam would listen with enchantment. She would admire Jalil for his vast and worldly knowledge. She would quiver with pride to have a father who knew such things.

"What rich lies!" Nana said after Jalil left. "Rich man telling rich lies. He never took you to any tree. And don't let him charm you. He betrayed us, your beloved father. He cast us out. He cast us out of his big fancy house like we were nothing to him. He did it happily." Mariam would listen dutifully to this. She never dared say to Nana how much she disliked her talking this way about Jalil. The truth was that around Jalil, Mariam did not feel at all like a *harami*. For an hour or two every Thursday, when Jalil came to see her, all smiles and gifts and endearments, Mariam felt deserving of all the beauty and bounty that life had to give. And, for this, Mariam loved Jalil.

Even if she had to share him.

Jalil had three wives and nine children, nine legitimate children, all of whom were strangers to Mariam. He was one of Herat's wealthiest men. He owned a cinema, which Mariam had never seen, but at her insistence Jalil had described it to her, and so she knew that the façade was made of blue-and-tan terra-cotta tiles, that it had private balcony seats and a trellised ceiling. Double swinging doors opened into a tiled lobby, where posters of Hindi films were encased in glass displays. On Tuesdays, Jalil said one day, kids got free ice cream at the concession stand.

Nana smiled demurely when he said this. She waited until he had left the *kolba*, before snickering and saying, "The children of strangers get ice cream. What do you get, Mariam? Stories of ice cream."

In addition to the cinema, Jalil owned land in Karokh, land in Farah, three carpet stores, a clothing shop, and a black 1956 Buick Roadmaster. He was one of Herat's best-connected men, friend of the mayor and the provincial governor. He had a cook, a driver, and three housekeepers.

Nana had been one of the housekeepers. Until her belly began to swell.

When that happened, Nana said, the collective gasp of Jalil's family sucked the air out of Herat. His in-laws swore blood would flow. The wives demanded that he throw her out. Nana's own father, who was a lowly stone carver in the nearby village of Gul Daman, disowned her. Disgraced, he packed his things and boarded a bus to Iran, never to be seen or heard from again.

"Sometimes," Nana said early one morning, as she was feeding the chickens outside the *kolba*, "I wish my father had had the stomach to sharpen one of his knives and do the honorable thing. It might have been better for me." She tossed another handful of seeds into the coop, paused, and looked at Mariam. "Better for you too, maybe. It would have spared you the grief of knowing that you are what you are. But he was a coward, my father. He didn't have the *dil*, the heart, for it."

Jalil didn't have the *dil* either, Nana said, to do the honorable thing. To stand up to his family, to his wives and in-laws, and accept responsibility for what he had done. Instead, behind closed doors, a face-saving deal had quickly been struck. The next day, he had made her gather her few things from the servants' quarters, where she'd been living, and sent her off.

"You know what he told his wives by way of defense? That I *forced* myself on him. That it was my fault. *Didi*? You see? This is what it means to be a woman in this world." Nana put down the bowl of chicken feed. She lifted Mariam's chin with a finger. "Look at me, Mariam."

Reluctantly, Mariam did.

Nana said, "Learn this now and learn it well, my daughter: Like a compass needle that points north, a man's accusing finger always finds a woman. Always. You remember that, Mariam."

23

(Nora Okja Keller, 1965—　)
诺拉·奥卡佳·凯勒

作者简介

诺拉·奥卡佳·凯勒（Nora Okja Keller, 1965—　），美国韩裔作家。凯勒的母亲是韩国人，父亲是德国人。从小跟着母亲在夏威夷长大，她认定自己是美籍韩裔人。她从夏威夷大学（University of Hawaii）获得了心理学和英语双专业学士学位，从加利福尼亚大学圣克鲁斯分校（University of California, Santa Cruz）获得了美国文学硕士学位和博士学位。目前她在火奴鲁鲁的普纳荷学校（Punahou School）担任英语教师。2003年诺拉·奥卡佳·凯勒荣获了夏威夷文学奖（Hawaii Award for Literature）。

诺拉·奥卡佳·凯勒迄今为止独立创作并已发表的两部作品分别是《慰安妇》（*Comfort Woman*, 1997）和《狐女》（*Fox Girl*, 2002）。这两部作品都是以第二次世界大战期间的韩国慰安妇的经历为题材，给世人展示慰安妇的血泪史，揭露第二次世界大战对慰安妇身心造成的摧残和创伤。

《慰安妇》是凯勒的处女作，也是她的成名作。这部小说斩获了美国图书奖（American Book Award）、艾略特·凯兹奖（Elliot Cades Award）和手推车奖（Pushcart Prize）等文学方面的重要奖项。这部小说主要描写了生活在美国主流社会边缘的母女两代人“保密”和“揭秘”的冲突故事。当女儿发现了母亲曾被迫作日本侵略军性奴隶的历史时，她将母亲努力掩盖的、视为耻辱的遭遇写下来公之于众，为母亲恢复了历史和身份的同时自己也获得精神力量和身份。

本故事中母女之间的“隔阂”在文章第17章母亲去世后得到了缓和。女儿在母亲去世后逐渐理解母亲以及她所遭遇的不堪回首的经历。女儿通过母亲遗留的录音机怀念母亲，反思历史与过去。

作品选读

Comfort Woman

Chapter 17

By Nora Okja Keller

BECCAH

According to my mother, the rituals that accompanied the major transitions in a woman's life—birth, puberty, childbirth, and death—involved the flow of blood and the freeing of the spirit. Slipping out of the body along pathways forged by blood, the spirit traveled and roamed free, giving the body permission to transform itself. Necessary but dangerous, these were times when the spirit could spin away forever, lost and aimless, severed from the body.

"This is the blood of a lost spirit," my mother told me when I first noticed the bloodied pad she unfolded from her panties each month. "Every once in a while a woman opens her mouth and a wandering spirit tries to take her body. I'm just spitting it out."

"What? How?" I mumbled, afraid to open my mouth.

"When women are forced to bleed, we have to take care to bind our spirits to us, or they will get confused and wander away. Ejected from our bodies, the spirit flows out on the river of blood, losing its name and its place. Sometimes that *yongson* spirit will try to invade another woman's body—maybe one that reminds them of the body they left behind. Sometimes they will catch a seed in a woman's body and be born again, but most times they will die. See? Like this one." My mother ripped the sticky pad from her panties, rolled it into a wad of toilet paper, and dropped it in the trash.

"Will that ever happen to me?" I asked, unsure if I was referring to losing my spirit or bleeding out a stray.

My mother reached into the box of maxipads and stuck a fresh one on her underpants to catch the blood of more dying spirits. "I will protect you, Beccah," she said, "when the time comes. And I will pray."

But despite my mother's prayers, her charms for my safety, her chants against Saja and Red Disaster, and despite my own efforts to still my body, I eventually bled.

When I felt the knot of pain pulling in my abdomen, pinning me to my seat in Mrs. Abernacke's ninth-grade homeroom, I folded my hands over my belly, picturing a beam of light soaking up the blood. The visualization had worked to suppress menstruation for more than two years, the flash of light cauterizing the wound between my legs, but this time I felt the light merge with my blood, rushing true and deep, thickening as it pounded against my tailbone and *poji* with heavy fists.

While Mrs. Abernacke called attendance, I dropped my head over my desk. I imagined blood, sweet and sticky as syrup, soaking through my jeans and onto the plastic seat. I stayed down, closing my eyes when first bell rang and everyone left for first period. When I opened my eyes again, I saw that the only ones left were me and, toward the back of the room, Fiaso Rialto—whom everyone called Fatso. Fatso, a cushioned cheek piled like dough on the desktop and his large, fat-ringed arms hanging down the sides so that his knuckles grazed the floor by his slippered feet, slept on even as Mrs. Abernacke stalked up behind him. She placed a hand against his neck, a caress really, and when he didn't move, she knocked the back of his head.

"Mr. Rialto!" His head snapped back and he looked around with red-rimmed eyes. "Naptime ended with kindergarten. Please gather up your belongings and proceed to your next class."

"Huh?" said Fatso.

"Go," said Mrs. Abernacke as she marched over to my desk. I expected a whack on the side of my head.

"Miss Bradley, first bell has sounded. If you don't want detention, please cell me why you are still lounging about in homeroom."

"I, uh, don't know," I stammered.

"Then go on." Mrs. Abernacke folded her hands across her chest, waiting for me to stand.

I slid off the seat, keeping my eyes down, expecting to see a smear of red blood on the chair. Relieved to see nothing but a heart someone had carved, I bent to retrieve my backpack.

"Oh, I see," Mrs. Abernacke said. "You should have just told me. I'm a woman too, you know."

"Huh?" I said.

"It's a natural, though unfortunate, function. Let me write you a pass for the nurse."

"For what?" I asked. I held my backpack between us.

"Please do not play games," she said, looking pointedly at my pants. Then she frowned. "Didn't you watch *The Time of Your Life* in fifth-grade health?"

Instead of going to the nurse, I changed into my PE shorts and went home. I tried to sneak my pants into the laundry without my mother seeing, but she found me as I was rubbing Stain Stick against the crotch of my jeans.

"It's time," she cried. "I delayed it for as long as I could, but now it's time." She grabbed the jeans from me, pulled the legs apart and wailed, "Oh, my poor baby! Does it hurt?"

I pushed her away as she tried to hug me. "Quit it," I told her. "It's no big deal, just the facts of life." And then I started to cry.

"*Aigu*," my mother clucked as she ushered me into her bedroom. "It does hurt. Lie down." She pulled the blankets to the foot of the bed, nestled me into her pillows.

"I swallowed a spirit, Mom," I said, half laughing.

"No," my mother said. "It's your own spirit fighting to get out, wanting to travel. We must make the way safe for it to go and then come back."

"I was only joking," I said. "I'm not a baby anymore that you can fool me with this stuff, you know." And then I groaned as a spirit raked its nails against my womb.

"Shh, shh," she crooned, stroking my hair. When I closed my eyes, I felt my mother move away from me, heard the glass doors open onto the garden.

I slept, sailing in and out of dreams, riding the waves of my first cramping. Through the night, my mother bathed my face and body with water that smelled sharp, like freshly cut grass, like newly unearthed roots. And as she stroked me, I dreamed I was swimming, then drowning, then climbing an embankment that eroded and dissolved as I scrambled toward the stars. I dragged myself over sand and stone, following the light, until I stepped on a bridge of fire and found a beautiful woman waiting for me.

At first I thought the woman was my mother, then I realized it was myself. "My name is Induk," the woman said through my lips. I looked into the face that was once my own and wondered who she saw, who stood in my place looking at the body that Induk now claimed.

I looked at my new hands, trying to find a clue to my present identity, but as I looked, the hands melted, then dissolved into ash. Quickly I looked at the arms, the feet, the legs, and they, too, disintegrated. I knew I was being devoured by flame ravenous as a dragon, fierce as the sun. I waited, a thin column of ash, for the dragon's breath, the wind that would blow my body apart.

"You must come back across running water," Induk said, exhaling, dispersing my ashes like pollen into the night air.

When I woke the next morning, my mother said, "You must return across running water." She pulled one of her white ceremonial gowns over my head and yanked my arms. "Come on."

I rubbed my stomach. "I don't feel so good," I whined, hoping she would leave me alone.

"I know," she said. "That's why we have to do this."

"No," I said, scrambling to the other side of the bed. "I have to go to school."

My mother ran to block the door to her room. "I already called, said you were too sick. That we have to go to the doctor."

"Oh," I said, pulling off my mother's gown. "Why didn't you say that's where we're going?"

My mother sighed, then spoke slowly: "Because we're not. I only told them something they could understand."

She lifted the white gown from the bed where I had thrown it, and handed it back to me. I put it on, and when the hem dropped to my ankles, I realized I had grown to my mother's height. "Come on," she said as she walked out the glass doors and into her garden.

I followed her to the back of our lot. When we reached the chicken wire enclosing our property, my mother raised her hands and, like Moses parting the Red Sea, stepped through the fence. I reached the spot where my mother had crossed over, expecting to see some kind of gate worked into the fence, but I couldn't see an opening of any kind. My mother waited. I slipped my fingers through the loops and shook. The fence rattled.

"Here," my mother said. "Look here." She grasped at the barrier between us and gently eased the wire apart. Creaking, the fence split wide enough for me to insert my body, then snapped shut behind me.

I followed where my mother led, watching the muscles of her legs flex as she scrambled over the thirsty tongues of tree roots and loose rocks scattered like broken teeth. I felt my body move like my mother's, bend and dip with hers, as if I lived within her skin. We climbed a skinny path among dank mulch and dying leaves, weaving our bodies through squares of sunlight that wavered and burst like overripe liliko'i as we stepped on them. And each step was accompanied by the music of the river, a white noise I became aware of only when we jumped over a small finger of water.

"She has crossed the dangerous stream in search of the spirit," my mother called out into the moist air.

"Dance," she said to me. "Free your spirit, Beccah-chan, let it loose." She leaped into the air, twirling and pivoting in a space of her own, dancing and singing a song with no words.

"Mom, stop!" I cried, looking about, afraid that—even here in the middle of nowhere, next to a small, unmarked runoff from the Manoa Stream—someone would see my mother as I saw her: flying unanchored to reality, her own dark waters soaking through her tunic until the lines of her used woman's body—the sloping shoulder bones jutting like wings out of her back, the sacs of her breasts swinging from her concave chest, the upturned bowl of her stomach—sharpened under the wet clothes.

"Please not now," I yelled, to both my mother and the spirits she danced with. I vowed that if she went into a trance, I would leave her here in the woods, making my own way back into sanity.

Spinning toward me, she grabbed one of my hands. "Dance with me, Beccah," she said. "Don't you hear the singing?"

She pulled and I jumped, hopping from one foot to the other. "That's it," she told me. "Let the river speak to you. Listen to what it has to say, to what you have to hear."

Her dance slowed. Still holding my hand, she slipped her fingers into the waistband of her tunic pants, pulled out a small pocket knife, and slashed the tip of my middle finger.

I yelled, then popped my finger into my mouth.

"Wait, not yet," my mother said, drawing my finger from my mouth. "Wash it first."

When I dipped my hand into the shallow water of the stream, my mother yelled, "Spirit, fly with the river, then follow it back home." She tapped me on the shoulder. "Okay," she said to me. "Now drink it."

I cupped some of the running water into my hands, brought it to my mouth. I tasted the metal of blood.

"Now you share the river's body," my mother said. "Its blood is your blood, and when you are ready to let your spirit fly, it will always follow the water back to its source."

Like the river in my blood, my mother waited for me to fly to her, waited for me to tell her I was ready to hear what she had to say. I never asked, but maybe she was telling me all the time and I wasn't listening.

Wanting to hear her voice once more, I unpacked the "Beccah" tape—my mother's last message, last gift to me—I had carried back from the Manoa house. But just as when I was a child listening in on my mother's sessions with her clients, just as when I listened to that one tape many years ago, I heard, when I first began playing my mother's tape in the apartment I had chosen for myself, only senseless wails, a high-pitched keening relieved by the occasional gunshot of drums. Still, I listened, but only when I stopped concentrating did I realize my mother was singing words, calling out names, telling a story. I turned the volume knob on the stereo until my mother's voice shivered up the walls, as if the louder the words, the easier I would be able to understand the story.

Kok: I howl into the night air, emptying my grief into the homes of my neighbors, announcing my loss and my love.

As the tape wound on, I rummaged through the kitchen cabinets for paper and pen, wanting to write down my mother's song. I scribbled words I recognized—*kok*, *han*, *chesa*, *chudang*, *Saja*, *poji*—words connected to blood and death. After filling several notebook pages with black scrawl, I stopped the recorder. The scraps of paper seemed inadequate, small and disjointed. Needing a bigger canvas, I stripped the sheet from my bed, laid it on the living room floor in front of the speakers, pressed Play on the recorder, and caught my mother's words.

Yom: Preparing your body for its final transition, I lay it down, stretched long against the mat in the main room. I boil ginger root, and with the cooled scented water, I bathe you for a final time. I massage your stiffening limbs, then tuck them close against your body. I wash your intimate places, pull your white hairs, and cut your nails. The loose trimmings I wrap in cloth to bury under you. And through it all I sing.

I sing Hanul, Pada, Ch-onji, sa-nam gwa irum, calling on Heaven, Sea, the four directions of Earth, and I sing your name. I mark the place where you are buried so that you will always find your way.

Abugi. Omoni. Kun Aniya. Mul Ajumoni. I sing the names by which I have known you, all of you, so that you will remember. So that I will remember. So that those who come after me will know. Induk. Miyoko. Kimiko. Hanako. Akiko. Soon Hi. Soon Mi. Soon Ja. Soon Hyo.

So many true names unknown, dead in the heart. So many bodies lefi unprepared, lost in the river.

Not once did my mother sing my name. And though primarily in English, this tape was not for me, was addressed not to me but to her mother, a final description of her mother's death and feast. Faithful in performing the death anniversary *chesa*, my mother proved to be dutiful and dependable as a daughter in a way she never was as a mother.

When the first side of the tape hissed to a stop, I realized that what I had thought were drums accenting my mother's lament was actually a dismal rapping at my door, incessant but faint. Flipping the tape over, I pressed Play and, with my mother's words wrapped around me, drifted to the door. Through the eye of the peephole, I saw the apartment manager leaning against the door, thumping listlessly with flattened hand, his bowed head a balloon on the string of his body.

"What?" I yelled through the closed door.

Hiram Hirano jumped away from the door, blinking his pink, watery eyes. "Sorry to bother you," he squeaked. "But there've been complaints about your, ah, music."

I watched him fiddle with his balding head, stick a finger into his ear. He snuffled at the door, trying to look into the peephole. "Hallo?" he stammered. "Did you hear me? Hallo? Could you turn it down?"

"My mother is dead," I said.

"Oh," he said, scuttling away from the door as if it were diseased.

Wishing I could turn up the volume even more, I added my own voice, an echo until I stumbled over a term I did not recognize: *Chongshindae*. I fit the words into my mouth, syllable by syllable, and flipped through my Korean-English dictionary, sounding out a rough, possible translation: Battalion slave.

Chongshindae: Our brothers and fathers conscripted. The women left to be picked over like fruit to be tastedy consumed, the pits spit out as Chongshindae, where we rotted under the body of orders from the Emperor of Japan. Under the Emperor's orders, we were beaten and starved. Under Emperor's orders, the holes of our bodies were used to bury their excrement. Under Emperor's orders, we were bled again and again until we were thrown into a pit and burned, the ash from our thrashing arms dusting the surface of the river in which we had sometimes been allowed to bathe. Under Emperor's orders, we could not prepare those in the river for the journey out of hell.

The Japanese believe they have destroyed an entire generation of Koreans. That we are all dead and have taken the horrible truth with us, but I am alive. I feel you, knowing you wait by my side until the time comes for me to join you across the river. I offer you this one small gesture each year, worth more than the guilt money the Japanese now offer to silence me: a bit of rice burned in your memories, and your names called over and over again, a feast of crumbs for the starving.

I rewound the tape where my mother spoke of the *Chongshindae*, listening to her accounts of crimes made against each woman she could remember, so many crimes and so many names that my stomach cramped. Without reference, unable to recognize any of the names, I did not know how to place my mother, who sounded like an avenging angel recounting the crimes of men.

"Mommy—Omoni—is this you?" I cried, but my mother did not pause in her grief, her song for the dead.

I could not view my mother, whom I had always seen as weak and vulnerable, as one of the "comfort women" she described. Even though I heard her call out "Akiko," the name she had answered to all my life, I could not imagine her surviving what she described, for I cannot imagine myself surviving. How could my mother have married, had a child, if she had been forced into the camps? And then, given new context, came the half-forgotten memory of the night my father was taken to the hospital.

From the little consistencies I could gather from her stories, we were living in Florida, in a bungalow adjacent to the chapel on the campus of the Miami Mission House for Boys. What I remember is a small yard in which I played and a small room where I slept by myself. That particular morning, a Saturday that I had been allowed to watch television, I saw *Curse of the Mummy*. Although, remembering its time slot, the movie I saw was more likely to have been *Abbott and Costello Meet the Mummy*, or even *Scooby-Doo and the Haunted House*. But whatever the movie, images of the resurrected dead chased me into the night, into my dreams. I remember the wrapped mummy shuffling toward me—strips of rotting, stinking cloth hanging from outstretched arms—stalking me even as I ran from sleep into the reality of my room. Screaming, feeling the mummy's breath rustle the hair on the back of my head, I jumped from my bed and stormed into my parents' bedroom.

Halfway across their room, I realized it was empty, that there was no one to save me. I waited for the mummy to devour me, but when she reached me, she merely turned my head toward the open window. I opened my eyes and, as if caught in another dream in which I had no control, saw my mother dancing in the alley of our yard and my father on his knees before her, begging her to come inside, come inside before someone saw them.

"Bow down before God, for He alone can heal your wounds," my father told my mother. "Remember the woman of Luke, chapter thirteen. She had been inflicted by evil spirits, suffering for eighteen years, before Jesus put His hands on her, saying 'Woman, you are set free from your infirmity.' Bow down, Akiko, just as that woman did, and you shall be free."

But my mother laughed and spat at my father. "I will never, never again lay down for any man," she said. And she swung around, spinning in circles about him.

My father stood and clasped his hands to his chest. "Forgive her, Father. She knows not what she speaks."

"I know what I speak, for that is my given name. Soon Hyo, the true voice, the pure tongue. I speak of laying down for a hundred men—and each one of them Saja, Death's Demon Soldier—over and over, until I died. I speak of bodies being bought and sold, of bodies—"

"'Put away perversity from your mouth; keep corrupt talk from your lips, or—,' " my father yelled.

"Of bodies that were burned and cut and thrown like garbage to wild dogs by the river—"

" 'Or ye shall be struck down!' " My father grabbed my mother's shoulders and shook her.

"I'm the one! I'm the one to strike you down, and God down too!" my mother screamed, charging my father, scratching at his face.

But my father was the one to strike *her* down, pushing her into the damp ground in an attempt to cover her mouth. "Quiet! What if someone hears you speaking like this? The boys, the brothers? What if Beccah hears you? Think of how she would feel, knowing her mother was a prostitute."

My father held my mother in his arms, cradling her as she moaned and pounded against him. "Shush," he murmured. "It is not for me to judge. But know that 'The sins of the parent shall fall upon their children and their grandchildren.' I ask you to protect our daughter, with your silence, from that shame."

I fell asleep in my parents' bed that night, listening to the sound of my mother crying, and when I woke, I was in the hospital. I spent most of the next few weeks in the hospital, roaming its corridors, dreaming in front of the candy machines, sliding on the slick white floors, waiting for my mother to emerge from my father's room. When I asked to see him, my mother said, "Wait, wait until he is better," but I never saw him again. On our final visit to the hospital, I remember hearing the words "heart failure," "complications," "pneumonia," "I'm sorry." And as the doctor bent toward my mother and me, offering his condolences, I asked not about my daddy, but about the candy in the vending machine.

I clawed through memory and story, denying what I heard and thought I remembered, and tried to pinpoint my mother's birth date, her age during World War II. Flooding my mind with dates and numbers, I wanted to drown my mother's voice, wanted to reassure myself that these atrocities could not have been inflicted on her, that she was just a child when she claimed to be a comfort woman. I began to scratch dates on the bedsheet—*1995, 1965, 1945, 1931-2-3*—when the manager came back. I recognized his feeble knocking, but the voice that called my name from outside the door was Sanford's, whom I had listed on the rental agreement as the person to contact in case of emergency.

I did not need to get off the floor in front of the speakers to know what was happening behind the door. Hiram, bug-eyed and sweating, would be backing away after having performed his obligatory knocking. Sanford would be waving the timid manager down the hallway while fretting with his hair and expression, concerned with looking supportive yet boyishly handsome.

I didn't rush to open the door upon hearing his voice, and I knew Sanford's mask must have slipped. "Beccah!" he roared, pounding the door. "It's me."

I turned the knob of the volume down. "Who?" I said, then twisted the knob back toward high.

Sanford stopped pounding for a moment, then yelled out his name as if it were a question.

About to take pity on him and open the door, I heard my mother call me, weaving my name into her chants, her prayers for justice.

Beccah-chan, lead the parade of the dead. Lead the Ch'ulssang with the rope of your light. Clear the air with the ringing of your bell, bathe us with your song. When I can no longer perform the chesa for the spirits, we will look to you to feed us. I have tried to release you, but in the end I cannot do it and tie you to me, so that we will carry each other always. Your blood in mine.

I remembered watching my mother lay out the offerings for the dead before she would feed me, remembered her dancing over me with strips of cloth torn from the sheets of my bed. And while I had felt invisible, unimportant, while my mother consorted with her spirits, I now understood that she knew I watched her. That in her way, she had always carried me with her.

Feeling my mother's arms around my waist, I walked to the door. "I'm speaking to my mother," I told Sanford through the cracks.

"Your mother is dead," Sanford said, speaking to me as I had spoken to my mother, as if she were unstable. Dangerous.

I looked at Sanford, made small through the tunnel of the peephole. When I was in high school, the art teacher taught us to look through a square made by our fingers, in order to focus on what we wanted to paint. I often looked at my mother through the finger frame, trying to put her in perspective. I liked the way my fingers capured her, making her manageable. Squinting my eye through my lens, I could make her any size I wanted. I could make her shrink, smaller and smaller, until she disappeared with a blink.

I looked at Sanford as I had looked at my mother, fitting him in the space between my fingers, and slowly, slowly, with infinite gentleness, brought my fingers together until he shrank smaller than the lines in a standard obituary, smaller than newsprint.

"I have to leave you, Sanford," I called our, while he slammed his weight against the door. I watched him rub his shoulder, then dropped my hand and closed my eyes. With my mother's voice filling the apartment, her words swirling around my shoulders, I thought how easy—in a pinch, with a blink—it was to make someone disappear. "Goodbye," I told him. "My mother is calling me."

24

(Thanhha Lai, 1965—)
赖昙荷

作者简介

赖昙荷（Thanhha Lai, 1965— ），美国越南裔儿童文学作家，出生于越南西贡（今胡志明市）。越战期间西贡沦陷时，她和家人被迫离开越南，到美国阿拉巴马州避难。她曾在纽约大学（New York University）学习，获得艺术硕士学位。毕业后，她在加利福尼亚州的一家报社工作，主要负责当地越南移民社会相关的新闻报道。在2005年，她发起了一个非盈利组织——“越南儿童”（Viet Kids Inc.）专门为越南走路上学的孩子买自行车。对越南的情怀以及对儿童的关爱促使赖昙荷创作出优秀的儿童文学作品。

迄今为止，她已出版两部小说。她的处女作《再见木瓜树》（*Inside Out & Back Again*, 2011）荣获2011年美国国家图书奖（National Book Award）与纽伯瑞奖（Newbery Honor），受到美国文坛的好评与读者的青睐，赖昙荷也从此成为家喻户晓的作家。2015年她出版了第二部小说《静静地听》（*Listen, Slowly*, 2015），同样得到如潮好评。

《再见木瓜树》从一位越南少女“哈”（Hà）的视角讲述了在越南战争期间“哈”（Hà）一家逃离越南西贡到达美国阿拉巴马州避难的故事。在美国，“哈”（Hà）一家受尽人间冷暖，被迫在美国主流社会边缘地带艰难生存。这部小说以半自传体小说的形式表现出赖昙荷作为越南难民在美国生活的心酸经历。

《一个吻》（“A Kiss”）和《邻居》（“Neighbors”）是本小说较为精彩的两个章节。《吻》讲述了美国的军舰以“救世主”的形象出现在越南难民面前，给他们以生存的希望。然而在《邻居》这一章节中，哈一家在美国白人社区受尽来自邻居的歧视，被迫在社会边缘地带苦苦挣扎。这两个章节均表达了作者对战争的反思，以及越南难民追求“美国梦”的真实写照。

作品选读

A Kiss

By Thanhha Lai

The horn on our ship
blows and blows
waking everyone
from a week-long nap.

A sure answer,
honk honk,
seems close enough
and real enough
to call everyone on deck.

A gigantic ship
with an American flag
moves closer.
Men in white uniform
wave and smile.
Our commander wears
his navy jacket and hat,
so white and so crisp.

Now I realize
why I like him so much.

In uniform,
he looks just like Father.

He boards the other ship,
salutes and shakes hands
with a man whose hair
grows on his face
not on his head
in the color of flames.

I had not known
such hair was possible.

We clap and clap
as the ships draw together
and kiss.

Boxes and boxes
pass onto our deck.
Oranges, apples, bananas,
cold sweet bubbly drinks,
chocolate drops, fruity gum.

The American ship
tows ours
with a steel braid
thick as my body.

Our rescue now certain,
the party blossoms
as food suddenly
comes up from below.
Ramen noodles, beef jerky,

dried shrimp, butter biscuits,
tamarind pods, canned fish,
and drums and drums of real water.

Mother says,
People share
when they know
they have escaped hunger.

Shouldn't people share
because there is hunger?

That night I stand behind
blowing blankets
and pour fresh water
all over my skin.

How sweet water tastes
even when mixed with soap.

Neighbors

By Thanhha Lai

Eggs explode
like smears of snot
on our front door.

Just dumb kids,

says our cowboy.

Bathroom paper hangs
like ghosts
from our willow.

More dumb kids,
says our cowboy.

A brick
shatters the front window,
landing on our dinner table
along with a note.

Brother Quang
refuses to translate.

Mother shakes her head
when Vu Lee pops his muscles.

Our cowboy
calls the police,
who tell us
to stay inside.

Hogwash,
our cowboy says,
then spits a brown blob
of tobacco.

I repeat, *Hogwash*,
puckering for the ending of
ssssshhhhhh.

Mother decides
we must meet
our neighbors.

Our cowboy leads,
giving us each a cowboy hat
to be tilted
while saying,
Good mornin'.

Only I wear the hat.

In the house
to our right
a bald man
closes his door.

Next to him
a woman
with yellow hair
slams hers.

Next to her
shouts reach us
behind a door unopened.

Redness crawls across
my brothers' faces.
Mother pats their backs.

Our cowboy leads us
to the house on our left.

An older woman
throws up her arms
and hugs us.

We're so startled
we stand like trees.

She points to her chest:
MiSSSisss WaSShington.

She hugs our cowboy
and kisses him.

I thought only
husbands and wives
do that when alone.

We find out
MiSSSisss WaSShington
is a widow and retired teacher.
She has no children
but has a dog named Lassie
and a garden that takes up
her backyard.

She volunteers
to tutor us all.

My time with her
will be right after school.

I'm afraid to tell her
how much help I'll need.

25

(Jhumpa Lahiri, 1967—　)

裘帕·拉希莉

作者简介

裘帕·拉希莉（Jhumpa Lahiri, 1967—　），美籍印度裔小说家。拉希莉生于英国伦敦的一个印度移民家庭，幼年随父母迁居美国罗德岛州。拉希莉毕业于伯纳德学院（Barnard College），继而在波士顿大学（Boston University）深造，获得硕士和博士学位。拉希莉现在普林斯顿大学教授创意写作课程。

拉希莉的主要作品有短篇小说集《疾病解说者》（*Interpreter of Maladies*, 1999）和《不适之地》（*The Unaccustomed Earth*, 2008），长篇小说《同名人》（*The Namesake*, 2003）和《低地》（*The Lowland*, 2013）。拉希莉的处女作《疾病解说者》获得美国笔会/海明威文学奖年度最佳虚构处女作和2000年普利策小说奖，拉希莉成为普利策小说奖史上最年轻的获奖者（33岁）。她的第一部长篇小说《同名人》出版后颇受欢迎，于2007年被改编成同名电影上映。《不适之地》出版后，登上《纽约时报》畅销书榜单，又获弗兰克·奥康纳国际短篇小说奖。拉希莉擅长短篇小说创作，她的短篇小说三度入选《美国最佳短篇小说年鉴》。拉希莉的小说有明显的自传色彩，多刻画她所熟悉的美国孟加拉裔移民，叙述他们在异国生活里遭遇的文化冲突，以及作为个体在社会生活里必然经历的悲欢离合、希望和失望、挣扎与困惑。她有学者般冷静客观、细致入微的写实主义的叙述，有小说家对故事结构的精心和灵敏的设计，又有对人的生存悲剧性犀利而深刻的领悟。她的语言精致、微妙，又很自然，在从容、冷静的叙述中蕴含着一种内在的力量。

《疾病解说者》（"Interpreter of Maladies"）选自短篇小说集《疾病解说者》，该篇获得欧·亨利短篇小说奖、《纽约客》杂志年度最佳处女作并入选《美国最佳短篇小说年鉴》。小说讲述一对美籍印度夫妇携带孩子回印度探亲旅行的故事，小说通过达斯夫妇（Das）一家探讨人与人的隔阂与理解困惑、失落与抗争、移民的移居困境。节选部分讲述达斯夫人向导游倾吐压抑在心底多年的婚外情和私生子的秘密。

小说《低地》讲述印度纳萨尔运动对于兄弟二人的命运影响，小说时间跨度长达半个世纪，跨越印度和美国，包含一个家族四代人的人生经历，将个人命运与国家命运融入叙事。节选部分选自小说《低地》，介绍故事主人公尤得彦（Udayan）和妻子格瑞（Gauri）的相识过程。

作品选读

Interpreter of Maladies (excerpt)

By Jhumpa Lahiri

Mr. Das headed up the defile with the children, the boys at his side, the little girl on his shoulders. Mr. Kapasi watched as they crossed paths with a Japanese man and woman, the only other tourists there, who paused for a final photograph, then stepped into a nearby car and drove away. As the car disappeared out of view some of the monkeys called out, emitting soft whooping sounds, and then walked on their flat black hands and feet up the path. At one point a group of them formed a little ring around Mr. Das and the children. Tina screamed in delight. Ronny ran in circles around his father.

Bobby bent down and picked up a fat stick on the ground. When he extended it, one of the monkeys approached him and snatched it, then briefly beat the ground.

"I'll join them," Mr. Kapasi said, unlocking the door on his side. "There is much to explain about the caves."

"No. Stay a minute," Mrs. Das said. She got out of the back seat and slipped in beside Mr. Kapasi. "Raj has his dumb book anyway." Together, through the windshield, Mrs. Das and Mr. Kapasi watched as Bobby and the monkey passed the stick back and forth between them.

"A brave little boy," Mr. Kapasi commented.

"It's not so surprising," Mrs. Das said.

"No?"

"He's not his."

"I beg your pardon?"

"Raj's. He's not Raj's son."

Mr. Kapasi felt a prickle on his skin. He reached into his shirt pocket for the small tin of lotus-oil balm he carried with him at all times, and applied it to three spots on his forehead. He knew that Mrs. Das was watching him, but he did not turn to face her. Instead he watched as the figures of Mr. Das and the children grew smaller, climbing up the steep path, pausing every now and then for a picture, surrounded by a growing number of monkeys.

"Are you surprised?" The way she put it made him choose his words with care.

"It's not the type of thing one assumes," Mr. Kapasi replied slowly. He put the tin of lotus-oil balm back in his pocket.

"No, of course not. And no one knows, of course. No one at all. I've kept it a secret for eight whole years." She looked at Mr. Kapasi, tilting her chin as if to gain a fresh perspective. "But now I've told you."

Mr. Kapasi nodded. He felt suddenly parched, and his forehead was warm and slightly numb from the balm. He considered asking Mrs. Das for a sip of water, then decided against it.

"We met when we were very young," she said. She reached into her straw bag in search of something, then pulled out a packet of puffed rice. "Want some?"

"No, thank you."

She put a fistful in her mouth, sank into the seat a little, and looked away from Mr. Kapasi, out the window on her side of the car. "We married when we were still in college. We were in high school when he proposed. We went to the same college, of course. Back then we couldn't stand the thought of being separated, not for a day, not for a minute. Our parents were best friends who lived in the same town. My entire life I saw him every weekend, either at our house or theirs. We were sent upstairs to play together while our parents joked about our marriage. Imagine! They never caught us at anything, though in a way I think it was all more or less a setup. The things we did those Friday and Saturday nights, while our parents sat downstairs drinking tea... I could tell you stories, Mr. Kapasi."

As a result of spending all her time in college with Raj, she continued, she did not make many close friends. There was no one to confide in about him at the end of a difficult day, or to share a passing thought or a worry. Her parents now lived on the other side of the world, but she had never been very close to them, anyway. After marrying so young she was overwhelmed by it all, having a child so quickly, and nursing, and warming up bottles of milk and testing their temperature against her wrist while Raj was at work, dressed in sweaters and corduroy pants, teaching his students about rocks and dinosaurs. Raj never looked cross or harried, or plump as she had become after the first baby.

Always tired, she declined invitations from her one or two college girlfriends, to have lunch or shop in Manhattan. Eventually the friends stopped calling her, so that she was left at home all day with the baby, surrounded by toys that made her trip when she walked or wince when she sat, always cross and tired. Only occasionally did they go out after Ronny was born, and even more rarely did they entertain. Raj didn't mind; he looked forward to coming home from teaching and watching television and bouncing Ronny on his knee. She had been outraged when Raj told her that a Punjabi friend, someone whom she had once met but did not remember, would be staying with them for a week for some job interviews in the New Brunswick area.

Bobby was conceived in the afternoon, on a sofa littered with rubber teething toys, after the friend learned that a London pharmaceutical company had hired him, while Ronny cried to be freed from his playpen. She made no protest when the friend touched the small of her back as she was about to make a pot of coffee, then pulled her against his crisp navy suit. He made love to her swiftly, in silence, with an expertise she had never known, without the meaningful expressions and smiles Raj always insisted on afterward. The next day Raj drove the friend to JFK. He was married now, to a Punjabi girl, and they lived in London still, and every year they exchanged Christmas cards with Raj and Mina, each couple tucking photos of their families into the envelopes. He did not know that he was Bobby's father. He never would.

"I beg your pardon, Mrs. Das, but why have you told me this information?" Mr. Kapasi asked when she had finally finished speaking, and had turned to face him once again.

"For God's sake, stop calling me Mrs. Das. I'm twenty-eight. You probably have children my age."

"Not quite." It disturbed Mr. Kapasi to learn that she thought of him as a parent. The feeling he had had toward her, that had made him check his reflection in the rearview mirror as they drove, evaporated a little.

"I told you because of your talents." She put the packet of puffed rice back into her bag without folding over the top.

"I don't understand," Mr. Kapasi said.

"Don't you see? For eight years I haven't been able to express this to anybody, not to friends, certainly not to Raj. He doesn't even suspect it. He thinks I'm still in love with him. Well, don't you have anything to say?"

"About what?"

"About what I've just told you. About my secret, and about how terrible it makes me feel. I feel terrible looking at my children, and at Raj, always terrible. I have terrible urges, Mr. Kapasi, to throw things away. One day I had the urge to throw everything I own out the window, the television, the children, everything. Don't you think it's unhealthy?"

He was silent.

"Mr. Kapasi, don't you have anything to say? I thought that was your job."

"My job is to give tours, Mrs. Das."

"Not that. Your other job. As an interpreter."

"But we do not face a language barrier. What need is there for an interpreter?"

"That's not what I mean. I would never have told you otherwise. Don't you realize what it means for me to tell you?"

"What does it mean?"

"It means that I'm tired of feeling so terrible all the time. Eight years, Mr. Kapasi, I've been in pain eight years. I was hoping you could help me feel better, say the right thing. Suggest some kind of remedy."

He looked at her, in her red plaid skirt and strawberry T-shirt, a woman not yet thirty, who loved neither her husband nor her children, who had already fallen out of love with life. Her confession depressed him, depressed him all the more when he thought of Mr. Das at the top of the path, Tina clinging to his shoulders, taking pictures of ancient monastic cells cut into the hills to show his students in America, unsuspecting and unaware that one of his sons was not his own. Mr. Kapasi felt insulted that Mrs. Das should ask him to interpret her common, trivial little secret. She did not resemble the patients in the doctor's office, those who came glassy-eyed and desperate, unable to sleep or breathe or urinate with ease, unable, above all, to give words to their pains.

Still, Mr. Kapasi believed it was his duty to assist Mrs. Das. Perhaps he ought to tell her to confess the truth to Mr. Das. He would explain that honesty was the best policy.

Honesty, surely, would help her feel better, as she'd put it. Perhaps he would offer to preside over the discussion, as a mediator. He decided to begin with the most obvious question, to get to the heart of the matter, and so he asked, "Is it really pain you feel, Mrs. Das, or is it guilt?"

She turned to him and glared, mustard oil thick on her frosty pink lips. She opened her mouth to say something, but as she glared at Mr. Kapasi some certain knowledge seemed to pass before her eyes, and she stopped. It crushed him; he knew at that moment that he was not even important enough to be properly insulted. She opened the car door and began walking up the path, wobbling a little on her square wooden heels, reaching into her straw bag to eat handfuls of puffed rice. It fell through her fingers, leaving a zigzagging trail, causing a monkey to leap down from a tree and devour the little white grains. In search of more, the monkey began to follow Mrs. Das. Others joined him, so that she was soon being followed by about half a dozen of them, their velvety tails dragging behind.

The Lowland
(excerpt)

By Jhumpa Lahiri

Normally she stayed on the balcony, reading, or kept to an adjacent room as her brother and Udayan studied and smoked and drank cups of tea. Manash had befriended him at Calcutta University, where they were both graduate students in the physics department. Much of the time their books on the behaviors of liquids and gases would sit ignored as they talked about the repercussions of Naxalbari, and commented on the day's events.

The discussions strayed to the insurgencies in Indochina and in Latin American countries. In the case of Cuba it wasn't even a mass movement, Udayan pointed out. Just a small group, attacking the right targets.

All over the world students were gaining momentum, standing up to exploitative systems. It was another example of Newton's second law of motion, he joked. Force equals mass times acceleration.

Manash was skeptical. What could they, urban students, claim to know about peasant life?

Nothing, Udayan said. We need to learn from them.

Through an open doorway she saw him. Tall but slight of build, twenty-three but looking a bit older. His clothing hung on him loosely. He wore kurtas but also European-style shirts, irreverently, the top portion unbuttoned, the bottom untucked, the sleeves rolled back past the elbow.

He sat in the room where they listened to the radio. On the bed that served as a sofa where, at night, Gauri slept. His arms were lean, his fingers too long for the small porcelain cups of tea her family served him, which he drained in just a few gulps. His hair was wavy, the brows thick, the eyes languid and dark.

His hands seemed an extension of his voice, always in motion, embellishing the things he said. Even as he argued he smiled easily. His upper teeth overlapped slightly, as if there were one too many of them. From the beginning, the attraction was there.

He never said anything to Gauri if she happened to brush by. Never glancing, never acknowledging that she was Manash's younger sister, until the day the houseboy was out on an errand, and Manash asked Gauri if she minded making them some tea.

She could not find a tray to put the teacups on. She carried them in, nudging open the door to the room with her shoulder.

Looking up at her an instant longer than he needed to, Udayan took his cup from her hands.

The groove between his mouth and nose was deep. Clean-shaven. Still looking at her, he posed his first question.

Where do you study? he asked.

Because she went to Presidency, and Calcutta University was just next door, she searched for him on the quadrangle, and among the bookstalls, at the tables of the Coffee House if she went there with a group of friends. Something told her he did not go to his classes as regularly as she did. She began to watch for him from the generous balcony that wrapped around the two sides of her grandparents' flat, overlooking the intersection where Cornwallis Street began. It became something for her to do.

Then one day she spotted him, amazed that she knew which of the hundreds of dark heads was his. He was standing on the opposite corner, buying a packet of cigarettes. Then he was crossing the street, a cotton book bag over his shoulder, glancing both ways, walking toward their flat.

She crouched below the filigree, under the clothes drying on the line, worried that he would look up and see her. Two minutes later she heard footsteps climbing the stairwell, and then the rattle of the iron knocker on the door of the flat. She heard the door being opened, the houseboy letting him in.

It was an afternoon everyone, including Manash, happened to be out, and she'd been reading, alone. She wondered if he'd turn back, given that Manash wasn't there. Instead, a moment later, he stepped out onto the balcony.

No one else here? he asked.

She shook her head.

Will you talk to me, then?

The laundry was damp, some of her petticoats and blouses were clipped to the line. The material of the blouses was tailored to the shape of her upper torso, her breasts. He unclipped one of the blouses and put it further down the line to make room.

He did this slowly, a mild tremor in his fingers forcing him to focus more than another person might on the task. Standing beside him, she was aware of his height, the slight stoop in his shoulders, the angle at which he held his face. He struck a match against the side of a box and lit a cigarette, cupping his whole hand over his mouth when he drew the cigarette to his lips. The houseboy brought out biscuits and tea.

They overlooked the intersection, from four flights above. They stood beside one another, both of them leaning into the railing. Together they took in the stone buildings, with their decrepit grandeur, that lined the streets. Their tired columns, their crumbling cornices, their sullied shades.

Her face was supported by the discreet barrier of her hand. His arm hung over the edge, the burning cigarette was in his fingers. The sleeves of his Punjabi were rolled up, exposing the veins running from his wrist to the crook of the elbow. They were prominent, the blood in them greenish gray, like a pointed archway below the skin.

There was something elemental about so many human beings in motion at once: walking, sitting in buses and trams, pulling or being pulled along in rickshaws. On the other side of the street were a few gold and silver shops all in a row, with mirrored walls and ceilings. Always crowded with families, endlessly reflected, placing orders for wedding jewels. There was the press where they took clothes to be ironed. The store where Gauri bought her ink, her notebooks. Narrow sweet shops, where trays of confections were studded with flies.

The paanwallah sat cross-legged at one corner, under a bare bulb, spreading white lime paste on stacks of betel leaves. A traffic constable stood at the center, in his helmet, on his little box. Blowing a whistle and waving his arms. The clamor of so many motors, of so many scooters and lorries and busses and cars, filled their ears.

I like this view, he said.

26

(Monique Truong, 1968—   )
莫妮卡·张

作者简介

莫妮卡·张（Monique Truong, 1968—   ），美国越南裔作家，出生于越南西贡（今胡志明市）。1975年，年仅6岁的她跟随母亲离开越南，以难民身份到美国避难和生活。她于1990年毕业于耶鲁大学（Yale University），获得文学学士学位，1995年从哥伦比亚法学院（Columbia Law School）毕业，获得法学博士学位。她曾担任美国亚太期刊副编辑。她荣获过纽约公立图书馆幼狮文学奖（New York Public Library Young Lions Fiction Award）等重要奖项。

她创作的作品有两部长篇小说《书之盐》（*The Book of Salt*, 2003）和《难言之隐》（*Bitter in the Mouth*, 2010）；与其他作家合著的作品《分水岭：美国越南裔诗歌和散文》（*Watermark: Vietnamese American Poetry & Prose*）。此外，莫妮卡·张还创作了一些短篇小说和散文。

《难言之隐》是莫妮卡·张的第二部小说。这部小说用“意识流”的叙事手法讲述了主人公在过去与现在的结合中试图找回迷失的自己，找回自己的身份定位，勇敢面对死亡、性侵、癌症和家庭矛盾等危险与灾难的故事。

本小说的第22章，即最后一章，随着身份谜底的揭开，主人公逐渐走出了过去遭受的各种痛苦和磨难的阴影，勇敢面对自己和未来，重新定位自己的人生，对未来充满了期待与希望。

作品选读

Bitter in the Mouth

Chapter 22

By Monique Truong

The story of my life, according to DeAnne Whatley Hammerick, began in the fall of 1955, thirteen years before I was born. Young Thomas, twenty-three years old, was in his third and last year of Columbia Law when he met a young woman named Mai-Dao. She was twenty years old and a senior at Barnard. She was a rare bird in his eyes. Young Thomas told her that he was from the South. She told him that she was from the South too. He, unlike many Americans at the time, knew that her country had been partitioned into North and South just the year before. Well, I would have never known; you don't have even a trace of a southern accent, he replied in his leisurely drawl. Then, he fell in love right there on the steps of Low Memorial Library, while the corridor of trees, which led from the street into the wide plaza before them, turned colors. He fell in love, even though Mai-Dao had told him that she was engaged to a young man back home. The school year ended, and she returned to her hometown and young Thomas to his. Before she left New York City, she gave him the photographs of their time together. What she couldn't say to him was that she couldn't keep the photographs. These things, if kept, were always found. They traded their mailing addresses, and he, like a teenage girl, promised to write. He did. He wrote to her many times after he returned home to Charlotte, once after he moved to Shelby, and one more time in 1960, on the day that he moved into the blue and gray ranch house in Boiling Springs with his new bride. Mai-Dao, like a teenage boy, didn't reply.

Over the years, as the name of Mai-Dao's country became a household word even in Boiling Springs, Thomas couldn't see the news of her country's civil war, the deployment of U.S. troops there, and the body bags that returned without thinking of her. In 1968, the year that she gave birth to me, though he didn't know that back then, he thought of her as he watched her hometown—it was the southern capitol, so he thought that it would keep her safe—exploding on his television set. He hoped that she was far away from there. He imagined her back in New York

City. He tried to imagine how her world had changed. He tried not to think about her, a married woman, as he was a married man.

On April 30, 1975, Thomas and DeAnne sat riveted in front of their television set as Dan Rather announced that Saigon was "now under Communist control." DeAnne remembered her husband closing his eyes and keeping them shut as he listened to the reporter announcing that Saigon had been renamed Ho Chi Minh City.

The letters addressed to Thomas began arriving at the blue and gray ranch house soon after. They were postmarked Chapel Hill, so DeAnne wouldn't have paid much attention to them, except for the foreign name in the return address.

Then came the telephone call on the night of July 5. It was 11:30 p.m., and DeAnne and Thomas were already side by side in bed. Thomas hung up the receiver and ran out of the house, still in his pajamas. DeAnne heard her husband's car door slam shut. When she heard his car door open, it was 4 p.m. the following day. She went to the front door of the blue and gray ranch house, and I was asleep in his arms.

Thomas had to tell DeAnne the story of my birth mother's life, or what he knew of it. That was DeAnne's precondition for agreeing to my adoption. DWH, the truth teller now, told me that she, in fact, didn't feel like she had a choice. Thomas had already made up his mind. She might as well get the whole story in the process, DeAnne thought. She also thought that it would be better (for her) if she made the decision then and there to believe that what her husband, Thomas, was telling her was true.

DeAnne asked to see the photographs. Then she asked to see the letters. She told Thomas that he had to throw everything away. He promised her that he would. He didn't. After he passed away, she found the photographs in his office. The letters she didn't find there. DWH said that when Thomas showed the letters to her she couldn't bring herself to read them. The handwriting was all curves and delicate loops, and all she could imagine was the body of the woman who wrote the words. DeAnne made Thomas read the letters aloud to her. So as I slept in the guest bedroom of their house, Thomas and DeAnne sat at the kitchen table and talked for the remainder of the day.

Mai-Dao wrote her first letter to Thomas on May 1, 1975, one day after the fall of Saigon. Mai-Dao had been in Chapel Hill for almost a year already. Her husband, Khanh, an assistant professor of economics at the University of Saigon, was a postdoctoral fellow at UNC, and after much bribing and string-pulling back in Saigon, she and their six-year-old daughter had been able to join Khanh in September of'74. Mai-Dao took with her to Chapel Hill the last letter that Thomas had sent to her in Saigon. Since the first day of her arrival in his home state, she had been taking mental notes of what she liked about his South, so that she could share them with him. Then she reread his letter, dated December 10, 1960—*he'd written to her on our wedding day, Linda*—and the letter reminded Mai-Dao that she knew nothing about his life in the fourteen years since then. Thomas must be a very different man now, Mai-Dao thought. So she set aside the idea of writing to him and tried as best as she could to settle into her new temporary home, a trailer that Khanh had rented for them in order to make the most of his small monthly stipend. She thought it was a storage shed when they first drove up to it. The interior was the size and width of a corridor in the three-story villa that her father had given to them as a wedding present back in Saigon. Khanh reminded her of how lucky they were to be here and not there.

That became her mantra in the months to come: lucky to be here and not there. She enrolled her daughter in the first grade and was amazed at how quickly a young child could pick up a new language, like it was just a shiny new toy. Mai-Dao audited classes in the art history department of UNC and thought often about traveling up to New York City and seeing the Metropolitan Museum of Art again and, of course, her beloved Central Park. Khanh told her that there was no money for such a pleasure trip. She looked at her husband, amazed at how the young man who had shown up for their dates in a chauffeured car had changed. She couldn't have imagined that he would become so serious and practical, with worry lines cut deep into his forehead. Lucky to be here and not there, she reminded herself. She went to the library and checked out a cookbook—the first one she had ever read—and fed her husband and daughter American-style meals, which the cookbook author, Betty Crocker, assured her were both economical and nutritious. Mai-Dao wasn't a very good cook, so every once in a while she and her daughter would go to the supermarket and indulge in the American snack foods and sodas that she had missed so dearly when she was in Saigon. "Thomas, did you know that there is a soda in Vietnam that tastes exactly like Dr. Pepper?" Mai-Dao asked, in the first of her eight letters to him. *I don't know why, Linda, but that always stuck in my head. Maybe because of your grandma. You know how she drank that stuff like water.*

On April 30, 1975, Mai-Dao and Khanh and their young daughter had sat in their rented trailer home in front of a small TV set, one of the few things they owned outright here, and had watched in disbelief as "there" disappeared. Mai-Dao started to cry when she saw the word YESTERDAY appear at the bottom of the tiny screen, the white text superimposed over the footage of the evacuation of Saigon. Khanh whispered in her ear that she shouldn't cry in front of their daughter.

Mai-Dao stopped, though she knew that it wouldn't change a thing. Her father was a general in the army. Khanh's father was one as well. When Dan Rather reported that South Vietnamese servicemen and their families were among the seventy thousand South Vietnamese who had made it safely to Thailand, Khanh turned to his wife and said that they would hear something from their families soon.

How? she wondered. Who would have had the forethought in the chaos of an evacuation to write down the address of a son and daughter who were lucky enough to be in a city called Chapel Hill? Even its name sounded distant and safe, Mai-Dao thought.

Over the next day or two, while her husband went to his office at the university to make the necessary telephone calls, listing their names with the International Red Cross, and trying to reach his distant relatives in Paris, Mai-Dao tried to keep herself from thinking about her mother being shoved and pushed into a helicopter or into a boat—*if* my mother was lucky, Mai-Dao reminded herself—by cleaning the trailer home, washing every item of clothing that the three of them owned at the Laundromat, and writing a long, belated letter to Thomas. "I'm here with my husband and my daughter" was how Mai-Dao began her letter. *Thomas choked up when he read those words to me, Linda. I could have told him to stop reading, but I didn't.*

DWH had been speaking very slowly, pausing in between words, stopping in midsentence. The incomings, given such a cadence, were acute and more assertive than usual, as if the tastes triggered by the words literally had more time to sink in. I had to excuse myself from the kitchen table. I went into the living room and telephoned Kelly at the Greek Revival. I asked her to bring over a bottle of whatever she had. It wasn't even noon, but Kelly, in true form, didn't ask why, didn't sound a bit surprised, and came by the blue and gray ranch house in less than fifteen minutes with a bottle of bourbon, two-thirds full. Kelly came to the back door of the house, said good morning to DWH through the screen door, handed me the bottle thoughtfully hidden inside of a fancy shopping bag underneath a layer of tissue paper, and was on her way again after she had squeezed my hands so hard that my fingers almost went white.

I poured for myself a juice glass full of bourbon and asked DWH if she wanted one as well. I couldn't remember at that moment whether I had explained to DWH about the ameliorative effects of alcohol. We had discussed cigarettes and their effects on my condition during our morning talks, but I wasn't sure whether the topic of alcohol or sex had reached the breakfast table yet. It didn't matter, because DWH answered yes. *You know, your grandma loved to mix that stuff with her Dr. Pepper.*

Iris's truth serum of choice, I thought.

Thomas, according to DWH, admitted that he immediately wrote back to Mai-Dao. He glossed over the contents of his letter, except to say that he had included his telephone number and had asked Mai-Dao to call him. She never did, but she did send a second letter to him at the blue and gray ranch house. *Your grandma told me that meant that he'd never been unfaithful to me before. A cheating man would've known to give his office number and mailing address, your grandma said.* Mai-Dao wrote that there was still no news about her or her husband's families. For once in her life she didn't mind so much that she was an only child. Her husband, Khanh, was unable to sleep or eat, worrying about his five younger brothers and their wives and children. In the middle of the night, Khanh would be in his office on campus trying to telephone them, one number after the other. Their lines had all been cut. How soon after the end of a war does the telephone service resume, Mai-Dao wondered. How about mail delivery? She didn't know these answers, but she wrote to her mother and father every day just in case they were there waiting to receive word from her. Mai-Dao thought often about her favorite building in Saigon, the Central Post Office, and she wondered if it had survived the last days of the war in one piece.

Mai-Dao wrote to Thomas that she felt guilty that she was worrying about a building, even if it was one designed by Gustave Eiffel, when the people who had gathered there were now so scattered and unaccounted for. She felt so guilty that she wouldn't dream of sharing these thoughts with her husband. Her daughter was too young, of course, to understand. Mai-Dao wrote that she was grateful that she had Thomas for a friend.

Thomas responded to Mai-Dao's second letter, asking her if he could come to Chapel Hill to see her. *I knew he didn't want to admit that to me, but he had to. That's how much he wanted you, Linda.*

Mai-Dao sent back a third letter, this one short and unequivocal. She wrote that a face-to-face visit wasn't a good idea right now. Maybe when things were more settled. Still not a word from my family or Khanh's, Mai-Dao added. Thomas swore to DeAnne that he never drove the 191 miles from Boiling Springs to Chapel Hill, until he received the telephone call summoning him there. He continued to write to Mai-Dao, though.

In her fourth letter to Thomas, Mai-Dao thanked him for his generous offer, but she thought that she and Khanh would be able to manage. *Thomas admitted that he had offered to send her money, Linda. He said he would have told me, if he had.* Mai-Dao wrote that she had found a part-time job at the main library on the UNC campus and was working during the hours when her daughter was at her summer school. The job kept her from thinking, which was what she wanted right now. The extra money was helping out too. Mai-Dao asked Thomas if his wife worked outside the house. *I knew he hadn't brought me up once in his letters. She had to*. Mai-Dao wanted to know because she was surprised at how much her husband had objected to the idea. Khanh had never been that sort of a man, not a dinosaur by any means. Khanh was caring, thoughtful, and one of the most intelligent men she had ever met. *It must have hurt Thomas to read that—the first time to himself and then again to me.* Still no word from our families, Mai-Dao wrote. Every night Mai-Dao dreamed that she was aboard an airplane that was about to land at the Saigon airport. The plane circled low over the southern capital, so low that she could see the red roof of the Opera House and the twin spires of the Basilica, the wide boulevards, and the cramped alleyways. Every night, she realized too late that it was a nightmare because the plane she was on would never land.

Thomas thought it was time that he became more involved. It was already the beginning of June. A month had passed since the fall of Saigon, and Mai-Dao and her husband still had no news about their families. Thomas wrote to Mai-Dao and offered another type of assistance, one that he knew she couldn't turn down. He asked for the names of her mother and father and of the immediate members of Khanh's family as well. Thomas wrote to Mai-Dao that he would contact a family friend who was a congressman. This man could make the right phone calls, Thomas assured Mai-Dao. *Willie Hoyle had just been elected to his first term, Linda. I know it's hard to imagine, but back then we thought that Willie could really get things done.*

Mai-Dao's fifth letter arrived soon after, and it was only a couple of lines long. Thomas knew that he had overstepped again. Mai-Dao wrote that Khanh thanked Thomas for the offer of assistance, but Khanh felt that this was a family matter. If Thomas would be so kind as to send them the name of the congressman, Khanh would contact the gentleman directly to inquire about what resources he and his office could extend to them. Thomas knew from the formal tone of the letter that Mai-Dao wrote the letter but that Khanh was either looking over her shoulders or dictating it. Thomas confessed to DeAnne that he had wanted to go to Chapel Hill right then and there and talk man-to-man with Khanh, to talk some sense into him.

Reasonable Man-to-Reasonable Man, I thought.

Before Thomas could write back, Mai-Dao's sixth letter arrived at the blue and gray ranch house. It was five pages long. This one was really from her, Thomas knew. She apologized for her previous letter. She confirmed that Khanh had asked her to write it, and she blamed its content on Khanh's lack of sleep. Her husband was becoming irritable and somewhat irrational, she wrote. He had been threatening to buy a plane ticket to go to Thailand to search for their families. Mai-Dao had to remind Khanh that he held a passport issued by the Republic of Vietnam, a country more commonly known as South Vietnam and one that no longer existed under either name. If Khanh, now a citizen of nowhere, left the United States, he might never be able to return.

Lucky to be here and not there, I thought.

Khanh, a man who rarely raised his voice in anger, yelled at Mai-Dao that night. He didn't need to be reminded of the obvious, he screamed at her. But he did, Mai-Dao insisted in her letter to Thomas. She wrote that she had brought up Thomas's offer to contact a congressman in the hopes of calming Khanh down. Her failure to anticipate Khanh's reaction she blamed on her own lack of sleep. Otherwise, she would have known, would have kept Thomas's offer to herself for another day, and sat there silently by her husband's side instead. Khanh demanded to know how she knew Thomas Hammerick, and how long the two of them had been keeping in touch. Khanh assumed the worst, that he had been cuckolded from the first day of their marriage, and that there had been other men. Mai-Dao sat there, stunned. When she became engaged, her mother had warned her that no man wanted to know about a woman's past. Her mother told her that it was best to pretend that you have been reborn, an innocent baby in his arms. Her mother, Mai-Dao wrote to Thomas, was always right. *You might want to take another sip, Linda. Just bring the bottle to the table.* Mai-Dao wrote that the worst part of the argument was that their daughter, Linh-Dao, was in the trailer and had heard everything that Khanh had said. The girl from birth had been a quiet child, so quiet that sometimes they would forget that she was in the room. Mai-Dao asked Thomas if he had any children of his own. *All those letters, Linda, and he hadn't told her anything about our marriage.*

Thomas saw that this sixth letter from Chapel Hill had a different return address. Mai-Dao had used her work address at the UNC library. He wrote back to her there. Thomas told DeAnne that he expressed his regret for the misunderstanding that had taken place between Mai-Dao and her husband. Thomas, however, reminded Mai-Dao that she didn't need her husband's permission to proceed. With or without Khanh's approval and cooperation, Thomas could still approach the congressman for assistance. Thomas urged her to send him a list of names immediately, but if she really wanted Khanh to make the call, enclosed was Congressman Hoyle's phone number and mailing address.

Thomas waited two and a half weeks before he received his seventh letter from Mai-Dao. Her letter wasn't what he had hoped for. There was no list of names. There was no "Thomas, I will call you soon." There was no "Thomas, I will see you in Chapel Hill." There was only news about Khanh's family. His youngest brother, Trac, and his wife were among the refugees who had made it to Thailand. There was still no news of the whereabouts of Khanh's four other brothers and their families. Trac had made contact with their second cousin in Paris, who had telephoned Khanh.

According to their second cousin, Trac and Khanh's father had shot himself in the early-morning hours of April 29. Their mother had refused to leave her husband's body alone and unburied when Trac came for them. Khanh received the news of his father's death with a kind of stoicism that surprised Mai-Dao. Khanh immediately concluded that it was better that way. A proud man like his father couldn't have survived a subjugated life, he told her.

What about your mother, Mai-Dao wanted to ask Khanh. Mai-Dao confided in Thomas that she felt that suicide was a cowardly act. Her father-in-law had deserted the woman who had been by his side for the past thirty years, who had borne him six sons, and whom he knew would be tethered to his body until the end of her days.

The news that Khanh didn't take as well was Trac's desire to emigrate to France instead of joining him in the United States. According to their second cousin, Trac felt that the United States had abandoned and betrayed South Vietnam. How could I live *there*, Trac had asked their kinsman. Khanh lost his temper when he repeated to Mai-Dao this part of the long-distance conversation. France colonized and humiliated us for eighty years, Khanh yelled at Mai-Dao. Had Trac forgotten *that*? Trac should have just stayed there, if he was so stupid and proud.

Or he should have just shot himself like your father, Mai-Dao thought and kept to herself. She wrote it in her seventh letter to Thomas, though. She also wrote that it made her feel guilty to do so, to send and receive personal letters at her place of work, hiding away more and more parts of herself. This wasn't how she had ever imagined her life to be.

Thomas, as was his habit by then, wrote back to Mai-Dao immediately. He didn't receive her eighth and last letter to him until July 7. Thomas wasn't the first person to read the letter. DeAnne was. *It was now my business too, Linda*.

On July 6, as the sun was beginning to set, DeAnne had agreed to my adoption. DeAnne told Thomas that her second precondition was that they would never speak about my birth parents again. *Otherwise how could I learn to love you, Linda*?

DWH remembered the letter shaking in her hands. DeAnne saw again the handwriting that seemed to her so alive with another woman's body and movement. The letter was only half a page long but full of sadness. Mai-Dao wrote that Khanh had found the letters that Thomas had sent to her and again had accused her of adultery. Khanh said that if it weren't for their daughter, he would leave her. Mai-Dao thanked Thomas for his kindness and his friendship, and she apologized for all the years in Saigon in which she had ignored his letters. She wanted him to know that she had kept all of his letters back then as well. Mai-Dao then asked Thomas not to write to her again. She would be in touch again in the near future, she promised. Mai-Dao's letter was postmarked July 3, 1975.

The bottle of bourbon was bone dry. The afternoon was almost gone. The late-afternoon sunlight was making every growing thing in the backyard look as if it were lit from within. All the windows in the blue and gray ranch house were wide open, letting in the sounds of birds and lawn mowers and the occasional passing car. The temperature inside and outside was the same, a rare equilibrium that we registered as the feeling of being comfortable in our own skin. DeAnne Whatley Hammerick and I were still the same. We didn't break into two or three or four pieces. Our limbs were all accounted for. Our internal organs were pumping and filtering. We were a bit light-headed, but that was just the bourbon talking. DWH and I, finally, had begun the complicated process of doing something that most people, especially a mother and a daughter, could never seem to do. We were forgiving each other for who we were, for how we came into this world, for how we changed or didn't change it for each other.

The story of my birth parents' final days in Chapel Hill was what my grandmother Iris, the secret bourbon drinker, had thought would break me in two. On her deathbed, my grandmother thought of these two people whom she had never met but who had changed her family, reinvented it in a way that she couldn't have foreseen.

DWH had skipped past the story of Khanh and Mai-Dao's death because she had no idea what really took place. I was the one who was there, the only one who had survived. But to bear witness I had to remember. What took place inside that trailer home in the days and hours and minutes before the fire on the night of July 5, 1975, was lost to me. Whoever carried me out, his or her face was blank to me. Whoever stayed inside, by force or by choice, became strangers to me. The years of my life with them, the life before *this* life, had been erased or, rather, my memories of them had been erased by my benevolent brain. The last word that this man or this woman had said to me was the only thing that remained, as a taste of bitter in my mouth. A fire had made everything else about them disappear.

This was what Thomas told his wife:

The firemen had found me on the gravel driveway of the adjacent trailer home. I was in a nightgown. I was wrapped in a sheet. I appeared to be sound asleep while a fire ate its way through the narrow corridor that I had called home. Tucked inside the pocket of my nightgown were my passport and the first letter that Thomas had sent to Mai-Dao in Chapel Hill, the one with the phone number of the blue and gray ranch house, which she had never dialed. A Chapel Hill police officer telephoned Thomas instead.

Thomas claimed me. He told the police and the social worker that night that he was related to Mai-Dao by marriage. That his cousin, who had died in the war—*that was the only part of the story that Thomas told that was true, Linda; his cousin Brett Hammerick died in the battle of Khe Sanh*—had been married to Mai-Dao's sister in Saigon. That no one on the American side of the family knew of their marriage. That the Vietnamese side of the family was all in Saigon, unaccounted for and unreachable. Thomas told DeAnne that it had been instinctual. He didn't mean the instinct to lie. He meant the desire to bring me home. A child needed a father and a mother, he said to DeAnne.

As Thomas recounted his sudden dash toward fatherhood, DeAnne sat at their kitchen table and thought about what he had told her years ago when they were still dating. Not all men have to become fathers, Thomas had assured her. They wouldn't need to have children in order to be a family, he had agreed with her. *I never thought I would hear a man say these things to me, Linda.* Though I had assumed otherwise, DeAnne had known from the time that she was in her early twenties that she didn't want to have children. *I didn't want to become another Iris, Linda.* Her mother, Iris, had told her that no man would think that was natural. DeAnne thought that meant that she would be alone for the rest of her life. But then she met Thomas, and he had made her believe that her fate would be different. Thomas, in a way, had kept his promise to her.

DWH told me that she was completely unprepared for motherhood. She was glad that I was such a quiet child. She admitted that during the first few years of my life at the blue and gray ranch house she sometimes would pretend that I wasn't there. She would close her eyes and imagine that everything had stayed exactly the same. This became more difficult to do as I grew older. *Thomas loved you so much, Linda.* What DWH meant was that as I grew older I began to look more and more like the young Vietnamese woman whom her husband had loved. As the years passed, the second precondition to my adoption—that they would never speak about my birth father or mother again—did little to alleviate this fact. Thomas and DeAnne didn't have to mention my birth mother's name. When I was in the house, Mai-Dao was in the house. As the years passed, though, the second precondition was what Thomas and DeAnne clung to. One silence had led to another, and eventually the silences became the life preservers dotting the dangerous ocean between them. In this way, Thomas and DeAnne survived.

DWH said that she had turned to Iris for comfort, though she knew that there would be little there but truth.

And you also turned to Bobby. This thought didn't keep me from reaching over the kitchen table and holding on to DWH's hands. I was understanding for the first time how lonely DeAnne must have felt in the blue and gray ranch house, even when Thomas and I had been around.

Iris told DeAnne that to have a child was to enter into a contract. The judge's wife explained to her daughter the basic concepts of contract law: promise, obligation, and duty. Iris, the truth teller, said that love wasn't required. In a pinch, "like" would do.

Thomas turned to Baby Harper. He entrusted my great-uncle with Mai-Dao's letters. DWH told me that after my great-uncle passed away she had found them in the bureau in his bedroom. *I've a set of extra keys to his house. Your great-uncle was always sweet on Thomas. We always keep the secrets of those we love.* DWH said that the letters were waiting for me now on the hallway table.

Of course, I had wondered how DeAnne Whatley Hammerick could have remembered in such plaintive details the contents of all those long-ago letters. I had thought, in between our sips of bourbon, that she could be making this all up. I decided that it didn't matter. At least it was a story, I thought. We all need a story of where we came from and how we got here. Otherwise, how could we ever put down our tender roots and stay.

27

(Justin Chin, 1969—2015)
贾斯丁·陈

作者简介

贾斯丁·陈（Justin Chin, 1969—2015），美国亚裔诗人、表演艺术家。贾斯丁·陈生于马来西亚，长于新加坡，后移民美国，定居旧金山。陈的父母都是华人医生，父母原本希望他能子承父业，但他对文学感兴趣，走上文学之路。

贾斯丁·陈除创作诗歌和散文以外，也为报纸和杂志供稿。贾斯丁·陈的作品有诗集《狠狠咬》（*Bite Hard*, 1997）、《无害的药》（*Harmless Medicine*, 2001）和《失望心烦》（*Gutted*, 2006），散文集《大杂烩：散文、谩骂和恶作剧》（*Mongrel: Essays, Diatribes and Pranks*, 1998）、《灰烬的负担》（*Burden of Ashes*, 2002）和《98 处伤口》（*98 Wounds*, 2011），剧本《食人莲花的攻击》（*Attack of the Man-Eating Lotus Blossoms*, 2005）。他的诗歌具有自传色彩，以坦诚的笔触在诗歌中探讨亚裔身份、种族刻板印象与冲突、移民经历、同性恋与性、美国消费主义和家庭等主题。他的作品以直接坦率的风格、幽默讽刺的语言和大胆的主题而著名。作为一名表演艺术家，他的作品在美国和世界各地上演。

诗歌《地理历史》（"A History of Geography"）选自诗集《狠狠咬》;《坟墓》（"The Grave"）选自诗集《无害的药》，诗歌记叙诗人对人生和死亡的思考。

作品选读

A History of Geography

By Justin Chin

America is a place far away,
as far as London/ Australia/ Canada
any Western country where people speak English,
All a page in an atlas/ a place on a map, can't drive/ walk/
take a bus to-
I want to go there, so I buy magazines, take a Biro felt pen,
draw arrows to people in the photographs & write my name
on their foreheads,
I want to go there so I fuck their people,
don't care if they're good-looking/ or turn me on or not,
I let them take me,
do what they want with me
even if it hurts me bad/ makes me bleed/ makes me bruise/ sore/ &
sad/ satisfied/ & happy/ mad/ desolate,
let them do what they want with a slab of meat
because they're giving me a place I cannot get to.
So I throw my legs up in the air,
spread them in toilets/ spread them in parks/ spread them in
hotel rooms
rich hotels/ with real fancy sheets and bedspreads/ with mint
chocolates and strawberries by starched white pillows &
fancy room service/ & nice uniformed bellmen/ &
receptionists who look at me and know what I'm doing/ cos
they want to do it too/ done it before,
maybe cheap rundown hotels/ with shared bathrooms & thin
walls/ creaky beds/ bed lice & stinking men.

But I don't care cos I'm in America/ in London/ in Australia/
in France/ in anywhere but this town.
This town where I am the son of a generation/ lost
to 25 years of what price paradise.
This town so clean and green, everything wiped over with
Dettol every week,
wiped so clean, they take away your insides
& give you dog biscuits & standard rations to replace what
they've disinfected.
I hold things I cannot say in my mouth,
I hold acts I cannot do in my chest,
hold a bitter stinking love in my groin.
Let them wipe away everything else,
wipe me/ disinfect me/ hose me down,
but I got what nobody else got
and they can't wipe that away
not even with their industrial strength bleach.
& I don't/ won't care what they make me sing/chant justice,
equality, peace, progress, prosperity, happiness for my
life,
it's all words that I sing/ chant/ move my lips/
know what it means,
and that is dangerous.
Wrap myself in newsprint,
wrap myself in satellite transmissions,
wrap myself in truth/ lies/ truth/ half truths,
believe what I wrap myself in knowing
I cannot go back.
They want to distill me,
take the queer sky out of my body.
Let it sit, simmer until my fire burns up in itself.
& when I am dark/ when I have no more life/ when I am no
more so abomination/ when I am no more shame/ when I am face

again/ when the collective being of me worships god, family,
education and the collective administrative silver spoon,
then I will be back in the fold.
The prodigal child, back from exile.
Please let me live
and rage in the realm of wonderment,
to know that the hand in the glove is not the fascist halal
rationed kiss that makes me feel like a stranger/ an
outsider in my own.
Let me live in all that my blood is mine,
in the color of spirits
backwards.
I am blind,
born blind, spirits come to me in polaroids of abstract
paintings that throw mud and saliva on my eyes to see
the new issue of Blue Boy,
who show me that love is deaf,
born deaf, spirits come to me as a bluesy lullaby, a
cat's howl at night that fills my ears/ that I can't
hear/ don't want to hear/ whispers yes that chokes me
till I can't speak, born dumb,
spirit is a voice that no one will hear because everybody is
born deaf, dumb and blind
in the bright lights holding us in a circle jerk, to the
music we speak of nothing that cannot find our minds
& I am in this world of pirates, prayers, ascensions, coups,
attacks, counterattacks, shadows, illness, deceptions
manipulations, addictions, metaphysicians, hyperboles
poetics, politics, plays, perspiration, and love.

The Grave

By Justin Chin

In the harsh glare of an easily
reprehensible life. The channel changer is lost
in the crack of an infinite sofa.
    Everything falls apart, everything breaks
down, torn into a million
fragments, Jericho everyday.

I want to be the blameless
victim in this canceled puppet show,
the marionette every mother loves, the one
souvenirs are modeled from.

> (In that lifetime, Elton John will write mushy ballads just
> for me. Michael Jackson will want to be my best friend. He'd
> take me to the Neverland Ranch, and by the llama feeding trough,
> he'd say something like, "You're a great guy, don't give up,
> stay positive!" And I'd say, "Michael, you fucking idiot, I *am*
> positive!" And he'd say, "Oh, you're so funny! Would you like
> to touch Bubbles?"
> And I would.)

In the crux of my hollow innocent youth,
I believed that my teddy bears had feelings.
    To cure me of this, my guardians made me give
them to the church missionaries' children.
Scrubbed-clean rosy-cheeked blonde kids who smelled
of sweat and talc, who were in constant
wide-blue-eyed bewilderment as to why

they were profusely perspiring in the tropics,
instead of living out some winter wonderland Bobsey Twins
fantasy, who were oblivious
to their parents' desperate efforts
to save the dusky masses, ignorant enough
to believe in the secret lives of stuffed animals.
I could not eat animal crackers
because I did not want to hurt the poor things;
but, braised the right way, I could eat
any part of a pig, starting with the head,
working on the soft flesh around the eyes,
savoring its raspy tongue with a dipping
sauce of ginger, chilies and lime.

Oh blameless innocent victim.
What measures a lifetime?

I used to have this theory about how
much life a human body could hold.
It all had to do with the number
of heartbeats. Each human is assigned a number
determined by an unknown power cascading
over the dark waters of the unformed Earth.

For some, it was a magnificently high number,
seen only in Richie Rich comics, and for others,
it was frightfully low, like twenty-six.
No bargaining, no coupons,
no White Flower Day sale, no specials. Once
you hit your number, you croak.
I imagined the angels in heaven
and the demons in hell gathering to watch
the counters turn, like how I enjoyed watching

the speedometer line up to a row of similar
numbers, and especially when the row of
nines turned into
                    the row of zeros.

Oh blameless innocent victim.
What measures eternity?

An eternal damnation. An everlasting love.

I could not imagine the night sky
stretched out forever, so I decided that it came
to an end at some point, by a velvet rope it ended
and beyond that rope were row after row of cushioned seats,
    a majestic cosmic theater,
playing every movie I can remember.

I want to be able to evoke
those blameless and innocent days, to revel
in their ignorance and goodness
as if they have the power
    to protect and to heal,
and to strengthen,
and to bring me to safety
    long after all other resource
      were exhausted.

But I emerge anew in the wreckage,
blinking in the sunlight,

the residue of salt water in my belly.

You know what they say,

God never closes a door before making sure
that the windows are barricaded
and the fire escape is inaccessible.

I used to know how to stop the revolution of planets.

I used to know how to save the world.

Now, I don't know anything anymore.

28

(Susan Choi, 1969—　)
苏珊·崔

作者简介

苏珊·崔（Susan Choi, 1969—　），美国韩裔小说家，出生于美国印第安纳州，9岁时随母亲搬到德克萨斯州的休斯敦居住。苏珊·崔从耶鲁大学（Yale University）获得文学学士学位，从康奈尔大学（Cornell University）获得艺术硕士学位。她荣获了2001年美国国家艺术基金会奖（National Endowment for the Arts Fellowship recipient）、2004年的古根海姆奖（Guggenheim Fellowships）与2010年的温弗里德·格奥尔格·泽巴尔德奖（PEN/W.G. Sebald Award）等。

迄今为止，她创作了四部长篇小说。她的处女作《留学生》（*The Foreign Student*, 1998）荣获亚裔文学小说奖（Asian American Literary Award for Fiction）与斯蒂芬·特纳奖（Steven Turner Award）。第二部长篇小说《美国女人》（*American Woman*, 2003）被提名2004年普利策奖（Pulitzer Prize finalist）与2010年的纽约公共图书馆小狮子奖（New York Public Library Young Lions Award）。第三部作品《嫌疑犯》（*A Person of Interest*, 2008）被提名2009年福克纳奖（Faulkner Award）；最近的一部小说《我的教育》（*My Education*, 2013）荣获浪达文学奖（Lambda Literary Award）。

《留学生》是苏珊·崔的代表作品。这部长篇小说主要讲述了主人公在日本侵略朝鲜期间历尽千辛万苦逃到了美国，试图摆脱国内动荡不安的政治。然而，战争阴影一直伴随着他，让他在无尽的痛苦中挣扎。直到美国白人女性凯瑟琳的出现给他的生活带来了光明，让他逐渐走出了阴霾。

小说第三章是本小说最为精彩的部分之一，主要讲述了主人公在美国的艰难生存以及美国社会对亚洲人，尤其是对朝鲜人的偏见和歧视。

作品选集

The Foreign Student

Chapter Three

(excerpt)

By Susan Choi

"I wanted you to see the country around here, before the leaves went away. You've been up on the mountain ever since you arrived."

"I have been to places. Last month I go to Mobile, Laurel, and Augusta," he said, enunciating each name with great precision.

"Really?"she exclaimed. She had hoped she was taking him on his first exploration of America. "What for?"

"There is something, the Episcopal Church Council. I go to churches belonging in this, and talk on Korea."

"Just for your own amusement?"

"No, I do it for the council, when they ask me. But I like to give a talk. I have a projector, and I show some slide."

"Of the war?"

"Not so many. Most of his pictures were from a set of National Archive photographs of Korea, in which it looked dim, impoverished, and unredeemable, in contrast with his presentation, which sought to be generic and not surprising or unpleasant. He generally explained that Koreans were farmers, that they enjoyed celebrating their holidays clad in bright costumes, that they were fond of flowers and children—that they were unremarkable, hardly worth the trouble of a lecture. The slides were never quite appropriate. Like his remarks, he kept them as generic as he could, and changed them often. He understood that people liked something to look at, and that even the least seasoned audience eventually lost interest in looking at him. He also gave a potted history of the war, and answered questions. "What kind?" said Katherine. "You must have found it annoying, when I asked you to describe what a war looked like."

"No. This isn't annoying."

"I didn't realize you had to answer people's stupid questions all the time."

"Your questions is not stupid. Nothing you say would be stupid."

She looked at him, surprised.

He blushed. "I tell you a very, really stupid one."

"All right."

"In Mobile, a man asks me if Koreans live in trees."

"Like monkeys!"

"In a tree house," he clarified.

"Like monkeys in tree houses! What did you say?"

"I say no, but maybe he's thinking of the kind of a house we do have, near the water. The kind of a house up on legs, like this."

"On stilts. You were too polite."

He smiled. "That was okay."

"You're polite to say yes to the church council."

"I don't mind it. They give Sewanee, for my tuition."

Katherine was embarrassed. The arrangement embarrassed her, but also the fact that it hadn't occurred to her that such an arrangement must exist. She was silent a moment.

"How do you get there?" she asked finally. "How do you reach these little towns?"

"I take Grey-Hound bus."

"That's terrible!"

He actually enjoyed it a great deal, but instead he said, noncommittally, "No."

"I'll drive you the next time you go. How far in advance do you get your marching orders?"

"It depends. Sometimes a lot of time, sometimes just a few, one or two days. I like this bus, though. It's a very quiet time."

"I won't hear of it."

"I do really," he laughed. "I sit, I watch this go by. Like going to the movies."

"Do you like the movies?"

"Yes. Very much."

"We must go sometime."

"Okay."

"But I still won't hear of your taking the bus. I'm going to drive you the next time. That's settled," she said, holding up a hand. He watched her eyes calmly scanning the road, until she glanced at him. "Do you give up?"

"I do," he said.

"You'll call me when you have a new assignment?"

"You make it sound like—you make it sound like I'm a spy," he said, smiling.

After she'd dropped him off he went upstairs to his room and sat on his bed. It was late. He'd missed supper. He wondered if Mrs. Wade had set aside something for him, but he couldn't get up.

Crane must have heard him come in. He came and hung off the door frame, the frame groaning in protest. Crane seemed morose and self-absorbed, as usual. After some time he said, "You want to come home for Thanksgiving with me? Where the hell are you going to go, right? I guess that you'll have to." Crane said this gloomily, as if it were a judgment on himself.

"Thank you. I think so."

Crane did a pull-up, and thrust his legs into the room. He hung there like a pendulum. "My folks don't know you're an Oriental," he puffed, swinging hard back and forth. "My folks are cracked." It was clear that the two statements had nothing to do with each other.

"Okay." He was not paying much more attention to Crane than Crane was paying to him. He no longer wondered at Crane's unlikely, unflagging attachment. He knew that for Crane he was an easy and dependable possession, as if at any time Crane might announce to someone, "My man Chuck." But he liked Crane. Crane was his only real friend, his only possible confidant.

"Where'd you say you were all day?" Crane asked. Without any hesitation whatsoever he lied, "At the library."

He was used to the constant pressure of the future, a dark hive of possibility that he had never learned how to ignore, until now. Now he ignored it completely. The outer limit of his vision sprang up right before his face and he refocused. He didn't think about his next church council lecture, or how he would arrive there, hoping the event, when it came, would escape his attention. It had taken days for him to realize that Katherine had offered to drive him in the way that he heard people say, when they met by accident, "We must see each other soon!" Hearing these exchanges it was never any problem for him to understand that the insistence was insincere, but talking with her, sitting right alongside her—he'd had difficulty judging her meaning. He would walk the paths of the campus with his head bowed, his algebra equations radiating in every direction, his latest dictionary words floating past like bits of floss on a fine summer day, lost in the landscape of his thoughts, but with the problem of her looming throughout, like a hill in the distance. It became clear that her offer of a ride had been no more than kind conversation. He blushed slightly to think it. He was embarrassed not only by his mistake, but by his sudden disappointment.

Dean Bower sent him a note saying that he had been invited to speak to the congregation of St. Paul's Episcopal Church in Jackson, Tennessee. He accepted ten dollars' pocket money for a round-trip bus ticket, a lunch, and some small improvement for himself he was left to decide on, like a new pair of socks. The first move was made, and nothing intervened to correct him, and so he went on, each elapsed day eroding the likelihood of his conversation with Katherine a little more, until he might have actually forgotten, because there no longer seemed to be anything to remember. Then she called him, on the telephone that sat on a glossy round vase-table out in the hall of Strake House. "I don't think I gave you my phone number," she began. "I'm sorry about that. I don't even think I gave you my name. My last name is Monroe." Hearing nothing but silence from him, she felt newly uncertain. But she said aloud, soldiering forth, "Of course, Mrs. Reston knows how to find me. Almost anyone does. But I should have made that simpler. In any case, I hear you're invited to give your talk in Jackson. That's lucky for me. It's a place I'd like to know." She listened carefully for possible signs. Until now she'd assumed he was afraid of imposing on her, but now it seemed she was imposing on him. When she hadn't heard anything from him for days she'd given way to curiosity and gone to ask the dean's secretary about the foreign student's lecture. "I thought that I might send my aunt to see him. Is he asked to speak anywhere lately? I have an aunt almost everywhere."

"He's going to go down to Jackson, Tennessee, next week," the secretary had said. "Have you got an aunt there?"

"No, I haven't."

"That's too bad. Have you met Mr. Ahn?"

"I met him with Mrs. Reston when he had just gotten here."

"He's a long way from home." She sounded vaguely critical saying it. "If you tell me where your aunt lives I'll let you know if he's going there, Katherine."

"That's all right," she'd said. She'd decided to wait and see if he would phone. But then he hadn't.

He had managed to locate his voice. "I just find out myself."

"You just found out."

"Yes. I just found out myself."

"I just heard, too, I'm sure not long after you did. In any case, I'd still like to drive you. I like to drive. I'd still teach you, if you still want to learn."

"I go Thursday. Not this one, the next one."

"If I teach you to drive, you won't need a ride anymore."

"I have no any car."

"Perhaps someone will give you one."

"Yeah!" he said, laughing.

"That would be fine, wouldn't it?" Her voice sounded so reduced. He was standing hunched over because the dried-out rubber coil of the phone cord refused to stretch straight, and his face brushed near the bush of fake flowers sticking out of the vase. He smelled dust.

In the week before their appointment she went to the library and looked for a book on Korea. All she found was a copy of Terry on the Japanese Empire, thirty years out of date. She remembered her father having Terry on everything, when she was a girl. All the flawlessly knife-scored, fragile colored maps, and ads for ancient travelers in the back: Nippon Cruise Lines, Bank of Taiwan, Southern Manchuria Railway. The Yamatoya Shirt Manufacturers, specializing in *silk, linen, and cotton crape*. Grimy photos of thin rigged canoes, with a sail like a sheet of notepaper impaled on a stick. She flipped to the part on Korea: *Korean ideas of hygiene are almost as negligible as those of a Hottentot. The average Korean well is little short of a pest-hole. The average Korean man is 5 ft. 4 in. tall, of good physique, well formed, with not unhandsome Mongoloid features, oblique dark-brown eyes, high cheek-bones, and non-curling hair that shades from a russet to a sloe black. The olive bronze complexions in certain instances show a tint as light as that of a quadroon*, and under "Seoul Entertainments," *Korean Dances (insipid and wearisome)*—

"Christ!" she burst out, tossing it aside.

Katherine came to pick him up early in the morning, with the giddy whirr of the engine floating far ahead through the still air and her scarf and a ribbon of car exhaust streaming behind. It was unusually warm for November in the mountains, and she was driving with the top down and no hat. When she arrived at Strake House he was waiting for her on the front steps in a thin-looking suit. He was holding a cardboard box that had the slide projector in it, with a brown bag on top. Mrs. Wade had made him a lunch, which saved him some money. Added to what he had saved in not buying a bus ticket and in deciding to stick with old socks, he had the whole ten dollars left over, the bill still folded in half in the envelope that had come from Dean Bower. It was in his power to make some kind of gesture. He wasn't nervous anymore when she pulled up.

They slid down off the mountain and found the road that would carry them west to Jackson, which lay five hours away on the highway from Nashville to Memphis. Autumn had left the hills not so much bare as rubbed dull, like an old sofa's cushions. The road surged and stuttered, unrolling with growing momentum and then braking hard against towns where a post office and drugstore would spring up across from each other, with one traffic light strung between them. The wind roared too loudly to talk. At first they worried that perhaps they should shout to each other, but eventually this worry was gone, as if the wind peeled it away. One hour passed, and then another, until their wordless cocoon of loud wind in the midst of dull hills pouring past seemed ancient and permanent, and not requiring anything more. Around noon they had to change roads and he leaned toward her with a finger on the map. She hardly glanced at it, taking the sharp right without slowing down, and they slammed hard together against her door, and then slowly came upright again as the car headed north.

Jackson was a considerable small city of six churches, but they were all close together on the neat grid of main street and side streets that made up downtown. They wound through these, their eyes trained together on steeples and signs. Now, in the drowsy noontime hush that they moved through, the silence between them seemed huge. They found St. Paul's and pulled into the white gravel lot alongside it. They had arrived very early. Katherine turned off the engine and they sat listening to its reluctant rattles and clunks as it spun to a halt, and when these were finished, they listened to the birds.

"You must want lunch," she said at last. "You'd better have eaten before you give your talk."

He understood now that he had been expecting the drive to transport him to a place in which he would find himself very calmly buying Katherine lunch with his ten-dollar bill. The simple and absolute logic of such a plan almost guaranteed that it would take place. He fingered the envelope in his pocket.

"Maybe we go find something," he said, accidentally sounding reluctant.

"Mrs. Wade is too good a friend of mine for me to let you waste your lunch. It would break my heart. And I'm not hungry."

"But it must be."

"I'm not." She took her case from her pocketbook and lit herself a cigarette. "I'm going to stretch my legs and take a look around. That's what I need most." She got out of the car, lifted her arms above her head for a moment, and then strode away.

He watched her recede. She crossed the lawn to the front steps, craned her head to look up at the steeple, and then vanished around the side of the building. She had left a thin ghost of smoke near the car. He got the lunch bag from between his feet and unrolled it. The crackling of the paper seemed deafening. He glanced around, but there was no one outside on this street, which was lined with old spreading oaks, stripped bare, reaching sideways for each other. Then he peered into the bag and caught his breath. It held two sandwiches carefully folded in wax paper, two red pears, two slices of cake, and a thermos of water.

They ate sitting together in the small churchyard. "Mrs. Wade is an artist of sandwiches," Katherine said. The churchyard was only half full of grave markers, most of them of the sturdy, prosperous-looking kind, shaped like fat slices of bread, although some were badly leaning and no longer legible. "I never used to notice a church," she went on, balling up the wax paper that had contained her sandwich. She produced a pocket knife from her bag and cut up her pear; if there was a seed she nicked it out and sent it flying. "Churches used to seem like part of the landscape, like rocks or trees. It never occurred to me that there was any difference between them. Not just differences in appearance, but differences in faith. I never gave it any thought at all."

"You do now?"

"I guess I give it a little more thought. For example, this is a plain white shingled church and there's nothing very surprising about the proportions of the steeple. And it's Episcopal, but I don't know what that means from Methodist, or Baptist, or any of the others."

"My mother," he said, surprised to hear himself saying it, "becomes Episcopal some years ago."

"My father was a Catholic. That meant he didn't want any religion in the house at all. I think my mother might have been a Lutheran, but she had to please my father, which was wonderful for her because I'm sure she never wanted to bother with religion in the first place. When I was twelve years old I had a great longing for God. I prayed and mooned about the house and threatened to become a nun. I thought my situation was very tragic. But I outgrew that. You know, when you're a child you want so badly to set yourself apart, and you imagine you're something you're not. Other things came along that I was better at."

"What things?"

"It sounds like you don't think I'm good at anything."

"No!" He flushed. "No."

"I don't know. Other things. In any case, I was thinking that it's strange, because now I'm older and I seem to have come full circle, and started noticing churches. Why did your mother become an Episcopalian?"

"A missionary."

"Are there many Episcopal missionaries in Korea?"

"And Catholic."

"And she didn't want to be Catholic? Or did the Episcopals get to her first?"

"I don't know."

When he didn't elaborate she said, "And your father?"

"No."

"And you?"

"No." She had handed him part of the pear and its scent filled his nostrils. Flowers' perfume, he remembered, is their prayer to God. Where had he read that? He prayed sometimes, but mostly as a reflex. He might be struck, and then it would fly out of him: *please God*.

They saw the priest coming across the yard, frowning and nodding in welcome. "I'm Katherine Monroe," she announced when he'd drawn near, rising to offer her hand. He was looking at Chuck as he groped for it. "I didn't realize Mr. Ahn would be accompanied."

"I'm Sewanee's most famous idler, Father, so I'm always trying to be useful. I thought it would be nice if Mr. Ahn didn't have to take the bus. Shall we get your machine from the car?" she asked, turning back to him.

He followed them, half hearing Katherine's elaborate replies to the priest's inquiries about Sewanee. The hem of her skirt snapped around her knees as she walked. At the car she lifted his box to him and set about raising the top; the priest helped her. "Can you suggest any interesting places in town, Father? I thought I'd take a walk. I've never been in Jackson before."

"You're not going to listen to Mr. Ahn's talk?"

"I don't want to make him nervous. I think it's easier to speak in front of people you don't know. That's all right, isn't it, Chuck?"

He didn't know whether he was relieved or disappointed. He and the priest stood watching as she resecured her scarf around her neck and stowed her gloves in the glove box. Neither of them seemed able to proceed while she was still there. She popped open a compact and glanced at herself, and as quickly shut it again.

"I'm all set. Did you think of anything I should see, Father?"

"Our town hall is a pretty impressive building. If you follow this street to the corner and go left, you'll find some shopping."

"That would be lethal," she laughed.

"If you were a southerner I could think you'd take an interest in our monument square, but you might find it interesting anyway."

Katherine laughed again. "I am a southerner, Father."

"I'm sorry. I wouldn't have guessed it."

"What would you have guessed?"

"Oh, no. It was my mistake to assume in the first place."

"I lived up East awhile. I think I must have lost my accent there."

"My goodness," said the priest. She knew they were watching her all the way to the corner, where she turned left as he had suggested. Then she'd moved out of sight.

Inside the church the priest showed him a screen he had brought from the Sunday-school room, and together they dragged out a table to set the projector on. Chuck brought an extension cord out of the box and the priest complimented him on how prepared he was. Until now his compact self-sufficiency on these journeys was the one thing that he could rely on to steady his nerves. He liked to board the bus, in his thin suit, with his roundtrip ticket, directions he'd made for himself from the library's atlas, a sum of money too small to seem unearned in his pocket, and the box in his arms that contained the projector and all of its needs: extension cord, slides, a spare bulb. All he required was electricity and a blank wall. He was an itinerant, as solitary as a country doctor, or the missionary who had converted his mother. He hadn't realized how much it gratified him to be independent this way until today.

He turned the projector on and a weak square of light swung around the room and fell short of the screen. He pushed a psalm book under the projector's front and glanced apologetically at the priest, but the priest was nodding and waving a hand. "That's just fine. I can tell that you've done this before."

"A few, two-three times." He put the slides in order and dropped them one by one into the carousel, checking that each had gone in right side up. Number one was the map: Korea After 1945. Number two was The U.S. Infantry Coming out of the Seoul Railway Station. He put his thumb on the slide-changer button and fired the carousel through the full rotation. Then he fiddled for a while with the focus. His palms were sweating. He asked the priest to show him to the men's room and once alone rinsed his face and scrubbed it dry with a coarse paper towel. He bent over to touch his toes, and dragged his knuckles back and forth on the floor. Then the door swung open and he sprang upright in embarrassment.

"We're ready for you," the priest said.

The audience was mostly older, charity and book-circle women, and a few intent men. "Hi," he croaked, and they all smiled at once, in response. "I am Chang Ahn. I study at Sewanee, University of the South, but before this I live in Korea."

"How old are you?" a woman interrupted.

"Now I am twenty-five years old."

"You look so young," she said sadly.

He usually began his address by saying that his presence before them was the direct result of MacArthur's Inchon landing. "I'm not here, if this doesn't happen," he said, feeling melancholy suddenly. The faces in the audience blinked at him. He turned on the projector and Korea After 1945 appeared on the wall. He ducked through the beam apologetically. "Here it is," he said, letting the shadow from his forearm mar the picture. "I am sorry the map is not more big."

He explained the positions of Japan, China, and the Soviet Union, around the edges of the fuzzy square of light. "This is makes the fate of Korea. The Japanese colonize, at the beginning of this twentieth century, so when the Second World War is beginning, they are already there."

He paused and looked around. "Okay?" he asked anxiously. A few people nodded.

"You remember," he went on, "in the Second World War it is United States and Soviets together, Japanese with the Italians and Germans. The Japanese are in Korea, this is a terrible time," he sighed. "Okay. The Soviets, in the Second World War, fight against the Japanese, and they fight in Korea." He threw his arms wide.

When the Japanese surrendered at the end of the war, the Soviets and the Americans split the job of overseeing the Japanese withdrawal from the Korean peninsula. A line was drawn at the thirty-eighth parallel, which split the country roughly in half. The Soviet military would administer the northern half, the Americans the southern. This was, in theory, a temporary arrangement. Provisional governments were set up on each side for the duration of Korea's reconstruction. The Soviets, on their side, enabled the return from exile of a great people's hero, a revolutionary who had fought the Japanese throughout the thirties. Chuck cut himself short. "This man become the leader of Communist North Korea," he concluded. The Americans, for their part, imported a committed anti-Communist expatriate named Syngman Rhee, who had graduated Princeton and lived in the U.S. for the preceding forty years. Rhee was put in charge of South Korea. Over time the rival governments dug in, and in June of 1950, went to war.

He always felt hopeless, called upon to deliver a clear explanation of the war. It defied explanation. Sometimes he simply skipped over causes, and began, "Korea is a shape just like Florida. Yes? The top half is a Communist state, and the bottom half are fighting for democracy!"

He would groundlessly compare the parallel to the Mason-Dixon line, and see every head nod excitedly. "In June 1950, the Communist army comes over the parallel and invades the South. They come by surprise, and get almost all to the sea." His hands swept: an amazing advance. The UN made a force to fight back, of the South's Republic of Korea army, ROKA, and the United States army, and some other armies, like Britain's.

The particularities of the UN force never interested anyone, and he quickly skipped ahead. "The Communists go fast, until the UN force is crowded into a very little space at the bottom of Korea, around the city Pusan." He pronounced it for them loudly: *Poos-ahn*. "This is like, if the war is all over Florida, and our side are trapped in Miami." Now MacArthur's genius showed itself: instead of trying to push back, over the land, he took his army to the sea, and sailed up the coast, to Inchon. He landed there and cut the Communists in half, off from themselves. Seoul was liberated, and the tide turned around.

He genuinely liked talking about the landing, and MacArthur. It all made for such an exciting, simple minded, morally unambiguous story. Each time he told it, the plot was reduced and the number of details increased, and the whole claimed more of his memory for itself and left less room for everything else. He punched the slide-changer now, and Korea After 1945 was replaced by The U.S. Infantry Coming out of the Seoul Railway Station, a soap-scrubbed and smiling platoon marching into the clean, level street. This image made a much better illustration of the idea of MacArthur than any actual picture of the Korean war could have. People were often surprised by the vaulted dome of the train station, and the European-looking avenue of trees. "That's Seoul?" a woman asked, vaguely disappointed. The file of troops looked confident and happy, because the picture had not been taken during the Korean conflict at all, but in September 1945, after the Japanese defeat. The photo's original caption had read, "Liberation feels fine! U.S. and their Soviet allies arrive to clean house in Korea." No one was dreaming there would be a civil war.

He followed the U.S. Infantry slide with Water Buffalo in a Rice Paddy, and then Village Farmers Squatting Down to Smoke, which satisfied the skepticism of the woman who had asked about the Seoul railway station. Everyone murmured with pleasure at the image of the farmers, in their year-round pajamas and inscrutable Eskimos' faces, and then the double doors at the back of the sanctuary creaked loudly and Katherine was standing there, with her pocketbook held to her chin, looking lost.

Each of the twelve or so heads clustered in the front pews turned to look at her. She let the door fall shut and slipped into the rearmost pew. "I'm sorry," she said. A flush appeared on her cheeks to match his.

He couldn't remember where he'd left off. The awareness that he was blushing made him blush even more deeply. He wondered if anyone could see it. Often the darkness of his skin seemed to guard his emotions from notice, as if the fact of the color blotted out all that happened within it. He fingered the slide-changer nervously, and the carousel shot ahead, throwing a new picture onto the screen. For a terrifying eternity he stared at this without recognizing what it was. The rough grain of the image, fine rubble, a burial mound. His gaze crisscrossed it wildly, searching for something that might help him locate himself.

When he remembered why the image was there, it was like remembering the plot of a childhood fable. Although the remembrance was deeply familiar, it wasn't convincing, because it didn't seem to make sense. The priest was in the front row, his eyebrows straining upward with encouragement. Chuck took a deep breath, and began again. "You maybe don't believe it, but Korea, the land, looks very much like Tennessee." He gestured at the picture of hills. So much, sometimes he woke in the morning and just for an instant was sure he was home. The mist coming out from the mountains. The soft shapes of hills. His hands formed them. At last he stopped seeing her.

29

(Paisley Rekdal, 1970—) 佩斯利·雷克达尔

作者简介

佩斯利·雷克达尔（Paisley Rekdal, 1970— ），美籍亚裔诗人。雷克达尔生于西雅图，母亲是华裔，父亲是挪威裔。雷克达尔获得华盛顿大学（University of Washington）学士、多伦多大学中世纪研究中心（Pontifical Institute of Mediaeval Studies）硕士和密歇根大学安娜堡分校（University of Michigan, Ann Arbor）的创意写作硕士学位（MFA）。她目前在犹他大学（University of Utah）任教。

雷克达尔著有诗集《犀牛的碰撞》（*A Crash of Rhinos,* 2000）、《没有裤子的六个女孩》（*Six Girls Without Pants,* 2002）、《万花筒的发明》（*The Invention of the Kaleidoscope,* 2007）、《动物眼睛》（*Animal Eye,* 2012）和《想象的船只》（*Imaginary Vessels,* 2016），散文集《我母亲遇见布鲁斯李的那个晚上》（*The Night My Mother Met Bruce Lee: Observations on Not Fitting In,* 2000）和回忆录《亲密：一个美国家庭的相册》（*Intimate: An American Family Photo Album,* 2012）。她的作品探讨种族、性、神话和身份等主题，风格清新自然却感情强烈。雷克达尔的诗歌多次获奖，包括古根海姆奖（Guggenheim Fellowship）、艾米·洛威尔诗歌旅行奖金（Amy Lowell Poetry Traveling Fellowship）、美国全国艺术基金会资助金、手推车奖和 2016 AWP 非虚构奖（AWP Nonfiction Prize），和其他各种州立艺术奖。她于 2017 年被授予犹他州桂冠诗人的称号。

诗歌《幸福》（"Happiness"）选自诗集《动物眼睛》，诗人以清新自然的语言、丰富的动物意象表达自己对于幸福的理解。诗歌《船只》（"Vessels"）选自诗集《想象的船只》，清新流畅，颇有意趣。

作品选读

Happiness

By Paisley Rekdal

I have been taught never to brag but now
I cannot help it: I keep
a beautiful garden, all abundance,
indiscriminate, pulling itself
from the stubborn earth: does it offend you
to watch me working in it,
touching my hands to the greening tips or
tearing the yellow stalks back, so wild
the living and the dead both
snap off in my hands?
The neighbor with his stuttering
fingers, the neighbor with his broken
love: each comes up my drive
to receive his pitying,
accustomed consolations, watches me
work in silence awhile, rises in anger,
walks back. Does it offend them to watch me
not mourning with them but working
fitfully, fruitlessly, working
the way the bees work, which is to say
by instinct alone, which looks like pleasure?
I can stand for hours among the sweet
narcissus, silent as a point of bone.
I can wait longer than sadness. I can wait longer
than your grief. It is such a small thing
to be proud of, a garden. Today

there were scrub jays, quail,
a woodpecker knocking at the white-
and-black shapes of trees, and someone's lost rabbit
scratching under the barberry: is it
indiscriminate? Should it shrink back, wither,
and expurgate? Should I, too, not be loved?
It is only a little time, a little space.
Why not watch the grasses take up their colors in a rush
like a stream of kerosene being lit?
If I could not have made this garden beautiful
I wouldn't understand your suffering,
nor care for each the same, inflamed way.
I would have to stay only like the bees,
beyond consciousness, beyond
self-reproach, fingers dug down hard
into stone, and growing nothing.
There is no end to ego,
with its museum of disappointments.
I want to take my neighbors into the garden
and show them: Here is consolation.
Here is your pity. Look how much seed it drops
around the sparrows as they fight.
It lives alongside their misery.
It glows each evening with a violent light.

Vessels

By Paisley Rekdal

Shouldn't it ache, this slit
into the sweet
and salt mix of waters
composing the mussel,
its labial meats
winged open: yellow-
fleshed, black and gray
around the tough
adductor? It hurts
to imagine it, regardless
of the harvester's
denials, swiveling
his knife to make
the incision: one
dull cyst nicked
from the oyster's
mantle—its thread of red
gland no bigger
than a seed
of trout roe—pressed
inside this mussel's
tendered flesh.
Both hosts eased
open with a knife
(as if anything
could be said to be eased
with a knife):
so that one pearl

after another can be
harvested, polished,
added to others
until a single rope is strung
on silk. Linked
by what you think
is pain. Nothing
could be so roughly
handled and yet feel
so little, your pity
turned into part of this
production: you
with your small,
four-chambered heart,
shyness, hungers, envy: what
in you could be so precious
you would cleave
another to keep it
close? Imagine
the weeks it takes to wind
nacre over the red
seed placed at another
heart's mantle. The mussel
become what no one
wants to:
vessel, caisson, wounded
into making us
the thing we want
to call beautiful.

30

(Viet Thanh Nguyen, 1971—　)
阮越清

作者简介

阮越清（Viet Thanh Nguyen, 1971—　），美国越南裔作家和批评家，出生于越南邦美蜀（Ban Me Thuot）。1975 年，在越南动荡的政治环境下，阮越清随父母到美国宾夕法尼亚洲难民营避难。1992 年，他从加州大学伯克利分校（University of California, Berkeley）获得英语与族裔研究本科学位，1997 年从同一所大学获得英语专业博士学位。毕业后阮越清到南加州大学（University of Southern California）任职。

阮越清迄今为止创作了颇多优秀的作品，有专著《种族与抗争：美国亚裔文学与政治》（*Race and Resistance: Literature and Politics in Asian America*, 2002）、非小说类书籍《永无消失的越南与战争记忆》（*Nothing Ever Dies: Vietnam and The Memory of War*, 2016）、长篇小说《同情者》（*The Sympathizer*, 2015）和短篇小说籍《难民》（*The Refugees*, 2017）。他创作的作品荣获或被提名诸多美国重要奖项。

阮越清的处女作《同情者》斩获 2016 年的普利策小说奖（Pulitzer Prize）、代顿文学和平奖（Dayton Literary Peace Prize）、卡耐基优秀小说奖（Carnegie Medal for Excellence in Fiction）、埃德加最佳处女作奖（Edgar Award for Best First Novel）与美国亚太文学奖（Asian/Pacific American Award for Literature）等诸多奖项。本小说讲述了一名北越南间谍，在越南政治动荡期间逃到美国避难，最后随着反共游击队回到了越南。在这期间，他在各种双重性之间挣扎和徘徊，最终选择顺从自己的内心，找回了自我。

本小说第 19 章主要围绕叙述者被刑讯逼供写忏悔书而展开。政治的动荡和不同文化背景让这位间谍迷失了自己，失去了“信仰”。通过写忏悔书，叙述者对自己的身份有了更为清楚的定位，明晰了自己的“信仰”。

作品选读

The Sympathizer

Chapter 19

By Viet Thanh Nguyen

Only from death? The commandant appeared genuinely wounded, his finger resting on the last words of my confession. In his other hand was a blue pencil, the color chosen because Stalin had also used a blue pencil, or so he told me. Like Stalin, the commandant was a diligent editor, always ready to note my many errata and digressions and always urging me to delete, excise, reword, or add. Implying that life in my camp is worse than death is a little histrionic, don't you think? The commandant seemed eminently reasonable as he sat in his bamboo chair, and for a moment, sitting in my bamboo chair, I, too, felt that he was eminently reasonable. But then I remembered that only an hour earlier I had been sitting in the windowless, redbrick isolation cell where I had spent the last year since the ambush, rewriting the many versions of my confession, the latest of which the commandant now possessed. Perhaps your perspective differs from mine, Comrade Commandant, I said, trying to get used to the sound of my own voice. I had not spoken to anyone in a week. I'm a prisoner, I went on, and you're the one in charge. It may be hard for you to sympathize with me, and vice versa.

The commandant sighed and laid the final sheet of my confession on top of the 294 other pages that preceded it, stacked on a table by his chair. How many times must I tell you? You're not a prisoner! Those men are prisoners, he said, pointing out the window to the barracks that housed a thousand inmates, including my fellow survivors, the Lao farmer, the Hmong scout, the philosophical medic, the darkest marine, the dark marine, and Bon. You are a special case. He lit a cigarette. You are a guest of myself and the commissar.

Guests can leave, Comrade Commandant. I paused to observe his reaction. I wanted one of his cigarettes, which I would not get if I angered him. Today, however, he was in a rare good mood and did not frown. He had the high cheekbones and delicate features of an opera singer, and even ten years of warfare fought from a cave in Laos had not ruined his classically good looks. What rendered him unattractive at times was his moroseness, a perpetual, damp affliction he shared with everyone else in the camp, including myself. This was the sadness felt by homesick soldiers and prisoners, a sweating that never ceased, absorbed into a perpetually damp clothing that could never be dried, just as I was not dry sitting in my bamboo chair. The commandant at least had the benefit of an electric fan blowing on him, one of only two in the camp. According to my baby-faced guard, the other fan was in the commissar's quarters.

Perhaps a better term than "guest" is "patient", the commandant said, editing once more. You have traveled to strange lands and been exposed to some dangerous ideas. It wouldn't do to bring infectious ideas into a country unused to them. Think of the people, insulated for so long from foreign ideas. Exposure could lead to a real catastrophe for minds that aren't ready for them. If you saw the situation from our point of view, you would see that it was necessary to quarantine you until we could cure you, even if it hurts us to see a revolutionary like yourself kept in such conditions.

I could see his point of view, albeit with some difficulty. There were reasons to be suspicious of someone like me, who had endured suspicion all his life. But still, it was hard for me not to feel that a year in an isolation cell from which I was allowed to emerge only an hour a day for exercise, blinking and white, was unwarranted, as I had informed him at each of these weekly sessions where he criticized my confession and I, in turn, criticized myself. These reminders I had given him must also have been on his mind, because when I opened my mouth to speak again, he said, I know what you're going to say. As I told you all along, when your confession reaches a satisfactory state, based on our reading of it and on my reports of these self-criticism sessions to the commissar, you will move on to the next and, we hope, last stage of your reeducation. In short, the commissar believes you ready to be cured.

He does? I had yet to even meet the faceless man, otherwise known as the commissar. None of the prisoners had. They saw him only during his weekly lectures, sitting behind a table on the dais of the meeting hall where all the prisoners gathered for political lectures. I had not even seen him there, for these lectures, according to the commandant, amounted only to an elementary school education designed for pure reactionaries, puppets brainwashed by decades of ideological saturation. The faceless man had decreed me exempt from these simple lessons. Instead, I was privileged by having no burdens except to write and to reflect. My only glimpses of the commissar had come on those rare moments when I looked up from my exercise pen and saw him on the balcony of his bamboo quarters, atop the larger of the two hills overlooking the camp. At the base of the hills clustered the kitchen, mess hall, armory, latrines, and warehouses of the guards, along with the solitary rooms for special cases like me. Barbed-wire fencing separated this interior camp of the guards from the exterior camp where the inmates slowly eroded, the former soldiers, security officers, or bureaucrats of the defeated regime. Next to one of the gates in this fencing, on the interior side, was a pavilion for family visits. The prisoners had become emotional cacti in order to survive, but their wives and children inevitably wept at the sight of their husbands and fathers, whom they saw, at most, a couple of times a year, the trek from even the nearest city an arduous one involving train, bus, and motorbike. Beyond the pavilion, the exterior camp itself was fenced off from the wasteland of barren plains surrounding us, the fence demarcated with watchtowers where pith-helmeted guards with binoculars could observe female visitors and, according to the prisoners, entertain themselves. From the elevated height of the commandant's patio, one could see not only these voyeurs but also the cratered plains and denuded trees surrounding the camp, a forest of toothpicks over which gusts of crows and torrents of bats soared in ominous black formations. I always paused on the patio before entering his quarters, savoring for a moment the view denied to me in my isolation cell, where, if I had not yet been cured, I had certainly been baked by the tropical sun.

You have complained often about the duration of your visit, the commandant said. But your confession is the necessary prelude to the cure. It is not my fault that it took you a year to write this confession, one that is not, in my opinion, even very good. Everyone except you has confessed to being a puppet soldier, an imperialist lackey, a brainwashed stooge, a colonized comprador, or a treacherous henchman. Regardless of what you think of my intellectual capacities, I know they're just telling me what I want to hear. You, on the other hand, won't tell me what I want to hear. Does that make you very smart or very stupid?

I was still somewhat dazed, the bamboo floor wobbling under my bamboo seat. It always took me at least an hour to become readjusted to light and space after my cell's cramped darkness. Well, I said, gathering the tattered coat of my wits about me, I believe the unexamined life is not worth living. So thank you, Comrade Commandant, for giving me the opportunity to examine my life. He nodded approvingly. No one else has the luxury I have of simply writing and living the life of the mind, I said. My orphaned voice, which had detached itself in my cell and spoken to me from a cobwebbed corner, had returned. I am smart in some ways, stupid in others. For example, I am smart enough to take your criticism and editorial suggestions seriously, but I am too stupid to understand how my confession has not met your high standards, despite my many drafts.

The commandant regarded me through glasses that magnified his eyes to twice their size, his poor eyesight a condition of having lived in cavernous darkness for ten years. If your confession was even just satisfactory, the commissar would let you proceed with what he calls your oral examination, he said. But my opinion of what he calls your written examination is that it hardly seems like a genuine confession to me.

Haven't I confessed to many things, Commandant?

In content, perhaps, but not in style. Confessions are as much about style as content, as the Red Guards have shown us. All we ask for is a certain way with words. Cigarette?

I hid my relief and merely nodded casually. The commandant inserted the dart of a cigarette between my cracked lips, then lit it for me with my own lighter, which he had appropriated. I inhaled the oxygen of smoke, its infusion into the folds of my lungs calming the trembling in my hands. Even in this latest revision, you quote Uncle Ho only once. This is but one symptom, among many in your confession, that you prefer foreign intellectuals and culture over our native traditions. Why is that?

I'm contaminated by the West?

Exactly. That wasn't so hard to admit, was it? Funny, then, how you can't put it into writing. Of course, I can understand why you didn't quote *How the Steel Was Tempered* or *Tracks in the Snowy Forest.* You wouldn't have had access to them, even though everyone of my generation from the north has read them. But not to mention To Huu, our greatest revolutionary poet? And to cite, instead, the yellow music of Pham Duy and the Beatles? The commissar actually has a collection of yellow music that he keeps for what he calls research purposes. He's offered to let me listen to them, but no thanks. Why would I want to be contaminated by that decadence? Contrast the songs you discuss with To Huu's "Since Then", which I read in high school. He talks about how "The sun of truth shone on my heart," which was exactly how I felt about the revolutions effect on me. I carried a book of his with me to China for infantry training, and it helped sustain me. My hope is that the sun of truth will shine on you as well. But I also think of another poem of his about a rich child and a servant child. Closing his eyes, the commandant recited a stanza:

A child lives in a life of plenty
With abundant toys made in the West
While the other child is an onlooker
Watching silently from far away

He opened his eyes. Worth a mention, don't you think?

If you would give me that book, I'd read it, I said, not having read anything for a year besides my own words. The commandant shook his head. You won't have any time to read anything in the next phase. But implying you only needed a book in order to be better read is hardly a good defense. Not quoting Uncle Ho or revolutionary poetry is one thing, but not even a folk saying or a proverb? Now you may be from the south—

I was born in the north and lived nine years there, sir.

You chose the southern side. Regardless, you share a common culture with me, a northerner. Yet you will not quote from that culture, not even this:

The good deeds of Father are as great as Mount Thai Son
The virtue of Mother is as bountiful as springwater gushing from its source
Wholeheartedly is Mother to be revered and Father respected
So that the child's way may be accomplished.

Did you not learn something as basic as this in school?

My mother did teach it to me, I said. But my confession does show my reverence for my mother and why my father is not to be respected.

The relations between your mother and father are indeed unfortunate. You may think that I'm heartless, but I am not. I look at your situation and feel great sympathy for you, given your curse. How can a child be accomplished if his source is tainted? Yet I can't help but feel that our own culture, and not Western culture, tells us something about your difficult situation. "Talent and destiny are apt to feud." Don't you think Nguyen Du's words apply to you? Your destiny is being a bastard, while your talent, as you say, is seeing from two sides. You would be better off if you only saw things from one side. The only cure for being a bastard is to take a side.

You're right, Comrade Commandant, I said, and perhaps he was. But the only thing harder than knowing the right thing to do, I went on, is to actually do the right thing.

I agree. What puzzles me is that you are perfectly reasonable in person, but on the page you are recalcitrant. The commandant poured himself a shot of unfiltered rice wine from a recycled soda bottle. Any urges? I shook my head, even though my priapic desire for a drink bumped against the back of my throat. Tea, please, I said, voice cracking. The commandant poured me a cup of lukewarm tinted water. It was quite sad watching you in those first few weeks. You were a raving lunatic. Isolation did you good. Now you're purified, at least in body.

If spirits are so bad for me, then why do you drink, Commandant?

I don't drink to excess, unlike you. I disciplined myself during the war. You rethink your entire life living in a cave. Even things like what to do with one's waste. Ever thought of that?

Once in a while.

I sense sarcasm. Still not satisfied with the camp's amenities and your chamber? This is nothing compared to what I went through in Laos. That's why I'm also puzzled by the unhappiness of some of our guests. You think I'm feigning perplexity, but no, I'm genuinely surprised. We haven't stuck them in a box underground. We haven't shackled them until their legs waste away. We haven't poured lime on their heads and beaten them bloody. Instead, we let them farm their own food, build their own homes, breathe fresh air, see sunlight, and work to transform this countryside. Compare that to how their American allies poisoned this place. No trees. Nothing grows. Unexploded mines and bombs killing and maiming innocents. This used to be beautiful countryside. Now it's just a wasteland. I try to bring these comparisons up with our guests and I can see the disbelief in their eyes even as they agree with me. You, at least, are honest with me, even though, to be honest with you, that may not be the healthiest strategy.

I've lived my life underground for the revolution, Commandant. The least the revolution can grant me is the right to live above ground and be absolutely honest about what I have done, at least before you put me below ground again.

There you go again, defiant for no reason. Don't you see we live in a sensitive time? It will take decades for the revolution to rebuild our country. Absolute honesty isn't always appreciated at moments like this. But that's why I keep this here. He pointed at the jar on the bamboo cabinet, covered with a jute cloth. He had already shown the jar to me more than once, though once was more than enough. Nevertheless, he leaned over and slipped the cloth off the jar, and there was nothing to do but turn my gaze onto the exhibit that should, if there were any justice in the world, be exhibited in the Louvre and other great museums devoted to Western accomplishments. Floating in formaldehyde was a greenish monstrosity that appeared to have originated from outer space or the deepest, weirdest depths of the ocean. A chemical defoliant invented by an American Frankenstein had led to this naked, pickled baby with one body but two heads, four eyes shut but two mouths agape in permanent, mongoloid yawns. Two faces pointed in different directions, two hands curled up against the chest, and two legs spread to reveal the boiled peanut of the masculine sex.

Imagine what the mother felt. The commandant tapped his finger on the glass. Or the father. Imagine the shrieks. *What is that thing*? He shook his head and drank his rice wine, its color that of thin milk. I licked my lips, and while the scratching of my dessicated tongue on my brittle lips was loud in my ears, the commandant did not notice. We could have just shot all these prisoners, he said. Your friend Bon, for example. A Phoenix Program assassin deserves the firing squad. Protecting him and excusing him as you do reflects poorly on your character and judgment. But the commissar is merciful and believes anyone can be rehabilitated, even when they and their American masters killed anyone they wanted. In contrast to the Americans and their puppets, our revolution has shown generosity by giving them this chance for redemption through labor. Many of these so-called leaders never worked a day on a farm. How do you lead an agricultural society into the future with no idea of the peasant's life? Without bothering to drape the cloth over the jar again, he poured himself another drink. Lack of understanding is the only way to characterize how some prisoners think they're being poorly fed. Of course I know they suffer. But we all suffered. We all must suffer still. The country is healing, and that takes longer than the war itself. But these prisoners focus only on their own suffering. They ignore what our side went through. I can't get them to understand that they get more calories per day than the revolutionary soldier during the war, more than the peasants forced into refugee camps. They believe they are being victimized here, instead of being reeducated. This obstinacy shows how much reeducation they still need. As recalcitrant as you are, you are still far ahead of them. Here I agree with the commissar about the state of your reeducation. I was just talking about you with *him* the other day. He's remarkably tolerant of you. He didn't even object to being called the faceless man. No, I understand, you are not mocking him, merely describing the obvious, but he's quite sensitive about his... condition. Wouldn't you be? He wants to meet you this evening. That's quite an honor. No prisoner has ever met him personally, not that you are a prisoner. He wants to clarify a few issues with you.

What issues? I said. We both looked at my manuscript, its leaves neatly stacked on his bamboo table and pinned down by a small rock, all 295 pages written by the light of a wick floating in a cup of oil. The commandant tapped my pages with a middle finger, its tip cut off. What issues? he said. Where to begin? Ah, dinner. A guard was at the door with a bamboo tray, a boy, his skin a sickly shade of yellow. Whether they were guards or prisoners, most men in the camp were this shade of yellow, or else a sickly, rotten shade of green, or a sickly, deathly shade of gray, a color palette resulting from tropical illnesses and a calamitous diet. What is it? said the commandant. Wood pigeon, manioc soup, stir-fried cabbage, and rice, sir. The wood pigeon's roasted haunches and breast made me salivate, as my usual ration was boiled manioc. Even when starving, I had to force the manioc down my gullet, where it cemented itself against the walls of my stomach, laughing at my attempts to digest it. Subsisting on a diet of manioc not only was culinarily unpleasant, it was also no fun from a gastroenterological perspective, resulting in either a painfully solid brick or its highly explosive liquid opposite. As a consequence, the inflamed piranha of one's anus was always gnawing at one's posterior. I tried desperately to time my bowel movements, knowing a guard would fetch the ammo box reserved for that purpose at 0800 hours, but the snarled firehose of my bowels erupted at will, oftentimes right after the guard returned with the emptied can. Liquids and solids then fermented for most of the night and day, a vile mixture rusting through the ammo box. But I had no right to complain, as my baby-faced guard told me. No one's picking up my shit every day, he said, peering at me through the slot in my iron door. But you're being waited on hand and foot, short of someone wiping your ass. What do you say to that?

Thank you, sir. I could not call the guards "comrade," the commandant demanding that I keep my history a secret, lest it be leaked. The commissar orders this for your own protection, the commandant had told me. The inmates will kill you if they know your secret. The only men who knew my secret were the commissar and the commandant, for whom I had developed feline feelings of both dependency and resentment. He was the one making me rewrite my confession with repeated strokes of his blue pencil. But what was I confessing to? I had done nothing wrong, except for being Westernized. Nevertheless, the commandant was right. I was recalcitrant, for I could have shortened my unwanted stay by writing what he wanted me to write. *Long live the Party and the State. Follow Ho Chi Minh's glorious example. Let's build a beautiful and perfect society*! I believed in these slogans, but I could not bring myself to write them. I could say that I was contaminated by the West, but I could not inscribe that on paper. It seemed as much of a crime to commit a cliché to paper as to kill a man, an act I had acknowledged rather than confessed, for killing Sonny and the crapulent major were not crimes in the commandant's eyes. But having nevertheless acknowledged what some might see as crimes, I could not then compound those deeds through my description of them.

My resistance to the appropriate confessional style irritated the commandant, as he resumed telling me over dinner. You southerners had it too good for too long, he said. You took beefsteak for granted, while we northerners lived on starvation rations. We've been purged of fat and bourgeois inclinations, but you, no matter how many times you've rewritten your confession, cannot eradicate those inclinations. Your confession is full of moral weaknesses, individual selfishness, and Christian superstition. You exhibit no sense of collectivity, no belief in the science of history. You show no need to sacrifice yourself in the cause of rescuing the nation and serving the people. Another of To Huu's verses is appropriate here:

> I'm a son of tens of thousands of families
> A younger brother of tens of thousands of withered lives
> A big brother to tens of thousands of little children
> Who are homeless and live in constant hunger

Compared to To Huu, you are a communist only in name. In practice, you are a bourgeois intellectual. I'm not blaming you. It's difficult to escape one's class and one's birth, and you are corrupted in both respects. You must remake yourself, as Uncle Ho and Chairman Mao both said bourgeois intellectuals should do. The good news is that you show glimmers of collective revolutionary consciousness. The bad news is that your language betrays you. It is not clear, not succinct, not direct, not simple. It is the language of the elite. You must write for the people!

You speak truthfully, sir, I said. The wood pigeon and manioc soup had begun dissolving in my stomach, their nutrients energizing my brain. I just wonder what you would say about Karl Marx, Comrade Commandant. *Das Kapital* isn't exactly written for the people.

Marx did not write for the people? Suddenly I could see the darkness of the commandant's cave through his magnified irises. Get out! See how bourgeois you are? A revolutionary humbles himself before Marx. Only a bourgeois compares himself to Marx. But rest assured, *he* will treat you for your elitism and Western inclinations. He has built a state-of-the-art examination room where he will personally supervise the final phase of your reeducation, when you are transformed from an American into a Vietnamese once more.

I'm not an American, sir, I said. If my confession reveals anything, isn't it that I'm an anti-American? I must have said something outrageously humorous, for he actually laughed. The anti-American already includes the American, he said. Don't you see that the Americans need the anti-American? While it is better to be loved than hated, it is also far better to be hated than ignored. To be anti-American only makes you a reactionary. In our case, having defeated the Americans, we no longer define ourselves as anti-American. We are simply one hundred percent Vietnamese.

You must try to be as well.

Respectfully speaking, sir, most of our countrymen do not think I am one of them.

All the more reason for you to work harder to prove that you are one of us. Obviously you think of yourself as one of us, at least sometimes, so you are making progress. I see you've finished eating. What did you think of the wood pigeon? I admitted that it was delicious. What if I told you that "wood pigeon" is only a euphemism? He watched me carefully as I looked again at the pile of little bones on my plate, sucked clean of every bit of meat and tendon. Regardless of what it was, I still longed for another serving. Some call this rat, but I prefer "field mouse," he said. But it hardly matters, does it? Meat is meat, and we eat what we must. Do you know I once saw a dog eating the brains of our battalion doctor? Ugh. I don't blame the dog. He was only eating the brains because the mans intestines had already been eaten by his fellow dog. These are the kinds of things you see on the battlefield. But losing all those men was worth it. All the bombs dropped on us by those air pirates were not dropped on our homeland. Not to mention that we liberated the Laotians. That is what revolutionaries do. We sacrifice ourselves to save others.

Yes, Comrade Commandant.

Enough serious talk. He threw the jute cover back over the pickled baby. I just wanted to give you my personal congratulations on having finished the written phase of your reeducation, no matter how barely, in my opinion. You should be pleased with how far you've come, even if you should be critical yourself for the limitations so evident in your confession. As good a student as you are, you may yet become the dialectical materialist that the revolution needs you to be. Now, let us go meet the commissar. The commandant checked the time on his wristwatch, which also happened to have been my wristwatch. *He* is expecting us.

We descended from the commandant s quarters and walked past the guard barracks to the stretch of flatland separating the two hills. My isolation cell was located here, one of a dozen brick ovens where we basted in our own juices and where the prisoners tapped messages on the walls with tin cups. They had developed a simple code for communicating, and it was not long before they taught it to me. Part of what they conveyed to me was how they held me in high regard. Much of my heroic reputation came from Bon, who often greeted me through my neighbors. He and they believed I was singled out for extended isolation because of my ardent republicanism and my Special Branch credentials. They blamed the commissar for my fate, for he was really the one in charge of the camp, as everyone, including the commandant, knew. My neighbors had seen the commissar up close during his weekly political lectures, and the sight was truly horrific. Some cursed him, taking delight in his suffering. But the facelessness compelled respect among others, the mark of his dedication and sacrifice, even if for a cause that the prisoners despised. The guards, too, spoke of the faceless commissar with mixed tones of horror, fear, and respect, but never mockery. A commissar must never be mocked, even among one's peers, for one never knew when one of those peers might report such antirevolutionary thinking.

I understood the need for my temporary detention and marginal conditions, for the revolution must be vigilant, but what I could not understand, and what I hoped the commissar would explain, was why the guards feared *him*, and, more generally, why revolutionaries feared one another. Aren't we all comrades? I asked the commandant at an earlier session. Yes, he said, but not all comrades have the same level of ideological consciousness. Although I am not thrilled at having to seek the commissars approval on certain matters, I also admit that *he* knows Marxist-Leninist theory and Ho Chi Minh Thought much better than I ever will. I'm not a scholar, but he is. Men like him are guiding us toward a truly classless society. But we haven't eradicated all elements of antirevolutionary thinking, and we must not forgive antirevolutionary faults. We must be vigilant, even of each other, but mostly of ourselves. What my time in the cave taught me is that the ultimate life-and-death struggle is with ourselves. Foreign invaders might kill my body, but only I could kill my spirit. This is the lesson you must absorb by heart, which is why we give you so much time to achieve it.

Ascending the hill toward the commissar's quarters, it seemed to me that I had already spent too much time learning that lesson. We stopped at the stairs leading up to his balcony, where the baby-faced guard and three other guards awaited. The commissar's in charge of you now, the commandant said, inspecting me from head to toe with a frown. I'll be frank. *He* sees much more potential in you than I do. You are addicted to the social evils of alcohol, prostitution, and yellow music. You write in an unacceptable, counterrevolutionary manner. You are responsible for the deaths of the Bru comrade and the Watchman. You failed even in undermining this movie that misrepresents and insults us. If it were only up to me, I'd send you to the fields for your final cure. And if things do not work out with the commissar, I still can. Remember that.

I will, I said. And, knowing that I had not yet escaped his power, I also said, Thank you, Comrade Commandant, for all you have done for me. I know I've seemed reactionary to you because of my confession, but please believe me when I say that I have learned much under your tutelage and criticism. (This, after all, was the truth.)

My show of gratitude mollified the commandant. Let me give you some advice, he said. The prisoners tell me what they think I want to hear, but they don't understand that what I want to hear is sincerity. Isn't that what education is all about? Getting the student to sincerely say what the teacher wants to hear? Keep that in mind. With that, the commandant turned and began his descent down the hill, a man of admirably erect posture.

The commissar's waiting, the baby-faced guard said. Let's go.

I gathered what remained of myself. I was three-quarters of the man I used to be, according to the commandant's scale, manufactured in the USA and appropriated from a southern hospital. The commandant was obsessed with his weight and enamored with the scale's statistical precision. Through a rigorous longitudinal study of bowel movements, sampled from both guards and prisoners, including myself, the commandant had calculated that the camp's collective bowels issued about six hundred kilos of waste per day. The prisoners collected and hand-carried this waste to the fields, where it served as fertilizer. Fecal precision was thus necessary for the scientific management of agricultural production. Even now, climbing the stairs ahead of the guards and knocking on the commissar's door, I felt the factory of my innards fashioning the wood pigeon into a solid brick that would be used tomorrow to help build the revolution.

Come in, said the commissar. That voice...

His quarters consisted entirely of one big, rectangular room as austere as the commandant's, with bamboo walls, bamboo floors, bamboo furniture, and bamboo rafters holding up a thatched roof. I had entered the sitting area, furnished with some low-slung bamboo chairs, a bamboo coffee table, and an altar on which sat Ho Chi Minh's goldpainted bust. Above his head hung a red banner imprinted with those golden words NOTHING IS MORE PRECIOUS THAN INDEPENDENCE AND FREEDOM. In the middle of the room was a long table stacked with books and papers, surrounded by chairs. Leaning against one of the chairs was a guitar with familiar curvaceous hips, and at one end of the long table was a record player that looked like the one I had left behind at the General's villa... At the far end of the room was a platform bed, draped in a cloud of mosquito netting behind which a shadow stirred. The bamboo floor was cool under my bare feet, and die breeze whispering through the open windows caused the netting to tremble. A hand parted the netting, its skin burned red, and *he* emerged from the bed's recesses, a visage of fearful asymmetry. I looked away. Come now, the commissar said. Am I really so horrible that you do not recognize me, my friend? I looked back to see lips scorched away to reveal perfect teeth, eyes bulging from withered sockets, nostrils reduced to holes without a nose, the hairless, earless skull one massive keloid scar, leaving the head to resemble one of those dried, decapitated trophies swung on a string by an ebullient headhunter. He coughed, and a marble rattled in his throat.

"Didn't I tell you," Man said, "not to return?"

31

(Lysley Tenorio, 1972—　)
莱斯利·特诺里奥

作者简介

莱斯利·特诺里奥（Lysley Tenorio, 1972—　），美国菲律宾裔小说家。莱斯利·特诺里奥生于菲律宾，毕业于俄勒冈大学（University of Oregon），目前任教于加州圣玛丽学院（Saint Mary's College of California）。

特诺里奥代表作是短篇小说集《女妖怪》（*Monstress*, 2002），获得手推车奖（Pushcard Prize）、怀丁作家奖（Whiting Award）、艾德蒙·怀特奖（Edmund White）。他的作品受到巴拉蒂·慕克吉（Bharati Mukherjee）、萨尔曼·拉什迪（Salman Rushdie）、石黑一雄（Kazuo Ishiguro）等作家和卡朋特乐队（The Carpenters）等的影响。他的作品大多以加州为背景，讲述菲律宾移民在美利坚大地艰难谋生的经历。他在作品中探讨爱情、家庭和身份等主题，他用幽默的语言和高超的写作技巧描绘了被排斥在美国社会之外的人群的生活，展现不同文化间的冲撞和融合，再现了柔情与权力、幻想和现实、日常生活与异国情调之间的对立。

短篇小说《爱情，CA》（"L'amour，CA"）选自短篇小说集《女妖怪》，小说以一个小男孩的视角讲述一个菲律宾移民家庭移居美国后的经历，特别是小男孩的姐姐伊莎（Isa）追寻爱却为爱所弃的悲惨遭遇。所选部分是小说开头一家人初到美国的经历，和结尾离家出走的伊莎被爱人所弃，身怀六甲回到家中。

作品选读

L'amour, CA

By Lysley Tenorio

Isa couldn't wait to leave the Philippines. But when we pull into an American town of foggy streets and gray, concrete houses, she looks confused, then panicked.

MY SISTER, ISA, speaks English and Tagalog. But one word, she could say in many languages: *koigokoro, beminnen, mahal, amor.* "It's the most important thing," she used to say, "the only thing. L-O-V-E. *Love*." So when we learned that we would be moving to California, to a city called L'amour, she called it home, the place where we were always meant to be. I believed her.

This was January of 1974, our final days in the Philippines. Isa was sixteen, I was eight, and we were from San Quinez, a small southern village surrounded by sugar-cane fields and cassava groves, with a single paved road winding through. Every house was like ours, made of bamboo and nipa and built on stilts, and every neighbor was somehow family. No one was a stranger where we lived.

Like many Filipino men at the time, my father joined the U.S. Navy, and after he had served in Korea and Vietnam, his request for a transfer to America was finally granted. "Our plan from the very beginning," my father said. My mother stayed silent, rubbing the leaf of a houseplant between her fingers until it ripped. My brother, Darwin, who was twelve, said he didn't care one way or another. But Isa started packing that same day. "L'amour, L'amour," she went on, like it was the name of a special friend she had that others never would. Friends and neighbors called her stuck-up and boastful; our oldest cousin called her an immigrant bitch. "*American* bitch," Isa corrected her, and called our cousin a village peasant who would never know a bigger world. "You're stuck here forever." As though no place was worse than the one you were from.

This is us on the plane, the day we leave: across the aisle my mother stares ahead, barely blinking, never speaking, and my father rifles through papers, rereading each document as though he can't figure out its meaning. Darwin sleeps next to me, so deeply that I double-check the rise and fall of his chest to make sure he isn't dead. On the other side of me is Isa, and only when she looks at me do I realize I'm crying. She unbuckles my seat belt and lets me sit on her lap, promises me that I'll be fine in L'amour.

We land in San Francisco but we keep moving. As soon as we claim our boxes and bags, we board a shuttle van and head south on the freeway, turn east hours later. I'm lying down for most of the ride, my head on Isa's lap, feeling our speed. We never traveled so quickly or smoothly on the dirt roads back home; I could almost sleep. But suddenly we're slow, and the driver yawns, "Almost there." Isa looks confused, then panicked, and when I sit up all I see are endless fields of gray stalks, the miles of freeway we leave behind, and, up ahead, we seem to be driving into a cloud. "Fog again," the driver says, and down the road, a sign becomes clearer. WELCOME TO LEMOORE, CA, it says, ENJOY YOUR STAY!

They sound the same—*L'amour, Lemoore*—but I know they're not. "Lemoore." I tug at Isa's sleeve. "What's that mean?" She doesn't answer.

We exit the freeway, turn into the Lemoore Naval Air Station. We drive through foggy streets to a section of military housing, passing rows of gray and concrete rectangular houses with low, flat roofs, then down a street that ends in a cul-de-sac. "That's ours," my father says, and we pull up to a house with a faintly lit doorway, newspaper-covered windows, a grassless yard. We step out, unload our cargo, drag boxes up the driveway to the front door. Most things are too heavy for me to lift, so I stand by the van to guard our belongings. Across the street, a balding blond man mows his dry, yellow lawn; two houses over, a lady with a shirt that says RENO! soaps her car, sprays it down, soaps it again. Then I see a family sitting in folding lawn chairs in a line along the sidewalk, their faces toward the sky. I have never had to *meet* a person before—back home, everyone knew everyone—and now is the time for someone to say *Welcome* or *How are you*? But by the end of the day no one says hello, not even us.

I hate my house. Too many walls make too many rooms, the hallway is long and dark as a tunnel. Nothing scared me back home, and I always knew where we were: you could hear a person breathe in the next room, and the floor shook when someone ascended the bamboo stairs. Now, brownish-orange carpet mutes our footsteps; I never know when a person is coming or going, who's here and who's gone.

Strangers come each day with heavy cardboard boxes on dollies—a refrigerator one morning, a kitchen table the next. When my father breaks down the box for our new oven, I drag it to the garage and build it again, turn it on its side, and wedge it between the washing machine and the wall. I crawl in, close the flaps. I fit perfectly. Minutes pass and I decide that I'm hiding, so I wait to be found, for someone to call out, *Where are you? Where did you go?* But no one searches, even as the afternoon fades and the garage darkens.

...

This is Isa's story: Malcolm got her pregnant. He didn't want the baby, and then he didn't want her. He paid for a bus ticket from wherever they were to Lemoore, and sent Isa on her way. That's all she told my parents; I never knew more than that. "But you shamed us," my father tells her in a voice so soft he sounds like he's speaking to the dead. "You shamed yourself. And if he shows up at my door—"

"He won't," Isa says, and she's right: I never see Malcolm again and he never calls, but now a baby is inside my sister. I think of its curled-up and freckled body, and wonder what will happen when it's born. Do I feed it when it's hungry? Hold it when it cries? No one talks about it, prepares me for it. This baby is like being in America—a thing that just happens, a thing you learn to live with.

My mother is proof of this. One afternoon I'm lying on my bedroom floor staring at the ceiling, when I hear her humming. I run to her room, find her laying out baby clothes, their tiny sleeves and pant legs splayed out like X's across her bed. "You wore these once," she says, then holds the smallest shirt I have ever seen against my chest. "Now look. How big you are." She breathes deeply, sits on the edge of her bed, puts her fingers on my cheek.

"Isa left us," I tell her, in case she forgot.

I haven't hugged or kissed Isa since she's been back. Whole days pass and I won't even say hello. She is the same way, and she joins us only at the dinner table, where all she does is stare at some spot on the table or the wall. Once, her stare is so long and steady she barely blinks, barely breathes, and I get suspicious: maybe she misses wherever she was, or is planning to leave us again.

I slam my hand on the table to bring her back. The forks and spoons rattle on our plates.

"Are you brain-damaged?" Darwin says, and when he kicks me hard under the table, I don't even flinch.

Days before Christmas, at the start of each night, the neighborhood houses glow and blink with colored lights, but ours is dim and plain. "They don't have Christmas trees back home," my father says one morning. "Maybe we should get one?"

They shop for a tree that afternoon, and as they pull out of the driveway I go running to my father's window. "I'll watch Isa," I say. But he barely nods, like he knows I'll fail again.

After they leave, Darwin goes outside to shoot baskets, and I sit in the dark hallway, on the floor in front of Isa's open door. She hasn't felt well all day, so she lies on her bed, facing the wall. But we are alone in the house, just Isa and me, and now is the time for all my questions—where she was all those months and the things she did; if she dreamed of me as often as I dreamed of her; and did she plan, from the very beginning, to leave us, knowing that I would wait for her, inside a box?

"You were gone" is the first thing I say.

She nods her head.

"When you left, nobody talked to me. For a long time. Even though I was here." I stare at the carpet, dig my finger into it. "We drove at night to find you. We couldn't." Outside, Darwin's basketball thumps and thumps, and I dig my finger deeper and deeper. "I walk by myself now. All the way to school. All the way home." When Isa turns to face me, I realize I'm crying, but I keep going, telling her more she doesn't know about me: new words I've learned in school, the teeth I've lost, how now I'm nine years old and can finally say *very* the way you're supposed to, but despite all these facts I always end up saying the same thing: "You were gone."

"But I'm back," she says, trying to smile. "I'm here." She takes a deep breath, sits up, rubbing her sides like the baby takes up too much room inside her. Slowly, she gets to her feet, reaches into her dresser, and from beneath folded dresses she takes out a cigarette and a book of matches. She lights it, breathes deeply, and a ring of smoke floats toward me. "Remember how much you liked these? How they made you laugh?" She breathes and breathes, and more rings float my way, but I let them fade.

She doesn't give up. She takes the cigarette to her lips, takes a long, deep breath, but instead of smoke rings all that comes out is a cough. She tries once more but coughs again, like she's forgotten how to smoke. She stubs out the cigarette against the window screen, sets the butt on the sill, and now she hunches over, holding her belly as though it's suddenly heavier than it was before. "I don't feel right," she says, squinting. She steps toward the bed, sits but misses the edge, falls to the floor. She looks funny and I almost laugh, but then I hear her say, "It hurts," and when she looks down between her legs, spots of blood are on her pink pajama bottoms. She puts her hand there, then looks at the blood on her fingers. "Something's wrong," she says. She tries to stand, but she hurts too much to move.

I get up, step into her room, reach for the box of tissues on her dresser and try handing it to her. But she pushes it away and asks for our mother, our father, then says she should get to a hospital, and now I think this baby will be born now, here. But I'm not ready. I don't want to be.

I pull out a tissue and lay it down by her hand. I tell her I'll get Darwin, that he will know what to do. "Just wait here, okay?" I close the door, tug on the knob to make sure it's shut tight, and tell her not to leave. I take a step back and listen to her shouting my name. "Just wait," I tell her again, then run to the end of the hallway. "I'll be back."

I head to the living room and walk out of the house. I go down the driveway past Darwin, who keeps bouncing his basketball against the garage door. "Where are you going?" he says, but I keep walking, even when he tells me to stay.

I continue down the sidewalk, count eleven houses. When I reach the end, I cross the street, and at the next house a lady is in the front window, holding a teacup in her hand. She sees me standing at the bottom of her driveway, but instead of drawing the curtain or looking away, she just waves, takes a sip of her drink. I don't wave back or even smile, but I nod to let her know I see her.

Then I turn back toward my street. Night is starting, but the air is warm, all the rooftops blink with colored lights, and Christmas trees full of ornaments and silvery tinsel light up every living-room window. Soon, our house will be this way too.

This is what L'amour was meant to be. This is the place my sister called home. Finally, after a long, long year, we're here. And so I go back, walking first, then running fast, because I can't wait to ask her, *Isa, how are you? Isa, how have you been?*

32

(Oliver de la Paz, 1972—　)
奥利弗·德·拉·帕兹

作者简介

奥利弗·德·拉·帕兹（Oliver de la Paz, 1972—　），美籍菲律宾裔诗人。他生于菲律宾马尼拉，长于美国俄勒冈州，毕业于洛约拉马利蒙特大学（Loyola Marymount University），后获得亚利桑那州立大学（Arizona State University）创意写作硕士学位（MFA）。奥利弗·德·拉·帕兹目前任教于圣十字学院（College of the Holy Cross）和太平洋路德大学（Pacific Lutheran University），同时也是昆迪曼（Kundiman）协会的主席。

奥利弗·德·拉·帕兹出版诗集《房子上的名字》（*Names Above Houses,* 2001）、《愤怒的摇篮曲》（*Furious Lullaby,* 2007）、《果园安魂曲》（*Requiem for the Orchard,* 2010）和《后主体：寓言》（*Post-Subject: A Fable,* 2014）。他荣获多个奖项，包括螃蟹果园奖（Crab Orchard Award）、阿克伦诗歌奖（Akron Prize for Poetry）、纽约艺术基金会奖金（New York Foundation for the Arts）等。他的诗歌形式多样，包括散文诗、晨曲、十四行诗等。帕兹与史黛丝·林恩·布朗（Stacey Lynn Brown）合编《一脸对众脸——当代人物诗歌选集》（*A Face to Meet the Faces: An Anthology of Contemporary Persona Poetry,* 2012）。

诗歌《喂麻雀的面包》（“Aubade with Bread for the Sparrows”）选自诗集《愤怒的摇篮曲》，诗人运用拟人、比喻等手法描述寻找面包的麻雀，清新自然，别有意趣；《我如何学会幸福》（“How I Learned Bliss”）选自诗集《果园安魂曲》，诗人从生活点滴着眼，探讨幸福的真谛。

作品选读

Aubade with Bread for the Sparrows

By Oliver de la Paz

The snow voids the distance of the road
and the first breath comes from the early morning
ghosts. The sparrows with their hard eyes
glisten in the difficult light. They preen
their feathers and chirp. It's as though they were one
voice talking to God.
                    Mornings are a sustained hymn
without the precision of faith. You've turned the bag
filled with molding bread inside out and watch
the old crusts fall to the ice. What's left
but to watch the daylight halved by the glistening ground?
What's left but an empty bag and the dust of bread
ravaged by songsters?
                    There are ruins we witness
within the moment of the world's first awakening
and the birds love you within that moment. They want
to eat the air and the stars they've hungered for, little razors.

Little urgent bells, the birds steal from each other's mouths
which makes you hurt. Don't ask for more bread.
The world is in haste to waken. Don't ask for a name
you can surrender, for there are more ghosts to placate.
Don't hurt for the sparrows, for they love you like a road.

How I Learned Bliss

By Oliver de la Paz

I spied everything. The North Dakota license,
the "Baby on Board" signs, dead raccoons, and deer carcasses.
The Garfields clinging to car windows—the musky traces of old coffee.
I was single-minded in the buzz saw tour I took through
the flatlands of the country to get home. I just wanted to get there.
Never mind the antecedent. I had lost stations miles ago
and was living on cassettes and caffeine. Ahead, brushstrokes
of smoke from annual fires. Only ahead to the last days of summer
and to the dying theme of youth. How pitch-perfect
the tire-on-shoulder sound was to mask the hiss of the tape deck ribbons.
Everything. Perfect. As Wyoming collapses over the car
like a wave. And then another mile marker. Another.
How can I say this more clearly? It was like opening a heavy book,
letting the pages feather themselves and finding a dried flower.

33

(Bryan Thao Worra, 1973—)

布莱恩·涛·沃拉

作者简介

布莱恩·涛·沃拉（Bryan Thao Worra, 1973— ）美国老挝裔作家和诗人，于1973年出生于老挝首都万象（Vientiane）。当他出生三天时被美国飞行员约翰·沃拉领养，几个月后被带到美国生活。从1991年到1997年，他就读于美国俄亥俄州的奥特本大学（Otterbein College），学习非西方文化中的交流与哲学。布莱恩·涛·沃拉获得过颇多重要的荣誉和奖项。他是首位获得美国国家艺术奖金（National Endowment for the Arts）与亚太领袖奖（Asian Pacific Leadership Award）的美国老挝裔作家，是国际科幻小说与幻想诗歌协会首位美国亚裔会长（The first Asian American president of the International Science Fiction and Fantasy Poetry Association），是职业恐怖小说作家协会首位美国老挝裔成员（The first Laotian American member of the professional Horror Writers Association）。在2012年代表老挝参加伦敦文化奥运会。

作为一名多产的作家，他创作了颇多优秀的作品。诗集有《引爆炸弹》（*Touching Detonations*, 2003）、《眼睛的另一边》（*On The Other Side Of The Eye*, 2007）、《冬墨》（*Winter Ink*, 2008）、《独轮车》（*BARROW*, 2009）与《无法看透的现实》（*DEMONSTRA*, 2013）。

《我们与集束炸弹共餐》（*Our Dinner With Cluster Bombs*）与《丑怪》（*Ecce Monstro*）是布莱恩·涛·沃拉具有代表性的两部作品。《我们与集束炸弹共餐》，顾名思义，讲述了老挝人在炸弹恐怖威胁中的艰难生存。这首诗的历史背景是20世纪六七十年代，在老挝战争期间，美国对老挝投放了几吨之重的炸弹，然而当时有超过三分之二的炸弹没有爆炸，这为老挝如今的稳定与重建造成了很大的威胁。布莱恩·涛·沃拉在诗集中揭露隐藏的炸弹对人们带来的恐慌以及美国对老挝犯下的罪行。《丑怪》这首诗非常具有创新色彩，作者以德语和英文混合的形式写作，创造出令人窒息的恐怖气息，表现出独特的哥特式怪诞之美。

作品选读

Our Dinner With Cluster Bombs

By Bryan Thao Worra

Our pilot packs a Makarov
Flying into the outskirts
Of the old province capitol
Long since delivered to kingdom come.

It's bleak, this once-thriving home of ours
Now just a pile of broken jars
Serenading the paint chips and charred spars
Of the human spirit.

Our hotel is ringed with bomb-tails
And inert Browning machine guns from distant days
Of immolation.

It's all the rage in décor.

The markets of carcass thrive because
There is no refrigeration to speak of:
Power fails them here, except from 5 to 11
When coincidentally, the best state-run TV is on.

The hills pulse with rank ghosts no one wants to mention.

These roads are emblems of narrow and nothing.

When it is time to eat, we have no difficulties finding
Empty seats, cracking, astral in their depths.

Our hostess strikes a match heavy with sulfur.

In the glow, we see their candleholders here:
Rusty yellow cans with brass fins and screw-on tops
Delivered direct from American aviation, yet flawed.
Failed agents of flame and whirlwind now somewhat tamed

Their menace barely noticeable
As she serves us her cream of mushroom soup.
She swears it's a local favorite these days.

We don't have the heart to compare it to Campbell's to her face.

Ecce Monstro

By Bryan Thao Worra

Als das Kind Kind war,
war es die Zeit der folgenden Fragen:
Warum bin ich ich und warum nicht du?
—Peter Handke, "Lied Vom Kindsein"

II

Began like pu, the uncarved block in a strange land.
Simulacrum, wood golem knocking about, dreaming of flesh.
Lies, truths, growths, recede and wonder what it is to be:

D'où Venons Nous
Que Sommes Nous
Où Allons Nous

Woher kommen wir
Wer sind wir
Wohin gehen wir

Where Do We Come From?
What Are We?
Where Are We Going?

How long have I got?

Father never answers. Why he is surprised when I bolt,
A prodigal arrow, into
The world, I can only suspect, among gears and puppets.

III

Wander the world.

I saw a boy herding ox.

I saw a dog dropping bones in the water, barking for more.
I saw a bathing woman with a beggar on a crutch of wood.

I saw a wretch with a dead albatross envy archers
Whose arrows were beyond them.

I may have seen a fleeting vanity fair, some carnival of souls.
I saw a Hmong orphan calling Naga kings from the riverbank,
Expecting nothing.

IV

Maw like Leviathan, peer of Melville's albino,
Abyssal gaze returned.
Within your belly like a worm,
After a lifetime of fighting, how

I've become like you,
Adrift

In the sea, Jonah, a leaf,
While the boy next to me has become a jackass.
And yet I still wish and yearn,
Dionysian, a destiny, if not a dynasty.

34

(Aimee Nezhukumatathil, 1974—　)
艾梅·内茨库马塔尔

作者简介

艾梅·内茨库马塔尔（Aimee Nezhukumatathil, 1974—　），美国亚裔诗人。艾梅·内茨库马塔尔生于芝加哥，母亲是菲律宾裔，父亲是印度裔。内茨库马塔尔获俄亥俄州立大学（Ohio State University）学士和创意写作硕士学位（MFA）。她目前在密西西比大学（University of Mississippi）任教，同时也是杂志《俄里翁》（*Orion*）的诗歌编辑。

内茨库马塔尔著有四部诗集，《奇迹水果》（*Miracle Fruit,* 2003）、《在驶入火山》（*At the Drive-In Volcano,* 2007）、《好运鱼》（*Lucky Fish,* 2011）和《海洋》（*Oceanic,* 2018），畅销故事书《鱼骨》（*Fishbone,* 2000），自然散文集《美妙世界》（*World of Wonder,* 2018），与罗斯·盖伊（Rose Gay）合编书信体自然诗集《花边和黄铁矿》（*Lace and Pyrite,* 2014）。《奇迹水果》获得全球菲律宾文学奖（Global Filipino Literary Award），《在驶入火山》获得 2007 年巴尔克内丝诗歌奖（Balcones Poetry Prize），《好运鱼》斩获埃里克·霍弗尔图书奖（Eric Hoffer Award）。内茨库马塔尔获得多个奖项，包括手推车奖（Pushcart Prize）、安戈夫奖（Angoff Award）、博特莱特奖（Boatwright Prize）、理查德·雨果奖（the Richard Hugo Prize）和美国国家艺术基金会的资助。多族裔的文化背景给她的诗歌创作提供独特的视角和丰富的内容。她的诗歌自然流畅、语言生动、意象鲜明、颇有意趣。

诗歌《咬一口》（“One Bite”）选自诗集《神奇水果》，诗歌以儿童的语气描绘吃到新鲜水果的惊喜之情。《一个地球仪只是一个星号，每个家庭应该有一个星号》（“A Globe Is Just An Asterick and Every Home Should Have An Asterick”）选自诗集《好运鱼》，诗歌以新奇的意象开篇，普通的地球仪也变得不平常，情感和历史感蕴含其中。

作品选读

One Bite

By Aimee Nezhukumatathil

Miracle fruit changes the tongue. One bite,
and for hours all you eat is sweet. Placed
alone on a saucer, it quivers like it's cold
from the ceramic, even in this Florida heat.

Small as a coffee bean, red as jam—
I can't believe. The man who sold
it to my father on Interstate 542 had one
tooth, one sandal, and called me

"Duttah, Duttah." I wanted to ask what
is that, but the red buds teased me
into our car and away from his fruit stand.
One bite. And if you eat it whole, it softens

and swells your teeth like a mouthful
of mallow. So how long before you lose
a sandal and still walk? How long
before you lose the sweetness?

A Globe Is Just An Asterick and Every Home Should Have An Asterick

By Aimee Nezhukumatathil

Before a globe is pressed into a sphere,
the shape of the paper is an asterisk.
The planet is holding our place in line:
look out for metallic chips of meteor
hurtling through the universe. On my drive
to work, I saw my neighbor's lawn boiling
over with birds. Like the yard was a giant lasagna
and the birds were the perfectly bubbled cheese,
not yet crisped and brown. And I was hungry
to keep driving, driving all the way down
to central Florida, to my parents' house
and into their garage, and up the pull-down stairs
in their attic to find my old globe from 1983.
I used to sit in the living room with Kenny Rogers
playing on Mom's record player. I spun and spun
that globe and traced my fingers along
the nubby Himalayas, the Andes—measured
with the span of my thumb and forefinger
and the bar scale that showed how many miles
per inch, I tried to pinch the widest part
of the Pacific Ocean, the distance between me
and India, me and Philippines. The space
between the shorelines was too wide. My hand
was always empty when it came to land, to knowing
where is home. I dip my hands in the sea, I net
nothing but seaweed and a single dizzy smelt.

35

(Hanya Yanagihara, 1974—　)
柳原汉雅

作者简介

柳原汉雅（Hanya Yanagihara, 1974—　），美国日裔小说家和旅行作家。柳原汉雅生于洛杉矶，童年时期，随家人在夏威夷、纽约、马里兰、加州和得克萨斯州居住过，现居纽约。柳原汉雅从女校史密斯学院（Smith College）毕业后，做过出版社营销助理、编辑，现在担任《纽约时报》旗下时尚杂志《T：纽约时报时尚杂志》（*T: The New York Times Style Magazine*）副主编。

柳原汉雅出版小说《林中秘族》（*The People in the Trees*, 2013）和《小人生》（*A Little Life*, 2015），获得高度评价。《林中秘族》以美国科学家、诺贝尔奖得主丹尼尔·卡尔顿·盖杜谢克（Daniel Carleton Gajdusek）为原型，讲述20世纪50年代，年轻的医生主人公在太平洋某座岛屿上进行人类学调查时发现岛上居民长寿并对此进行研究，最终获得诺贝尔奖，可是在他功成名就后却因性侵儿童而锒铛入狱、身败名裂。小说《小人生》入围曼布克奖和美国国家图书奖。《小人生》以第三人称讲述四个大学同学毕业后在纽约的追梦和自我发现之旅，小说按照时间顺序展开，中间穿插着回忆和倒叙。小说探讨痛苦、创伤、记忆和友情等主题，但是小说包含的虐待、暴力、同性恋内容也遭到少数批评家的批评。《小人生》描写细腻到位，文笔犀利，震撼人心，文学性强。

选读部分选自小说《小人生》第一章，介绍四个老友在纽约重聚的场景。

作品选读

A Little Life

Chapter 1

(excerpt)

By Hanya Yanagihara

The eleventh apartment had only one closet, but it did have a sliding glass door that opened onto a small balcony, from which he could see a man sitting across the way, outdoors in only a T-shirt and shorts even though it was October, smoking. Willem held up a hand in greeting to him, but the man didn't wave back.

In the bedroom, Jude was accordioning the closet door, opening and shutting it, when Willem came in. "There's only one closet," he said.

"That's okay," Willem said. "I have nothing to put in it anyway."

"Neither do I." They smiled at each other. The agent from the building wandered in after them. "We'll take it," Jude told her.

But back at the agent's office, they were told they couldn't rent the apartment after all. "Why not?" Jude asked her.

"You don't make enough to cover six months' rent, and you don't have anything in savings," said the agent, suddenly terse. She had checked their credit and their bank accounts and had at last realized that there was something amiss about two men in their twenties who were not a couple and yet were trying to rent a one-bedroom apartment on a dull (but still expensive) stretch of Twenty-fifth Street. "Do you have anyone who can sign on as your guarantor? A boss? Parents?"

"Our parents are dead," said Willem, swiftly.

The agent sighed. "Then I suggest you lower your expectations. No one who manages a well-run building is going to rent to candidates with your financial profile." And then she stood, with an air of finality, and looked pointedly at the door.

When they told JB and Malcolm this, however, they made it into a comedy: the apartment floor became tattooed with mouse droppings, the man across the way had almost exposed himself, the agent was upset because she had been flirting with Willem and he hadn't reciprocated.

"Who wants to live on Twenty-fifth and Second anyway," asked JB. They were at Pho Viet Huong in Chinatown, where they met twice a month for dinner. Pho Viet Huong wasn't very good—the pho was curiously sugary, the lime juice was soapy, and at least one of them got sick after every meal—but they kept coming, both out of habit and necessity. You could get a bowl of soup or a sandwich at Pho Viet Huong for five dollars, or you could get an entrée, which were eight to ten dollars but much larger, so you could save half of it for the next day or for a snack later that night. Only Malcolm never ate the whole of his entrée and never saved the other half either, and when he was finished eating, he put his plate in the center of the table so Willem and JB—who were always hungry—could eat the rest.

"Of course we don't want to live at Twenty-fifth and Second, JB," said Willem, patiently, "but we don't really have a choice. We don't have any money, remember?"

"I don't understand why you don't stay where you are," said Malcolm, who was now pushing his mushrooms and tofu—he always ordered the same dish: oyster mushrooms and braised tofu in a treacly brown sauce—around his plate, as Willem and JB eyed it.

"Well, I can't," Willem said. "Remember?" He had to have explained this to Malcolm a dozen times in the last three months. "Merritt's boyfriend's moving in, so I have to move out."

"But why do you have to move out?"

"Because it's Merritt's name on the lease, Malcolm!" said JB.

"Oh," Malcolm said. He was quiet. He often forgot what he considered inconsequential details, but he also never seemed to mind when people grew impatient with him for forgetting. "Right." He moved the mushrooms to the center of the table. "But you, Jude—"

"I can't stay at your place forever, Malcolm. Your parents are going to kill me at some point."

"My parents love you."

"That's nice of you to say. But they won't if I don't move out, and soon."

Malcolm was the only one of the four of them who lived at home, and as JB liked to say, if he had Malcolm's home, he would live at home too. It wasn't as if Malcolm's house was particularly grand—it was, in fact, creaky and ill-kept, and Willem had once gotten a splinter simply by running his hand up its banister—but it was large: a real Upper East Side town house. Malcolm's sister, Flora, who was three years older than him, had moved out of the basement apartment recently, and Jude had taken her place as a short-term solution: Eventually, Malcolm's parents would want to reclaim the unit to convert it into offices for his mother's literary agency, which meant Jude (who was finding the flight of stairs that led down to it too difficult to navigate anyway) had to look for his own apartment.

And it was natural that he would live with Willem; they had been roommates throughout college. In their first year, the four of them had shared a space that consisted of a cinder-blocked common room, where sat their desks and chairs and a couch that JB's aunts had driven up in a U-Haul, and a second, far tinier room, in which two sets of bunk beds had been placed. This room had been so narrow that Malcolm and Jude, lying in the bottom bunks, could reach out and grab each other's hands. Malcolm and JB had shared one of the units; Jude and Willem had shared the other.

"It's blacks versus whites," JB would say.

"Jude's not white," Willem would respond.

"And I'm not black," Malcolm would add, more to annoy JB than because he believed it.

"Well," JB said now, pulling the plate of mushrooms toward him with the tines of his fork, "I'd say you could both stay with me, but I think you'd fucking hate it." JB lived in a massive, filthy loft in Little Italy, full of strange hallways that led to unused, oddly shaped cul-de-sacs and unfinished half rooms, the Sheetrock abandoned mid-construction, which belonged to another person they knew from college. Ezra was an artist, a bad one, but he didn't need to be good because, as JB liked to remind them, he would never have to work in his entire life. And not only would he never have to work, but his children's children's children would never have to work: They could make bad, unsalable, worthless art for generations and they would still be able to buy at whim the best oils they wanted, and impractically large lofts in downtown Manhattan that they could trash with their bad architectural decisions, and when they got sick of the artist's life—as JB was convinced Ezra someday would—all they would need to do is call their trust officers and be awarded an enormous lump sum of cash of an amount that the four of them (well, maybe not Malcolm) could never dream of seeing in their lifetimes. In the meantime, though, Ezra was a useful person to know, not only because he let JB and a few of his other friends from school stay in his apartment—at any time, there were four or five people burrowing in various corners of the loft—but because he was a good-natured and basically generous person, and liked to throw excessive parties in which copious amounts of food and drugs and alcohol were available for free.

"Hold up," JB said, putting his chopsticks down. "I just realized—there's someone at the magazine renting some place for her aunt. Like, just on the verge of Chinatown."

"How much is it?" asked Willem.

"Probably nothing—she didn't even know what to ask for it. And she wants someone in there that she knows."

"Do you think you could put in a good word?"

"Better—I'll introduce you. Can you come by the office tomorrow?"

Jude sighed. "I won't be able to get away." He looked at Willem.

"Don't worry—I can. What time?"

"Lunchtime, I guess. One?"

"I'll be there."

Willem was still hungry, but he let JB eat the rest of the mushrooms. Then they all waited around for a bit; sometimes Malcolm ordered jackfruit ice cream, the one consistently good thing on the menu, ate two bites, and then stopped, and he and JB would finish the rest. But this time he didn't order the ice cream, and so they asked for the bill so they could study it and divide it to the dollar.

The next day, Willem met JB at his office. JB worked as a receptionist at a small but influential magazine based in SoHo that covered the downtown art scene. This was a strategic job for him; his plan, as he'd explained to Willem one night, was that he'd try to befriend one of the editors there and then convince him to feature him in the magazine. He estimated this taking about six months, which meant he had three more to go.

JB wore a perpetual expression of mild disbelief while at his job, both that he should be working at all and that no one had yet thought to recognize his special genius. He was not a good receptionist. Although the phones rang more or less constantly, he rarely picked them up; when any of them wanted to get through to him (the cell phone reception in the building was inconsistent), they had to follow a special code of ringing twice, hanging up, and then ringing again. And even then he sometimes failed to answer—his hands were busy beneath his desk, combing and plaiting snarls of hair from a black plastic trash bag he kept at his feet.

JB was going through, as he put it, his hair phase. Recently he had decided to take a break from painting in favor of making sculptures from black hair. Each of them had spent an exhausting weekend following JB from barbershop to beauty shop in Queens, Brooklyn, the Bronx, and Manhattan, waiting outside as JB went in to ask the owners for any sweepings or cuttings they might have, and then lugging an increasingly awkward bag of hair down the street after him. His early pieces had included The Mace, a tennis ball that he had de-fuzzed, sliced in half, and filled with sand before coating it in glue and rolling it around and around in a carpet of hair so that the bristles moved like seaweed underwater, and "The Kwotidien," in which he covered various household items—a stapler; a spatula; a teacup—in pelts of hair. Now he was working on a large-scale project that he refused to discuss with them except in snatches, but it involved the combing out and braiding together of many pieces in order to make one apparently endless rope of frizzing black hair. The previous Friday he had lured them over with the promise of pizza and beer to help him braid, but after many hours of tedious work, it became clear that there was no pizza and beer forthcoming, and they had left, a little irritated but not terribly surprised.

They were all bored with the hair project, although Jude—alone among them—thought that the pieces were lovely and would someday be considered significant. In thanks, JB had given Jude a hair-covered hairbrush, but then had reclaimed the gift when it looked like Ezra's father's friend might be interested in buying it (he didn't, but JB never returned the hairbrush to Jude). The hair project had proved difficult in other ways as well; another evening, when the three of them had somehow been once again conned into going to Little Italy and combing out more hair, Malcolm had commented that the hair stank. Which it did: not of anything distasteful but simply the tangy metallic scent of unwashed scalp. But JB had thrown one of his mounting tantrums, and had called Malcolm a self-hating Negro and an Uncle Tom and a traitor to the race, and Malcolm, who very rarely angered but who angered over accusations like this, had dumped his wine into the nearest bag of hair and gotten up and stamped out. Jude had hurried, the best he could, after Malcolm, and Willem had stayed to handle JB. And although the two of them reconciled the next day, in the end Willem and Jude felt (unfairly, they knew) slightly angrier at Malcolm, since the next weekend they were back in Queens, walking from barbershop to barbershop, trying to replace the bag of hair that he had ruined.

"How's life on the black planet?" Willem asked JB now.

"Black," said JB, stuffing the plait he was untangling back into the bag. "Let's go; I told Annika we'd be there at one thirty." The phone on his desk began to ring.

"Don't you want to get that?"

"They'll call back."

As they walked downtown, JB complained. So far, he had concentrated most of his seductive energies on a senior editor named Dean, whom they all called DeeAnn. They had been at a party, the three of them, held at one of the junior editor's parents' apartment in the Dakota, in which art-hung room bled into art-hung room. As JB talked with his coworkers in the kitchen, Malcolm and Willem had walked through the apartment together (Where had Jude been that night? Working, probably), looking at a series of Edward Burtynskys hanging in the guest bedroom, a suite of water towers by the Bechers mounted in four rows of five over the desk in the den, an enormous Gursky floating above the half bookcases in the library, and, in the master bedroom, an entire wall of Diane Arbuses, covering the space so thoroughly that only a few centimeters of blank wall remained at the top and bottom. They had been admiring a picture of two sweet-faced girls with Down syndrome playing for the camera in their too-tight, too-childish bathing suits, when Dean had approached them. He was a tall man, but he had a small, gophery, pockmarked face that made him appear feral and untrustworthy.

They introduced themselves, explained that they were here because they were JB's friends. Dean told them that he was one of the senior editors at the magazine, and that he handled all the arts coverage.

"Ah," Willem said, careful not to look at Malcolm, whom he did not trust not to react. JB had told them that he had targeted the arts editor as his potential mark; this must be him.

"Have you ever seen anything like this?" Dean asked them, waving a hand at the Arbuses.

"Never," Willem said. "I love Diane Arbus."

Dean stiffened, and his little features seemed to gather themselves into a knot in the center of his little face. "It's DeeAnn."

"What?"

"DeeAnn. You pronounce her name 'DeeAnn.'?"

They had barely been able to get out of the room without laughing. "DeeAnn!" JB had said later, when they told him the story. "Christ! What a pretentious little shit."

36

(Vu Tran, 1975—)

陈武

作者简介

陈武（Vu Tran, 1975— ），美国越南裔作家，出生于越南西贡（今胡志明市）。他从塔尔萨大学（University of Tulsa）获得学士学位，从爱荷华作家研究会（Iowa Writers' Workshop）获得硕士学位，从内华达大学拉斯维加斯分校（University of Nevada, Las Vegas）获得博士学位。目前在芝加哥大学（University of Chicago）教授创意写作课程。他荣获过怀丁奖（Whiting Award）和劳伦斯基金奖（Lawrence Foundation Prize）等重要奖项。他的作品在南方评论（*Southern Review*）、哈佛评论（*Harvard Review*）、密歇根季评（*Michigan Quarterly Review*）与安提俄克评论（*Antioch Review*）等重要期刊上发表。陈武的作品充满恐怖色彩，把读者一步一步带到他设计好的悬疑谜团中，任其探索和挣扎。

《龙鱼》（*Dragonfish*, 2015）是陈武的处女座，也是目前为止唯一一部已出版的作品。这部小说讲述了一名奥克兰警察在拉斯维加斯历经千辛万苦寻找越南裔妻子的故事。作者用巧妙的文笔，精心勾勒出复杂而有趣的连环故事。细读文本，读者会发现，看似简单的故事背后隐藏着种族歧视、身份困惑和历史溯源等严肃而深刻的内涵。

本小说的第二章和最后一章主要围绕罗伯特与他越南籍妻子之间悬妙的关系展开。最后，罗伯特发现，他与妻子之间存在的不仅仅是感情问题，而是种族歧视与殖民历史等更为严肃的问题。

作品选读

Dragonfish

Chapter 2

(excerpt)

By Vu Tran

WHEN SUZY LEFT ME, it was easy at first. No children. No possessions to split up. No one really to care. I was an only child, my parents both years in their graves, and her entire family was either also dead or still in Vietnam. After eight years together, I'd gotten to know maybe two or three of her friends, and the only things my police buddies knew about her was her name and her temper.

She gave me the news after Sunday dinner. I was sitting at the dining table, and she approached me from the kitchen, her mouth still swollen, and said, "I'm leaving tomorrow and I'm taking my clothes. You can have everything else." She carried away my half-empty plate and I heard it shatter in the sink.

The first time I met her, I knew she was fearless. I was responding to a robbery at the flower shop where she worked. She'd been in America almost a decade, but her English was still pretty bad. When I arrived, she stood at the door with a baseball bat in one hand and bloody pruning shears in the other. Before I could step out of the patrol car, she flew into a tirade about what had happened, as though I'd been the one who robbed her. I understood about a quarter of what she said—something about a gun and ruined roses—but I knew I liked her. That petite sprightly body. Her lips, her cheekbones: full and bold. Firecracker eyes that glared at people with the urgency of a lit fuse. We found the perp two miles away, limping and bleeding from a stab wound to his thigh. The pruning shears had done it. Suzy and I married four months later.

I was thirty-five then, an age when I once thought I should already have two or three kids, though I suspected she, at thirty-three, had given little thought to her own biology, let alone the passage of time. When I proposed, she agreed on the spot, but only if I was okay with not having children. She was not good with kids, she said, and having them would hurt too much, two reasons she repeated when I brought it up again a year later and a third time the year after that. I always figured she'd eventually change her mind.

Her real name was Hong, which meant "pink" or "rose" in Vietnamese. But it sounded a bit piggish the way Americans pronounced it, so I suggested the name of my first girlfriend in high school, and *this* she did give me, though her Vietnamese acquaintances still called her Hong.

When we married, neither of us seemed to have any worldly possessions beyond our clothes and the car we drove. It was like we had both, up until the time we met, lived our adulthoods at some cheap motel, so that we knew nothing about domesticated life beyond paying bills and doing laundry. We combined all our savings and bought an old townhouse near Chinatown that I repainted and she furnished—a luxury she'd apparently never had and one she indulged in with care and sincerity, down to the crucifixes that adorned every room and the two brass hooks on the wall of the entryway, the one for my coat a little higher than hers.

In our first year, we bonded over this novelty of owning a home, of living with another human being and building a brand-new life together with chairs and tables and dishes and bath towels. We were happy, I realize now, not because of what we actually had in common, but because we were fashioning this new life out of things that had never existed for either of us.

I'd stop by the flower shop every afternoon during my patrol to visit her. We had two days of the week together, and we spent it fixing up the townhouse, exploring local consignment shops, trying out every cheap restaurant in Chinatown, then going to the movies (Westerns and old black-and-white detective films were her favorite) or walking the waterfront, where the smell of the ocean reminded her of Vietnam. For a long time I didn't mind losing myself in her world: the Vietnamese church, the food, the sappy ballads on the tape player, her handful of "friends" who with the exception of Happy hardly spoke a lick of English, even the morbid altar in the corner of the living room with the gruesome crucifix and the candles and pictures of dead people she never talked about. That was all fine, even wonderful, because being with her was like discovering a new, unexpected person in myself.

But after two years, I realized she had no interest in discovering *me*: my job, my friends, my love for baseball or cars or a nice steak and potato dinner. She hardly ever asked me about my family or my upbringing. She must have assumed, because of her silence about herself, that I was equally indifferent to my own past. She didn't know that until her I had not thought of Vietnam since 1973, when I was eighteen and the draft ended and saved me from the war, and that all of a sudden, decades later, this distant country—this vague alien idea from my youth—meant everything again, until she gradually embodied the place itself, the central mystery in my life.

The least she could do was share her stories, like how happy her childhood had been and how the war upended everything, or what cruel assholes the Communists were, or how her uncle or father or neighbor had died in battle or survived a reeducation camp, or *something*. But she'd only say her life back home was "lonely" and "uninteresting," her voice muted with hesitation, like she was teaching me her language and I'd never get it anyway.

Gradually, an easy distance settled between us. I found I loved her most when she was sick and had no choice but to let me take care of her. Feed her. Give her medicine. Keep her housebound, which she rarely was for more than a day. And since I'd apparently reached the limit of what she was willing to give me, I grew fond of any situation where she'd talk about herself, even if it was her waking in the night from a bad dream and then, in the grip of her fright, waking me too so I could lie there in the darkness and listen to her recount it.

She had bad dreams constantly. Recurring ones where I had cheated on her and hurt her in some profound way and she's beating me with her fists as violently as she can and yet all I'm doing is laughing and laughing as she throttles me in the face. Sometimes it's another man in this dream, though she'd never say who that might be—perhaps a lover from her past whose sins she was now mistaking for mine. Then there were the dreams where she's murdered someone. Not just one person but a lot of people. She doesn't murder them in the dream, she's only conscious of having done it and must now figure out how to cover it up. In one version, she has buried them under piles of clothes in the closet. In another, she has shoved them into the washer, the dryer, that large cabinet in our laundry room where she kept all the strange pickled foods I could never force myself to like. And the entire time, all she can think about it is that she has killed people and that her life is now over.

I remember her describing one dream where she's walking for hours through an empty furniture store and someone is following her as she makes her way across beautiful model bedrooms and kitchens and living rooms. Even as she climbs the stairwells from one floor of the store to the other, the person keeps following her, their footsteps loud and steady. I asked if she ever saw what the person looked like, and she said she couldn't make herself stop or turn around in the dream, and that all she wanted was for the person to catch up to her, take her by the shoulder, and show their face.

To church every Sunday, she brought along a red leather-bound journal, worn and darkened with age, and held it in her lap throughout Mass like a private *Bible*, except she never opened it. She said it was a keepsake from the refugee camp and that it made her feel more right with God at church, whatever that meant. At home, it lay on the altar beneath the crucifix. I opened it once.

The first few pages, brittle and yellowed, were written in someone else's handwriting, the rest in Suzy's tiny Vietnamese cursive, which was already hard to read. I tried translating the first page with a bilingual dictionary but could get no further than the opening sentence. Something about rain in the morning and someone's mother yelling at them. Suzy once forgot the book at church and didn't realize it until bedtime. She wanted to go right then and there to retrieve it, insisting, "Someone is always there!" But I refused to let her go. At dawn the next morning, after a long, sleepless night, she drove to church and came home with the journal clutched to her chest like a talisman, her eyes red from crying. She did not speak to me the rest of the day.

She could go an entire week without speaking. A way at first to punish me for whatever I had done to anger her, though gradually, almost every time, her silence outlasted her anger and became a retreat from me and into herself, an absence actually, as though she had gotten lost in whatever world she had escaped into. Her temper—that flailing beast inside her that she herself hated—would retreat as well, and the only thing left between us until she spoke again was what we had said and done to each other when we fought: about money we didn't have and the children we weren't having, about what to eat for dinner, about my poor driving and my poor taste in clothes and a million other things I can't remember anymore. I always played my part, stubborn and mouthy as I am, my own temper always burning brightest before hers exploded. She'd go from yelling at me to lunging at me, those eyes erupting out of her face as she slapped and punched my chest or seized my neck with both hands. Both of us knew she was not strong enough to hurt me, and on a certain level I think she went out of her way to avoid it, never throwing or breaking anything in the house, never once using anything but her hands and her words. Even as I held her wrists and let her scream at me, let her kick me in the stomach or the legs, it sometimes felt as though she were asking me—with her hateful, pleading eyes—to hold her back and tie her to the mast until the storm passed. Because inevitably she'd crumple to the floor and cry herself into a numb silence and eventually into bed, where she would begin withdrawing from me and the world.

Sometimes we didn't need an argument. She'd be talkative and affectionate in the morning, and then I'd come home in the evening and she'd seem afflicted with some flu-like melancholy that only silence and aloneness could treat. So I learned to let her be. I turned on the TV in the kitchen during dinner. I turned up the music in the car as she sat staring out the window. I spent more and more time with friends at the bar or at our weekly poker game. I slept in our spare bedroom, which was otherwise never used.

Once or twice a year, I'd startle awake in the middle of the night and find myself alone in bed, the house empty, her car still parked in the driveway. An hour later the front door would open and she'd be barefoot in her nightgown and a jacket, having taken one of her nocturnal walks through the neighborhood, God knows what for or where to. She'd crawl back into bed without explaining anything, despite my stares and my questions, and in the morning I'd notice the dirty bottoms of her feet, the stench of cigarettes on her clothes, the whiff of alcohol on her breath. One evening I came home from work and every single light in the house was on, and she was out back beneath the apple tree, curled up and asleep on the grass, empty beer bottles lying beside her with crushed cigarettes inside.

Then, after a few days, sometimes as long as two weeks, without any hint whatsoever of reconciliation, she'd crawl into my arms while I lay on the couch watching TV, roll over in bed and bury her face in my chest, join me in the shower and lather me with soap from my head to my feet. I never knew how to feel in these moments, whether to love her back or commence my own week of silence. Not until she started talking again, recounting some funny incident at the flower shop two weeks before, or describing some movie she'd seen on TV at three in the morning, would I then feel her voice burrow into me, unravel all the knots, and bring us back to wherever we were before the silence began. Then we'd make love and she would whimper, a childlike thing a lot of Asian women do, except hers sounded more like a wounded animal's, and that would remind me once again of all the other ways I felt myself a stranger in her presence, an intruder, right back to where we were.

And yet we still kept at it, year after year of living out our separate lives in the same home, of needing each other and not knowing why, of her looking at me as though I was some longtime lodger at the house, until I came to believe that she was both naive and practical about love, that she'd only ever loved me because I was a cop, because that was supposed to mean I'd never hurt her.

The night I hit her was a rainy night. I had come home from the scene of a shooting in Ghost Town in West Oakland, where a guy had tried robbing someone's seventy-year-old grandmother and, when she fought back, shot her in the head. I was too spent to care about tracking mud across Suzy's spotless kitchen floor, or to listen to her yell at me when she saw the mess. Couldn't she understand that blood on a sidewalk is a world worse than mud on a tile floor? Shouldn't she, coming from where she came, appreciate something like that? I told her to just fuck off. She glared at me, and then started with something she'd been doing the last few years whenever we argued: she spoke in Vietnamese. Not loudly or irrationally like she was venting her anger at me—but calmly and deliberately, as if I actually understood her, like she was daring me to understand her, flaunting all the nasty things she could be saying to me and knowing full well that it could have been gibberish for all I knew and that I could do nothing of the sort to her. I usually ignored her or walked away. But this time, after a minute of staring her down as she delivered whatever the hell she was saying, I slapped her across the face.

She yelped and clutched her cheek, her eyes aghast. But then her hand fell away and she was flinging indecipherable words at me again, more and more vicious the closer she got to my face, her voice rising each time I told her to shut up. So I slapped her a second time, harder, sent her bumping into the dining chair behind her.

I felt queasy even as something inside me untangled itself. There'd been pushing in the past, me seizing her by the arms, the cheeks. But I had never gone this far. The tips of my fingers stung.

Everything happened fast, but I still remember her turning back to me with her flushed cheeks and her wet outraged eyes, her chin raised defiantly, and how it reminded me of men I'd arrested who'd just hit their wives or girlfriends and that preternatural calm on their faces when I confronted them, the posturing ease of a liar, a control freak, a bully wearing his guilt like armor. It made me see-myself in Suzy's pathetic show of boldness. She'd never been as tough as I thought, and now I was the bad guy.

She spit out three words. She knew I understood. *Fuck your mother*. She said it again, then again and again, a bitter recitation. I barked at her to shut her mouth, shoving my face at hers, and that's when she swung at me as if to slap me with her fist, two swift blows on my ear that felt like an explosion in my head. I put up an arm to shield myself and she flailed at it, still cursing me, until finally I backhanded her as hard as I could, felt the thud of my knuckles against her teeth.

She stumbled back a few steps, covering her mouth with one hand and steadying herself on the dining table with the other until she finally went down on a knee, her head bowed like she was about to vomit. Briefly, she peered up at me. Red milky eyes, childish all of a sudden, disbelieving. I watched her rise to her feet, still cradling her mouth, and shamble to the sink and spit into it several times. I watched her linger there, stooped over like she was staring down a well. I didn't move—I couldn't—until I heard her sniffling and saw her raise herself gingerly and reach for a towel and turn on the faucet.

As I walked upstairs, I listened to the water running in the kitchen and the murmuring TV in the living room and the rain pummelling the gutters outside, and everything had the sound of finality to it.

In the divorce, she was true to her word and I was left with a home full of eggshell paintings and crucifixes and rattan furniture. It was a testament to the weird isolating vacuum of our marriage that she was able to immediately and completely disappear from my life. Her flower shop had closed down a year before and she had been working odd jobs around town: cutting hair, selling furniture, I rarely kept up. I had known so little about her comings and goings or the people she knew that once she was gone I had no way of even finding out where she was living. Even Happy had quietly disappeared.

Months later, after the divorce was finalized, with a little help from within the department I found out she had moved to Las Vegas. I sold the townhouse and everything in it and tried my best to forget I had ever married anyone. I went on a strict diet of hamburgers and steaks.

But two years later, a few months before my trip to Vegas, I bumped into Happy at the supermarket. Instead of ignoring me or telling me off, she treated me like an old friend, which didn't surprise me too much. She had always lived up to her name in that way, and actually looked a lot like Suzy without her glasses: a taller, more carefree version. She said she, too, had moved to Vegas for work and was in town for the summer to visit family. I asked her out to dinner that night. Afterward she came home with me. We shared two bottles of wine and I let her lead me to the bedroom, and it wasn't until we finished that I realized—or admitted to myself—my true reason for doing all this. With her blissfully drunk and more talkative than ever, I asked about Suzy. She told me everything: how Suzy had become a card dealer in Vegas and met up with this cocky Vietnamese poker player who owned a fancy restaurant and a big house and apparently had some shady dealings in town, and how she quit her job and married him after knowing him a month, and how everything had been good for about a year.

"Until he start losing," Happy declared casually, sitting back against the headboard. She fell silent and I had to tell her several times to get on with it. She looked at me impatiently as though I should already know, as though anyone could've told the rest of the story.

"He hit her," she said. "She hit him too, but he too strong and he drink so much. Last month, he throw her down the stair, break her arm. I see her two week before, her arm in a sling, her cheek purple. But he too rich for her to leave. And always he say he need her, he need her."

"Did she call the cops? Why didn't she go to the cops?"

I stood from the bed, my head throbbing from the wine and all that I was imagining. I knocked the lamp off the nightstand.

Happy flinched. She had put her glasses back on, as if to see me better. After a moment, she said, "Why you still love her?" There was no envy or bitterness in her voice. She was simply curious.

"Who said I did?"

She checked me with her eyes as though I didn't understand my own emotions.

I tried to soften my voice, but it still came out in a growl: "Is it just the money? What—is he handsome?"

"Not really. But you not either." She patted my arm and laughed.

"You know what? I'm gonna go to Vegas and I'm gonna find this fucker. And then I'm gonna hit him a little before I break *his* arm."

This time she laughed hard, covering her mouth and regarding me with drunken pity. "You a silly, stupid man," she said.

Chapter 18

As I DROVE OUT of the city, the sun shone as intensely as it had the previous morning. The sky was the color of the Pacific in July. The farther south I drove on the 15, the less snow I could see. Only a few unmelted patches on the shoulders of the highway, the broken lumps on the tops of passing cars, spitting flurries onto my windshield. It was strange to see green palm trees swaying in the breeze and beyond them the vague warm mountains, because in the bright sunlight, if you squint, it all seems like a vision from some tropical island.

I held on to that thought to lessen the pain in my head. To bury as much as I could of the last two days.

It was my second and my last time leaving Las Vegas. The farther away I got, the more I felt I was shedding some pitch-dark side of myself that the place had awoken. Maybe it was my most genuine side. It doesn't matter ultimately—who you think you are. Sonny and Happy had died, and mourning one and cursing the other made me no more wiser about the things that people do to each other. In the end, good and bad people perish all the same.

I felt inside my duffel bag for the videotape. It was still there, though its value was lost on me now. It would never tell me where Suzy went or what new life she would find for herself. It would never tell me what she had actually written me or what else had happened in that hotel room. All it contained were darkened glimpses of two people whose love for each other somehow lasted for over twenty years.

Two hours out, I stopped at a gas station to fill up my car and change out of my bloody clothes. I threw away the food and painkillers Junior had given me and bought a bottle of ibuprofen, some cold sandwiches and hot coffee, and a pair of cheap sunglasses to cover up my bruised eye and shade myself from the harsh sunlight.

It was still desert all around me, gray mountains behind brown mountains, miles of hoary creosote bushes blanketing the flat land like a bed of thorns. I ate all the sandwiches sitting on the frigid hood of my car and drank my coffee slowly and decided I was never coming back to this or any desert.

Only then did I call Tommy.

As soon as he heard my voice, he said, "What the hell did you do, man?"

"I can explain the girl," I said.

"What girl? There's no girl. All I see is a suitcase at my front door with fifty fucking grand inside and a note with your name on it. And oh yeah, your badge."

He grilled me with a string of questions, but I wasn't listening. I hung up without saying another word.

I sat in the car for a while, sifting through my surprise, my disappointment, and eventually the realization that I shouldn't have been surprised at all.

I considered tossing the videotape then. Run over it with my car first. Burn it and let it melt into the desert dust. If Mai was gone now, why hold on to anything else, especially this?

But I kept it. I would never watch it again, but somehow it felt right to save this one reminder. At least it wasn't some heartfelt memento of something we once had. On the tape was everything I knew about her and everything I would never know. That wasn't enough, but at least it was real.

37

(Cathy Park Hong, 1976—)
卡西·朴·洪

作家简介

卡西·朴·洪（Cathy Park Hong, 1976— ），美籍韩裔诗人和作家。洪在洛杉矶长大，从欧柏林学院（Oberlin College）毕业后，赴爱荷华大学作家工坊（Iowa Writers' Workshop）进修，获创意写作硕士学位（MFA）。洪目前在罗格斯大学（Rutgers University）教授创意写作，也是《新共和》（*The New Republic*）的诗歌编辑。

卡西·朴·洪著有诗集《翻译元音》（*Translating Mo'um*, 2002）、《跳舞跳舞革命》（*Dance Dance Revolution,* 2007）和《发动机帝国》（*Engine Empire: Poems*, 2012）。诗集《翻译元音》获得手推车奖（Pushcart Prize），《跳舞跳舞革命》获得伯纳德女诗人奖（Barnard Women Poets Prize），第三部诗集《发动机帝国》出版后受到诗歌界和评论界的好评。《发动机帝国》是一部叙事抒情诗三部曲，运用民谣、十四行诗、抒情诗等多种体裁和叙事声音，涵盖过去的美国西部边疆、当下的工业化中国和未来社会三个不同的时空体，气势恢弘，历史感强。她获得古根汉姆奖金、富布莱特奖金、美国全国艺术基金会奖金等。洪是一位颇有创新精神的诗人，她的诗歌具有语言杂糅、非线性叙述和历史意识等特征，包含英语、韩语、西班牙语等多种语言，标准语、方言、俚语、口语等多种变体。她的诗歌充满孤独的边缘人形象。

诗歌《A的民谣》（"Ballad in A"）和《杀婴民谣》（"Ballad of Infanticide"）选自《发动机帝国》。《A的民谣》全诗几乎只包含一个元音字母A；《杀婴民谣》则包含美国西部边疆的风土人情与民俗习惯，赋予诗歌一种残忍的真实感和厚重的历史感。

作品选读

Ballad in A

By Cathy Park Hong

A Kansan plays cards, calls Marshall
a crawdad, that barb lands that rascal a slap;
that Kansan jackass scats,
camps back at caballada ranch.

Hang's kack, ax, and camp hat.
Kansan's nag mad and rants can't bask,
can't bacchanal and garland a lass,
can't at last brag can crack Law's balls,

Kansan's cantata rang at that ramada ranch,
Mañana, Kansan snarls, I'll have an armada
and thwart Law's brawn,
slam Law a damn mass war path.

Marshall's a marksman, maps Kansan's track,
calm as a shaman, sharp as a hawk,
Says: That dastard Kansan's had
and gnaws lamb fatback.

At dawn, Marshall stalks that ranch,
packs a gat and blasts Kansan's ass
and Kansan gasps, blasts back.
A flag flaps at half-mast.

Ballad of Infanticide

By Cathy Park Hong

Near starved, we find a fort of teetotalers
who begrudge us their succor.

While we eat up all their salt pork,
Our Jim sings for them in his strange high voice
of an Injun killing ranger who hitches up
with his Comanche guide.

She bears him a strapping son and is ramped
with another, when the ranger hives off
with a fair-haired sheriff's daughter.
He then banishes his squaw and his sons
like they're prairie beeves.

But she won't go quietly:
she poisons his new wife with a malarial dress,
and that ain't the worst of her sins, that tar-eyed witch
strangles her own newborn,
and the other son flees—

The ladies cry: enough of this devil song.
Then it done occurs to us, looking at his dusky skin—

Our Jim's a two-bit half-breed.

38

(Porochista Khakpour, 1978—   )
波罗齐思达·哈科波尔

作者简介

波罗齐思达·哈科波尔（Porochista Khakpour, 1978—   ），美国伊朗裔小说家。哈科波尔生于伊朗德黑兰，长于加利福尼亚州南帕萨迪纳。哈科波尔毕业于莎拉劳伦斯学院（Sarah Lawrence College），获约翰·霍普金斯大学（Johns Hopkins University）硕士学位。她曾在哥伦比亚大学、约翰·霍普金斯大学和莎拉劳伦斯学院等高校教授创意写作课程。她目前任教于佛蒙特学院（Vermont College）。

她的处女作《儿子和其他易燃物》（*Sons and Other Flammable Objects*, 2007）讲述"9·11"恐怖袭击对于一个伊朗裔家庭的影响，斩获第77届加利福尼亚图书奖。小说探讨移民身份、归属感、父子感情等主题，感情真挚，语言流畅。她的第二部小说《最后的幻影》（*The Last Illusion*, 2014）反思"9·11"事件，结合古老的波斯神话和现代美国社会，想象奇特，文字优美，出版后好评如潮。小说讲述一个自幼脱离人类社会的伊朗裔青年在"9·11"事件期间被带到纽约的奇遇记，具有魔幻现实主义色彩。她的首部回忆录《生病》（*Sick: A Memoir,* 2018）以诚实的笔触记录作者与莱姆关节炎的长期斗争过程，她的痛苦与焦虑、希望与失望。《生病》记录作者的心路历程，探讨疾病对于女性心理与生理的影响。哈科波尔的散文、书评、专栏文章等见于《纽约时报》、《洛杉矶时报》、《华尔街日报》、《纽约客》和《巴黎评论日报》（*The Paris Review Daily*）等报纸杂志。

《乱写：作家、金钱和谋生的艺术》（*Scratch: Writers, Money, and the Art of Making a Living*, 2017）收录当代美国作家关于写作与金钱、文学与商业、生活与工作等话题的思想感悟。《初出茅庐的艺术家画像：债务、抑郁和名字被读错的各种读法》(“Portrait of the Artist as a Debut Novelist: on Debt, Depression, and the Many Ways a Name Can Be Mispronounced”)选自《乱写：作家、金钱和谋生的艺术》，记叙哈科波尔创作时的巨大压力、等待期间的焦灼心情和身为作家的囊中羞涩，语言幽默风趣。

作品选读

Portrait of the Artist as a Debut Novelist: on Debt, Depression, and the Many Ways a Name Can Be Mispronounced (excerpt)

By Porochista Khakpour

The Very Bad Summer

There is a season where it seems like maybe I won't make it.

I spend much of the summer finishing the novel, in the midst of serious anxiety, panic, depression, chronic fatigue, gastritis, carpal tunnel, God knows what else, all the shattered states in the nightmare nation of chronic insomnia. Any normal person would assume I am on drugs, and I am. At any given time, it's a combination of two to five types of pills, prescribed by people who don't know about each other, given to me by my second general practitioner, all three of my psychiatrists, the ER internist from my third summer visit to the ER, and a gastroenterologist. I am sedated at all times yet so introspective I am paralyzed.

I turn the novel in. I go out to a celebration dinner with a very normal guy I have somehow fallen into dating. I pick at a whole fish and order dessert. I make bathroom visits devoted solely to dropping benzodiazepine crumbs under my tongue, licking any residue off my finger.

The novel made it, but I didn't.

Back at home, my parents' home, which was to be my summer editing and writing retreat, I look at the box of pills. It isn't me—Ambien, Ativan, Klonopin, Celexa, Trazodone. They are like names for weapons, an army of futuristic knives, jagged and unforgiving. They will get me a few hours of sleep that will keep me alive. I am terrified. My whole life is doctors and ERs and shrinks, and they all shake their heads when they hear the answer to their question, "Has anything traumatic happened in the last few months?"

Yes, I tell them.

"Traumatic means bad," one doctor informs me.

They seem skeptical when I say I have a novel on the way, like

A washboard-stomached woman complaining about third trimester pains—just another part of the crazy talk, they must think. All they can recommend is shrinks, and I have four. I pay for the visits without insurance, in cash or with plastic gold. I collect cards, any card.

I have gone to post-book deal hell and all I got was this serious debt. But it's an okay place to be. There are no surprises in debt.

The novel is out of my hands and in purgatory before entering the world. I love that phase: the middle of the road trip, someone else driving, seeing a world outside pass by, deftly escaping resignation to thoughts, assignment to words.

Waiting

August 2007: My publisher tells me the *New York Times* is going to review my book, and it's tentatively slated for a date in September. I will lazily say that it is impossible to describe just how exciting that is, but it is also stressful, when there is a whole month to kill until the judgment.

Suddenly, there is time. Time has a way of injecting herself into the picture when there is waiting to be done. I remember this from childhood Christmases, a holiday we should have never celebrated in the first place. But there we were, my brother and I, with lists in hand and our eyes glued to the small department-store plastic tree and its ribboned droppings. Time kept on and on, like the cheapest toilet paper.

This time, though, because I am in it alone, the waiting is unbearable. It must be filled. I try yoga, massage, acupuncture, more therapy, but there is only one thing that does the trick.

Crank calls. This is a truth, sadly.

Even worse is this truth: I have a long history with this sort of thing. In elementary school with friends, calling an old man and telling him we were leggy blond *Playboy* models and being certain the joke was on him. International calls to Kenya, the globe seeming so surreal to me, a kid who was lonely in school and at home, never quite an American, never quite an Iranian.

In college, I went through a phase of calling my parents at odd hours and saying I was with the IRS or the FBI or CIA or the local police, whatever could get struggling immigrants on political asylum really going.

But this time, I began crank-calling my friends. I created characters. I called famous people, professional contacts. Some never found out who it was. Some did. To this day, I have not patched up things with about half a dozen victims of the Great NYTBR Waiting Period. The review was good in the end, but I lost friends I'd had for more than twenty years. What do you say? How do you explain it?

There are very few people going through what I'm going through, you imagine telling them. Very few people ever have, you know?

CLICK.

Portrait of the Starving Artist

October 2007: It is a fact that even a NYTBR-approved novelist can still find herself in highly undignified positions at certain times. Two months later, I am sitting Indian-style on the dirty linoleum floor at the JFK Delta baggage claim, hugging my carry-on like it's a pillow and trying to sob subtly into my cell phone.

I'm crying about money, something I have a negative amount of, according to a robot at my bank. I have some change in my jacket, but it is not even enough to get a cookie from the concession stand in front of me and I am starving.

I haven't had money for weeks. My paperwork from the new university job has not gone through. My publisher has paid for some flights and hotels, but I have not had more than what a struggling boyfriend could spare. I have a million fancy dresses to wear and a lot of good face to put on, but all I've been doing is eyeing the prices on every menu and pretending cookies and chips are my food of choice, that Subway is my adorably ironic passion, that the McDonald's breakfast menu is my kitschy little crush.

But the most disturbing part of being overdrawn is that it results from a certain check, made out in the summer, that I have no memory of. It is a three-figure check, written out to... my psychic.

I call people, but I don't want to ask for help. I want them to think of it as a humorous anecdote but not that it's real, that my life is that difficult. After all, certain friends who are not involved in publishing think I am rich and famous. Why burst that bubble?

In the end, I borrow money from a friend of my boyfriend and take that walk of shame to a yellow cab, when I know there are buses and shuttles and subways and all sorts of only semi-impossible ways to get back to Brooklyn.

Later, when my publicist finds out, she is shocked. Why didn't you call us?!

I give her some gloss-over answer, but I want to say, I don't know whom to call, when to call, why to call. I am learning everything over again. I have become what the publishing world and media suspect of a debut novelist—suddenly, I am new to the universe, not just to being a novelist. I suddenly don't know what the hell I'm doing.

Weeks later, I discover during another bad moment—as the value of the dollar plummets and oil is sky-high—that gold is at its peak. I sell what is left of family heirlooms to an old Iranian man in the Diamond District, who listens to a fraction of my story, gives me a decent deal, and tells me, "My boy in medical university; my girl, married and with baby. Your fault for being a starver of an artist, daughter."

39

(Paul Yoon, 1980—　)
保罗·尹

作者简介

保罗·尹（Paul Yoon, 1980—　），美国韩裔小说家，出生于美国纽约。他于1998年毕业于菲利普艾斯特中学（Phillips Exeter Academy），于2002年毕业于卫斯理大学（Wesleyan University）。目前在哈佛大学任教。虽年纪尚轻，保罗·尹以他超人的写作天赋和优秀的作品荣获了诸多重要的荣誉和奖项。在2010年国家图书基金会选他为“35岁以下近五年发表首部小说的作家”（5 Under 35 Honoree）。

迄今为止，他发表了短篇小说集《昔日的岸边》（*Once the Shore*, 2009）、《大山》（*The Mountain*, 2017）与长篇小说《猎雪人》（*Snow Hunters*, 2013）。其中，处女作《昔日的岸边》（*Once the Shore*, 2009）登上《纽约时报》（*New York Times*）、《旧金山纪事报》（*San Francisco Chronicle*）、《洛杉矶时报》（*Los Angeles Times*）、《出版人周刊》（*Publishers Weekly*）与《明尼阿波里斯星坛报》（*Minneapolis Star Tribune*）等重要报纸杂志的最佳年度图书榜，被选为美国国家公共广播（National Public Radio）“年度最佳处女作”。他的长篇小说《猎雪人》同样受到了读者的青睐和文坛的好评，荣获2014年幼狮小说奖（Young Lions Fiction Award）。

《昔日的岸边》这部短篇小说集中的故事发生时间跨越了近半个世纪，从朝鲜战争爆发前到战争结束后的几十年，主要描绘了战争对人们带来的苦难以及人们对战争和生活的反思。

《昔日的岸边》（“Once the Shore”）和《在残骸中》（“Among the Wreckage”）这两部

短篇小说选自短篇小说集《昔日的岸边》。《昔日的岸边》主要讲述了一位美国老妇人带着沉重的心情来到南朝鲜半岛寻找她的丈夫曾经打仗时逗留过的洞穴，寻找丈夫的“痕迹”，寻找过去的“线索”。《在残骸中》描写了一对年迈的夫妇拜访曾经儿子遇难的荒岛，踏上了寻找爱和亲情的旅程。这两部小说辞藻优美，以精湛的笔墨刻画出悲凉的画面，给人留下深刻的印象。

作品选读

Once the Shore (excerpt)

By Paul Yoon

It was morning and she sat at her usual table closest to the stone ledge, occupied by the distant strokes of a swimmer in the outdoor pool. Beside her, at another table, a Canadian man was reading aloud portions of the news to his companion. The incident with the US Submarine caused the American widow to shift her attention. The bodies had not yet been recovered. An admiral gave a press conference and formally apologized for this tragedy, unable to give further information at this time.

Her husband used to clip articles out of the newspaper. Anything having to do with the Pacific. It was a type of hobby, she assumed, like collecting butterflies. He tucked them inside photo albums. He never showed them to her. She only knew about it because, cleaning out his study, she had opened one, thinking they contained pictures. Years' and years' worth of collecting. She immediately shut the books. It was as though she had opened her husband's diary and felt it wrong to do so, even if he was no longer present."It just isn't right," she muttered to herself, returning the album to its spot on the shelf.

The waiter called Jim approached the diners with a tray of orange juice in highball glasses and when he placed two on the table with the Canadians, he lifted his hand very slowly, as though attempting to slow time. He furrowed his brows and rubbed his eyes and the widow stiffened her back as he passed and quickly took the order of another table without meeting their gaze. He had forgotten to slick his hair, she noticed, so it seemed dull under the morning sun.

She raised a hand. "Hello, Jim," she said. "I've been up since four. And I called room service because your dining room is never open so early. You should look into that, you know."

He tucked his empty tray under his arm and promised he would. She told him she had yet to see Tamra Mountain and he offered her suggestions on reliable drivers, who appeared at the entrance to the hotel every hour. To all of this she nodded vaguely, "Yes, yes," she added. "Tell me what else you know of this place."

Jim began to describe it as best as he could. If you were to think of the island in terms of circles, then the outer circle was mostly residential including the cities and the resorts; farther inland were the farms and the forests, and at the center was the untain that stood behind then. She had only glanced at it through the taxi window on her way here. And although it was always visible, she made no effort to take the time to observe it.

She wasn' t interested. Not in its presence or its impressive height or how most guests were determined to hike along its trails. For her, it was simply what identified the island. She had come to the right place. That was all.

It takes no longer than one hour to get from here to anywhere, Jim said.

"Anywhere," she repeated, then smiled, although Jim didn't join in the merriment.

She concluded the boy was tired—that he had been up late and needed sleep. She could tell from the redness of his eyes, the way his shoulders slouched. There was a question she wanted to ask him but decided it could wait. Instead, she pointed her head as discreetly as possible toward the Canadians and said, "Terrible business. I suspect you won't look fondly on Americans after this."

The expression on his face was that of confusion.

"My husband. He was here, you know. Many years ago. Not here, exactly, but over there." She lifted a finger toward the coast. Somewhere over there, I think. I' m not really sure, to be perfectly honest. But I can imagine it. And it would take exactly one hour. That's what I think, Jim. Like you said. Exactly one hour and we'd find it.

The boy asked whether he could get her anything else.

And here, before being conscious of it, she took his hand between hers and patted his knuckles. His skin was warm, his circulation excellent. She imagined that the blood that flowed underneath these fingers, rivers of it, splitting like highway systems. How healthy he must be with such warm hands. He was a boy, she was certain, who didn't grow cold easily.

Among the Wreckage
(excerpt)

By Paul Yoon

EARLY ONE WORNING IN THE SFRING of 1947, a dark blue trawler, once used for fishing, moved slowly across the flat of the Pacific. It had been abandoned by the Japanese on the banks of a river in Solla island, and the old farmer named Bey had claimed it as his own. He now stood at the helm, above the deck. He was shirtless, his skin dark and speckled moles. His pale beard hung past his neck, cinched at the bottom with a piece of twine. Below him, his wife, Soni, lay near the bow. She was asleep. Her right arm covered her eyes to shield the sun. Her hair, like a thin cloud, curved over her shoulder and across her chest. The sea was calm. Above them, in the shape of teardrops, flew albatross. The birds headed east, toward Japan. Bey was following them.

Two days had passed since they heard thunder and the trees shook as a cluster of long-winged planes stormed over their village. When they rushed to the coast, they saw what resembled a vaporous tsunami rise up in the east, whitening the midday sky. And then the waves sped away, followed by a long echoing shudder. They recalled the bombs of two years before and remained silent. The noise faded. The waves calmed, the air stilled. Their world returned as it was before.

They did not learn of what happened until the following morning, when the salt peddler arrived from the mainland.

The Americans, they were told, had been testing. This had become common. They targeted uninhabited islands. It had been this way since the end of the Japanese occupation. What the pilots were unaware of, however, was that the coasts of this particular island, east of Sollawere used by fishermen to collect sea weed and shellfish. And so the belly of these planes opened, releasing over seventy red-fisted bombs, and out of the hundred men who were missing was Karo, Bey and Soni's forty-year old son.

They waited a full day for his return. And when he didn't come they set out to find him.

This was at dawn. Now they had been at sea for an hour. Already they felt the heat of the sun. Soni, for the first time in two days, slept. Though as soon as she was settled into it, the engine of a plane woke her. She rose, startled, her hair slipping off her chest. Bey descended the helm, gripping the rails. "It's nothing," he assured her, as the engine noise faded. He wasn't certain, it was something to say. He listened to their breathing and they kept in rhythm with each other. In the sky contrails were dissipating.

She believed him. He could tell by the way her face calmed, as though she were returning to sleep. She yawned and the sun hit what remained of her teeth. But then something caught her attention and she stood and pointed down at the waters. "Look," she said.

Bey attempted to follow the path of Soni's finger. He searched the vague shadows, the empty distance. She leaned closer to him. Her hair had become brittle. Her eyes dim, her back arced like the blade of a scythe from her years in the fields. He used to cup his hand under her soft chin and bring her to him.

"Over there," she said, her voice gone quiet. "Do you see them?"

"What is it?"

Dolphins, she said. "Look they're leaving."

She was so certain. She kept pointing Bey scanned the surface of the sea. Nothing. And so he shut his eyes and recalled their image, silver-backed and quick as spirits. He thought of his son and could not remember when he had last embraced him. He saw the boy in a field. He saw him wrapped in sails, running. He turned away from his wife who did not know his thoughts, and he said, "Yes, they are leaving."

Bey and Soni had known each other as children. In those early years, as their parents spent the days in the fields, they would do their chores together. The houses there were raised on stilts and the ground beneath was used as a pen for pigs. They fed off the family's waste which Bey and Soni threw down through a hole in the kitchen. They washed clothes and bathed in the river, scraping each other's back with rough cotton rags, their bodies bent and shivering from the dawn water. They braided each other's hair. They wove wide-brimmed hats and moccasins out of straw. Every year, when the Japanese inspectors visited, they filled sacks of barley as offering for the Emperor.

Bey was thirteen when he asked the officials whether they took the grains for themselves. He was struck on the side of his face with the butt of a rifle. They were standing in front of Bey's house. He fell and Soni kneeled to cover his head, and when she looked up at the men they hit her mouth. When Bey regained consciousness, he saw her lying there, beside him, covering her face. What resembled the juices of berries leaked out between her fingers.

She lost her front teeth. They found one on the ground. The other, she told Bey, she had swallowed. Like a seed, she said. It was growing already. She opened her mouth for him to pour drops of water down her throat.

When he first kissed her, he slipped his tongue into that space where her teeth had been. She pressed her other teeth together and surrounded his tongue. In this way he filled a space.

Their marriage took place when Bey turned sixteen. It was dusk and the winds from the sea cut through the trees and blew against the bonfire. They celebrated through the night and at sunrise the newly weds went on a treasure hunt in the forest. The wedding presents—candies wrapped in wax paper, chopsticks, bean curd, pouches filled with small cakes—had been hidden throughout the village by the women and children.

Bey and Soni looked inside trees, on branches, under rocks, and moss. They searched without bothering to change out of their wedding clothes. Soni wore a silk gown with a ballooned skirt and wide sleeves, the top folding over her breasts and tied around her waist by a ribbon. Bey was dressed in clean linen pants that fell to his shins and a new pair of straw moccasins that Soni had made him. They stopped several times to face each other. In the early morning, sleepy and drunk with wine they rested under a tree and she braided his hair and twisted it into a bun above his head the way all the married men did. They fell asleep there with their pockets stuffed with gifts.

With the treasure hunt, the amount of presents you were unable to find was the amount of children the wife would bear, the undiscovered gifts returning through a life. They found all but one. What that lost gift was no one ever identified.

Soni gave birth to their son a year later, on the floor of their house. Bey, along with his father, remained outside facing the forest. They heard her and the frightened pigs brushing up against the pen. And then they heard the child. The infant was given to Bey to hold. He brought him close to his face. From his skin rose the copper smell of Soni's insides. Bey licked his thumb and wiped away the stains across the infant's head. He had his mother's nose and his father's thick eyebrows.

During the monsoon season when the thatch of the roof whistled from the leaking winds and the floors shook. Karo learned to walk across the house with care as an old man would. First he touched Soni, who was attempting to boil rice, and then he returned and touched Bey on the top of his head. Back and forth he went like this. After the winds calmed and the house settled the child ventured to the window and looked outside in awe, as if they were somewhere else.

In the winters Bey carried him on his back to watch the sea at dusk. When it darkened, they witnessed the constellations appear, one by one, and the child held onto his father's ears and leaned back as far as he could swinging his braided hair. His breath puffed above the masked his father what kind of fish swam among the stars.

They were happiest then.

Karo grew to love the sea. And distances. When he was old enough, he joined a fishing crew. Soni wanted him to stay. To help with the fields. He would be at sea for weeks, months. Bey wished the same though he did not voice his concerns.

He left at the age of fifteen on a ship with mud-colored sails. Bey and Soni stood on the river bank to watch him depart. Their son waved until the ship disappeared around a bend. They stayed there, standing, long after the ship's wake faded and the lanterns began to glow through the trees.

From that moment on, they would see him when time allowed it. And all the days that had gone so quickly, slowed and lengthened. Both Bey and Soni's parents passed away. It was the two of them now, and in each other's company grew the overwhelming reminder of absence.

Bey began to remain in the fields long after sunset, unwilling to return home. On some evenings Soni ate alone. While she slept, he took walks through the forest. Beside the river he imagined the limbs of trees as the masts of ships. He smelled the night water, light and cool. As the years progressed he walked farther to the coast. There he undressed and swam into the sea, to the spot where the moon lay reflected.

Afloat, he recalled the treasure hunt and the single gift they had not discovered. He wondered what it was and where it now lav. He wondered whether an animal had taken the gift for its own purposes or whether it was still there, buried, or high up in a tree.

There were now days when it seemed that all his life he had been looking. As though he could not account for all the years gone, as though he could not yet claim those years as his own.

In the Pacific, a war had begun. And his son lived within it.

And Bey bathed in the luminous dark of the coast, scrubbing his back and soaking his hair and his beard. He stood upright to clean his chest. In his sadness he opened his mouth up toward the metallic stars and waited for one to fall.

40

(Ocean Vuong, 1988—)
王洋

作者简介

王洋（Ocean Vuong, 1988— ），美国越南裔诗人和散文家，出生于越南胡志明市（Ho Chi Minh City），1990 年移民到美国。王洋幼年时患有阅读障碍症，直到 11 岁才学会阅读。他曾就读于布鲁克林学院（Brooklyn College）并获得 19 世纪英国文学学士学位。他曾师从著名诗人和小说家本·勒纳（Ben Lerner）。目前他是马萨诸塞大学安姆斯特分校（University of Massachusetts Amherst）的助理教授，讲授硕士写作课程。

作为文坛新星，王洋荣获了露丝·丽莉与萨珍特罗森博格奖（Ruth Lilly/Sargent Rosenberg Fellowship）、手推车奖（Pushcart Prize）、伊丽莎白·乔治基金奖（Elizabeth George Foundation Fellowship）、史丹利·库尼茨青年诗人奖（Stanley Kunitz Prize for Younger Poets）、怀丁诗歌奖（Whiting Award for Poetry）与 T. S. 艾略特奖（T. S. Eliot Prize）等众多重要奖项。

他创作的作品有《燃烧》（*Burnings*, 2010）、《不》（*No*, 2013）与《带着伤口的夜晚的天空》（*Night Sky with Exit Wounds*, 2016）。王洋的作品充满了血腥和阴暗的色调，如同恐怖故事一般，牵引着读者，去揭开现象背后的真相。

《与燃烧的城市晨歌》（"Aubade with Burning City"）与《曾让我们一度辉煌的土地上》（"On Earth We're Briefly Gorgeous"）是王洋诗歌中的经典作品。《与燃烧的城市晨歌》本是沉痛、紧张的战地事役，在王洋的笔下，带着欧文·博林《白色圣诞节》音乐的进行曲，阴柔、绵长而怪诞。《曾让我们一度辉煌的土地上》这首诗歌以唯美的语言描绘出了越南战争给人民带来的苦难以及难民们为了保命，拼尽一切努力搭上美国的“救命航班”的故事。这两首诗歌表达了越南人民在战争阴霾下惶惶不可终日的心情，值得人们进行深刻的反思。

作品选读

Aubade with Burning City

By Ocean Vuong

South Vietnam, April 29, 1975: Armed Forces Radio played Irving Berlin's "White Christmas" as a code to begin Operation Frequent Wind, the ultimate evacuation of American civilians and Vietnamese refugees by helicopter during the fall of Saigon.

Milkflower petals on the street
like pieces of a girl's dress.

May your days be merry and bright...

He fills a teacup with champagne, brings it to her lips.
Open, he says.
She opens.
Outside, a soldier spits out
his cigarette as footsteps
fill the square like stones fallen from the sky. *May all*
your Christmases be white as the traffic guard
unstraps his holster.
His hand running the hem
of her white dress.
His black eyes.
Her black hair.

A single candle.
Their shadows: two wicks.
A military truck speeds through the intersection, the sound of children
shrieking inside. A bicycle hurled
through a store window. When the dust rises, a black dog
lies in the road, panting. Its hind legs
crushed into the shine
of a white Christmas.
On the nightstand, a sprig of magnolia expands like a secret heard
for the first time.
The treetops glisten and children listen, the chief of police
facedown in a pool of Coca-Cola.
A palm-sized photo of his father soaking
beside his left ear.

The song moving through the city like a widow.
A white... A white... I'm dreaming of a curtain of snow
falling from her shoulders.
Snow crackling against the window. Snow shredded
with gunfire. Red sky.

Snow on the tanks rolling over the city walls.
A helicopter lifting the living just out of reach.

The city so white it is ready for ink.
The radio saying run run run.
Milkflower petals on a black dog
like pieces of a girl's dress.

May your days be merry and bright. She is saying
something neither of them can hear. The hotel rocks
beneath them. The bed a field of ice
cracking.

Don't worry, he says, as the first bomb brightens
their faces, *my brothers have won the war*
and tomorrow...
The lights go out.
I'm dreaming. I'm dreaming...
to hear sleigh bells in the snow...
In the square below: a nun, on fire,
runs silently toward her god—
Open, he says.
She opens.

On Earth We're Briefly Gorgeous

By Ocean Vuong

Tell me it was for the hunger
& nothing less. For hunger is to give
the body what it knows

it cannot keep. That this amber light
whittled down by another war
is all that pins my hand

to your chest.

You, drowning
between my arms—
stay.

You, pushing your body
　　　　into the river
only to be left
　　　　with yourself—
stay.

¿

I'll tell you how we're wrong enough to be forgiven. How one night, after backhanding
mother, then taking a chainsaw to the kitchen table, my father went to kneel
in the bathroom until we heard his muffled cries through the walls.
And so I learned that a man, in climax, was the closest thing
to surrender.

¿

Say surrender. Say alabaster. Switchblade.
　　Honeysuckle. Goldenrod. Say autumn.
Say autumn despite the green
　　in your eyes. Beauty despite
daylight. Say you'd kill for it. Unbreakable dawn
　　mounting in your throat.
My thrashing beneath you
　　like a sparrow stunned
with falling.

¿

Dusk: a blade of honey between our shadows, draining.

¿

I wanted to disappear—so I opened the door to a stranger's car. He was divorced. He was still alive. He was sobbing into his hands (hands that tasted like rust). The pink breast cancer ribbon on his keychain swayed in the ignition. Don't we touch each other just to prove we are still here?

I was still here once. The moon, distant & flickering, trapped itself in beads of sweat on my neck. I let the fog spill through the cracked window & cover my fangs. When I left, the Buick kept sitting there, a dumb bull in pasture, its eyes searing my shadow onto the side of suburban houses. At home, I threw myself on the bed like a torch & watched the flames gnaw through my mother's house until the sky appeared, bloodshot & massive. How I wanted to be that sky—to hold every flying & falling at once.

Say amen. Say amend.

Say yes. Say yes

anyway.

In the shower, sweating under cold water, I scrubbed & scrubbed.

In the life before this one, you could tell
two people were in love
because when they drove the pickup
over the bridge, their wings
would grow back just in time.

Some days I am still inside the pickup.
Some days I keep waiting.

It's not too late. Our heads haloed
        with gnats & summer too early
to leave any marks.
        Your hand under my shirt as static
intensifies on the radio.
        Your other hand pointing

your daddy's revolver
        to the sky. Stars falling one
by one in the cross hairs.
        This means I won't be
afraid if we're already
        here. Already more
than skin can hold. That a body
        beside a body
must make a field
        full of ticking. That your name
is only the sound of clocks
        being set back another hour
& morning
            finds our clothes
on your mother's front porch, shed
          like week-old lilies.

图书在版编目（CIP）数据

美国亚裔文学作品选：英文 / 郭英剑，张国庆，张龙艳主编. —北京：中国人民大学出版社，2018. 9
（美国亚裔文学研究丛书）
ISBN 978-7-300-26119-5

Ⅰ. ①美…　Ⅱ. ①郭…②张…③张…　Ⅲ. ①文学－作品综合集－美国－英文　Ⅳ. ①I712. 11

中国版本图书馆 CIP 数据核字（2018）第 187706 号

美国亚裔文学研究丛书
美国亚裔文学作品选
总主编　郭英剑
主　编　郭英剑　张国庆　张龙艳
Meiguo Yayi Wenxue Zuopinxuan

出版发行	中国人民大学出版社		
社　　址	北京中关村大街 31 号	**邮政编码**	100080
电　　话	010-62511242（总编室）		010-62511770（质管部）
	010-82501766（邮购部）		010-62514148（门市部）
	010-62515195（发行公司）		010-62515275（盗版举报）
网　　址	http://www.crup.com.cn		
	http://www.ttrnet.com（人大教研网）		
经　　销	新华书店		
印　　刷	北京东君印刷有限公司		
规　　格	185 mm×230 mm　16 开本	**版　　次**	2018 年 9 月第 1 版
印　　张	22	**印　　次**	2018 年 9 月第 1 次印刷
字　　数	446 000	**定　　价**	65.00 元

中国人民大学出版社外语出版分社读者信息反馈表

尊敬的读者：

感谢您购买和使用中国人民大学出版社外语出版分社的 ________ 一书，我们希望通过这张小小的反馈卡来获得您更多的建议和意见，以改进我们的工作，加强我们双方的沟通和联系。我们期待着能为更多的读者提供更多的好书。

请您填妥下表后，寄回或传真回复我们，对您的支持我们不胜感激！

1. 您是从何种途径得知本书的：

☐书店　☐网上　☐报纸杂志　☐朋友推荐

2. 您为什么决定购买本书：

☐工作需要　☐学习参考　☐对本书主题感兴趣　☐随便翻翻

3. 您对本书内容的评价是：

☐很好　☐好　☐一般　☐差　☐很差

4. 您在阅读本书的过程中有没有发现明显的专业及编校错误，如果有，它们是：

____

____

____

5. 您对哪些专业的图书信息比较感兴趣：

____

____

____

6. 如果方便，请提供您的个人信息，以便于我们和您联系（您的个人资料我们将严格保密）：

您供职的单位：________________________

您教授的课程（教师填写）：________________________

您的通信地址：________________________

您的电子邮箱：________________________

请联系我们：贾乐凯　黄婷　程子殊　鞠方安

电话：010-62515580，62512737，62513265，62515576

传真：010-62514961

E-mail：jialk@crup.com.cn　huangt@crup.com.cn　chengzsh@crup.com.cn

jufa@crup.com.cn

通信地址：北京市海淀区中关村大街甲 59 号文化大厦 15 层　邮编：100872

中国人民大学出版社外语出版分社